Loving and Writing, Writing and Loving

Loving and Writing, Writing and Loving

D. B. Reynolds

iUniverse, Inc.
Bloomington

Loving and Writing, Writing and Loving

iUniverse books may be ordered through booksellers or by contacting:

iUniverse
1663 Liberty Drive
Bloomington, IN 47403
www.iuniverse.com
1-800-Authors (1-800-288-4677)

ISBN: 978-1-4620-1468-2 (sc)
ISBN: 978-1-4620-1473-6 (hc)
ISBN: 978-1-4620-1471-2 (ebk)

Printed in the United States of America

iUniverse rev. date: 09/02/2011

In memory of
Ernest and Hilda Reynolds,
my parents.

INTRODUCTORY:

ANOTHER COUNTRY

Of course, nobody said I had to or should do this: write my own story. Or, for that matter, write about anyone or anything, much less about someone or something conjured up in my own head, my usual thing. But something of that last sort is what I've been up to with this, having presented certain studied versions of myself and others. In fact, from my first to last page, what else would anybody have expected other than this: a reality of sorts, a reconstruction of events and the parts played in them by myself and others? As any psychologist will tell you, what is recoverable from the past represents not so much the facts themselves as their appearance.

Working with autobiographical material, there are decisions to be made bearing not only on the narrator's artistic sensibilities and storytelling abilities, but also on one's personal integrity and honest-to-goodness objectivity as well. Keeping the ego, with its accumulated pride and conceit, in check, and resisting any conscious manipulation of what you know to be true is mandatory. Also, from start to finish, the mind, in recall mode, can play tricks on you, skewing the truth. The protagonist/narrator in L.P. Hartley's *The Go-Between*, for instance: 'The past is another country. They do things differently there.'

Still, the philosophers, the think-a-thing-through ones, have long been on record about the benefits of looking back to learn what's to be learned in going forward. And it's possible, in exploring my past like this, that I've arrived occasionally at certain points in that journey when, as T.S. Eliot posited poetically, I've got to 'know the place for the first time.'

T.C.H.
Hammersmith, London
September 2003

RECENTLY

The telephone was chirping; that's what it was. Not the dawn chorus from the treed city green outside my Hammersmith flat, I'd realized, after a befuddled moment or two. Sprawled at sixes and sevens, I'd been out like a light on the sofa in the lower floor drawing room.

'Hello.' In a roupy voice; my mouth like a wadi in the dry season.

'Timothy?'

'Yes?'

'I woke you up, ol' chum, didn't I? You must have just walked in the door and fallen into bed, right?'

It was Kell—Kellison Marleau. Half Irish, half French, a good talker, his mind as sharp as a tack, Kell was Canada's Stratford Festival's artistic director, a position he'd quickly shaped in his own artistic image. He, Jace and I—in that order—went back quite a few years together. (Jace—Jacinth Glyn-Davies—beautiful, intelligent, blonde English rose star of stage and screen, who'd once meant so much to me, and who would never stop meaning something to me.) Whatever the subject, it was best to be wide awake, on your toes, whenever talking to Kell, nearly always half a step ahead of you at every turn.

'Had a long, exhausting weekend, have we, Tim?'

'Indeed we have, Kell. Listen, d'you realize it's going on for one a.m. here? Forget the time diff, did you?'

'Hardly. I'm in London—at the usual place in Bayswater. And no, Tim, I couldn't leave this until tomorrow, if that's what you're thinking. I'm out of here first thing in the morning. To Dublin for Christmas with m' mam's side of the family, then to Cork, for ten days—one binge after another. Then over to Paree to see in the new millennium with mon pere and his new wife, who I've never met, and their sophisticated coterie. God, I hope I can stomach this stepmother better than I could the first one! Anyway, ol' chum, I've been trying to reach you all weekend. Tried your place in Oxfordshire too. You weren't cavalierly ignoring my messages, I trust. Also, your agent wouldn't give me your mobile number to save his life.'

'Good for Gerry.'

'Under strict orders, I suppose. Where were you, anyway?'

'Ben Layzell's place in Hertfordshire.'

'Oh, were you now? In very interesting company too, I'm sure.'

'No, Kell, it wasn't that sort of weekend. We were working on the "Congravino" script.' The film version of my latest and, some say, my best play. 'Practically working round the clock, in fact. I've not had much sleep, about seven hours total, in two days.'

'And how is the lovely Mrs. Layzell? It still is Lesley Kyle, is it?'

Lesley and I had dated a few times a year or so prior to her marriage to Ben, nearly twenty years her senior.

'Lesley wasn't there. She's on location somewhere.'

'Well, lucky for you. You might not have got any sleep at all. How is the script coming along, anyway?'

'It's getting there.'

'Is it true Layzell wanted someone else to do the adaptation?'

'Well, if he did, we've not had any problems working together, anyway. The usual differences of opinion, of course—but nothing we haven't been able to resolve amicably.'

'Well, at least someone isn't doing unspeakable things to your lovely story.'

He wished me all the very best for Christmas and the New Year. And: 'And as for all that—with the new millennium bearing down on us—I don't know about you, Tim, m' lad, but I feel pressured, I really do. To do something about myself. Shut myself down for a bit; get in some serious introspection; get myself sorted. What's it all about, Kelli? That sort of thing. What you and Jacie and me used to talk about until the wee hours, remember?'

'As I remember it, Kell, it was mostly just you and Jace. The way it'd been before I showed up.'

'Oh, really?' As if he didn't remember. 'Well, anyway, Tim, the rather scary thing is, it's the big Four-O for me next month. And near enough the same thing for you and Jacie, isn't it? For all our lot. The question is: if now isn't the time for an honest-to-God mid-life crisis, when the hell is it? What are we waiting for, I'd like to know?'

'Good question, Kell. Only right now you happen to be talking to a seriously sleep-deprived person. In other words, I'm just not up to contributing anything useful to a discussion like that—or any other sort of discussion, for that matter.'

As a matter of fact, I never have been up to discussing anything very much with Kell, except the usual shop talk. We've always gone easy on the more personal stuff, and especially if it had anything to do with Jace and me. Kell and I had never been 'ol' chums,' actually. We were friends mostly by default, linked only by our common interest in Jace. From the outset, Kell had regarded me as a Johnny-come-lately who'd interrupted what he liked to think of as a very special story of love and friendship he and Jace had been collaborating on since first meeting at RADA (the Royal Academy of Dramatic Art) in London in 1981. Albeit a love story with a 'wondrous strange' quality about it; what with Kell's penchant for loving both men and women in approximately equal measure, and Jace's strictly conventional sexual preferences. Most other things that came up for discussion between them Jace and Kell were essentially in agreement on, however. (But any discussion about her relationship with me, she'd always vetoed, she assured me.)

'I hear you, Tim. I'll not keep you up much longer. Just wanted to say hello, pass on season's greetings, ol' chum—something I'd have preferred to do in person, mind, but there you are. And a couple of things I wanted to ask you too.'

Why wasn't I surprised? 'Oh, yes?'

'Tell me you're not going to be moving soon—permanently, I mean—to your bolt hole in the country.' He was referring to Hook Norton, near Banbury, where I was spending as much if not more time than I was in London.

'No, I'm not, Kell. There've been rumours, I know, but nothing more.'

'Well, that's good to hear, anyway.' Good, as he saw it, because he knew Hook Norton wasn't really Jace's sort of place, just possibly? 'You know how it is, though, the loads of people from here I hear from, and having to sort out the facts from the fiddle-faddle.'

'And the other thing?'

'Oh, yes. You haven't seen Jacie or talked to her since New York, have you?' A few weeks before, in November, this had been.

I might have known that Jace's name, in connection with mine, would be brought up. Kell has this thing about Jace and me as it could affect him. Having to adjust to me as someone who wasn't just a passing phase in Jace's life, Kell had got to thinking that he and I, with our individual qualities and strengths, were better able together to provide the comfort and support a complex, multi-faceted woman such as she was always going to require. And that not only Jace, but he and I too would be much the poorer for not keeping a three-way relationship like ours in place and in good nick. And later, odder still, Kell continued to talk and behave as if this complementary triad was still functioning—some five years and counting since Jace and I had gone our separate ways. The good thing was, though: with Kell far away in Canada, this wasn't something either Jace or I were faced with except during his bi-annual visits to London. (Although I'm sure Jace had had a steady diet of the same from Kell while working with him and the Stratford Festival for much of the past year.)

Anyway, I told Kell I'd not seen or spoken to Jace since returning from New York, where she'd appeared with the SF company in my play *Congravino*.

Kell said, 'Well, just thought you might have run across one another. I just missed her. She's taken off for Emma Burnett's place near Sheffield for Christmas. Which worries me a bit, I have to admit.'

'Oh? Why's that, then?'

'Well, you know just how closely she listens to her dear Emma. Hangs on her every word, it seems like.'

Jace's only close friend other than Kell while at RADA, Emma had left the stage to become the wife of an academic and a mother. Judging by her own experience, Emma couldn't see why any woman given a clear choice of one or the other—a career, or love and marriage—would happily choose any differently than she'd done. Also, she thought the chances of succeeding in mixing the two were slim at best. She'd said to Jace, 'You must know that, anyway, being your mother's daughter.' Jace's mother, Ursula Bentley, a former actor—and a good one—had had more than her fair share of problems trying to keep her career and marriage and motherhood nicely balanced, eventually having to give up the one for one or the other. Kell seemed to think Jace always made a point of seeing Emma when she wanted 'agony column' advice about some man or other.

'You wouldn't have a number for the Burnetts, would you?' he asked.

'Afraid not, Kell. Ursula might have it, though.'

'No, she says she doesn't. Probably didn't want to give it to me. Julian doesn't have it either. He did say, though, Jacie will be back here for a millennium eve's party he's throwing. Quite a splash, I hear—on a boat on the Thames.'

AD for the Chichester Festival, Julian Caverley went a way back too with Jace and I. For me, back to my Nottingham days in the early '80s; to my first play, *Writing and Loving, Loving and Writing*. And to the hard-to-forget Sam (Samantha) Tolliver. Very heady days for me, writing and loving, mixing the two.

After he'd enquired I told Kell I'd also be going to Julian's bash on the river, probably going alone; that I wasn't keen on seeing in the new millennium with a casual date. He said, 'I get your point, Tim—I think. Starting a new era, turning the page, as it were, with a clean slate, romantically speaking, has its advantages, I dare say. And besides, I'm sure you and Jacie will enjoy spending some time together, having a good chinwag.'

Yes, and I could guess what he'd most like the two of us to be having a good chinwag about, too. Convinced as he was that the one, big reason neither one of us had had much luck finding other partners since we'd split up was by now, surely, staring us in the face. That one of these fine days it would finally dawn on us as well, as it had on almost everyone else. And looking into each other's eyes, we'd put our pride and stubbornness aside and do the right thing, the best thing, for both of us. I could hear the violins playing.

Of course, I had to assume that Kell didn't have a clue about me and Leona Fielder. (But Jace might have had, though.) Then again, what really was there for Kell or Jace or anybody else to know, anyway? Come to that, Leona and I didn't know either if there was anything much between us; we'd not had the time, quality time, to find out. And for that matter, although it looked as if we'd find some time for that in the New Year, I couldn't be too sure about that either.

ONE

1

The sudden loss of my mother not long before my eleventh birthday broke in on me and marred my childhood, to say the least of it. And yet, some twenty-eight years later, I find I can look back on and write of my early years in Westcliff-on-Sea on the S.E. Essex coast in a predominantly positive and uncomplaining frame of mind. Despite sorely missing Mum's always giving and comforting presence, I'd managed eventually to just get on with things without feeling too sorry for myself—as I knew she'd have wanted me to. Mum had sometimes called me her 'brave little man,' which I'd gone on trying to be for her whenever she'd come to mind.

In keeping with the archetypal Christian tenets my parents lived by (and my father diligently taught), my brother Paul and I were raised with all due loving care and attention. For our lasting good, they believed, Mum and Dad instructed us patiently in the things of God as evidenced in the life, death and resurrection of Jesus Christ—'The Way, The Truth and The Life'. But not so much pointed out and explained to us as shown them by example in the varied course of life's day-to-day doings and circumstances. Little wonder, then, for my brother and I, that what it meant to love God and please him in thought, word and deed amounted to much the same thing as loving and pleasing our parents.

But childhood ends, and in youth the questions start to form. What one feels and believes isn't quite so clear-cut as sometimes it was just the day before. And so it was for me; and my increasing lack of attention in my teens to matters of Christian faith and practice started to show.

Whether my father has ever blamed himself for not taking me to task for this I'm sure I'll never know; but there's never been any hint of reproach in his dark, pensive eyes for my having failed him at all. (Dad doesn't have a judgmental bone in his body, actually.) Just occasionally, however, there's a glancing expression from him not unlike the one on the face of Jesus in a church vestibule portrait, with that same welcoming 'Come, let's commune together' look about each of them—a picture I'd found difficult to ignore without feeling I'd offhandedly snubbed the Good Lord himself. The elegantly framed, non-reflective glassed print of Jesus Christ was titled 'The Constant Friend'.

Arthur and Daphne Hainault's joint design for living was in all respects a well-ordered one. Each week, from day one, the routine at 66 St. John's Road in Westcliff scarcely ever changed. Our shared lives that day revolved around morning and evening services and afternoon Sunday school at CPM—Cliff Place Methodist—in neighbouring Southend. And it was the same old thing on weekdays, too. Before the rest of us were up, Dad was en route for London on the Fenchurch Street line to his commercial sales job with Aylesworth's, a legal publishing firm located conveniently beside the Royal Courts of Justice in the Strand, as it had been for donkey's years. Dad joined Aylesworth's, a family concern in business since 1805, when he was eighteen in 1949. By the time he got home again every evening Paul and I had eaten and made ourselves scarce. The family ate together only on the weekends—for Saturday tea, three meals on Sunday, all squeezed in hurriedly between church activities. On Saturdays, Dad would prepare for Sunday—he was the CPM's long-serving Sunday school Superintendent—attend to some household repairs or improvements, or tinker with the second-hand clocks he collected. In the summer he'd work in the garden or get out into the S.E. Essex countryside for some hiking and birdwatching, sometimes with Paul, who also liked that sort of thing. I, on the other hand, would usually be off somewhere watching or playing cricket (and football in the winter). Other than our summer holidays together, usually in Oxfordshire or on the Norfolk coast near Cromer, we spent only a limited amount of time doing things as a family outside the confines of CPM. But a sense of togetherness stayed with us. Our prayers—perhaps even my own increasingly perfunctory, less frequent ones—may have helped keep the family ties strong and binding. After all, we were the Hainaults—one in Christ, sticking together, the four of us against the world and its many harmful ways. United we stood, presenting a solid, safe and secure front to the world at large—one strong, cohesive family unit; as my parents and Paul too would have reckoned us to be, at any rate.

At home on winter evenings, after dinner (as he always called it) and a good chat with Mum—she always waited to eat with him—Dad would rise from the table and pointedly pass the downstairs middle room where the television was, and head for the bay-windowed front room. There he'd settle in front of the electric fire and listen to the occasional radio concert, talk or documentary; mostly, though, to get his nose into a good book. And there he'd stay until Mum would go in with his nightly cup of Horlicks and a plate of cheese and cream crackers, signalling time for bed as she did so; never a minute before or after ten o'clock.

At least three-quarters of Dad's collection of books in the front room were housed in a floor-to-ceiling, solid mahogany, glass-doored, early Victorian bookcase—his only self-admitted 'worldly possession' for which he'd coughed up, he said, 'much too much in a premeditated act of fiscal irresponsibility.' For the most part, the contents of this 'hard-to-regret extravagance' of his—classic novels, some modern ones, short story, poetry and play collections, history, biographies, natural history, travel books, philosophy, Bible commentary, Christian apologetics and inspirational titles (with a Wesleyan slant)—he'd inherited from Anthony Timson, his second father, as Dad has always seen him as such. As a World War II evacuee from London's East End, Dad had gone to live with Anthony and his wife Agnes in Hook Norton in Oxfordshire. He'd ended up staying with the Timsons, who were childless, for nearly five years.

A considerably smaller, more modest bookcase—an Art Deco-style knock-off—contained new and second-hand volumes Dad had picked up himself including two shelves of titles he'd got for Paul and me, as well as Sunday school attendance prizes we'd been presented with. (Dad had made sure that the CPM's annual prize-giving tradition had carried on; getting a good book into the hands of a kid was important to him, as it had been as well to Anthony Timson, who'd been in charge of the Hook Norton Methodist Chapel Sunday school when Dad was in the large-sized village.)

Our front room library's children's section included many of the usual favourite titles, all of which Paul and I had read with little parental persuasion. We'd both enjoyed Kenneth Grahame's *The Wind in the Willows* a great deal (and later had seen A.A. Milne's dramatic version in

London). On the whole, though, I preferred humans to talking animals. King Arthur, Robin Hood and Elizabethan and Napoleonic sea captains and their stout crews were more to my taste. I'd lapped up Scott's *Ivanhoe*, Kingsley's *Westward Ho*! and Forester's Hornblower books before I was out of junior school.

Of course, as a reader in a seriously Christian household, one starts early with the Bible. To begin with, with large-print, copiously and colourfully illustrated storybooks meant to catch the young eye and imagination as well as stir one's awakening conscience. Stories peopled by bronze-skinned, grey and raven-maned, fine figures of men and decorous, subtly seductive women in exotic, sun-bleached, palm-treed surroundings. Easy-on-the-eye specimens of man-and-womanhood who'd have looked good on a poster for a passionate, blood-on-the-sand Hollywood epic, every one of them. And despite my northern hemisphere, slate-grey environs, my pale Englishness—all that Anglo-Saxon heritage—these were people and places I seemed to relate to without any trouble whatsoever. These were tales in which hot-blooded, action-oriented men would do both marvellous and also bloody awful and ruinous things to one another, and to themselves; and just as likely too when there was a 'very fair to look upon' woman somewhere in the frame. It was irresistible stuff for a kid like me.

High on my Top Ten list among such books was a somewhat tattered, clothbound, dog-eared volume, *Great Short Stories from the Bible for the Older Child*—a gift from the Timsons to my father on his twelfth birthday in 1943. The inscription said how such stories help the reader appreciate the way well-written, truthful literature improves you in both mind and spirit. On into my teens, this book ran just about neck and neck in my estimation with a collection of Sherlock Holmes stories by Conan Doyle. In a way, the two books had for me a common overall theme: the discovery of truth and the overcoming of evil by people with their hearts in the right place, and with minds clear and bright enough to see the wrong, the danger, and send it packing. And, I suppose, challenging me, and cautioning me too, to live and strive on the side of the angels, the good guys.

In the 1960s and '70s, when Paul and I were growing up, the whole concept of God in his heaven—like the sun in the western sky—was sinking fast. Huxley's grinning Cheshire cat, fading from sight—that was the image, the idea of God the majority was choosing to see, to adopt, to adapt to as a given. No more of all that 'pie-in-the-sky', metaphysical malarkey to bother with, to be bothered by, then.

Paul and I, of course, could see, hear and read about the things filling the void of godlessness as well as the next chap. At school, even in the juniors, our apartness as believers was starting to show itself in one way or another. And later, in our teens, we felt marginalized—out of the swing of things—among the kids we rubbed shoulders with at school, many of whom couldn't see what the Bible had to do anymore with anything.

My brother, however, coped better than I seemed able to in the face of this everyday reality. In Paul's view—one he shared with just about everybody in the congregation at CPM—there wasn't that much going on the faithful hadn't seen before; the same array of false gods and wolves in sheep's clothing to mess you up, to plague mankind. But also, along with that, the same promises of God firmly in place to aid and protect his every faithful follower. Without being uppity, holier-than-thou about it, Paul knew where he stood as a Christian. No shilly-shallying with him. He was in the world all right—but definitely not of it; and that being so, the other kids at school could take him or leave him. That was about the size of it with Paul.

My brother was so much more his father's son than I will ever be.

The fact is, Paul and I never did have very much in common. He was only two years older than me—a time gap between us, though, we'd let affect our companionship more than most other kids seemed to allow. Paul rarely sought me out to play with him, and I'd not felt any urge to hang onto his coat-tails; even at an early age we'd preferred doing our own thing, playing our own games, pursuing our own interests. Unlike me, he was a dedicated model maker, made complicated Meccano constructions, did large jigsaw puzzles. Physical activities, other than hiking, he could take or leave—mostly the latter. Also, in taking what some might see as a typical, no-nonsense Protestant approach to literary consumption, Paul wasn't much of one for fiction of any sort—my food and drink as a reader. All in all, however, we got on very well together. We respected the other's right to see things in his own way—but not necessarily that much differently from one another, we both thought, I'm sure.

Paul and I assumed, I think—probably he more than I—that the path each of us was taking ran more or less parallel with and in the same general direction as the other's.

A short while after my ninth birthday, while still at West Road Junior, the idea came to me. Reading as much as I was—newspapers (particularly sports) and magazines (my mother's too) as well as novels and short stories—I thought: why not have a go myself and see what I could do as a would-be writer? What to write didn't take much thinking about. I decided on sports journalism—football match reports, specifically. But not something I'd have to leave the house to do, however. The matches, the teams, the league, all of it, I'd dreamed up myself.

Keeping at it, I spent four, five hours a week writing the copy (with my byline) and fastidiously printing it by hand in very small letters, mocking up a newspaper page carrying the report, usually with an accompanying drawing (a goal) purporting to be a match action photo, along with a caption. The matches I reported were fixtures featuring 'St. John's United'—the only club in my version of the English First Division with a make-believe existence—and played Saturday mornings on the large, extra-leafed table in the front room on an always perfect green baize pitch. I played a still popular, table-top football game, using three-dimensional players mounted on rocker-stands, for all of St. John's U.'s home matches. Away match scores and other league results I generated through a combination of another football game, a board game, home-made playing cards and dice, filling an exercise book with weekly league tables and other statistics.

About halfway through the first season, running from August through to May, I tried my hand at a trio of player profiles, making up careers and lives for them. And this led, the next season, to a thirty-page biography of St. John's U.'s Danny Potts, a brilliant striker and an English international by the age of twenty.

That second year too I branched out into storytelling, pure and simple. Dipping into the past—England's, of course—I wrote three short stories about a Round Table knight at King Arthur's court in Camelot called Sir Kelvain the Good. As one might suspect, Sir Kelvain was handsome, honourable, an excellent swordsman and all-star jouster—and womanless; but greatly admired by the Queen and ladies of the court. Sir Kelvain didn't seem to have the time for the ladies, however—not even, at first, for love of a courtly fashion.

None of this, the journalism or the fiction, I showed to anyone—little worlds of my own I chose to keep to myself, hidden away in a cardboard box in the storage space under the stairs. Partly, perhaps, for fear of being looked at sideways by Paul or my parents, but more likely by some of my school, games-playing pals. And also because I thought, knowing myself no better than most kids of my age, that making up things like that was a phase I'd grow out of as I got older and put off childish things.

Then, enter Miss Ozanne—my new home room, English and History teacher at West Road Junior School.

In her mid-twenties, the dark-haired, blue-eyed Miss Ozanne was quite a smasher. King Arthur's Guenevere had nothing on her. She had French Channel Islands connections—and a Gallic name that in our part of the world only amplified her charm and womanly mystique. Her first name was Aimée. which in English meant 'Beloved.' I'd looked it up, and thought it suited her very well. For me, one smile, a look of approval from Miss O. was like being given a large bag of Quality Street sweets. Also—no surprise—my English and History marks shot up to class-leading levels.

In my eleventh year—and also my last at West Road—Miss O. set the class a 750-word essay on how the summer holidays had been spent; the usual thing. She'd said, however, she didn't want a list of one thing after another—I did this, and then that, and so on. If we wanted to, we could write about one particularly interesting thing that had happened. 'What I want you to tell me is what you thought and felt about whatever it was,' she said. Miss O.'s word was my command. My pet teacher would get nothing less than what she wanted from her devoted pupil—and maybe something more beside.

Miss O. knew that I'd been to Canada that summer, visiting relatives in Ontario. And thinking possibly I might have something out of the ordinary to tell; something different from the kind of things she'd heard too often before. But whatever she'd been expecting, I'm pretty sure it wasn't *The Girl from Maple Cottage*. Quite a lot more words than she'd asked for, for a start. But more significantly, I'd turned in what had started out as an essay all right—but had then, about halfway through, morphed into a short story.

Miss O. must have had her suspicions as soon as she'd read the piece. I'd been hoping she would, quite possibly. Taking me aside, my hybrid effort in hand, she said, 'Well, Tim, this really is a surprise, a big surprise. It's one of the best essays I think I've ever had the pleasure of reading from someone your age.' And: 'I was wondering, Tim, if you'd like to read this to the rest of the class?' She'd kept her eyes on me while asking this, and saw my expression. 'Or maybe you'd rather not?'

'No, Miss.'

'You would or you wouldn't?'

'I wouldn't, Miss.'

'All right, then. But would you care to tell me why?' I shrugged, my only response. 'You think your friends will think things about you you'd rather they didn't because of what you wrote—about their games, about fighting battles; and what they think about girls, maybe?'

I shrugged again, but this time I felt the redness spreading across my face. In a History class, Miss O. had commented that 'fighting wars is the worst way for people to settle their differences.' Little more than an aside, this—but I'd heard and taken note, hanging on her every word as I did. And, in English, talking about *Anne Frank: The Diary of a Young Girl*, she said, 'Because people are different than us, and believe different things than we do, that doesn't give us any right whatsoever to look down on them, to treat them as if they don't matter; and maybe even get to hate them.' The girl from Maple Cottage had also been against war—and just happened to have been Jewish as well.

'Of course, it could be, Tim, that you just don't like showing off in front of the class,' Miss O. continued. 'But you certainly wanted to show off for me with this, didn't you, right? But maybe you went a little bit further than you meant; got carried away, trying so hard to impress me. So tell me, Tim, am I right in thinking some things in this didn't quite happen the way you described them? Or maybe didn't happen at all?'

I couldn't lie to Miss O. I told her there had been a Jewish girl staying at Maple Cottage, next to my uncle's place on the lake, but admitted that I'd not got to meet her, seeing her only from a distance. 'We never got to talk, me and the girl. I made all that up.' Miss O. wasn't cross. She didn't even have a 'I thought so' expression on her face. After a silence, she said, 'Well, the thing is, I'm afraid, this isn't what I asked for, is it, Tim? And which means, unfortunately, I can't give you a good mark for it.' Then, after the shortest of pauses, she smiled, making everything right for me in a flash, and said, 'But I will tell you this, Timothy Hainault: I thoroughly enjoyed reading what you wrote from start to finish. In fact, I've the feeling you have the makings of becoming a writer, a good one, when you're a few years older, I really do.' I must have looked pleased silly. 'You do know what this means, though, don't you, Tim? From now on,

I'm going to be seeing you in quite a different light than before. And if you write any other out-and-out stories—you know what I mean by that, Tim, I'm sure—I'd like to see them, and maybe we could have a chat about them. If you wanted to, that is.'

I think I'll always remember what Miss Aimée Ozanne said to me that afternoon at West Road. Come to that, she may well have settled my hash, occupationally speaking, right there and then. Also, Miss O., I think, has affected the way I've since regarded women—that different, rather mysterious half of the human race I'd just then started to get interested in, as she'd guessed—and more than she'd realized, or will ever realize, I wouldn't wonder.

2

The moment I first saw Samantha Tolliver—as Hero in *Much Ado About Nothing*, on its second preview night at the Nottingham Playhouse—I was beguiled by her. I couldn't keep my eyes off her. I was at her mercy.

Ms Tolliver hadn't had a word to say until Act Two. But the way she looked and moved—or just stood there, for that matter—kept getting my attention no matter how good the action and reactions were elsewhere onstage. She reminded me of a younger and dark, straight-haired Julie Christie. And when she got to say something, her low-to-middle range, slightly husky voice—as exquisite as cut glass, but not at all plumy—was enchantingly seductive in its own right as well. From where I was sitting in the cheap seats, the lady had me in the palm of her hands. Smitten though I was, however, I was well aware too that the subject of my affection was merely a woman on public display as someone other than herself—and that that would be it for me, the extent of all this ado of mine.

And that was how things remained for the rest of the play's run, during which I'd laid down good money to see two more performances from better seats I could ill afford. As a bike-riding university student on a tight budget, I didn't fancy my chances with Ms Tolliver as a Stage Door Johnny. But things were about to look up.

The surprising kindness of a stranger with whom I shared an interest in playwright and novelist David Storey introduced me to the world of professional theatre and, as a result of that, opened up my way to Sam Tolliver. Following a seminar at the university on new directions in English drama, I got to talk to the keynote speaker, Julian Caverley, the young and talented assistant artistic director at the Playhouse. He'd just started rehearsing Shaw's *You Never Can Tell* in which Sam would be playing the fascinating but also 'dangerous' Gloria, as GBS described her;

and Julian invited me to sit in on rehearsals anytime it was convenient for me. I took him up on his offer with no delay, heedlessly skipping lectures to do so.

During coffee breaks at the Playhouse, Sam quite openly took note of me, no doubt having noticed me taking note of her. She didn't appear to be looking down her nicely contoured nose at me, anything like that. Two-and-a-half years older than me, Sam wasn't a London or Home Counties girl, I found out; born in Gloucester, she'd grown up near Hereford where her father was a veterinarian. If she had any airs about her none were apparent; her feet seemed to me well planted on the terra firma. She struck me as a person I could be comfortable with in next to no time.

One afternoon, leaving the theatre at the same time, Sam and I found ourselves heading for the same street corner, where we'd parted company. But before we did, she asked, 'What d'you do on Sundays, usually, Timothy? If you don't mind me asking, that is.'

'Well, the usual thing: hit the books, do essays, that sort of thing. Always having to catch up on things, it seems.'

'Maybe you shouldn't be spending the time you do hanging around the theatre.'

'No, you're right, maybe I shouldn't.'

'Well, anyway, Timothy, one of these Sundays, if you ever get caught up on your school work, and feel like it, give me a call.' She gave me her number. 'Maybe we could have a drink or eat somewhere—later in the day, I mean. I don't get up until one.'

'Yes, I will. I'd like to very much.'

'Good. Actually, most Sundays, I find myself not doing very much at all.'

'You don't?'

'That's right. And don't seem so surprised. I don't have a parade of men lining up to see me, you know—at least not the sort of men I want to see.'

It was good timing. *You Never Can Tell*—no more than Sam and I could, for that matter—was opening the next night, with rehearsals just about over with. This—conveniently—would allow me more weekday time to get my school work done, to be able to give it a rest on Sundays. (As if I'd miss a chance of seeing Sam for whatever the reason.)

Going around with Sam on a Sunday became a habit I couldn't have broken if I'd tried; and which she seemed as eager as I was to keep up on a regular basis. I couldn't get enough of her company; when we were together it must have been written all over my face. When Sam put an arm through mine or around my waist while strolling the streets I could have been walking on air. I felt like a commoner who'd somehow snagged a gorgeous, egalitarian princess all for himself.

There were one or two things Sam left me to wonder about, however. Around the theatre you'd not have realized she knew me as well as she did. She didn't want us to mix with anyone else in the company. We never saw one another except on a Sunday, the way she wanted it. And she'd not as yet invited me over to her flat. In fact, I wasn't as sure as I'd have liked about how serious or not she wanted to be with me. She'd told me once that one of the things she appreciated most when she was with me were all the things I seemed to have on my mind other than getting into her knickers—and I'd taken my cue from that.

But not a cue, that, I wanted to keep on taking indefinitely. I'd fallen in love with Sam; I was crazy about her, actually. How could I not want to make love to her? And the way she touched and embraced me, as freely as she did, I couldn't see her not wanting me to make love to her, either. It was just a matter of time before we'd become full-blown lovers, I believed. When the time was right, it would happen. And I went on believing this despite what Jack Stafford had told me over a coffee in the green room.

Another of the Playhouse's bright, young up-and-comers, Stafford had had his eyes on Sam as well. He told me, however, he wasn't holding his breath waiting to get anywhere with her. 'She's a very dedicated career girl is our lovely Sam,' he said. 'And if she's keen on anybody around here some think it has to be Julian. But if she is, she's keener, I'd say, on what he can do for her professionally rather than personally. Julian's been seeing an actress who's working in Leicester, I think it is, for quite awhile—everybody knows that. Mind you, I wouldn't put it past Sam trying it on with him. You know, mixing in a bit of pleasure with business as and when required. Then again, Julian's not slow; he'd probably see her coming a mile off.'

Apparently, Stafford didn't know about Sam seeing me. But I could have been wrong about that, though.

Sam said, 'You haven't said much lately about your Lawrence play, Tim. How's it coming?'

'It's finished, actually,' The play I was working on was another thing I'd sometimes given priority over my studies for no good reason. 'Well, the fourth draft is finished, anyway.'

'How many drafts are you planning on, then?'

'One more, maybe two, I'm not sure.'

'Will you ever be sure, d'you think?'

'Well, I would really like to be sometime, Sam, if I can pull it off.'

'And you still haven't shown it to anybody?'

'Not yet. Nor even talked about it to anyone—except you, of course.'

'Well, maybe you should. Maybe get some actors to read it for you. Hear how it sounds, how the lines bounce back and forth between characters. And maybe show it to somebody at the university.'

'Yes, I was thinking of that. There's someone I thought might be a possibility—in the English department, where else? And where Lawrence still rules like a god; where you have to be careful what you have to say about him.'

'Well, Tim, write a play like you have and what can you expect? Bound to bring the literati scurrying out of their cubbyholes, isn't it?'

Sam was right about that. Perhaps I should have written something else—or, for that matter, nothing at all. But for my sort it doesn't work like that; get a burning idea for something and it's rarely a matter of just letting it go on a whim.

And so it was for me in this case. I'd taken it on, and it had taken me over. But this time, perhaps, the blame wasn't entirely my own. A certain amount I could surely plonk down, with some justification, on the narrow shoulders of The Monk—Sidney Monkwell, a D.H. Lawrence aficionado and my English teacher at Blenheim Park High School in Westcliff. The Monk had patiently endeavoured to make the dense, both hard-edged and sensitive world of Lorenzo, as he called Lawrence, as fascinating and enriching for his sixth form class as it was for him. It had worked pretty well in my case, anyway.

The book we were studying was the autobiographical novel *Sons and Lovers*, in which Lawrence's Paul Morel and Miriam Lievers mirrored himself, the young Bertie, and his first love, Jessie Chambers. A story about young love and becoming a writer I'd have had trouble resisting no matter how I'd been introduced to it; and it got me reading other D.H.L. novels, short stories, poetry and some biographical material into the bargain. And before I knew it, I was trying my hand at writing a play about Bertie and Jessie—and this with my A level school exams less than four months distant. It wasn't my first attempt at a piece for the stage. I'd written a comedic one-acter and a full-length drama, the one presented at Blenheim Park High, the other at Cliff Place Methodist. I reckoned I'd learned a thing or two about doing something for the stage, and also from the number of plays I'd seen and read. In the summer holidays I'd worked three to four hours a day on the play. And after getting in to Nottingham, I was looking forward to the opportunity to do some relevant, in-depth research there to help my cause.

Cradling her glass of red, Sam said, 'I've been thinking, Tim. Why don't you let Julian have a look at it?'

'Yes, that crossed my mind too—but no, I don't think so, Sam. I don't want to embarrass myself, or him.'

'Yes, I thought you might say that. So here's another idea. Why not let me read it—as it is now? No matter how many drafts you do, if it ever goes into production it's going to change again, anyway. I'd say what you need right now, Tim, is a knowledgeable assessment, from a reliable source, that is. See if it's shaping up as something an audience would want to see. And that's something I think I can provide for you, Tim—in fact I know I can, no problem—as the actress said to the playwright, without a blush to be seen. And I promise you, Tim, what you'll get from me is an honest-to-God opinion, nothing less. No beating around the bushes, no sugar-coating. And if that means you won't want to speak to me again for God knows how long, then so be it.'

A risk she was much readier to take than I was at that moment, obviously. But also, maybe, the sort of test a relationship in the making like ours needs to undergo from time to time to determine its chances of going anywhere. And the next day, I'd left at the theatre a copy of what I'd provisionally titled *Writing and Loving, Loving and Writing* for Sam to take home with her at the Christmas break.

For the young Bertie Lawrence, perhaps, there had had to have been a Jessie Chambers. And after Jessie, an Agnes Holt, an Alice Dax, a Helen

Corke—and then a Louise Burrows, to whom he got himself engaged but never married. With someone like the individualistic Bertie, would-be lover and neophyte literary artist, the loving and the writing would always go hand in hand, side by side, if not always in the same order of choice.

In time, however, when Frieda Weekley came on the scene—she was a von Richthofen, of aristocratic German descent—the romantic running around came to an abrupt halt. The strong-minded, wilful and randy Frieda left her husband—a Nottingham academic who'd taught Lawrence—and their three children to run away with Lorenzo. And as soon as they could, the two elopers got married, forming a once-and-for-all marital alliance. Despite the example of his parents' chronically unhappy union, Lawrence never doubted that marriage was right for him. Quite early on he'd begun articulating the idea that any greatness in a man, no matter his choice of livelihood, is founded on the woman at his side. And before Frieda he'd measured every woman he was involved with by whether or not she was marriageable for him.

But to begin with, it had been Jessie Chambers. The quiet, reserved country girl's faith in Bertie as a writer, and her love for him, knew no bounds. Her father farmed near Eastwood in Nottinghamshire at The Haggs, where Bertie hung around a lot mainly because of Jessie; and where he showed the intelligent and sensitive Jessie drafts of his stories, pressing for her opinions. Jessie became Bertie's only source of encouragement as a writer; he couldn't count on any from family members. She was the first to recognize Lorenzo's very special gift, and acted as an agent of sorts for him as well.

Although he'd given Jessie sufficient reason to believe he was interested in her romantically, Bertie decided she wasn't the woman he could ever see himself marrying. He told her he couldn't love her 'as a husband should love a wife'; that he could give her only what he would 'a holy nun'. But later, while Jessie was visiting him in Croydon, he persuaded her to have sex with him, putting at risk both her good name and teaching career. And giving Jessie cause to believe, erroneously, that he'd changed his mind about her and their prospects of becoming man and wife. Instead, however, the insensitive Bertie (to say the least) informed her that as a lover she was too passive, like 'a sacrificial virgin'—and with that squashed her hopes of ever becoming his life partner and muse.

Jessie believed that Lydia Lawrence, his mother, was at the root of Bertie's problems with her. Mrs. L. didn't consider Jessie good enough for her Bertie. Jessie wrote (in a memoir) that Lydia had an unassailable belief in her rightness in all things; that she 'ruled by a sort of divine right of motherhood' over Bertie. Jessie characterized Lydia as 'the priestess rather than the mother', and that questioning her authority would have seemed like sacrilege to Bertie. Also, Jessie knew—as Bertie must have too—that he couldn't expect any support from his mother so far as his aspirations as a writer were concerned. Lydia never did acknowledge or appreciate his talent. She'd been singularly unimpressed by the early drafts of his first novel, *The White Peacock*, he'd been so keen to have her read. All that mattered to Bertie's mother was her son's success in a traditional and secure position of respectability—and not at all his desire to write, to use and serve his gift, his art. For this reason too, then, Jessie couldn't understand why Bertie was unable to see how good in so many ways she would have been for him.

But the evidence is thin on the ground, if it exists at all, that she'd have served Lorenzo as well as the woman he eventually chose to marry. Lawrence came to regard Frieda as his lodestar, the source of all good for him—his very life source. (He did go on a bit, of course.) And with that, presumably, responsible for all he was able to make of himself as a man and as a writer. Ostensibly, Lorenzo's passion for his art and his chosen woman went hand in hand.

In the new year (1981), with a play going into rehearsal, Sam returned to Nottingham a week ahead of me. And when I got back she had some surprises for me.

She told me she liked my play, liked it a lot. 'It's well constructed, reads very smoothly. Your Lawrence and Jessie jump off the page at you. And very well researched, I'm sure.' What perhaps surprised me more, though, was how emotionally exercised Sam was by what she'd read. 'I know what shits artists can be, of course—but there were times when I felt Lawrence needed smashing in the face, or maybe lower. And times when I wanted to give Jessie a good shaking; to tell her to wake up and start looking after herself, to care for herself better.'

Then, the next day, she invited me over to her place for dinner. That was a surprise; something she'd never done before. When I complimented her on the meal—a made-from-scratch chicken pie with wine sauce, and an apple crumble dessert topped with freshly whipped cream—she said, 'Yes, I thought you'd be surprised, Tim. I don't tell my friends I can cook.

They'd laugh and not believe me, or ask me to prove it to them. So let's keep it just between you and me, all right? And besides, something like that wouldn't do a thing for my image as a dyed-in-the-wool feminist, would it?'

Then another surprise from Sam awaited me—a surprise and a half, in fact. She said, 'I hope you won't be annoyed when I tell you this, Tim, but here goes, anyway. I gave your play to Julian. And he likes it so much he wants to workshop it; and also thinks there's a chance it could be included in next season's lineup. So what d'you think of that?' Some great news she thought well worth celebrating together, she said. And raising her glass: 'So here's to your little gem of a play, Tim. And may she soon be sparkling under the lights here, there and everywhere.'

Then, came her biggest surprise for me. When it was about time for me to leave, Sam said, 'Well, this has been lovely, Tim, it really has. So lovely in fact I don't want it to end. And if that's how you feel too, why end it? So why don't we make a night of it? Why don't you say for breakfast? And in any case, Tim, I don't really see much point anymore in delaying the inevitable any longer, do you?'

This rather amazing turn of events hadn't seemed in the least inevitable to me, actually; and which, I think, served to make our love making that night so much the more surprising and sweeter for me. The next morning, I felt like the prince in a happy fairy tale.

There were some other such nights to come over the next year or so. But not on a regular basis, by any means. With Sam's flat the venue for these meetings it was always her call to make; only when she was in the mood, in other words.

Julian workshopped the play that winter and into the spring. I did what amounted to a complete rewrite. I wasn't to be seen around the university very much. In March the Playhouse announced its 1981-82 season—and there it was, in black and white: '*Writing and Loving, Loving and Writing* by Timothy Hainault. A fresh, searching look at D.H. Lawrence's early days in Nottinghamshire and London. A fascinating, finely-drawn portrait of the artist as a young man, warts and all.'

Directed by Julian, with Jack Stafford as Lawrence and Sam as Jessie (she liked the challenge of playing someone so different from herself), the play opened in the second half of the season in April, three weeks before my twentieth birthday. The entire experience—the rehearsals, the promotion, the previews and performances—left me periodically in a state of near disbelief. Seeing my name in the advertising, the programme and the press had a dream sequence quality about it. There were even occasional moments when what I was watching onstage seemed to have little if any connection with me.

Every interlocking part of the production was pulled off superbly, and had the critics, academics and punters all on the same page, chorusing their approval with hardly a dissonant note. The box office was quickly under siege, and every seat sold out for the entire run within three days of opening. And all of this very exciting and exhilarating stuff for me, of course.

And all the more so when a London group came in with solid plans and a good offer for a West End production. But business being business, the London would-be producers had in mind another director and a 'name' actor for both the Bertie and Jessie roles. Even so, though, everyone at the Playhouse exuded happiness for me when the London production was confirmed. Julian kindly linked me up with a London agent who secured a good advance and royalties deal for me. He told me, 'Tim, don't think of this as a fluke, a one-off, will you? Your play deserves to be in London. And no matter what happens with it there, see it as a stepping stone to your next one, won't you?'

I'd had to tell Dad about the play. Not that I'd not wanted to; I'd been bursting to tell him. But I wasn't sure how he'd react. And I was feeling guilty too, having neglected my studies; and, in a way, having misappropriated his money, hard-earned or from insurances, either way.

He came up to see the play on the second Saturday. Congratulating me, he said he was very impressed. 'It's excellent, Tim—although I'm not by any means an expert on things theatrical, of course.' And said later, 'As the play unfolded I was trying to tell where your sympathies lay—with Lawrence or with Jessie.'

'Were you? And what did you decide?'

'I didn't. I couldn't be sure, one way or the other. Which is how you wanted it to be, I expect.'

I introduced him to Sam after the show. I think he could see what I saw in her. 'She's charming,' he said; an adjective I'd never heard him use before. 'And in person not at all like Jessie, is she? She's a very good actress, obviously.'

Dad went back to Westcliff the next day, not in any way displeased with me, it would seem.

After *Writing and Loving . . .* closed at the Playhouse, Sam and I remained on friendly terms. But she'd stopped phoning, suggesting we do something. Something was up. I did remember her once, during rehearsals, saying she might be realizing why, in deciding on the play's title, I'd put the 'writing' first and last, and the 'loving' in-between. (And in saying that, had she identified me with Bertie and herself with Jessie, and suggesting she'd always come second to the writing with me?) In any case, I was very unhappy with the cooling off that seemed to be going on between us. I didn't think it was my fault, for one thing. And as it continued on, the more miserable I felt, the more despondent I was. I saw her on one occasion in a pub with Julian, but made sure they didn't see me. I never did know if anything had been going on between them, but if so it was short-lived. Sam didn't sign on with the Playhouse for another season, moving on instead to the prestigious Birmingham Rep.

Sam and I parted amicably enough—closing a chapter in our young lives during which our shared experiences had perhaps at times overlapped emotionally and psychologically into Bertie and Jessie's at a similar point in theirs; and maybe partly explaining our attraction for one another in no small way.

About a year later, *Writing and Loving . . .* got good notices in London and looked set for a pretty good stay. (It ended up running for more than eleven months.) If Dad had needed any reminding of my surprising success he got it from his firm's managing director, Sir Henry Aylesworth, a well-known theatre arts patron. 'It's the first time Sir Harry's ever spoken to me,' Dad said. 'I think he's got this odd idea that I must have had something to do with you being the promising playwright he obviously thinks you are, Timothy—something to do with genes, I suppose it is.'

When I informed Dad I was skipping my last year in university to move to London—I'd already lined up a small basement flat in Putney—he said he understood why I might have wanted to do that. 'You can always catch up on your degree some other time,' he said. A promising playwright I may well have been—but in my father's view, I think, there could be a time, perhaps in the not-too-distant future, when I'd be scouring the 'Help Wanted' ads for a steady job of some sort.

3

THE GIRL FROM MAPLE COTTAGE

by Tim Hainault

In the summer I went to Canada with my family, my mum and dad and my brother Paul, for our holidays. It was the biggest holiday we've ever been on. We stayed with the Bannerman family, my Uncle Wally, Auntie Pam and my cousins Barbara who is 12 like Paul and Jimmy who is about my age. Everybody calls Barbara Barbie.

We went to London and caught a very big Canadian jet airliner. The plane was so big I didn't think it would get off the ground, but it did and it flew very smoothly. We were high over the clouds and we didn't seem to be going at all, just floating. The Atlantic Ocean was below us most of the way. Dad said we were crossing what some people call The Pond, doing the opposite to exaggerating.

Uncle Wally met us at the airport in Toronto which is a round building the planes go right up to. He drove us a long way into the country in a big and long motor called a Country Squire. It looked like it had wooden sides but they were really made of metal. Uncle Wally said it was called a station wagon. There was lots of room in it for all of us and the luggage, and it could go fast with a big load like us.

The Bannermans live in Minden which isn't a very big place. Uncle Wally said everybody knew each other in Minden which he liked the idea of for some reason. My uncle's and aunt's house is on a long and pretty wide lake called Hall's Lake you can fish in for trout, I think it is. It is quite a big house with wooden sides painted white with green shutters, they call them. The back of the house is nearest to the lake and has a veranda as wide as the house with white wooden chairs on it, and a sofa that swings like a seat on a Ferris wheel at the fair. There is a big lawn and a garden on one side of the house, and trees and bushes with plenty of places to hide in on the other side. A stone path and steps goes down to the lake and to a wooden jetty. In the lake about 30 yards out there is a raft covered by a rubber mat you can dive from. It is chained to something in the water to keep it from floating away. Not far from the jetty is a small boathouse with a metal motor boat and two rowing boats in it.

I think that Uncle Wally must be pretty well off. He has a big shop in Minden called Bannerman's Hardware that sells all sorts of things like tools, taps, pots and pans, tents for camping, fishing rods and what you need to play baseball, which is like rounders, ice hockey and tennis, and lawn mowers you push and also ones you sit on and drive like small tractors.

I didn't think it would be but every day it was hot, hotter than in England. The air felt sticky to me, so it was good to have the lake to go in. The water in the lake was clear and cool but not too cool on the skin.

My cousin Barbie and her friend Francie were swimming or lying around on the raft most of the day. They also used to water ski, and Jimmy did too, pulled along by Uncle Wally or Auntie Pam in the motor boat. Mum used to wonder at the things Auntie Pam used to do like that. Paul and me had a few goes at water ski-ing too but we weren't very good at it. When we did Barbie and Francie used to try not to laugh, but Jimmy didn't try not to at all. He laughed out aloud.

Sometimes we went fishing with Uncle Wally. I found it boring. We stared at the water a lot, for ages, and hardly ever caught anything. After a few days Jimmy and me stopped going out, and then Paul did too, so it was just Dad and Uncle Wally.

Paul didn't want to play very much with Jimmy and me. He went for walks in the woods that were everywhere, and also spent quite a lot of time swimming and on the raft with Barbie and Francie. I think he was keen on Francie.

"Your brother must like girls" said Jimmy and made a face.

Jimmy and me did some swimming and also some other things together. He taught me some card games using real playing cards and when Dad saw us playing he didn't like it very much I could tell.

I also learned some sports from Jimmy I had never played that Dad didn't mind me playing. Jimmy talked a lot about baseball and about teams that played in America. There didn't seem to be any that played in Canada. But he also talked about ice hockey that he said is played inside on ice that men have to make themselves. The team he supported and knew all about was in Toronto and was called the Maple Leaves that had won a lot of cups and is famous in Canada like Arsenal is in England for football.

On the lawn we put on big leather gloves Jimmy called mitts and threw around a baseball that is made of white leather but isn't as hard as a cricket ball. We were not allowed to hit the ball hard at all, just take gentle taps. We played shuttlecock as well, and in a sand pit at the end of the lawn we threw some real horse shoes trying to get them around a metal stake which is called getting a ringer. You use underhand tosses to throw the horse shoes.

We also played cowboys and Indians with silver cap guns and rifles, chasing each other in the trees and bushes.

Jimmy also liked to play with toy soldiers. He had a big plastic box full of them with lots of Germans too, and another one with jeeps, lorries, tanks, big guns and rocket launchers. He didn't have any redcoats like I do. He said Uncle Wally had won some medals fighting against the Germans in Italy. Jimmy called the Germans Gerries and the Italians Eyeties.

One day we were playing with the toy soldiers on a rocky bit of ground near the lake. I was always the Germans. Jimmy said stop the battle and he stood up. He was looking towards the bushes.

"Hey, what are you looking at?" he shouted.

I looked to where he was looking, and I saw a girl in the bushes. I could only see her head and shoulders. She had a dark sun tan and was nice looking. She had long black, very straight hair. She had a red piece of cloth tied around her forehead. She was maybe a bit older than me. She looked quite a big different from an English girl. Most English girls have fair skin and lighter hair.

"What are you spying on us for?" Jimmy called out.

The girl didn't answer.

"You're not supposed to be there anyhow" said Jimmy. "You're on our property. Go on, scram! Vamoose!"

The girl still wouldn't say anything. She gave Jimmy a long look and me a shorter one. She sort of laughed like people do who think you're not up to much and not worth listening to, and disappeared.

"She's from next door, she's staying in Maple Cottage" said Jimmy. "In summer you get all sorts in there."

"Was she on your property?" I asked.

"Maybe, I dunno" said Jimmy.

"I guess you don't like her" I said.

"No I don't, who likes girls anyhow?" said Jimmy. "And I don't want her hanging around watching us like that."

"Maybe she wants to be friends" I said.

"No, she don't, and we don't want to be friends with her" said Jimmy. "The sort she is, they're not our sort. They're like hippies. Her dad's got his hair in a pony tail. And I think they're Jews as well as being hippies. Maple Cottage belongs to Mister Berg who teaches school and that's what he is, and Mister Berg has long hair and looks like a hippie guy too."

The next day Jimmy went into Minden with Auntie Pam for something. I walked down towards the lake and sat down where Jimmy and me had seen the girl from Maple Cottage. She wasn't there. But she suddenly appeared in about the same place she'd been in the day before. This time I could see all of her. She had on a long skirt that had lots of different coloured patches on it. She had a cloth strap around her with a camera on it.

"Where's the other boy?" she asked

I told her he was away for the afternoon and she smiled and said "Good." She really was pretty.

She wasn't a bit shy. She said her name was Rebecca Jacobs and that she was from Toronto. I told her who I was and where I was from. She said she liked the name Timothy, and after I'd said a few things she said she also liked the way I talked, the accent and everything.

When I asked her she said she liked taking photos of chipmonks. Chipmonks are small brown animals like squirrels with darker stripes on their fur. She said she liked to draw and paint coloured pictures of the chipmonks copying from her photos.

"Sometimes I give them names and put clothes on them and make up stories about them which maybe you think is silly" she said.

I said no, I didn't think that. I was thinking of "Wind in the willows." I don't think she believed me.

"I like writing stories too" I said.

"Do you?" she said. "What kind of stories?"

"About knights in olden times" I answered.

"They fight and kill people I suppose" she said.

"Evildoers, they do" I said.

"Do you like playing games killing and blowing up people?" she asked.

I said I sometimes did but not all the time.

"Maybe it's okay for boys to like stories and play games like that, but there are boys who want to do that for real when they grow up, and I don't think anybody should want to do that, but they do. But if they didn't there wouldn't be anybody to fight the wars, would there?"

I said I guess not.

She asked if she could take a photo of me and I said fine and she did. I asked if I could take one of her with her camera and she wondered why, but let me.

"If you give me your address I may write and send you the photos, but I'm not promising" she said.

I was disappointed and maybe I looked like I was.

"Well, I don't think you're Jewish like me, are you?" she said.

I said it didn't matter to me that she was Jewish.

"Do you go to church?" she asked.

I said yes.

"Well, maybe I'll write, and maybe I won't" she said.

I didn't get to talk to her anymore after that.

Rebecca hasn't sent anything to me yet. I'm really hoping that one day she will. I would like to have a photo of her. I would also like to write her and for us to become pen pals. And if anybody ever said we shouldn't be pen pals I'm pretty sure I wouldn't take any notice of them. And if anybody said that to Rebecca I'll be hoping she won't take any notice either.

4

Getting a true take on the more distant past, getting it straight, isn't a doddle. Sometimes it takes some reading between the lines.

James Hainault, my grandfather, an East Ender born and bred, was sometimes called 'Gentleman Jim.' Because he looked the part—handsome, well-groomed and Brilliantined, nicely turned out; like a First Class passenger on a between-the-wars art deco railway poster. Jimmy wouldn't have been seen dead in anything bought at The Co-op. He got his suits made-to-measure in Stepney; his shirts, ties, hats and shoes further west on Oxford Street. He liked to sound the part as well. He modified his vowel sounds, sounded his 'h's, avoided common-speaking contractions and never used double negatives. Henry Higgins would have been proud of him—but not fooled for a moment by him either.

By Manor Park E12 standards, Jimmy Hainault was quite a catch—and knew it too. He'd got most of his high-flying ideas about himself honestly from his mother, and none at all from his father. Enid Hainault had lived to make her boy James (she never called him Jim or Jimmy or even Jamie) what her husband Henry (Harry) never had amounted to as she saw it: a man going places, a somebody. Enid had married and appropriated Harry and the sweets, fags and newspaper shop on Church Road he'd inherited from his father, and the upstairs flat that went with it, before he knew what was happening to him. Sizing up the quiet, diffident, dutiful son Harry had always been, Enid took over from where her husband's typically Victorian father William had left off, getting him sorted out and running the business, doing things exactly the way she wanted them done.

After Jimmy had put in his appearance—an experience Enid swore she'd never go through again, and never did—Harry quickly found himself relegated to a distant second place in his wife's affections; a state of affairs he accepted without a murmur. Young James was now the centre of the Hainaults' universe for Enid, and, needless to say, for Harry as well.

The boy was bright enough to get into a grammar school in nearby Ilford, and Enid was as sure as she was proud of him that he was on his way. But Jimmy didn't take to scholastic activities. He said he'd only end up as a teacher, anyway. That he didn't want to stay in schoolrooms all his life—not with a big, bright and interesting world out there just waiting for him. He had no intentions either of being a shopkeeper, he told Enid and Harry, which was all right with her. She also thought he was destined for better things.

After working for a wholesale grocery firm for a couple of years, Jimmy reckoned his talents as a salesman were going to waste on penny-pinching shopkeepers, and that his commissions were not large enough. He moved on to a well-known Wolsley car dealership and its fancy showroom in Ilford; and where, by the age of eighteen, he was outselling everyone else on staff. He told Enid that the owner had his eye on him, and not having a son of his own could be thinking of him as one. And that if he continued to do well and play his cards right there was a good chance he'd be able to take over the firm in his twenties.

But that was Jimmy talking—his usual big talk. Jimmy being Jimmy, who else? With confidence coming out of his ears and full of himself, courtesy of his mother, Jimmy at eighteen thought he could talk himself into getting anything he wanted, and out of anything he didn't.

Like many of his sort, Jimmy liked to play the big shot, to impress people, particularly the ones he thought could help him, and flashing his money around. He never had any trouble attracting people who were out to get something from him either—the sort of people, along with the girls among them, his mother would not have approved of, if she'd known anything about them. Jimmy was careful to keep the way he spent his evenings and days off from Enid. He'd tell her all sorts of things. He was going to night school; attending sales seminars; had joined a chess club; even taking in Young Conservatives meetings—all of which his mother seemed to have swallowed whole. If Enid had ever had any idea about the company her James was getting into, and about the gambling habit he'd acquired—cards, the horses, the dogs, even betting on darts and snooker—she'd have convinced herself it wasn't possible, quite out of the question. What, her clever, lovely boy? There'd have been no losing faith in her James for Enid. (She wouldn't have had any of Harry's occasional doubts about him, of course.)

The name may have had an Arcadian ring to it, but Greenhill Grove wasn't what it sounded like. The Grove was just another drab, nondescript Manor Park street, with Church Road at one end and the busy Romford Road at the other, and sided by small, very modest, grey-stoned, look-alike row housing. Only the paint on the doors, the way the lace curtains in the front bay windows were hung, distinguished one house from another. Not entirely a residential street, the Grove had small businesses with yards and a cluster of shops at opposite ends; and towards the middle, a public house on one side and a Salvation Army hall, home of the Manor Park Corps, on the other, reminding residents and passers-by of the pull of both God and his fallen angels in everyday life—if many on the street ever thought of such matters, of course.

Stanley and Millie Linton and their only child Mavis lived across the street from the Salvation Army hall and only a few doors from the pub. Stanley was a ticket collector at the Woodgrange Park railway station. Woodgrange Park was another misleadingly-named district adjacent to Manor Park. When he wasn't working, Stanley spent a lot of his time in the very handy pub in the Grove or in a snooker hall on East Ham High, and on Saturdays watching West Ham United at Upton Park. Millie, on the other hand, didn't go out very much, only to work—she was a part-time seamstress—or to do the shopping. Now and again, though, she crossed the road to attend the Home League, the women's group meeting at the Salvation Army. Also, Millie sent Mavis to the Sunday school at 'the Army.'

At Sunday school Mavis used to sing 'I'll be a sunbeam for Jesus and shine for him each day', which even then she seldom did, and which she didn't do at all as she developed into a pretty, blonde-curled, long-legged, perky-breasted, very wilful teenager. Mavis didn't like being told to do anything, preferring to do what she'd been told not to do. She took to pinching her dad's fags. And liking boys as much as she did—and they her—she frequently lied to her mother about the company she'd been keeping. Stanley was tacitly proud of his daughter. He liked her spirit, the way she wouldn't be intimidated, and laughed off much of her misbehaviour, to Millie's exasperation. Also, he knew Mavis knew a few things about him he didn't want getting back to his wife.

After leaving school and a couple of shop jobs, Mavis went to work in the office at a commercial laundry on Church Road. The Advance Laundry was on the same side, only a few doors down from Hainault & Son's on the corner. It was only a matter of time before Mavis Linton and Jimmy Hainault met up with one another. One morning, Mavis was being served by Enid when Jimmy came downstairs into the shop. Ignoring Enid's stony glare, Jimmy chatted up Mavis. They both knew straight away that things could heat up very quickly between them, if that was what they wanted, which it was.

Mavis wasn't the melting sort, and far from a fool she wasn't taken in easily by anybody. She was onto Jimmy in a jiffy; she recognized the type. She had her dad to go by, for a start. She guessed that Jimmy wanted her only for one thing, and she was right. There was too much Manor Park in the girl for his liking. But suspecting Jimmy wasn't to be trusted any further than she could throw him, Mavis took up with him just for the sexy fun of it. She could play his sort of games as well as he could.

So the fast dance, the free-and-easy frolicking went on for Jimmy and Mavis for several months. They were mad for each other—and not always as careful as they'd meant to be.

In the spring of 1927, Jimmy and Mavis had a very small, very quiet wedding at a register office in Woodford. Mavis was five months pregnant with my Aunt Pam. Back then, having an abortion wasn't really an option. Jimmy was twenty, Mavis only seventeen—but given the checkered parental control the two had had, they were hardly two kids who didn't know which way was up.

If it hadn't been for their respective mothers, the less-than-ecstatic couple probably wouldn't have got married at all. To save face, Enid insisted her James do his gentlemanly duty, gritting her teeth as she did so; and hinting there'd be no more infusions of money for Jimmy if he didn't go along with her. At the same time, Millie convinced Mavis that she'd never be able to give her child up for adoption, and that single motherhood wasn't a very good idea at all. Good men were scared off by an unmarried woman with a child, Millie told her.

Enid may have been counting on the marriage falling apart before too long. Her fine boy James had made a very foolish if very human mistake, getting himself trapped by a pretty and scheming and tarty woman, she reasoned. She was sure he'd see Mavis for what she was, and get free of her; that he'd put the whole unfortunate business behind him, and find himself an infinitely more suitable wife, preferably as far away from E12, from the East End altogether, as possible. As it stood, Enid herself wasn't content to stick around in Manor Park for very much longer. Getting after Harry to sell the shop and flat and get a nice bungalow somewhere, Enid didn't take long getting her way. With their move to Loughton, Essex in '28, Hainault & Son's on Church Road was no more.

But then again, it was a time when divorce wasn't so easily obtained, and there was more of a stigma to it as well. And as the thirties dawned, Jimmy and Mavis were still together and living in Manor Park—together after a fashion, anyway. Jimmy had left the Wolsley firm in Ilford under some sort of cloud and was selling gramophones, records and sheet music in Leytonstone. In nearby Snaresbrook, he'd frequently stay overnight with a buxom widow in her thirties with some money to her name. And back in Manor Park, Mavis, in turn, was partial to some occasional male company in Jimmy's absence.

In 1931, shocking Enid and mystifying Millie, along with everybody else, Mavis gave birth to Arthur, my father. Aunt Pam told me that Jimmy and Mavis had never stopped sleeping together—that that was about the only thing they were good at together. And although some said he'd said as much, Jimmy never did deny the boy was his. 'And besides, Tim, your dad is the spitting image of his father—and you're not unlike him either, you know, if you look at the photos I've got of him,' Pam said.

In the recession-plagued thirties, Jimmy managed to survive. Always the main chancer, he went where there still was some money in evidence, working in a West End nightclub and its illegal gambling annex in the basement as an undercover security man, looking good in white tie and tails. He was popular with the ladies, of course—with one, a chorus girl, in particular.

Mavis and the kids were not seeing much of Jimmy in their cramped Shakespeare Avenue flat. (Incongruously, perhaps, several Manor Park streets are named after great literary figures such as Byron, Coleridge, Wordsworth, Tennyson and Browning as well as The Bard.) With only some spotty financial help from Jimmy, Mavis was nevertheless getting on with it, and getting by. She was back working as a clerk at The Advance Laundry, and getting regular and willing babysitting help from her mother.

By the time Neville Chamberlain got back from Munich, waving a piece of paper and chuntering on about peace in our time, Jimmy and Mavis had decided to bring their own hot-and-cold war to an end. They hardly saw anything of one another after that. (Enid Hainault was too sick and Harry too busy looking after her to care very much, apparently.) Jimmy and Mavis did talk about getting a divorce, but never got it done.

Mavis, however, was starting to worry about her kids. Following in her mother's footsteps, Pam, thirteen, was rebellious and secretly seeing boys, while nine-year-old Arthur was running the streets with some pals he made sure his mum and grandma never got to meet. Millie Linton was by then a Christian convert, having got 'saved' at the Salvation Army across the street. (Stanley complained that she wasn't the woman he'd married anymore—the woman he'd largely ignored and cheated on.) Mavis routinely ignored her mother's opinion that the children could do with some Christian education, some spiritual care and attention at the Army.

But something was going to have to be done pretty soon, Mavis realized. In particular, young Artie—a Smart Alec and an Artful Dodger in the making—was becoming a regular little blighter and getting out of control. After he'd got caught shoplifting for a second time, Mavis—this time agreeing with Millie—began fearing for the boy's safety, moral as well as physical, on the dangerous wartime streets of E12. Mavis finally agreed to Arthur's evacuation to the Oxfordshire countryside, arranged by Millie through the Salvation Army's Manor Park Corps officers. Artie, to say the very least, was reluctant to go. He believed he was being abandoned by his mother, calling her 'a rotten cow' for doing a thing like that to him. Mavis had had second thoughts, but her mother persuaded her to stick to the plan. (Jimmy hadn't wanted to know.)

With Artie in the country, Mavis made noises too about sending Pam out of London as well. But the girl made even more fuss than Artie had, screaming at her mother, accusing her of wanting her out of the way to make it easier to carry on with men. Mavis quickly backed down, letting Pam have her way.

Mavis continued carrying on with men, with Pam there or not; and continued to argue with Millie because of it. But not with Pam. Mother and daughter were pretty much in agreement when it came to seeing how the land lay in that one respect.

In 1943, Mavis started taking sixteen-year-old Pam up West with her to dance with women-hungry servicemen from Auckland to Arkansas. Developing nicely and pretty with it, Pam looked closer to twenty. Mavis had a serious falling out with Millie over these Saturday night jaunts, creating a rift between them the two never did quite get over.

Meanwhile, in Hook Norton, Oxfordshire, young Artie had undergone a personal transformation neither Mavis nor Pam could hardly credit, his mother in particular. Amazed and also perplexed, Mavis said she didn't really know her son anymore. The one-time little devil had joined Grandma Linton on the Lord's side, turning himself into a Christian; and telling his mother she could leave him in Hookey until the war was over, that that would be fine with him—according to Aunt Pamela. Hiding her hurt, something she'd always done well, Mavis told Artie that that would be best, anyway, with the Germans launching their V-1 'buzz bombs', aimed at London. This was in the summer of '44.

The next year, with the war over, Artie moved back to London. He was fourteen. He lived with the Lintons in Greenhill Grove until until he'd finished school. With Pam still at home, Mavis's flat was too small for the three of them. Artie and his mother didn't see a great deal of one another—something Mavis thought her mother might have had a hand in. But Artie told his sister that Millie had in fact encouraged him to see his mum more often—more often than he wanted to, actually. He wasn't comfortable around his mother, nor was she around him, he said.

Pam told me: 'Your dad didn't like the way Mum made him feel, like he'd betrayed her or something. He didn't care for her smoking and drinking either, specially the drinking. And he couldn't stand the bloke she was seeing a lot of, who didn't want him around, anyway.' And when Artie told Pam that she too could do better than the chap she was seeing, they'd had a big row. 'I said that if that's how it was—if he thought he was better than Mum and me—he could go and hang around with his friends at the Methodist church, and just leave us alone.'

It's hardly a revelation: it's not only death that breaks up families—but also life as it's lived, in one way or another, as well.

Gran Gadsden, on my mother's side, was the only grandparent who was still alive when I was born. She lived on into my thirties, happily. Her husband was in the Royal Air Force and was killed in WWII. Mavis

Hainault survived the war (as did the Lintons and Jimmy's parents), but not by a lot. Except for Jimmy, they were all gone by the early '50s.

Next to Charlie Gadsden, Mavis died the youngest at forty-one in 1949, succumbing quite suddenly to ovarian cancer. She'd kept up appearances, not saying anything to anyone about her illness; even Millie didn't know. Her husband Jimmy wasn't told. Dad had made countless enquiries, but neither he nor Pam could find out where their father was living.

Jimmy died in 1960 after a heart attack at the age of fifty-four. Dad got a late-night phone call from his father's Clapham landlady and companion, a Doreen Featherstone. Before suffering an earlier heart attack, Jimmy had been driving a taxi cab in the West End. Dad said that at the funeral Doreen had been very distraught.

Pam's marriage in Toronto in 1946 to a Canadian airman she'd met at the Lyceum in London during the war was dissolved in '51. She'd had two miscarriages. She stayed in Toronto doing part-time office work and instructing at an Arthur Murray dance studio. She didn't marry again until 1957 after meeting another WWII ex-serviceman and 'confirmed bachelor,' Wally Bannerman. In Toronto for a trade show, Wally had gone to a hockey game in Maple Leaf Gardens where Pam, working as an usherette, had shown him to his seat.

If it wasn't for Pam, what I'd know about the Hainault side of the family wouldn't be extensive. Recently, though, Dad has opened up to some extent about his early Manor Park and Hook Norton days, with Gran Gadsden filling in certain gaps he'd left, including a thing or two he'd have preferred to have been left untold, I'm sure.

5

Charles Dickens said he found it difficult to write when he was away from London—from the city he'd called 'the magic lantern.' And for me too, as a youngster, London had a magic show quality about it I was always hankering to experience once again, and the sooner the better—and never more so than at Christmastime.

For my family, it was always the first or the second Saturday in December: time for our Christmas season trip to the centre of our known world.

All of us were up early—no later than 6:15 a.m. We'd dodge around one another to get into the bathroom. The boiled eggs, toast and marmalade were scoffed, the sweet tea gulped down. By eight o'clock, after scurrying down Hamlet Court Road to Westcliff station, we'd be click-clacking our way on the Fenchurch Street line to The Big Smoke.

The train always stops at Barking. It was in and around this East London suburb on one such trip I'd first heard the joke newspaper headline 'Barking Man Bitten By Dog,' and also: 'If you're mad for Barking, you have to be barking mad.' Days such as these were days for jokes. A good time was being had by all.

After Barking it was non-stop all the way to Fenchurch Street; a station without the cachet of termini such as Kings Cross, Waterloo and Victoria, perhaps. But one's point of access to a city that 'contains no less than everything', that's 'a true vision of the world' (Peter Ackroyd in his remarkable *London The Biography*), is really neither here nor there.

But what London is, and what's gone on there over the centuries as well, is all part of its fascination for me. Walking its streets, whether just visiting or there to make a living, wherever you go, the evidence of two millennia of history is all around you.

Taking the five-minute walk from Fenchurch to the nearest underground station, for instance, you'll pass by St. Olave's, Hart Street—frequently mentioned in parishioner, plague and Great Fire survivor and Restoration playgoer Samuel Pepys' diary (and literary classic). And on entering the station one's view is monopolized by the imposing Tower of London, begun by William the Conqueror in the tenth century, and evoking as it does England's glorious and also tempestuous and bloody past in the shaping of a nation.

Every Christmas, travelling the tube from Tower Hill, we'd alight five stations later at Westminster, coming up to street level to find ourselves, as we knew we would, across from Big Ben and the Houses of Parliament, and a short walk from Westminster Abbey. We'd make an annual pilgrimage-like visit to the Abbey where we paused for any length of time only at the tomb of the 'Unknown Warrior'; before the Coronation chair in Edward the Confessor's chapel (where several English kings are buried), and in the Poet's Corner area. Dad gave Dickens's last resting place more attention than anybody else's except Sir Walter Scott's, possibly. And then, after exiting the Abbey and before heading north up Whitehall, Dad liked to reflect for a minute or two at the statue of Winston Churchill in Parliament Square. The great man's *A History of the English-speaking Peoples* in four volumes and his *The Second World War* in six are among Dad's more cherished literary possessions. Dad considers Churchill Britain's greatest hero, and God's man in a time of the nation's greatest ever need in the face of so great an evil. And has long believed the survival of Westminster Abbey and St. Paul's Cathedral in the Blitz had made clear enough which side, in God's sight, was in the right.

From that point the day's long route march was off and walking, with Dad leading the way—but never with any complaints from Mum, Paul or me. Each of us knew what lay ahead. We took the same route every year. And all of us, getting foot-weary or not, looked forward to every step along the way, every sight to be seen. For Paul and myself, particularly, there was always excitement in the damp or the crisp air.

Making our way along Whitehall, heading for Trafalgar Square, we'd pass Downing Street—a gated courtyard, actually—where the Prime Minister resides at Number 10. Then it was Indigo Jones' banqueting hall, on the balcony of which Charles I lost his head; the WWI Cenotaph in the centre of the street; and Horse Guards Parade, where the Trooping of the Colours takes place.

Entering Trafalgar Square, eyes are immediately drawn, of course, to the 185-foot-high Nelson's Column, on a central island and guarded by four bronze lions, commemorating the defeat of the French and Spanish fleets off Cape Trafalgar in 1805 by the nation's greatest and most celebrated admiral. Also, on the north side of the square, stand the National Art and National Portrait galleries, and one of London's best known churches: the early eighteenth century and Corinthian-porticoed St. Martins-in-the-Fields, where Handel sometimes popped in to take a turn on the organ. But in the square too at Christmastime, a towering Christmas tree, culled from a Scandinavian forest, festooned with cascading strings of glittering white lights, vied with Nelson's monument for one's attention, and got its full share especially from the kids in the crowd.

For Paul and I, the Christmas tree in Trafalgar Square seemed to signal our imminent entry into the magical, theme park-like world of Christmas into which West Central London had turned itself.

The city's West End is a year-round Vanity Fair, in any case—with its shops, restaurants, clubs and pubs, theatres and cinemas. But add to all that on every side, indoors and out, a brilliant, flashing array of festive Christmas trimmings—multi-coloured street illuminations of every size, shape and description, the floodlit buildings, the shop window displays and interior decorations. Carefree kids and not-too-jaded adults alike find themselves completely caught up in an extravaganza of beckoning attractions and sensory delights.

The loafing and looking around in Trafalgar Square over with, it was onward in earnest: up Haymarket to Piccadilly Circus, with its swirl of traffic and pedestrians, the latter probably making equally as much progress as the former. Eros got a glance or two but not much more than that. I recall my father saying that although he, for one, couldn't see much rhyme or reason in erecting a statue of a Grecian god of love to memorialize a prominent Victorian like Lord Shaftesbury, 'somebody must have known what he was doing, I suppose'. (Dad is curious to a fault and, if asked, a mine of information; he seldom goes anywhere, in town or country, without a pocket guide or natural history book to refer to.)

Branching off the Circus onto Regent Street, where many of Britain's flagship, most exclusive shops are congregated, it was the usual mob scene. Nothing else for us to do but to join the pavement parade's shuffling ranks. We were virtually at a standstill a lot of the time as we craned to get a better view of one spectacular, cleverly designed and artfully lit, frequently mechanized window display after another. In that district, that's what we'd come to do. Most of the street's department stores—high fashion merchants, jewellers and giftware shops—went unvisited by the Hainault family; and which, of course, was no skin off the establishments' sales staff's well-draped backs. We were not prospective customers, not at those prices. If we'd stepped inside any one of these shops we'd have been quickly sized up as lookers only and pointedly ignored, which would have been just fine with Mum and Dad.

One Regent Street shop was an exception to the rule for us, however. It was Hamley's—the well-known, long-established, five-floored toy box and treasure chest of a shop. In Hamley's, just a walk-through definitely wasn't on. Paul and I could roam the aisles at our leisure, having been allowed to look at what we wanted to and as long as we wanted to. Two hours could pass very quickly in Hamley's. But it was clearly understood: it was just to look, nothing more. Any pleas to have something or other bought for either one of us were a waste of breath; we knew they'd be ignored. At the same time, though, staying discretely in the background, Mum and Dad were in fact carrying out a shopping undercover operation.

How else explain, then, the toys and games that made our every Christmas Day morning so brilliant for Paul and me? It was the same thing every year. Dad would return to Hamley's after work to pick up certain items he'd made a note of; and back in Westcliff later that night he'd smuggle them into the house through the back door. He was taking no chances of being spotted. (Most Christmases, I'm sure, he and Mum would settle happily for less extravagant presents for one another, probably purchased in Westcliff or Southend, to help offset the money laid out in Hamley's on Regent Street.)

By the time we'd got through our circular W1 tour—up to, then east on Oxford Street and south on Charing Cross Road, with occasional detours into the surrounding maze of side streets (including Carnaby Street, of course)—it was dusk. We'd be back by then in Trafalgar Square, again admiring the Christmas tree. As the night sky closed in, the city's light show was so much the more effective and eye-catching—fantastical, almost.

Finally, getting off our aching feet, in a restaurant on the Strand—with white tablecloths, good tableware and cutlery, and waiters to serve us—we'd dine, if not like kings, like somebodies of some sort, it seemed to me. We didn't often eat out back home, not even in caffs; some occasional fish and chips on the seafront or on the London Road across from the Palace Theatre, and that was about it.

'Well, isn't this grand?' I remember Mum saying in the restaurant, smiling at Dad and Paul and me, a picture of contentment. What Mum thought was the grandest thing of all, though, I think, was being together like that, the four of us, for the whole day, enjoying each other's company; and maybe with some happy anticipation too of what we were still about to share together that evening.

After the restaurant and a taxi ride—another rarity, and in a London cab on such busy streets an adventure in itself—what awaited us next topped off the day splendidly. We had good seats—front row centre, lower balcony—for a big-time West End pantomime at the Coliseum; a spectacular, rollicking, time-honoured British theatrical tradition at Christmastime, of course. An amazing show, put on and pulled off with long-practised perfection—with star talent, a top-notch supporting ensemble, and costumes, scenery and special effects to knock your eyes out. (By comparison, the local panto at The Palace in Westcliff was Second or Third Division stuff—but an unfair comparison to make, though, given the differences in budget and technical capabilities.)

Mum's idea, going to the panto, without a doubt. As a child she'd been taken to London to see a panto from the age of five and on into her teens, and seemed to have wanted the delight and wonder she'd experienced at such times for her own children as well ; and any expectations Mum had had of that sort she would have most certainly seen fulfilled in me had she lived long enough. She would have been surprised, though, by the long-term effects of those London pantos on me. (I'd seen *Jack and the Beanstalk, Mother Goose, Cinderella* and *Dick Whittington*, the genre's classics, by the age of nine.) Then, getting into my teens, aided and abetted by what I'd gone to see at The Palace as well—in some instances without Dad knowing what I was seeing—live theatre had undoubtedly found itself a permanent place in my imagination and affections.

Having turned sixteen, I was getting up to London, mostly on Friday nights, to see as much theatre as I could afford, at student prices, in the cheap seats. Also, there were school trips to museums, galleries, places of historical interest; and the occasional football match and a day's cricket as well. And so it was, the more I went to London, the more convinced I'd become that it was there I'd feel as free as I'd need to be to explore myself intellectually and emotionally; to work out how I could best make something of myself, personally and professionally.

London had begun to get its sure and steady hold on me—and one, I'm certain, the city has never quite relinquished. (Peter Ackroyd again—his final words in his London biography: that the city 'contains every wish or word ever spoken, every action or gesture ever made, every harsh or noble statement ever expressed. It is illimitable. It is Infinite London.')

6

I'm certain my father has read Graham Greene—his earlier novels, at any rate: *Stamboul Train, England Made Me, Brighton Rock* and *The Power and the Glory*. These titles and others of Greene's were to be found in our front room library in Westcliff, courtesy of Anthony Timson. Anything Dad's mentor and father-figure in wartime Hook Norton had considered worth reading he would have as well. Greene, a Catholic convert—converts are usually the eager ones in the flock—wrote stories in which issues of religion, morality, personal salvation and redemption have a prominent place. Characterizing what he saw as an essential theme in much of his work, Greene quoted Robert Browning's *Bishop Blougram's Apology*:

> 'Our interest's on the dangerous side of things,
> The honest thief, the tender murderer,
> The suspicious athiest . . .'

And all of which might also have explained Anthony Timson's sympathetic feelings for the scruffy, hard-eyed, fractious nine-year-old evacuee from Manor Park E12 that he and his wife had landed themselves with in 1940. The already slightly bent Artie Hainault, who just three days under their roof had helped himself to some rings and things of Agnes Timson's—to raise the train fare to London; to get himself back to a broken home in a bomb-blasted city. But the only home he knew, of course.

When the Timsons took Artie into their home in Hookey—what the locals have called Hook Norton since time immemorial—they must have known it wasn't going to be easy. The kid from The Big Smoke didn't give a toss for the peace and quiet, the safety of the place, only some sixty-five miles from the capital, though it was; where no barking dogs of war were to be heard, and the good, fresh and plentiful grub to be had was so much better than the tinned variety, the lab-made substitutes, the meagre rations on offer in London. So far as the unhappy Artie was concerned, he was a deportee, and had been sentenced to exile in a dead-and-alive hole nobody had heard of for good reason. And where he was to be surrounded and pushed around by complete strangers who talked funny, and some of whom he suspected of having a screw loose, or maybe two.

And yet, for my father, looking back over the years on all that, his landing in Hookey may well have been that moment in his childhood when 'the door opened to let in the future' for him—a phrase of Graham Greene's in one of his novels (*The Power and the Glory*, I think it is). It was in Hookey, Dad said in church on one occasion, that he'd slowly started to learn the meaning of love, and how transforming it could be; and where he'd first realized that goodness for its own sake really existed. And also that goodness can in fact come out of evil and all sorts of personal hardships. And in saying so, whether he'd realized it or not, Dad had touched on another theme running through a good many novels of Greene's—what the author described as 'the appalling strangeness of the mercy of God.'

Bringing young Artie to Hookey was mostly Agnes Timson's doing. Nobody in a government office had had anything to do with it. The boy had been brought to Agnes's attention by the Snelgroves, the Salvation Army officers in charge of the Manor Park Corps in the earlier years of the war. Mrs. Adjutant Snelgrove was a cousin of Agnes's.

Anthony Timson, who wasn't in the best of health, had his reservations. Agnes hadn't pressed him at all, though. But the more Anthony thought about it—his wife had wanted a child the couple could never have—the more it seemed to him as something they should do. And they'd readily agreed, something they could do, God helping.

Anthony did what he could to make the transition as easy as possible for the boy. He'd travelled to Manor Park to meet Mavis and also Millie Linton. He spent an hour or so alone with Artie, letting him say what he was feeling and ask questions. The boy didn't say very much at all. He hardly ever looked at Anthony. Mavis told Anthony that Artie believed that if she and his dad reconciled he wouldn't have to go away; that Jimmy had lied to the boy, saying that that was what he wanted but his mum didn't. She said Artie always believed his dad rather than anything she said, making it almost impossible for her to deal with him; that it was all starting to get too much for her.

A week later, Anthony returned to Manor Park to take Artie back with him to Hook Norton. On the journey the boy had hardly spoken. On the train, most of the time he'd tried looking out of the steamed-up, rain-streaked carriage window, probably not seeing very much.

In Hookey, walking from the station—about a fifteen-minute walk—Artie maintained his silence. Then, quite suddenly, he said, 'M' mum and dad are goin' t' get back togevver soon, you'll see. And when they do, I'm goin' t' be back in Lunnon wiv 'em as quick as a wink, you watch. Betcha anyfing.'

Anthony replied, 'Well, we'll see, Arthur, won't we? But until then, we'll have to wait. And while we're waiting, Mrs. Timson and me are going to do all we can to make you feel at home with us, all right?'

But nothing more was heard from Artie after that.

Three days later, the unfortunate business of Mrs.Timson's trinkets gave Artie his first big surprise, living with his new caregivers. (Or his keepers, as he thought of them.)

'Believe me, Arthur, we do understand,' Anthony told him. 'How hard it is for you being here, something of what you're feeling. And why you did what you did.' And he and his wife smiled at him, seeming to mean what they were saying.

Artie was promptly forgiven, the incident never mentioned again.

And it was much the same thing too with his spell of truancy—something he'd been able to get away with for awhile, with school classes being held in various locations around the village, not just in the school next to St. Peter's. Getting soaked in a sudden, heavy shower had given him away—flippin' bad luck, in other words.

Sometimes, though, in certain situations, forgiveness is harder to take than none at all—particularly when you're getting it from people whose good books you're not looking to get into in the first place. Artie wanted the Timsons to run out of patience with him, and the sooner, the better.

In 1918, at the age of twenty, physically shattered and psychologically scarred by the Great War—his golden youth gone forever—Anthony Timson was like many of his contemporaries: ready to revolt against 'the old men' and what they stood for. About to jettison the preceding generation's 'father knows best' ideas; having to live your life in line with a code of morality and value system in place since year dot that was fast eroding into just so much meaningless nonsense.

A year or so later, however, Anthony had eventually chosen to resist 'throwing the baby out with the bath water' by abandoning the time-proven Judaeo-Christian values he'd grown up with. He could no longer blame God, he'd found, for the ills his prodigal offspring had brought upon themselves, seeing this as 'the great cop out of his generation'—an all-too expedient rationalization, intellectually and in moral terms as well. And, as Anthony told everybody, meeting Agnes Lockwood had had a lot to do with his change in thinking about God. (This from a former rector of St. Peter's in Hookey, a friend of Anthony's who'd officiated at his funeral in 1957.)

Anthony and Agnes Lockwood first met in 1918. A librarian, four years older than he was, Agnes had wheeled a book trolley into the sunroom of the military convalescent home Anthony was in near Cirencester. Their eyes had met, and the die was cast for both of them; there could be no future without the other being a part of it.

What sort of future together, though? Anthony had no prospects; he wasn't even sure he'd ever be able to work. The year before he'd sustained severe, life-threatening stomach wounds on the Western Front. Born in Swansea, at eighteen he'd been all set to go to training college in Cardiff to become a teacher. Also, he'd had a promising sports career in the offing. A quick and tricky three-quarter, he was already playing regularly for his local rugby union club, and was being touted as a future Welsh international.

His father, who owned and ran a men's clothing and accessories shop in the centre of town, was proud of his handsome, bright and athletic only son. But as a staunch Methodist, Richard Timson had some reservations about one or two of Anthony's liberal-sounding ideas on Christian faith and practice. He did his best, however, to understand his son and the crisis of faith he was going through after his experiences in the trenches. But it was Agnes's firm but less conservative Christian beliefs that helped keep Anthony from going beyond the pale into full-blown faithlessness.

Agnes had spent her childhood in Rhodesia, where her father, a surgeon, had been a layman staff member in an Anglican hospital before having to return to England because of malaria-complicated health problems.

Anthony and Agnes married in 1921 despite her parents' misgivings. Living in Gloucester they'd got by. Agnes continued on with her library work and Anthony got a part-time position with the city preparing communications of one kind or another.

In 1934, Rose Heath, a widowed favourite aunt of Agnes's who lived in Hook Norton, persuaded the Timsons to run her small grocery and post office in the village for her and live in the house that went with the business. Rose moved to nearby Banbury to live in a retirement home. Three years later Rose died and left the house and the business to Agnes.

The Timsons had settled into Hookey quite quickly. They were well-liked, as Rose and her husband Tom had been. They became active in community affairs and in both the Anglican and Methodist churches. They'd fitted in—being seen, possibly, as country rather than city people.

When Artie came to Hookey, a rumour was still in circulation that Anthony's war wounds were so bad that he'd been left virtually 'tackleless,' without any fully functioning 'dangly bits.' (In actual fact, it had been Agnes and a problem of hers that had been responsible for the couple's childlessness.) When Artie first heard the rumours about Anthony he'd been in Hookey for some six months—and he didn't care for any of it, not thinking it was funny in the least. He told the pair of sniggery kids he'd heard it from to belt up or he'd give them one in the chops; that he could take both of them with one hand tied behind his back.

And he would have—and, most likely, could have. But on his way back to the Timsons, he couldn't help wondering why, though. Why those two country bumpkins—thick as a plank, each of them, in his reckoning—had got up his nose like they had.

'Sorry about all the church-going, Arthur—but if we go, which we always do, you have to go too, I'm afraid,' Anthony had told the boy. And on Sundays that was all the Timsons did: go to church. It was St. Peter's in the morning for matins, and back there again after tea for evensong. And in the afternoon, just down the street to the Methodist chapel for Sunday School, and for another service after that, both conducted by Mr. Timson. (Hook Norton Methodist, not having a minister, relied on faithful lay people and itinerant preachers.) But as Anthony went on to assure Artie: 'You don't have to sing the hymns and pray, anything like that, not if you don't care to—or listen to anything, or believe anything you hear, you understand? All that's something you have to make up your own mind about, if you've a mind to, of course.'

What went on in church the boy couldn't make neither head nor tail of, anyway.

What Artie hadn't counted on, though—another surprise for the boy—was looking forward to going to Sunday school; to the stories he was hearing there for the first time. It wasn't just the stories in themselves; it was also the telling of them by Mr. Timson. With an imaginative flair, good timing and his expressive voice—it was his Welsh genes, perhaps—Anthony told his stories so well his listeners could not help but be carried along with them. Every Sunday afternoon he had his young audience in the palm of his hands.

There was another thing he'd sometimes do, too. He'd get kids—partially costumed and using props provided by Mrs. Timson—to act out Bible stories using their own words. Although Artie refused to take part in any of this improvised play-acting—that sort of thing wasn't for him—he'd listen and watch closely, taking it all in. And, very likely, only partially realizing just how much he was getting from it, what it was teaching him.

Artie was sure he'd be home for Christmas, '41, and not long after that, home for good. But he was wrong on both counts.

Instead, his mum and sister came to Hookey that Christmas, staying for a couple of nights at the Station Hotel. Their visit went quite well; but there were awkward moments, however. A comment of Mavis's, for instance, the Timsons were not meant to hear but did, unfortunately—about 'all that virgin birth malarkey' after attending the Christmas Eve service at St. Peter's. Also, Mavis had had her moments when she'd seemed very put out about the way Artie was with the Timsons, and they with him—how comfortable with one another the three of them seemed to be—and at which times Agnes in particular was on the receiving end of some dark, undisguised looks from her.

Artie got a comic book annual and a wooden RAF bomber plane from his dad for Christmas, and which he later found out his mum had got for him.

Just before Mum and Sis left to return to London, Artie realized the Christmas festivities were well and truly over with, getting a wintry shot of reality from Pam. She told him he'd better stop dreaming about getting home anytime soon. She said, 'Dad's living with another woman all the time now, and Mum says a bloke at the laundry told her he's going to leave his wife for her, and she believes him, the silly thing she's being. But if it does happen, just say it does, I get the feeling that me and you, kid, are going to be in the way. If you ask me, Artie, you're much better off where you are right now—out of the mess we're always in around our place.'

In May, Artie got the news that the chap at the laundry had changed jobs, but not his wife, and had left Manor Park; and that his mum already had her eye on his replacement in the office. (By this time, Grannie Linton had given up and didn't want to know about any of it.)

Soon after that, Artie started playing the lone wolf, keeping to himself more than ever, speaking only when he had to, and tramping the fields and woods around Hookey for hours at a time. He had a hideaway under the railway viaduct. He'd sit there, looking at nothing, sometimes chewing on watercress leaves he'd pulled from a nearby stream. One day he stayed out for several hours until after dark.

The Timsons were forming a search party when he walked into the house, and went straight to his room without a word. Anthony said the boy probably didn't want to explain himself in front of the others.

The next morning, at the breakfast table, it was a different story. The Timsons found Artie readier to talk than he'd ever been. He told them he knew how worried they'd been the night before; that they'd probably thought he'd done a runner on them. He said he was very sorry; that he'd not do anything like that again. 'That's over with, things like that, over with for good,' he promised them. He kept his promise.

His sister thinks Artie must have come to a decision: that he really was better off being with the Timsons; that he could be happier there than back in Manor Park. And that maybe too he'd made up his mind about some things he wanted for himself as he got older—and that the way his mum and dad lived their lives wasn't one of them.

A few days after his disappearing act, Artie started calling the Timsons Uncle Tony and Auntie Agnes.

Just about everything about the Timsons had at first struck Artie as more than a little peculiar. It wasn't only their church-going and church-related activities, which were odd enough. It was also how the couple occupied themselves at home; the way they spent the time they'd always find for themselves.

In their upstairs living room over the shop, they'd sit around, each in an armchair for their own exclusive use, in a library-like silence, their heads buried in a book. (They had a permanent discount with a bookshop in Banbury.) It was either that or listening to the wireless—to newscasts, talks, discussions, plays, choral and orchestral concerts, that sort of thing. Only occasionally would they turn the knob on the dial to the BBC's Light Programme to get a few laughs or a variety show. And it was the same with the records they played on a free-standing, rather grand ebony-black gramaphone with an oriental, red-and-gold lacquered design on it. *The Messiah, The Warsaw Concerto* and the like always got the nod over dance bands, Vera Lynn and Bing Crosby etcetera. Not exactly an East End kid's cup of char, any of it. (Although Anthony did like listening once in awhile to traditional jazz, which Artie rather took to.)

In time, though, Artie got used to how things were under his guardians' roof. And he started to find the peace and quiet around the house relaxing as well. There was a calm, settled feeling about it; and the very noticeable absence of the arguing, the rows, the full-scale blow-ups he'd been used to at home in Manor Park had a settling effect on him, too. But it wasn't only this, the way the Timsons were with one another—what Artie thought of as lovey-dovey and a bit soppy when he'd first encountered it. It was the way the Timsons were with him as well. Both Anthony and Agnes had time for him. They listened to him, and treated him kindly without letting him get away with anything, which he got to respect. They were always fair with him, as he got to appreciate more and more. And he got to learn that their word was to be trusted, leaving him knowing where he stood at all times with either one of them.

The overall effect on the boy from Manor Park was practically inevitable. Living with the Timsons, observing them closely, was beginning to alter his view of people in general. And also, gave him a different slant on at least what life doesn't necessarily have to be like; such as always getting in the first whack before anyone else could get in theirs at your expense, for one thing.

At the end of August '41, Winston Churchill sent a memo to the RAF's Chief of Air Staff. The PM wanted to know what was going on at Bomber Command. That month more than 200 aircraft had been lost, gone missing or been pranged up. The PM was very concerned. It was the first time since the beginning of the war in September, 1939 that Bomber Command had had such alarming statistics. And with numbers like that, of course, there'd been a heavy loss of aircrew personnel. And among whom was bomber-navigator Sergeant Charlie Gadsden, one of the RAF's fast-disappearing company of seasoned pre-war flyers. He was killed in a Blenheim shot down over Rotterdam. Charlie Gadsden was my grandfather. And left to mourn him were his wife Elizabeth (Liz) and daughter Daphne, eleven, my mother.

Liz Gadsden moved to Northampton a few months later, and worked in her in-laws' family bakery. A little over a year after that, following her mother's demise in Hook Norton, she returned to the village she was born and raised in to keep house for her father, George 'Pop' Easton.

'Pop' Easton worked in his own smithy in Queen's Lane, across the yard from his home, the large 'L'-shaped, three-storey Queen's House. He occupied the larger of the two residences in the house, renting out the other located in the shorter arm of the 'L'. Queen's House had at one time been an inn called The Queen's Arms going back to the early 1800s. Plough horses were still being used in the district in the 1940s, helping keep 'Pop' in business. He also did some farm machinery repair work. 'Pop' said he'd think about retiring when there were no more horses to shoe. He and the huge, sometimes skittish equines he sent on their well-shod way seemed to get on very well with each other.

After the pretty, auburn-haired Daphne Gadsden's arrival in early in '43, Hookey was never again the boring, confining place it once had been for the fast-growing Artie Hainault. He was from then on as happy as a sandboy to be right where he'd got landed: where the vivacious, one-year-older Daphne G. lived. All of a sudden Hookey was his kind of place.

Artie got out of bed looking forward to going to school—something new for him—and he jolly well knew why as well. When anywhere in Daphne's vicinity, he felt alive in a new and exciting way he could never quite explain, not completely—and had no intention either of asking someone to try explaining it to him. He started racking his brains how to tell Daphne how much he liked her. He had the feeling, though, that he couldn't hold off much longer on this. He knew how popular Daphne was with everybody, including three other boys; he could see it in their eyes. The question was, though: how to approach her without being spotted by all and sundry? He was apprehensive, too. What if Daphne told him she didn't feel the same way about him?

Then he got an invitation to attend her thirteenth birthday party at Queen's House that May. He was the only boy to be invited who wasn't in her school class. And some girls in his class, teasing him, said that must be because Daphne must want him to be her sweetheart. And they said too that if he didn't make an excuse not to go, it had to be because he wanted her to be his.

Artie went to Daphne's party. The girls at school had been right about his invitation, of course; and they didn't soon let him forget it, either.

Agnes Timson and Liz Gadsden knew soon enough there was an attraction between Artie and Daphne; but they doubted anything much would come of it. And Daphne, listening to her mum, whom she loved very much, thought like her that Artie and her were too young for anything serious, anyway. Childhood sweethearts are just that, and rarely anything more than that, Liz told her. (Although, by this time, neither Daphne nor Artie saw themselves as children anymore, naturally.)

Liz moved Daphne to a girls' school in Banbury as a day student in September that year. Gran G. wanted better things for her daughter than quite a few Hookey girls seemed to end up getting. Daphne didn't see as much of Artie as she had; mostly on Sundays only, in the pews at St. Peter's. Not only that, Artie had that summer attended some Methodist youth meetings in Oxford; and as Liz learned from Agnes, he'd come back and told Anthony that he'd decided to become a Christian, a Christian just like him. In other words, Agnes presumed, a Methodist—or at least more Methodist than C. of E. (Agnes tended to be the other way round.) Liz had to wonder. And like mother, like daughter, Daphne thought the Methodists were a bit too much on the straight and narrow for her liking. Liz Gadsden, as everybody knew, as well as singing in the choir and a women's guild member at St. Peter's, liked her ten Gold Flakes a day, the occasional drink and went to dances and whist drives, having 'a good old time of it'. Like her father, Liz didn't make a big show of her religious beliefs. ('Pop' Easton, a sidesman at St. Peter's, after taking up the Sunday matins collection, always skipped the sermon and went across the road to The Sun for a pint.)

And yet to Daphne Artie didn't seem likely to become stuffy and sniffy or a killjoy, or anything like that—no more than Anthony Timson, in her mum's view, was that sort of chap. But Daphne had her doubts, all the same, that she and Artie would make a good match for one another. In fact, she wasn't expecting to ever see or hear anything of him once he'd returned to London after the war.

But Daphne couldn't have been more wrong about that. Back in London, Artie wrote to her at least twice a month. And after leaving school and getting a job, he got himself to Hookey just as often as he could—and not just to visit with the Timsons, either.

7

A wet and windy day in October 1985—for the time of year, the usual thing. For Julian Caverley and I there'd been delays on the District Line getting out to Hornchurch, Essex. But once there and inside The Queen's theatre—in that closed-in, underground-like atmosphere theatre auditoriums have, where natural light never reaches and exterior noise is seldom heard—we were immediately in a world of our own making; to make theatre happen, to create onstage another world to our own liking, for us to determine what happens. On this particular day, however, still at the earliest stage in that driven, all-involving process; there to hopefully wrap up auditions for *Entrances and Exits*, my second play. And like the original production of my first one in Nottingham, my trusted friend and collaborator Julian C. would be directing.

The play was cast except for the female lead: the role of the promising, young actress, Natasha Fenner. We'd seen four such actresses who'd all read well across from Maurice Laxton as Derek (Del) Fortune, a fellow actor in the 'kitchen sink' drama they were playing the leads in. (*Entrances and Exits* was set in the early 1960s, when theatre, like the world at large, was riding a tidal wave of social change.) But so far, Maury—from the Michael Caine school of acting, and a natural for Del—hadn't seemed to get anything much going with any of the Natashas he'd read with. 'The chemistry just wasn't there,' Maury claimed. Julian wasn't giving anything away, whether he agreed with him or not.

There were only two more possible Natashas to see that day. One of them—Jacinth Glyn-Davies—Julian had been phoning for a month asking her to audition, which she'd finally agreed to after asking to read the script. Neither I nor Maury knew anything about her. Glyn-Davies wasn't much more than a year out of RADA, where she'd won the Bancroft, the student-of-the-year gold medal award, in a year when there'd been plenty of talent on hand on Gower Street. She'd turned down the RSC after finishing school; she wasn't interested in a play-as-cast contract even though an instant Equity card came with it. Instead, she'd made a first big leap to the Bristol Old Vic—where her mother Ursula Haldane, an actress's daughter herself, had once starred along with the likes of Peter O'Toole—and had turned in a terrific Kate Hardcastle in *She Stoops to Conquer*, Julian informed us. He said, 'Believe me, Tim, the girl's got the right genes, the talent and the looks; she's the complete package. I'm keeping fingers crossed on both hands.'

'Well, let's hope she'll pass Maury's chemistry test.'

'Pass it? She'll blow the pointer off his meter.'

Glyn-Davies had been called for three. But when she arrived in London she phoned to say her train from Brighton had been delayed; that she'd be about an hour late. (With British Rail coming up with one of its large stock of imaginative excuses, no doubt.)

'That all right with you, Maury?' Julian asked.

'Do I have a choice?'

Julian smiled. 'Well, thanks, anyway, Maury. It'll be worth the wait, you'll see.'

'Well, let's bloody well hope so, Julian.'

Julian turned to me and winked.

With the reality of the 'Angry Young Man' phenomenon—in the wake of John Osborne's *Look Back in Anger* and his Jimmy Porter at the Royal Court, London in 1956—the revolution was on in British theatre. The play that Angus Wilson said had 'saved the English theatre from death through gentility' had quickly spawned others in a similar vein. Shows such as teenager Shelagh Delaney's *A Taste of Honey*, Brendan Behan's *The Hostage*, and Joan Littlewood's Theatre Workshop production of *Oh What a Lovely War!* at Stratford—the other Stratford, the one in London's East End. Productions that spoke to a younger, non-traditional audience, to a new breed of playmakers and playgoers; and the critics were cheering on every would-be Osborne and Jimmy Porter in sight, along with an emerging raft of less privileged counterparts of theirs. Writing plays at that point in time was 'extraordinarily and deeply attractive . . . plays were sexy . . .' and 'a young writer having his or her play performed without decor on a Sunday night at the Royal Court would have more critical attention poured into this tyro piece than someone publishing an eighth novel.' (As playwright Tom Stoppard described it.)

As expected, there were those inside the theatre community who didn't welcome the changes so drastically affecting the profession and jeopardizing their livelihood. The foundations of the world they knew so well, that had been so much a part of their working lives, were crumbling under their feet. Writers, directors and actors with anything but 'Anyone for tennis?' backgrounds were moving in on the old guard's territory and networks, lessening their influence in the process. Well-known 'names' started to disappear from the scene and were immediately replaced in what was perhaps an upheaval in British theatre history not seen since the Restoration period—a shaking of the theatrical firmament I'd tapped into exuberantly in writing *Entrances and Exits*.

I happened to be looking at my watch—it was ten minutes to four—when Jacinth Glyn-Davies made her not-to-be-missed entrance that afternoon. Wafting her way down an aisle with springy steps and bouncing hair, she called out in that melodious, sirenesque voice of hers, 'Sorry about this, everybody. You will forgive me, won't you?'

Women with looks like hers are forgiven practically anything, let alone a misdemeanour like that—by the men in the crowd, anyway.

About her looks Julian hadn't gilded the lily. Jacinth G-D was tallish, with a Royal Doulton figurine figure and a peaches-and-cream complexion—that's what you noticed to begin with. And after that, you kept on looking, of course. With her flowing, softly-waved, ash-blonde hair; the large, lively grey-green eyes; the nicely proportioned nose and mouth, the one with a hint of an upturn and the other with fullish, very kissable lips—and what you had with Ms Glyn-Davies, no two ways about it, is your classic Anglo-Saxon beauty. And beautifully spoken too; but not to the point of sounding to-the-manor-born, in any sort of superior way like that. (She was much like Sam Tolliver in that respect.) And like Sam as well—even in a business in which one's physical attributes and quality of voice count as much as they do—Jacinth Glyn-Davies was a rarity, in a class of her own.

Julian introduced her to everybody. When it was Maury's turn—he'd hardly taken his eyes off her—she smiled easily enough; but at the same time giving him a quick once-over, it looked like to me. She may have seen his critically acclaimed West End debut earlier in the year, and also talked to someone who'd worked with him. (And she'd no doubt checked out Julian as well.)

Having read the play she didn't need a preamble from Julian, I'm sure, but listened intently to what he had to say, gleaning from him anything he might be looking for in a Natasha Fenner he could live with. No indication from her, then, that the role was hers for the taking. In his concise, to-the-point way, Julian talked about the significant differences, personally and professionally, between Natasha and Del Fortune—and also what was developing in like manner between Delia Winstanton and Bernie Glazer in the Terry Hankin play the two were auditioning for in the fledgling Stage E1 company's converted warehouse on the Mile End Road. And also the apprehension being felt, trying to impress Oliver Hawkes, the play's director, by Natasha, if not by the swaggery Del Fortune.

Maury and Jacinth went onstage, moving into a pool of downstage light where some folding chairs served as a sofa and armchair in what was supposed to be Stage E1's green room. 'When you're ready, then,' Julian called out. After Maury's usual walkabout, deep in thought—Julian would remain remarkably patient with him and his pre-scene psychological preparation—the scene in which Del and Natasha meet for the first time got underway.

Although a minute at least had passed before a word was spoken, we were left in no doubt that the scene had begun. Maury/Del and Jacinth/Natasha had swapped quick, sly glances, nicely timed to avoid any eye contact. Their instant interest in each other had about it a compelling compulsiveness that was already registering with me. Although carrying scripts, of course, neither one was referring to the lines very much, getting the words off the page, inhabiting their characters. The dialogue crackled like bacon frying in the pan:

> DEL: Hey, Tasha, just relax with it, okay? You're gonna be fine—I'm gonna be fine—we're both gonna be fine. Just go in there and do what they taught you at jolly ol' RADA, and I'll stick to what I learned at Saint Joanie's knee at Stratford East. And you know what? Between the two of us, we'll knock Ollie's and Terry Boy's ruddy socks off. They'll just sit there and marvel. We'll be the Bernie and Delia they could only dream about.
>
> NATASHA: You think so?

DEL: Trust me, luvvie. It'll be you—Delia—and it's gonna be me—Bernie. They won't be able to tell the diff, to save their lives, they won't. You watch.

NATASHA: Well, I hope you're right. (*She looks away, then back.*) Just so long as you and me can tell the difference, all right?

And in the look they'd exchanged then—in that stage moment—any difference between Maury and Del, and Jacinth and Natasha, wasn't anywhere in sight; not for me, at any rate.

Three scenes later, Julian called it a day. No need for a brains trust in the stalls; we'd all seen and heard what we'd seen and heard. A few minutes later Julian and Jacinth emerged from the office looking pleased with themselves, and with each other. We'd got our Natasha Fenner. The play's other centre piece was now in place. And already, for me, anyone else other than Jacinth as Natasha and Maury as Del was unthinkable. The chances of my second play being a success had just improved immeasurably.

Later, in a pub, Julian and I were hoisting a celebratory glass or two. He said, 'Well, Tim, I think we're on our way at last, wouldn't you say?'

'I certainly would. Like a train leaving the station.'

We both knew that getting the casting right is half, maybe three quarters of the battle. There are those who believe, though, that in professional theatre getting the casting right is easy—but that's not always the case. The fact is, whatever actors purport to be onstage and how ever good at this they are, they are always, first and last, what they are in their own heads and under their skins.

Rehearsals started the following Monday. Julian said to me, 'Come back in a fortnight and not before, all right, Tim? I don't want you doing a Hankin-on-Hawkes thing on me. I'll send you packing if you do.'

'Don't worry, Julian. I know when I'm not wanted.'

I wasn't worried, anyway. I'd trust Julian with my life—so why not with just a play of mine? But then, it wasn't just a play, of course. There was more at stake with my second play than with my first—much more. The second one is the hardest; and proves more than the first was ever capable of doing.

Julian relented and let me sit in on rehearsals any time I wanted to, but asked me not to talk to anyone other than himself about anything I thought should or should not be going on onstage. Julian liked to run a tight ship.

I enjoyed watching him work. He had a bag of tricks, or strategies, to help make things work as he wanted them to. One ploy of his was to make use in one subtle way or another of similarities in background and personality between actor and character. And sometimes would make use of things he himself had in common with a character—in this instance with the play's stage director, Ollie Hawkes, with whom he shared a public school education and a penchant for leftwing politics. (He thought I'd conveniently left myself off the hook by not landing my playwright, Terry Hankin, with any noticeable similarities to me.)

While writing the play, however, I'd had no one person in mind as a pattern of sorts for either Del Fortune or Natasha Fenner. I didn't know either Maury Laxton or Jacinth Glyn-Davies in the slightest. But in Maury's case in particular, the similarities between him and Del are plentiful. The two had an East London upbringing and staunch union and Labour Party sympathies in common; and each had overridden the opposition of a dominant, working class father to get into a 'chancy and poncy game' like theatre. Maury and Del also shared a built-in distrust of both Julian's and Ollie's 'silver spoon in mouth' background, their theoretical political beliefs and intellectualizing. (Internal problems of trust with a basis in class differences seem to have always dogged the Labour Party and socialism in general.) Also, there were some hardly incidental likenesses between Jacinth Glyn-Davies and Natasha Fenner. Both were third generation actors with a conventional upper middle class, conservative background, and an establishmentarian theatrical heritage. I'd given Natasha's father—having followed in his own father's iconic, classical theatre footsteps—an almost King Canute-like disaffection with the new directions, along with a 'pinky' social agenda, that the theatre seemed bent on taking.

But Julian wasn't about to let similarities and differences like these affect company morale and togetherness and, therefore, the play's onstage effectiveness. Also, as usual, he wasn't one to ride roughshod over any subtleties he was looking for in a scene. So, accordingly, one key element in *Entrances and Exits*—the confusions and complications arising from Natasha's various dealings with Hawkes, Fortune and Hankin—would not be allowed to foreshadow anything of that sort occuring in reality between Jacinth and the actors playing those parts, or with Julian or me. As a director Julian was an animal of a different stripe altogether from the play's vacillating, out-of-his-depth Ollie Hawkes. For which the theatre gods be praised!

On opening night, *Entrances and Exits* couldn't have gone very much better than it did. The audience lapped it up from beginning to end, and the next day the critics, almost to a man, were complimentary as well. At the after-show reception, Julian said, 'I think we've pulled it off, Tim'—and we did our level best, the two of us, not to be seen glowing triumphantly.

A bit later, Jacinth came over to me, saying, 'See that tall woman over there—the one in the turquoise suit?'

I turned to look. 'The older, rather dishy lady, you mean? Rather dishy from here and in this light, anyway. Who's she when she's at home, then?'

'Ursula Haldane. One of London's top talent agents. She's also my mother.'

Oh, God, Hainault!

Seeing my expression Jacinth laughed delightedly. 'Walked you into that one, didn't I? Still, don't let it worry you too much. I won't tell her what you said. And as we speak, here she comes, working her way over here to be introduced. Just one quick word of warning for you, though.'

'Oh?'

'My mother will be checking you out, sizing you up. It may not seem she is, but she will be. And I'll be getting her notes on you in due course—quite unasked for, I assure you.' I made a face, and she laughed again.

Ursula Haldane was upon us. She was indeed rather dishy—close up and in any light—and very personable and easy to talk to, too. She warmly congratulated me on the play. 'I enjoyed it immensely. No undue sentimentalizing, no self-serving aggrandizement about the business, which I liked.' Acknowledging her daughter's fine performance almost perfunctorily—she'd already congratulated her, obviously—she said Jacinth's decision to leave the Bristol Old Vic to take the role might turn out to be a good one after all. 'Made against my advice, I have to admit. But then I'm not your agent, am I, darling?' Soon after which Jacinth gracefully excused herself. And for the rest of our conversation Ursula stayed with just the one topic: the play. She said it had seemed to her an accurate reflection of life in the theatre at the time. 'And I should know; I was there, wasn't I?' And as Jacinth had said, if her mother had been sizing me up, I'd not been able to tell.

Jacinth told me later, 'From here on in, my dear mumsie will be trying to determine how close you and me are getting—and claiming it's only for my protection, as always.'

'How close we're getting? You and me? You must be joking. We've not spent more than a few minutes alone together since we met, have we?'

'Yes, well, I can't account for the ideas my mother gets about me and men. But I do know I don't need anybody protecting me from them, professionally or personally. Either way I know how to look after myself, and always have.'

Knowing Jacinth socially as well as an actor—he'd directed her once at RADA—Julian had told me a thing or two about her, as she'd probably guessed he would have. His advice: never take her or anything to do with her for granted. Also, she may have reckoned, going by my Natasha Fenner, that I wasn't unfamiliar with women of her type and personality, as well as what they had in common as actors. In other words, when it came to dealing with women like her I could look after myself as well, very probably.

With the Hornchurch cast intact except in the case of a minor role, *Entrances and Exits* transferred to the Criterion in London in January '86; and where it played for a further nine months. As with the Lawrence play's London run, a good sampling of theatre notables came to see it, quite a few of whom had gone out of their way to pass on their congratulations. There were times when it was hard to believe to whom I was talking and getting complimented by. No fluke my first play, then, the concensus seemed to be among those in the know.

But I had no illusions about the business I was in and at what point I may have reached as a playwright. I'd been given a perch—twice, now—from which to have a song of mine sung, and sung very well; and one a good many punters had paid good money to hear, presumably because they'd considered it worth listening to. The reality, though, is that there are only so many such perches to go around, and with no guarantee I'd ever get another made available to me. It was my father, probably, who'd helped keep my head on straight in this respect—we'd occasionally have a meal together in London at the end of his working day.

But keeping my heart on an even keel, however, that was another matter altogether—and no guarantees in that department either, of course. Having someone like Jacinth Glyn-Davies in your life makes keeping one's emotional equilibrium at all times something of a challenge. Although we'd been dating fairly regularly by then—lunch or dinner somewhere, a play, film or a concert—no commitments had been made, and none seemed imminent. I was as willin' as Barkis in Dickens's *David Copperfield* but on Julian's advice I wasn't about to press her to see me as something more than a good friend. Anything more than that I could only keep dearly hoping for in reluctant silence. (While at the same time, though, sometimes still coming achingly to mind, was what I'd gone through in Nottingham with Sam Tolliver—another beautiful actress playing so beautifully a character of mine I'd so lovingly created.)

8

It was the Easter weekend, 1973—Saturday, April 21.

I ran the usual early-morning errands for Mum. I had to be on my way by eight to get what she wanted: the freshly baked white and brown loaves, sponge cake and scones at the bakery she favoured, and the prize-winning pork sausages from a butcher's on Westborough Road. At my second stop, delayed by a bike tyre flat, I'd had to settle for beef sausages. Her country roots showing, Mum was choosy about the meat, fish and vegetables and the baked goods she served up. My shopping done, back at the house, it was straight to the front room for a 'First Division' football match between St. John's United and Liverpool on the extra-leafed table—a 1-1 draw—then back to the living room, where we ate, for a cheese sandwich with Branston pickle and a mug of Bovril for lunch.

In the afternoon it was more football; but this time the real life kind. I went to Roots Hall with a West Road school pal, Kenny Coulter, to watch Southend United—the Blues—play Chesterfield in a Third Division encounter, the club's final home match of the season. As I was leaving the house, Mum asked if I wanted to bring Kenny home with me for tea. I'd told her he wouldn't come, anyway, and she'd asked why. I said, 'He'll think it's just another way of getting him to come to Sunday school with me'. Mum laughed and said, 'Go on with you!'

The Blues won 5-1 that afternoon, with Scottish veteran Billy Best and a nineteen-year-old newcomer from Newcastle, Chris Guthrie, each netting a pair of goals. (And the day before, on Good Friday, Best (2) and Guthrie (3) had shared all the goals in a 5-0 drubbing of Port Vale—nine out of ten goals in two games just a day apart.) After the match, sauntering home along West Road, Kenny enthused, 'The dynamic duo strike again! I can't wait for next season. They're going to rip the league up, those two are.' By then the Blues' hopes of promotion that season were long gone. It seemed that Kenny, a dedicated Blues fan, which I wasn't—I'd already developed a taste for top drawer stuff on view in London—had visions dancing in his head of promotion to Division Two for the first time in the club's sixty-five years of existence. 'Pie-in-the-sky' stuff, Kenny, I thought. Reaching Glenwood Avenue, where Kenny lived, we parted company. From across the street he yelled, 'See yer, Timbo! Up the Blues! Yeah, yeah, yeah! Up the Blues!"

I didn't know it then, of course, but this was to be a day I never have forgotten—but certainly not for how things had gone up to that point. In fact, I can't explain why minutiae such as this, these trivialities have stayed in my head for such easy recall as well as with what the rest of that terrible, life-changing day was to bring with it.

It was about half past five when I turned onto St. John's Road and recognized the dark blue Vauxhall Velox parked across from the house, belonging to the Reverend Trevor Midgley. In his mid-forties, the Reverend, a quietly spoken but also resolute man, had been Cliff Place Methodist's minister for some fifteen years. It was unusual for him to be doing some home visitation on a Saturday, though, particularly on a busy Easter weekend. He was still in the car. Wasn't anybody home? Had he dropped by without phoning? Dad's car wasn't on the street. But why wasn't Mum in? We always had tea at six.

As I came level with his car, the Rev rolled down the window. 'Ah, there you are, Tim. I've been waiting for you.' Waiting for me? He didn't smile and ask me how I was doing, which wasn't like him. He didn't look himself at all; he looked tired, older. He asked me to get in, told me he had to take me somewhere—but before he did, he had to tell me something. I got the wind up. I knew I wasn't going to like what he was going to tell me.

I hadn't dreamed, however, it was going to be as bad as it was. About two hours before, a delivery van turning onto St. John's had narrowly missed Mum on her way home from the greengrocers on Hamlet Court Road. Very shortly afterwards, about fifteen yards further on from the corner, Mum had suffered a massive heart attack—untouched by the van, but struck down, all the same. Neither she nor Dad had ever talked about her heart condition in our hearing, but Paul and I had overheard things and noticed the medications in the bathroom cabinet.

When Dad got back to the house that afternoon—he'd been gone since eleven—the ambulance had left for the hospital. A neighbour told him what had happened. He'd called the church where he knew Paul was, helping hang an Easter mural he'd designed; and the Rev had volunteered to drive him to the hospital and then return to the house to wait for me. Neither Dad nor Paul knew where I'd got to that afternoon.

The Rev and I got to the hospital around six. We joined Dad and Paul in the visitors' lounge. Dad was putting on a brave front, remaining calm and composed, not wanting to alarm Paul and me. A few minutes later a doctor came in to talk to him. Dad had his back to us. His head dropped and his shoulders sagged. The doctor had left before he turned. He came over to Paul and me, put his arms around us, and said, hardly audible, 'Mum's gone.' We'd not really needed telling. But for me it was like a blow to the pit of the stomach.

His face as stricken as ours must have been, the Rev came over and prayed with us, just briefly. He could well have been using a foreign language. Saying nothing, crying silently, we stood there, still holding on to one another. Then, like blind men, with blank, blanched faces—like WWI soldiers gassed in battle (I'd seen pictures)—we sat down and stared ahead with dead, unseeing eyes.

Dad finally broke the silence: 'I've got to phone Gran'—Gran Gadsden in Hook Norton. He told the Rev he'd delayed calling, hoping to have better news for her. 'I'll phone as soon as I get home.' No mobiles then, of course.

Then more silence. Still numb with shock, we were trying to deal with this new and awful reality each in his own way. I wasn't even sure if what had happened was real—or if I was simply refusing to acknowledge such a thing. I didn't want to have to think at all. I'd willed my mind to go blank. And what I remember most about the rest of that day was the blankness of mind and the numbness of feeling I was experiencing. I seemed to have been anaesthetized.

Returning to the house, there was a faint whiff of the sea in Dad's car—no doubt the fresh shrimps he'd picked up that afternoon in old Leigh town for Mum's tea salad.

Mum and Dad's old CPM friends, the Harwoods, and their daughter Pippa, came to the house. We were just sitting or shuffling aimlessly around the place. We were hungry, but didn't feel like eating. Mrs. Harwood made a large pot of tea and served the scones I'd got that morning with some of Mum's home-made blackberry jam.

Again Dad said he'd have to phone Gran—twice, in fact—but remained at the table. Finally, he admitted he couldn't tell her over the phone. 'I have to drive up there—now, tonight,' he said. The Harwoods didn't think that that would be wise, but Dad wouldn't be persuaded otherwise. Mister Harwood then offered to drive him to Hookey, which he did. We had a sofa bed in the middle room and Mrs. Harwood and Pippa stayed the night. Mrs. H. kissed Paul and me goodnight. And Pippa had wanted to kiss me too, I thought. I might have been imagining it, though.

I knelt by the bed and tried to pray but couldn't get a word out, not even the name of Jesus. I couldn't cry either—not that anyone would have noticed, anyway. Thankfully, I fell asleep quickly. I wanted to sleep; I needed to. If I'd dreamed that night, there was no memory of it when I woke up—again, thankfully.

The next day there would be no church for us. No Easter Sunday worship, singing hymns of praise, thankfulness and celebration to mark Christ's triumphant victory over the grave and mankind's sin for the rest of time.

I never did see Paul's mural at the church, but later saw a photo of it. Its inscription, from a Charles Wesley hymn: 'Lives again our glorious King! Where, O death, is now thy sting?' (A few years later, in Blenheim Park High School's production of *Oh What a Lovely War*! I would sing: 'O death, where is thy sting-a-ling-a-ling, where death thy victoree?')

Pippa, Paul and I went for a walk on the seafront in the afternoon just to get out of the house. We didn't talk much. One thing I do remember. Paul said that we ought not to be mad at God, that Mum wouldn't have wanted that. Pippa gave me a look—agreeing with Paul or not, I couldn't tell. I did think, though, that Pippa understood how hurt I was.

As Dad had expected, Gran wanted the funeral and commital services to be held at St. Peter's in Hook Norton. Again, for me—and perhaps for Dad and Paul too—it was good to be getting out of the house, doing something, going somewhere.

So Mum joined three earlier generations of Eastons in the family plot in Hookey, not much more than a stone's throw from Queen's House where she'd had so many happy times growing up; and where she and

Dad had first acknowledged their early stirrings of love for one another. The elegantly-worded, well-ordered formality of the C. of E. Book of Common Prayer's rites probably helped lessen the day's emotional wear and tear. Gran's brave, chin-up composure had helped as well.

Making our way from the graveside, her arm around me, Gran said, 'I can't be like your mum for you, Tim—but I do love you, like I did your mum. So always remember that, won't you, Tim, dearie?' She'd probably said much the same thing to Paul.

The following Sunday, there was one more difficult public thing to get through: an afternoon memorial service for Mum at Cliff Place Methodist in Southend. The church was packed; people were standing at the back. Gran said to Dad later that Mum must have made a good Methodist after all.

Much of what was spoken and sung that afternoon I'd tried to block out—to help me handle it—but not easily done, however; and the choir's rendition of one of Mum's favourite pieces, *All in the April Evening*, in particular. Mum said that the song's words—pointing to Christ as the sacrificial Lamb of God—always reminded her of the lambing season in Hookey. Also, there was one visible reference to Mum's passing I'd found hard to take all through the service: her chair in the choir's alto section had been left vacant in silent tribute to her.

I felt a guilty wave of relief when the service was over. I was relieved too to get away from the church. To get away from everybody there—from their words, however well-intended; from their eyes, however compassionate their expressions. But getting away only so far as 68 St. John's Road, where the sad fact of Mum's absence was everywhere.

It was still home for the three of us, of course—but for me it would never be the same place again.

That summer I'd get my bike out, but with no place to go—just to ride around. The exercise helped put the mind in neutral gear. And if not thinking very much at all, seeing life going on as usual all around me I'd found unsettling.No sign out there of what had happened to Mum, or to us because of it, obviously. I'd thought there should have been, for some reason; that it might have made the loss of Mum a bit easier to deal with, to adjust to. That was the hopeful idea, anyway.

9

Entrances and Exits was in its fifth month at the Criterion, still doing well at the box office. I'd not been in for six weeks. I was due for a look-see—by my estimation, not anyone else's. The playwright isn't invited after opening night. After the show, I went back and knocked on Jacinth's dressing room door.

'Go home, Maury!' she called out. 'I told you, we'll talk about it some other time.'

'Does that go for me too, Jacinth?' I called back.

'Oh.'

She opened the door. 'Sorry about that, Tim. Please come in.'

To my surprise she was alone. Being a Saturday I thought she'd have company. She was in her usual kimono-like wrap, getting her stage make-up off. She sat down to finish the job in the mirror, motioning to me to take a seat. 'Well, how lovely to see you, Tim. How are you, then?'

'Very well, thank you, Jacinth. And you?'

'Fine—well, with the odd cloudy period. Were you in tonight?'

'I was.'

'Up to scratch, were we?'

'In pretty good nick, I would say.'

'I'm glad to hear it, coming from you, Tim. You've been quite the stranger, haven't you? I can't remember when you were last in. Your absence has been noted, you know—by me, anyway. I've missed you.'

'Have you?'

She looked at me in the mirror. 'Yes, Tim, oddly enough, I have.' She didn't ask if I'd missed her; giving men openings wasn't really her thing. But she did complain about me not having phoned.

'You havn't phoned either,' I said.

'Yes, well, I don't think it matters who should have phoned first, do you? We're past that stage, I thought.'

'What stage is that, then, Jacinth?'

Another look then from her via the mirror. 'Tim, you've not come to argue, I hope. Although I should be grateful, I suppose, that you've come at all.'

'I'm not in the way, then?'

'In the way of what, exactly? No, forget I asked. I don't want to encourage you.' She went to the sink to wash up. 'Mind you, I'm sure Maury would have thought you were in the way tonight. You didn't bump into him, did you?'

'Almost, but not quite. He was leaving as I was arriving. He didn't see me, though.'

'Good. Not that it matters if he did, mind. It's just that he can be funny at times. He's always cooking up plans of some sort for the two of us—and when I don't fall in with them, which is most of the time, depending on what they are, he can be a bit of a pillock, he really can. Deflating for his ego, I expect it is. Still, for all that, Maury's always the professional, I'll say that for him. Night after night I couldn't be getting anything more than I'm getting from him onstage.'

After drying off, she sat down again, applying make-up, fixing her hair. She said, 'But now I've got you here, Tim—at long last—why are we talking about Maury?' I didn't think I was, actually. 'Let's just talk about you and me; about finding some time, making time for one another, for a start. To stop fluffing around and get on with things between the two of us.'

'And what things would they be, then, Jacinth?'

She made a face in the mirror. 'Tim, I wish you wouldn't do that. You're always insisting on being so precise about everything; wanting to dot the "i"s, and so on.' (That was much like a line of Natasha's.) 'Let's just ease our way along, shall we? To whatever seems to be the next thing for us, all right?'

But we'd not be getting on with such things right away, apparently—not that night, anyway. She said she wouldn't be getting her usual Sunday morning lie-in the next day because Kellison Marleau was in London and would be calling for her on the dot of nine. 'We're going to spend the day together. And please, don't look at me like that, Tim. You know how it is between Kell and me. And don't say "Do I?" either. Kell's got a job in Canada; he's leaving on Tuesday. This'll be our last chance of getting together for ages and ages.'

Marleau, her bosom buddy since their days at RADA, had accepted an offer to teach and direct at the National Theatre School in Montreal, as well as getting himself in on the ground floor with a new bi-lingual stage company in the autumn. He'd been assisting at Plymouth in Devon and had lost out getting the AD's job there. After failing to find anything as a director in the U.K., he'd had to make up his mind quickly on the Montreal opportunity.

Jacinth said she had mixed feelings about his departure and the distance between them—sad, because she'd miss seeing him regularly and his professional advice; but also glad because it might help stop the annoying talk about her dependence on him in all areas of her life. 'To hear some talk, including my mother, you'd think I'd be lost without Kell—that he's been playing Svengali to my Trilby, rubbish like that.' Her mother and Kell never had hit it off. She'd told Jacinth that he was too ambitious and pushy for her liking; too ready to use and then discard people he thought could help him. (Of course, not a rare thing in theatre, this, as Ursula would surely have known; or in any other business, for that matter.)

Anyway, we settled on seeing each other the next Sunday—for dinner, somewhere quiet and intimate, when and where we could spend the whole evening 'concentrating on just you and me,' she said. 'And no begging off, either—unless one or the other of us is in hospital, or prison.'

She stood up and shed her wrap, her scanty bra and knickers leaving little to the imagination. I looked away; but with the room's wall mirrors, it was difficult not to seem to be looking her over. In her mind, though, I think I was welcome to the view—if to nothing more than that. But then, with Jacinth, I was never sure if she was testing me—and if she was, what I had to do or not do to pass the test.

A knock on the door, and a man's cockney voice: 'Miss Glyn-Davies, yer ride's arrived. And not parked legal eiver.'

'Thank you, Nobby. That'll be Mumsie for me.'

Since returning to London to do the play Jacinth was back living with Ursula in her spacious, two-level flat in Hammersmith, and planning to stay there at least until *Entrances and Exits* closed. Actors are not in the habit of planning too far ahead.

She gathered up her coat and handbag. 'Tim, d'you mind if we say goodnight here? If my mother sees you with me she'll have even more reason to ask about you, which I don't need, as I've told her umpteen times if I've told her once.'

We shared a long kiss. 'Hmmm. If Mumsie had seen us saying goodnight like that she'd have had another lecture for me,' she said.

I waited a minute or two before leaving by the stage door, as she'd asked me to. I'd resisted the urge to step outside sooner to see if indeed it was her mother with whom she'd driven off into the night.

10

Perhaps I'd been closer, more attached to my mother than I'd realized, not having fully appreciated how much she'd meant to me. Something to do possibly with not wanting to be taken for a mummy's boy; I was only a kid, after all. Psychiatrists say that adjusting well to the mother's temporary absence from the home as a youngster is the key to being able to deal with her permanent absence in later childhood. Be that as it may, though, one thing is certain: when it comes to adjusting to the loss of a loved one, sudden or otherwise, no matter at what point in life you've reached, you are on your own.

I thought a lot to begin with about the last time I saw Mum. Quite pointlessly, of course, I asked myself why I'd not stayed at home that Easter Saturday afternoon, speculating that if I had I would probably have gone to the greengrocers on Hamlet Court Road for her. And her laugh and her last words to me kept coming back to mind. A memory, though, that in time I'd been able to take some comfort from. Mum would often say, as she had that day, 'Oh, go on with you!' to either Paul or me, usually when we were seeing something in the wrong light as she saw it. And eventually I came to think of those last words of Mum's as a useful piece of advice to live by; a reminder to get myself sorted, to make the best of things, to never give in—to just go on and keep going on with the business of being myself, the self I hoped one day to be.

In the meantime, however, Mum had left me with some adjustments to make, I knew, as young as I was. And I knew too that making those necessary adjustments wouldn't be a quick or easy thing to do.

A second sea change of circumstances on the heels of an earlier, achingly sad and totally negative one can sometimes, surprisingly, work out positively for you; give you a better outlook on what may be awaiting around the next corner for you. That's how it was for me, at any rate. Within four months of Mum's passing, I'd moved on from West Road Juniors to Blenheim Park High School in Westcliff's Belfairs area—a move giving me new surroundings to explore, new kids to get to know (or not). It would be a fresh start for me, as I viewed it, with the expectancy and hopes, a sense of adventure and the prospect of new opportunities that come with that. I'd chosen Blenheim Park over Southend and Westcliff High for Boys for two reasons. My brother Paul went to Southend, where he'd had two good years, with all-round high marks—and I'd not fancied having comparisons of any sort made between us. Also—not entirely beside-the-point factors in my decision—there were, for one thing, girls at BPH; and for another, the school played football, the round ball game, not rugby.

But I didn't jump headlong into life at BPH. That wasn't my style. In fact, that summer, I'd started cultivating something of a lone wolf persona that seemed to suit me better than perhaps it should have done. My first year at BPH, I'd applied myself to my school work, racking up good marks and staying out of detention trouble, getting myself the only sort of attention I was looking for from any of my teachers. I didn't rush willy-nilly into any new friendships, either. Also, I wasn't keen on hanging around with any of the kids who'd been with me at West Road. And it was much the same thing for me at CPM as well. I wasn't old enough for youth group at the church, where three nights a week both Dad and Paul would be for something or other, leaving me at home to do my homework; read (mostly novels and serial story comics); or watch the telly (sports, comedy or drama series, mainly) in what represented for me comfortable, if not splendid isolation.

And for a few hours every week I'd continued on with my tyro literary efforts—arguably as solitary an activity one can get into and become obsessed by as any. I was still doing some ersatz football journalism and 'newspaper' mock-ups, but less of that and more short fiction. I completed three further adventures of Sir Kelvain the Good at Camelot. In my latest story, I'd introduced a fair and virtuous court lady called Genevieve, a princess whose father, ruler of a French Channel Islands-like kingdom, was ostensibly in an alliance with King Arthur, but who in fact had invading and conquering Camelot on his treacherous mind. Genevieve had almost certainly been inspired by West Road Juniors' Miss Aimée Ozanne—something she'd have likely cottoned onto when she read the story.

I'd sent the story to her, and she'd invited me to tea at her Prittlewell flat to discuss it. Recently married, she now went by the name of Mrs. Gilbert. (I thought she'd have pronounced it the French way, but she didn't.) She'd edited my story, showing me how it could be improved. Realizing I was crestfallen by the number of changes and suggestions she'd made, she said, 'You know, Tim, your writing is coming along very nicely. I'm impressed. So you really must keep working at it. Good writing is a lot about keeping at it. And if you don't keep at it, Tim, I'm going to be very disappointed, and I will probably let you know it, too.'

Of course, I hadn't the slightest intention of ever disappointing the one-and-only Miss Ozanne—Mrs. Gilbert, rather—even if she had gone off behind my back and got herself married to some very lucky bloke whose existence I'd not even known about. For some reason I'd thought she should have told me about the chap.

'Well, Tim, laddie, are you going to try out for us or not?' Chris Penlow said.

'I'm not sure yet.'

'What sort of answer's that? Just get your finger out and make up your strange little mind, okay?'

'I told you, Chris, I'm still thinking about it.'

'Scotty's not gonna come running after you, yer know. Not ready to put your feet on the pitch as well as in your mouth, is that what it is?' But this said in his usual, good-natured way.

Getting on for two years older than me, Chris was on his way to becoming a hero at BPH. He was a fast and tricky, high-scoring striker with the school's junior version of the Blenheim Park Battlers. After a few down years, football was again experiencing a resurgence at BPH because of Chris, and as well an influx of others like him and some good coaching. I'd been overheard, unfortunately, while watching the junior Battlers in action that September, saying that the midfield could do with a player with two good feet and some imagination, hadn't I? This had got back to Chris soon enough, of course; and he'd not let me forget it, naturally.

So, two weeks later, there it was, in black and white: T. HAINAULT. My name included with some fifteen others on the junior Battlers' roster for their next fixture the following Saturday at Billericay. I wasn't in the starting line-up, but for a twelve-year-old in only his second year at BPH, something of an achievement, all the same. The Battlers' junior squad was made up exclusively of thirteen-to-fifteen-year-olds. Not exactly a life-changing moment, seeing my name posted on the gymnasium notice board that October afternoon in '74—but certainly a sign of things to come for me at BPH.

But it wasn't the only sign. Because of my good marks I'd been moved up to the A form after the summer holidays—and where I was to meet and get to know the very individualistic, articulate and academically-gifted Jeremy Burgess. Actually, he'd met me—a meeting of his choosing, not mine. Like Chris, Jeremy drew me in—just as inevitably in the one case as in the other, each one in his own, hard-to-resist way. The two of them had induced me, with no obvious intent in mind, to run and keep up with each of them at the same time—but along quite separate paths and in different directions. As a fellow traveller of both Chris and Jeremy, I'd sensed I'd be in for a contrasting mixture of interesting experiences—an intuition that proved to be bang on the mark. And I'd reckoned too, also correctly, my days as a would-be lone wolf were well and truly numbered.

So for me it was football, football, football—or, if you prefer: soccer. The 'beautiful game' and the 'funny ol' game'—both things.

I played only three full games in my first season with the BP Battlers. Just one game into my second, however, my subbing days were over. I started in the midfield for the rest of the season and also all through the next one. And I'd kept my place for three more seasons after we'd moved up, practically en masse, into the senior team, along with our demanding but respected coach, Scotty Alexander. With the mentally relaxing escape that football offers and the sheer enjoyment I got out of playing or practising—the two amounted to much the same thing with me—I'd not given the time, effort and commitment involved a second thought. (My first glimmers of understanding in respect to the idea the ancient Greeks had put about for the need to pay heed to and keep in balance the body, mind and spirit?) Also, there is the camaraderie, the sort of tribal solidarity that asserts itself in competitive group activities for an unambiguous common cause.

Since taking over the junior Battlers, Scotty Alexander was dead set on putting together a team of 'Sassenachs who play like Scots'—never-say-die battlers, that is; a team made in Scotty's own Highland 'braveheart' image. A terrier-like side, putting itself about, scrapping for every ball, playing smartly on or off the ball, heads and hearts always in the game—and all this with an 'all for one, one for all' attitude. 'If you don't want to play football like that, you don't play for me,' Scotty rasped. We got the message.

It had taken Scotty two years to whip the juniors into shape. In his third season—and my first—we started beating teams that had owned BPH for years. The following season we lost in extra time in the league cup final. The next year, however, we copped the cup for the school for the first time in nine years, with Chris notching two goals as well as topping the league in scoring for the second year running.

Also called Alexander the Great by some, Scotty had provided the continuity in coaching and plain football knowhow the senior Battlers had been crying out for since the late '60s. It came as no surprise, then, when his charges, the team he'd moulded, repeated its junior successes at the higher level. We were league cup winners two years in a row and runner-up in the third. (We'd lost three regulars to graduation that year.)

Ah, the sweet smell, the exultant clamour of success on the footer field after a long, hard-fought season! There is nothing like it. It's a rite of passage of a special sort. And there'd been the bonding between Chris and myself as well. In the five full seasons we'd been teammates on the Battlers, we'd developed an almost uncanny understanding on the pitch, so often thinking alike, anticipating each other's next move. A clockwork-like partnership we revelled in every match; something we'd probably remember happily for the rest of our lives. But it wasn't only the football we'd played together, however. Chris and I had also had three satisfying summer terms on the cricket field with the school's first XI, with both the bat and ball. And it was in the summer of '79—with the sounds of leather on willow and 'howzat?'s in the air—when the two of us had had our last hurrahs on the playing fields of Blenheim Park High School.

And also for me, it was theatre, theatre, theatre—or, if you prefer: the theatre. In many respects, also a game: a game like none other, the ultimate team sport. And the making of which is another thing altogether from just sitting there in the audience, enjoying or being moved (or not) by what's taking place onstage.

In the autumn of 1976—at the start of my fourth year at BPH—drama teacher Barry Maxwell was faced with the same old problem he ran into every year: a shortage of actors of the male gender. There were those, of course, who thought he should have known better, choosing to do as he had Joan Littlewood's *Oh What a Lovely War!* for Stage Blenheim's main production. Still, pressing on manfully, the youthful-looking Maxwell—we called him 'Barry Boy'—went looking for recruits to fill all the male roles going begging, and in particular the bunch of WWI trench Tommies he needed. He even went so far as to canvass among the school's crowd of jocks, the ballsy, ball-chasing lot.

Interestingly, for me, anyway, as I was to find out some years later, it was around the same time as this that the young, football-playing Kenneth Branagh had gone onstage for the first time at school in Reading; in the same show, and in exactly the same way as I had. In his memoir he'd titled *Beginnings*, Branagh writes how he and his teammates needed 'to be persuaded that playing soldiers had great girl-pulling potential and could easily be as macho as their activities on the football field.' More or less the reasons I'd had as well for going onstage for the first time and playing a range of characters, after a fashion, in the entertaining but also biting and poignant ensemble piece. Possibly, too, the show's knock-about, music hall-influenced theatricality and its anti-establishment message—from a cannon-fodder conscript's point of view—had had an appeal for me as well. The girl-pulling opportunities on offer were the main attraction, however. And like Branagh too, as he'd recalled his own efforts, what I did in Stage Blenheim's version of the show had nothing 'much to do with acting, but it was a great laugh.'

My charismatic classmate Jeremy Burgess, along with Barry Boy, loved *Oh What a Lovely War!*—reflecting as it did the leftist leanings the two shared. Barry Boy's assistant director for the show as well as appearing in it, the multi-talented Jeremy was Stage Blenheim's most trusted and dedicated member. And between the persuasive two of them they convinced me, without too much difficulty, to become a regular, fully-fledged colleague of theirs with Stage Blenheim. Jeremy said, 'Come join our brave, little band of brothers and sisters, fighting the good fight against the philistinism blighting the sad, pathetic world we have inherited for no fault of our own'. He actually talked like that—like an obsessive aesthete in an Evelyn Waugh, between-the-wars novel, taking on the 'hearties' who handled, kicked or struck balls of one kind or another to prove their manhood. Jeremy was fascinated by the political, social, cultural and moral upheaval in Britain after WWI, and liked to go on about the Sonnenkinder, or 'Children of the Sun'—the Oxbridge, anti-patriarchal, arts-obsessed 'dandies' who surfaced between the wars. Oddly enough, though, surprising myself, I could listen to Jeremy all day long.

He'd also told me: 'I've very little competition for roles around here, and I think you're the one who'll provide me with some.' I'd doubted that; and I wasn't sure either how much competition he'd really wanted. 'Or at least have someone who'll give me something, who I can play off,' he'd added, probably having read my mind.

After joining Stage Blenheim—I'd not really known what I was letting myself in for, of course—Jeremy gave me much more of his attention than previously. As I remember it, I think I reckoned I should listen closely to what he was saying and get to know him as well as possible for my own protection. Finding my theatre education sadly lacking, he loaned me or recommended plays, books and articles to rectify my 'sins of omission' on the subject. Sometimes we'd go to something at the Palace in Westcliff or in London—but never to see what he called 'show-me-your-knickers tripe'—after which we'd analyze what we'd seen content-wise as well as the performances and production values. Mostly, Jeremy talked and I listened.

Having played increasingly larger roles in one full-length and three one-act plays, I'd have given *Romeo and Juliet* a miss if it hadn't been for Jeremy. He said, 'You're not afraid of the Bard, are you, Hainault? Come on, gird your loins, stand like a man! Get your nice teeth into some real meat. Show us all what you're made of. Go on, surprise me!' So I did. I didn't try for Romeo, of course; Jeremy had the role sewn up, in any case. I was cast as Mercutio, which suited me fine. I did all right, handling the language reasonably well, I think—while realizing, though, one can never make an assessment like that. Along with a few well-meaning compliments I'd got for my efforts, there'd been a strange look or two from some of my teammates on the BP Battlers, however.

What I really did enjoy during my three years with Stage Blenheim, however, was my offstage collaboration with Jeremy's Juliet, Marnie Boulting. (My attempts at girl-pulling had finally paid off.) Our fine romance had finally bloomed soon after *Romeo and Julie* had finished. At a party for a select group of cast members at Jeremy's house, Marnie told me, sotto voce, she'd wanted me to play Romeo. 'If you'd been my lover, Tim, I'd have been so much better as Juliet, I'm sure of it.'

Jeremy seemed a bit put out by my attachment to Marnie. He said I should be careful, describing Marnie as 'a bona fide cock teaser who can disguise the fact like no ther girl I've ever known'—and advised me to play the girl at her own game. I wondered if he was having a hard time accepting the fact that Marnie had designated me her Romeo of choice. I never did think that Jeremy was right about Marnie—but I did have my moments when I doubted she was as keen on me as I was on her.

Not long after my first and only attempt at Shakespeare, I got an idea for a play, a one-acter, about two kids wondering if it's love they're feeling while playing the leads in a school production of *Romeo and Juliet*. (No mystery about where that idea came from, then.) And two months later I came up with *Star-Cross'd*, which Barry Boy liked and staged after I'd rewritten large parts of it. Jeremy surprised Barry Boy—but not me so much—by declining the student/Romeo role. He claimed he needed to concentrate more on his studies than he'd been doing of late; a likely story. So Marnie and I ended up doing the two leads. The play was only a three-hander. Directed by Barry Boy, we'd had a fine old time playing ourselves to all intents and purposes. We'd not fooled many who'd watched it about how we felt about each other. *Star-Cross'd* won an original play award and best production at a regional schools' drama festival later that year. Jeremy asked drily, 'Tell me, Hainault, what's it to be in your future, then—the Royal Court or Stamford Bridge?' With his vacuum cleaner-like mind, I shouldn't have been surprised he'd know that London's Chelsea F.C. played at Stamford Bridge.

By this time I'd not written any short stories for more than two years, what with the homework, the Battlers, Stage Blenheim and my developing social life; and also, more than likely, because of my growing acquaintance with good literature. But the urge was still there, lying low: and when it surfaced again, nothing else but writing a play seemed to fit the bill. Tom Stoppard realized his métier was writing plays after seeing *The Tempest* staged outdoors beside a lake; when, with the help of planks placed just below the lake's surface, and fireworks providing sound and lighting effects, Ariel made a spectacular exit by skipping across the water and disappearing into the dusk. (The stage direction in the text: Exit Ariel.) Stoppard's biographer, Ira Nadel, wrote that for him this was 'the essence of theatre—imagination and the freedom to create a scene that makes the text an event.' (As a playwright I make no comparisons between Stoppard and myself except that an ardent desire for any higher education to speak of seems to have escaped us both—and also that each of us loves playing and watching cricket, a game whose mystique is as difficult to demystify and describe as the one at the heart of the business of making theatre, especially good theatre.)

Dad enjoyed my exploits with the BP Battlers, but possibly less so my prowess (?) with Stage Blenheim. He was always complimentary in his never effusive manner, of course. But with at least two of the roles I'd played—and also with my play, which had reflected the post-Beatles, free-and-easy, boy-girl relationships of the majority of my BPH peers—these may have given him cause to wonder if I too might be going to the dogs, or at least going in that general direction.

11

'God help me, but they are lovely, aren't they?' Horatio Lambert smiled and shook his head in wonder as he'd said this; Jacinth, her mother Ursula and her dearest girlfriend Emma Kirk, he was talking about. 'And dangerous to know too, everyone of them, I'm telling you. Before you know it, m' boy, with women like that, a chappie's life isn't his own anymore—and that's a fact.'

On a Sunday evening in late autumn, we were having a pre-prandial sherry in Ursula and Jace's upstairs flat in Brook Green, Hammersmith. Ursula was in the kitchen; Jace with Emma in her part of the flat, a bedroom and sitting room on the top floor. Horatio, who was known to everyone as Raich, had made his way up the communal hallway stairs from his ground floor flat.

A semi-retired actor in his mid-seventies, and very dapper with it—his stock-in-trade, a ladies' man's urbane, awfully good-mannered randiness—Raich was Ursula's landlord; and a kind and generous one, apparently. 'He prefers to think of himself as family,' Jace told me. 'He and Mumsie go back a long way. We're as close to family as he's got—no siblings or children, just two ex-wives, and that's it. We're his dear, dear girls, you see: a pseudo wife and daughter. I think he's been in love with Mumsie from the day they met, working together somewhere or other. A bit of a lad, a rascal, for all his years, really—but definitely a loveable one.' Raich had inherited the Brook Green house from his mother, who'd forgiven him for going on the stage. His father, a departmental head at the Bank of England, never had, however.

Emma Kirk, whose waifish short hair wasn't quite in keeping with her Italianate beauty in my estimation, was three years older than Jace. Also an actress—the two had been practically inseparable at RADA—she and

Jace had contrasting dark and fair looks; not unlike Walter Scott's Rebecca and Rowena in *Ivanhoe*, I thought. Emma had recently completed playing William Congreve's fascinating Millamant in *The Way of the World* at the Birmingham Rep. I could well imagine her, with dark, flashing eyes, telling the clever, dashing man-about-town, Mirabell, and her husband-to-be, that she won't be called names—'wife, spouse, my dear, joy, jewel, love, sweetheart, and the rest of that nauseous cant.' And that they should 'be as strange as if we had been married a great while; and as well-bred as if we were not married at all.'

Coming in with something for the table, Ursula said, 'Timothy, I really should warn you about Raich, you know. He's a lovely talker all right—but when he's talking about women, he's not always as objective as he ought to be. Interesting, yes—but his judgment could at times be rather better.'

Raich said affably, 'Well, thank you, Ursula, dear. You put that as nicely as I've ever heard you put it. But I must say, my dear girl, when it's you I'm talking about, you know very well that you can look as closely as you want into my eyes, the windows of my soul, and see there nothing but the truth, so help me God.'

Ursula laughed. 'Well, that's a new one, I'll give you that, Raich. A bit creaky, though, isn't it? Sounds like a dreadful line from some old play you were in—for your sins.'

'It is, actually. "The Heart of the Storm," Clacton, 1947. Or was it "The Storm of the Heart"?'

Ursula laughed again and returned to the kitchen.

Turning back to me, Raich confided, man to man, 'That's the thing with women, m' boy. Keep your sense of humour, no matter what. Never let them rattle you. And always leave them wondering where you're comng from as well, if you're really smart.'

Did he learn that before or after his two wives?

This was an evening needing to be got over with, as Jace had put it to me. 'Bringing you home to meet m' mum, and all that. And the way my clever mumsie arranged it, for you to meet my surrogate dad as well.' She said Raich had an open invitation every week for Sunday night dinner up at their place. 'And this time too, I suspect, for you to meet Emma, my surrogate sister.'

As Jace explained it, Ursula talked a lot to Raich about her daughter, about her career—and about anybody she was interested in, particularly men. 'She talks to him about her own men too—like asking your hubby if you can have an affair or something, for heaven's sakes!' She said her mother would most likely be basing her opinions of me on Raich's. 'And then in dribs and drabs, she'll carefully and artfully pass them onto me. But doubting she can influence me much, she's brought in Emma for that; to give me the straight goods. She thinks I hang onto Emma's every word. Mumsie respects Emma's views on most things, you see—and always when it's the opposite sex she's talking about. Mainly, I think, because Emma's never been that keen on Kell Marleau either, and any influence he may or may not have on me. And by-the-by, because of Emma's openly expressed views on men, Raich is very wary of her. The thing is, of course, she can read him like a book—and he knows it.'

And could read me too, perhaps? For Jace's benefit?

But the evening shouldn't be an ordeal for me; not a third-degree-over-dinner sort of thing, she said. 'They'll all be going easy on you. If they don't, they know I'll know, and not be happy about it. I'm sure Raich, for one, will keep things rolling merrily along. Any audience, new or old, large or small, is just his cup of tea.'

Jace was proven right. I enjoyed the evening. I didn't feel under the microscope at all; that I'd have to mind my Ps and Qs. And any curiosity around the table about me—what feelings I might have for Jace especially—was kept well hidden from me.

Jace set the tone she wanted the evening to have when Raich got into something about Vanessa Redgrave and her leftwing activism. Jace said,"Sorry, Raich, but no politics or religion tonight, if you don't mind, thank you. I say we should all just eat, drink and be merry—let good cheer abound, and all that.'

And so we did, so we were, so it came about.

With theatre people, as with soldiers, there's an instant camaraderie abroad when they meet, new to each other or not. But unlike many soldiers who have seen action, theatre people will share their experiences under fire at the drop of a hat—and none more eager than Raich, old trouper extraordinaire, to fill the bill in that respect.

'Just a fast-dwindling few of us left now to tell the tales, of course,' he said. To tell of playing venues like Wigan; being on the road for months on end, making a pittance, living like DPs. 'That's displaced persons or dramatis personae, take your pick.' For six nights a week and two matinees, speaking Shakespeare's language and attempting to get his timeless truths across the footlights 'in one Satanic mills of a place after another.' And all in a constant struggle 'to dig audiences out from under that awful, deadening weight piled on them in the classroom by generations of bloody pitiful schoolteachers. And sometimes that actually happened, and we'd rejoiced together, players and audience alike. A marvellous feeling, that.'

He spoke about one actor-manager he'd worked with by the name of Edward Dunstan, who'd never played the primary circuit houses in the provinces, let alone ever get to London. 'But this was a chappie who could rivet some of the toughest audiences in the country to their seats.' Nobody could have looked less like an actor than Dunstan, he said. He was in his fifties, bald, with a large droopy nose and a stoop—too old to play the parts he did. 'But like Kendal says, good old Eddy—in full costume, make-up and wig, and heel lifts in his boots—he was handsome as blazes, and could play any part like it was his and his alone to play.' Dunstan was the best actor he'd ever seen or worked with, in London or anywhere else, Kendal had written. (Geoffrey Kendal, Felicity's father, in his newly published memoir, *Shakespeare Wallah*.)

'It can't help have you wondering, though, you know,' Raich went on. 'All the God-awful stuff you put up with—the grimy trains, the down-at-heel theatres, the cold and dreary lodgings, the hard men's pubs and caffs, continually on your uppers, the rootlessness of it all. Really, where was the rhyme and reason to it? Like kids playing games; on the run all the time, avoiding what most people think of as being a man, facing up to the responsibilities of making a normal life for you and yours. What did we think we were up to, for God's sake?'

'But admit it, Raich, dear,' said Ursula. 'You've never ever regretted being an actor, not once. Not on your life.'

'Perhaps not, Ursula, my dear. But that's not to say I haven't wondered the odd time over the years. I've never forgotten my pater telling me that I wasn't a fool, ordinarily speaking—but a fool for the theatre I certainly was, which amounted to exactly the same thing, he said.'

Nodding, Emma said, 'Yes, my father told me pretty much the same thing—only a few weeks before he died, it proved to be. As an actress I wasn't taking myself and my life seriously enough, he said; and asked why should I expect anybody else to take me and what I was doing seriously? And said he doubted if anybody remembers for long what actors do onstage, anyway, and maybe he was right. So as with your talented Mr. Dunstan, Raich, so with us all. Come to that, Timothy, what was it your playwright

Hankin tells Natasha? That no matter what actors say and how well they say it, soon enough it all drifts away into the ether like smoke signals in the sky.' Earlier in the evening Emma had had something else to say about *Entrances and Exits*, telling me that Natasha's belief she'd find all she'd want in life as a an actor she herself had disavowed for 'self-protection'.

With a sudden smile—like sun after rain—Jace said, 'Well, luvvies, as true as all this may or may not be, I say enough of all that. Or all the good cheer wafting around us tonight will be floating off someplace and we'll never find it again.'

As I was to discover, quickly changing the subject was de rigueur with Jace, which she effected sometimes to defer something that clearly needed discussing; or, as in this instance, when she wasn't in the mood for whatever it was.

Ursula said, 'Well, whether it's fools for theatre or fools for love, what's the difference, anyway? When you're in love, who's going to tell you you're a fool and be believed? Doing theatre and being in love—what choice do you have in either case, I ask you?'

If anyone knew of which she spoke, it was Ursula, as none of us there needed any telling.

Later on, I got into another discussion—Raich was off answering a call of nature—about my first play about D.H. Lawrence. I'm never comfortable talking about my own work, but always obligingly try to keep my end up. Emma said I'd been wise to have stayed out of the debate it had set off between the late F.D. Leavis's so-called 'thought police'—like him, ardent D.H. Lawrence devotees—and some other literary critics, and those with feminist sympathies in particular. The two factions had argued back and forth about Jessie Chambers' influence on the young Bertie and his work. And whether or not he'd have become the writer he did if he'd loved and married Jessie instead of Frieda Weekley; if his understanding of man-woman relationships would have been different in any way. I didn't contribute much to the conversation. I was relieved when Raich returned and immediately got us onto something else altogether.

Before calling it a night, Raich said one more thing on the q.t. to me—about Jace. 'Remember, m' boy, gently does it with that sweetie-pie. Try pushing things with her and you'll be looking for trouble. A word to the wise in your shell-like, I hope.'

'You can count on it, Raich.'

'Good lad. Oh yes, another thing. Don't get to worshipping the girl, idealizing her, will you? Writers, particularly them, tend to do that with women, you know. Even Will Shakespeare—and where did that get him with the ladies? If you ask me, Will scared them all off, making goddesses out of them. And ends up coming up with his Imogen, his dream woman and wife. Ended up having to do with a sweetie he made up—a woman he could only love in his imagination.'

It was Emma who got in the last word. She said, 'When you think about it, there's a case to be made when it's writers you're talking about, and not a very complimentary one at that: that they find it impossible to avoid using people—even people who are close to them, and maybe especially them—for their own literary needs and purposes.' A comment duly noted by Ursula, who shot a quick glance her daughter's way. But Jace quickly switched her attention to Raich, asking him something or other about nothing very much.

Downstairs in the hallway, seeing me out the front door, Jace said, 'You enjoyed yourself tonight, Tim, didn't you?'

'Yes, I did. I enjoyed myself very much.'

'Yes, I thought you would. You went down very well with Raich and Mumsie, you know. And our Emma was impressed too, I could tell.'

'I thought you said it wasn't going to be that kind of evening for me?'

'No, Tim, I wasn't saying you wouldn't be under any scrutiny tonight—just that you wouldn't have anything to worry about. That whatever anyone there may decide to think about you after tonight, I'd not be giving a fig for any of it, unless it's good, of course.' She smiled. 'They don't know you like I do, you see. In my eyes you're a lovely man, Tim. And I can't see you being anything other than a lovely man. In other words, you've got my approval in the bag, Timothy Hainault—and that's all that matters to me. And to you too, right?'

'Right, Jacinth Glyn-Davies.'

'It's just you and me, kid, then? Okay?'

'Okay.'

'That's how it is, then?'

'Yes, that's how it is.'

We kissed goodnight, like parting was such sweet sorrow. And parted quite sure that tomorrow would look after itself more than nicely so far as the two of us were concerned.

12

I don't remember the three of us—Chris Penlow, Jeremy Burgess and myself—ever spending time together as a group, in or out of school. The Three Musketeers we were not. Both Chris and Jeremy seemed to think I wasn't capable of adequately explaining my attachment to the other; neither one ever asked me to do so, anyway. As each saw it, I suppose, this was no less a puzzlement than my passion for and wholehearted involvement with both football and theatre. After doing my first Stage Blenheim show, it didn't take me long to realize that my friendships with the two of them would have to be kept in separate compartments. As it worked out, however, I didn't share anywhere near equal time with them, seeing considerably more of Jeremy than I did of Chris—an inequality having to do with geography as much as anything. Jeremy lived on Crowstone Road in Westcliff, which was on my way home from school, while Chris lived a considerable distance further east in Southend near Southchurch Park on the municipality's east side. (The High Street in Southend, running north-south in line with the mile-and-a-quarter pier stretching out into the Thames estuary, represented an east-west boundary of sorts over which residents on the western Westcliff-Chalkwell-Leigh side only occasionally crossed.) Consequently, spending after-school time with Jeremy rather than with Chris was the norm for me.

Also, more weeknight evening time was spent with Jeremy, going to the theatre with him, and sometimes along with his more-or-less steady girlfriend Helen Bartlett, who like him attended St. Andrew's C. of E. church in Westcliff. I didn't see anything of Jeremy on weekends, church and football or cricket accounting for that. But I'd occasionally see Chris on a Saturday night at a Southend youth club dance or to go to the cinema—mostly on double dates, his girlfriend at the time usually having arranged for my date. Telling me I was welcome anytime, Jeremy's mother sometimes invited me to stay for an evening dinner. Mrs. Burgess had taken a shine to me. There wasn't a Mr. Burgess on hand; there hadn't been for several years. An engineering designer, he'd worked abroad a lot, mainly in the Middle East, and the marriage had broken down when Jeremy, an only child, was seven—with an '*Arabian Nights Entertainments* beauty' mixed up in the whole mess, according to him. Once in awhile, Jeremy got put out if his mother spent more time than he liked talking to me. He complained to me, 'I don't think my mother realizes that you're my friend, not hers.' (Echoes of the father-forsaken Sebastian Flyte's complaint to his Oxford friend Charles Ryder about his interfering mater in Evelyn Waugh's *Brideshead Revisited.*) And on another occasion: 'You know what it is with my mother and you, Hainault, don't you? Mama's never been comfortable having to rear me by herself. In the absence of a father, she thinks a brother would have been good for me—someone just like you, Hainault, would you believe? A boy with a good, solid Christian father, shaping you in his likeness. Mama's hoping that some of this will rub off on me—make a fine, wholesome, upstanding young man of me.'

But it didn't seem I was helping him much with that. When I first got to know Jeremy he was attending St. Andrew's regularly. He told me, 'Helps keep Mama and Grandmama happy, if nothing else. And I have to admit that the rituals and the dressing up has a theatrical flair about it I'm quite fond of, actually.' His late grandfather on his mother's side, the Reverend Edward Lockyer, was St. Andrew's much revered rector for many years. Jeremy had lived with the Lockyers for three years after his parents' divorce while his mother was back in school at Birmingham getting her M. Ed. degree.

Headmistress of a private girls' school in Thorpe Bay, Estelle Burgess was an Anglican liberal who thought Bishop John Robinson was as close as the C. of E. would get in her lifetime to having a saint and a prophet in one of its dog collars. (Robinson was a defence witness in the famous *Lady Chatterley's Lover* obscenity trial at the Old Bailey in 1960, and his *Honest to God* was a controversial best-seller in 1963.) Mrs. Burgess was also an undercover socialist, having to be wary around her school's governors and fellow parishioners. Jeremy knew very well what she stood for theologically and politically, and she'd influenced him in both areas of contention. By the age of sixteen, however, Jeremy had moved on beyond his mother's positions—if not politically, but certainly theologically. He said his mother was 'clinging to the wreckage in a messed-up world in which God is still supposedly on top of things'; that he was becoming increasingly baffled by her intransigent 'faith-riddled world view.' He announced that he was now a practising agnostic, with atheism his likely next step. And added, as he was prone to say: 'It's logic, not magic, isn't it? If in doubt, Hainault, use your head—that piece of anatomy sitting on your shoulders.' And to which all I said in reply—about all he'd listen to right then, I'd convinced myself—was that being religious is all about having faith; that if there are no doubts, there isn't any faith to speak of, either. That in other words, lacking in faith is not such a bad thing after all, and certainly better than self-righteousness. And, in fact, proof of the possibility of belief in its own roundabout, through-a-glass-darkly way.

Jeremy looked at me sideways and said, 'Well, thank you, Hainault, for that illuminating "thought for the day." You're not thinking, are you, of going over to the Catholics and joining the Jesuits? Thinking like that is right up their street.'

'Hainault, I know how much you like Helen—as she does too, I wouldn't be surprised,' Jeremy said. 'But I must ask you if you think Helen and me make a good match. Do we make a good match, would you say?'

'Must I?'

'Well, no, you don't have to—but I might start getting a bit suspicious if you don't.'

'All right, then, if I have to. Obviously, Burgess, you know very well why I like Helen—the extremely pleasant and personable, very bright and pretty girl she is. Helen's just about all a chap could ever ask for, I would say. But that's not to say, not at all, that I'm a chap who's thinking of asking for her, okay?'

'Yes, well, that's it, isn't it? I really don't think that I'm a chap who's asking for Helen, either.'

'You're not? Are you sure? I could have sworn you were. And I think she thinks you are too.'

He nodded. 'Yes, she probably is.' No question of that for him. 'But that doesn't mean we'd make a good match, does it? I mean, people often turn out to be different from what they seem to be—more often than not, I'm inclined to think. And another thing: since when does the one for you just happen to be there, right under your nose, which Helen has been since I was eight?'

'It can happen—and it does happen, you know.'

'Yes—but to me, to Helen, to us? And that's the only statistical possibility I'm interested in right now.'

What lay behind his question about Helen came next. 'Strictly entre nous, you understand, Hainault—but I have to let you in on something. On Saturday night, Helen and I made love. And to say the least of it, we didn't exactly set the world on fire. What one might call a missed connection between us, I'd say, without going into any embarrassing details. It could have been something psychological with the two of us—to do with our upbringing, being friends since Sunday school, and so on. Just as long, though, that Helen doesn't start dwelling on what didn't happen. I don't want her to think we've got a problem we deserve to have—one we ought to pray about, needing forgiveness for wanting one another like that. And God forbid she gets the idea, that despite my best intentions I'm not capable of satisfying a girl that way; and that maybe I need some sort of divine intervention to solve the problem. I couldn't stand the thought of her thinking that.' He paused, shaking his head. 'Tell me something, Hainault—if you want to, of course. Have you ever had the sort of problem I'm talking about? With a nice girl or a naughty girl—with any sort of girl?'

'No, I havn't, actually.'

'No braggadocio?'

"No, none at all. But not surprising, really, since about all I've ever done is think about it. It's not that I havn't had my chances, though. Maybe the Methodism runs deeper in me than I thought, keeping my hormones from raging out of control.'

'Well, I never, Hainault! Or rather, Hainault: you never!' He grinned. 'No, seriously, though, thank you for that.'

'You're welcome, Burgess. But what you're welcome to, though, I haven't a clue, to tell the truth.'

'Well, boys will be boys, won't they?'

Sometimes, Jeremy liked to dole out his subtle reasonings in incremental doses to let you savour and appreciate each and every one of them all the more.

'And?'

'Well, boys being boys, they lie like hell to one another about their sexual exploits, don't they? They always have, and always will. But not you and I, Hainault, right?'

'Oh? What makes us different, then?'

'Because we are different, that's why.'

'Oh?'

'We are different. I think our friendship is proof of that, don't you? We like and respect one another far too much to tell each other porkies, to be dishonest with one another. If that was the case, I very much doubt we could talk the way we do. True blue birds of a feather, that's what we are, matey. David and Jonathan didn't have a thing on us, Hainault, not one blooming thing.'

Taking me by surprise, Jeremy hugged me like a long-lost brother. That's how it seemed to me it was, anyway. Not any different, really, from the way Chris and I and the other BP Battlers celebrated after putting the ball in the net.

Chris was a Catholic. But like his father and younger brother Simon, he was more often than not a no-show for Sunday mass at the Sacred Heart church on Southchurch Road. Before turning sixteen, Chris was already playing football and cricket for men's teams on Sundays, with his dad providing rides to games, and along with Simon cheering him on, win or lose, in fair weather or foul. Mrs. Penlow, on the other hand, wasn't going to miss mass for anything other than what she hoped both Father Gough and God would consider a good enough reason. If Chris went to confession, I could only wonder about how detailed an account he'd ever given the priest of his shortcomings.

With Chris, without a doubt, if it wasn't football and cricket and his snooker, it was girls. A game that came as naturally to him as any other sport; and like the others, a game he played flat out. His readily given advice: 'You get in there, mate, and get as much playing time as you can. And always get in there thinking positive. Be confident, pal—the girls like that. But don't swagger—they don't like that. And don't ever get the idea that girls don't want to come out to play as much as we do, because they sure as hell do. And hey—hey-nonny-no!—why not? You're only young once, right? And we'll never look as good to each other as we do right now, and that's a fact. Like the man said, when it's girls you're talking about, it's always open season.' In Chris's estimation, obviously, 'the man' (whomever he was) was an eminently quotable source of reliable information.

Of course, by the '70s, the glorious sexual revolution begun in the '60s had been won hands down. In the years of my youth the prevailing 'new morality'—the 'all you need is love' creed, with no strings attached—had taken hold like a fire in a bone-dry forest. Very heady times (and lower down, too) for a lot of kids. And which were probably no better captured on the written page than by a pudgy, balding, bespectacled university librarian by the name of Philip Larkin. And never more so than in his short but landmark poem, *Annus Mirabilis* (1967):

> 'Sexual intercourse began
> In nineteen sixty-three
> (Which was rather late for me)—
> Between the end of the *Chatterley* ban
> And the Beatles' first LP . . .'

Until then, as Larkin had it, there'd been between the sexes, in the flush of youth, 'a wrangle for a ring, a shame that . . . spread to everything.' And so it was, thank God (or one's lucky stars, if you preferred), that all that sad, repressive and guilt-ridden stuff was over and done with for good. For most of us in my generation—having accepted ourselves for the sexual beings we were—life was now 'a brilliant breaking of the bank, a quite unlosable game.' Now we could openly embrace an honest, realistic and psychologically healthy approach to sexual politics and behaviour.

But it wasn't all clear sailing for me, however. At Cliff Place Methodist this new, joyful anthem of freedom was regarded as anything but liberating—but rather a dangerously seductive siren song that only served to cheapen and distort the true meaning of love; and if you were not careful, would leave you at the mercy of your own selfish self and a whole raft of self-destructive ideas and undesirable desires. What a Christian education provides you with is an alternative view to many things the world at large would have you believe, my brother used to say. And also, I remember: 'What the world wants now is freedom from guilt, no matter what you think or say or do—and for that, God's just got to go. But like Dostoevsky said, if God goes, then anything goes—and the West's Judaeo-Christian culture along with it. We're talking rubbishing the lot of it here—throwing the baby out with the bath water.'

From time to time Jeremy and I—he couldn't help it, he said—got into the always current 'new morality' debate. As he leaned more and more away from mainstream Christian thinking, he was generally amused rather than irritated by my usual 'on the fence' position. 'Trying to get at where you are on this, Hainault, is like shying at a fairground coconut filled with cement,' he remarked ruefully. But with Chris, on the other hand, there wasn't any discussion whatsoever about such things. I think we each thought the other preferred to sort such things out for himself—as being nobody's business but our own. Again, then, I could only imagine what Chris might have owned up to in the confessional about his feelings for and dealings with girls. He did tell me once, though, that maybe, if he tried hard enough, he might sometimes identify with Saint Somebody or Other—who, as he told it, prayed as a young man to be chaste and free of women to save his soul, only to add, 'But, Lord, if you don't mind, not for the time being, all right?' And Chris followed this up with a devilish grin.

Jeremy and I agreed that we both theorized too much about girls; that we were far too bookish on the whole subject of male-female relationships. He said, 'Let's face it, Hainault, the two of us spend too much time, wasted time, looking for a certain kind of girl we've read about, mostly in novels, who doesn't exist. Real girls don't live in books, do they? You know what we are, dear chum? We're a couple of Guenevere chasers—like courtly lovers looking for The Holy Quail; for the Bird of Paradise, the Bird of all Birds, the Perfect One. And which is, of course, a figment of our own idiotically idealistic, fuzzy-headed imaginations.'

I was glad I'd never told him about my Sir Kelvain the Good stories. He also said it might have helped if we'd had sisters—to assist us with 'the process of de-mystification of the fairer sex.' And added, 'Or should that be the darker sex? As in: too dark to see through?'

On another occasion, on the same subject, Jeremy said: 'Of course, I realize there are those—artists of one kind or another, for example—who don't need to find themselves and their future in someone else; to find fulfilment in life through a lasting relationship with some special other. I mean, who says our lives can only be considered worthwhile if measured by the success of our relationships with others? But then, talking of artists, there are all the failed ones kicking around, isn't there? They're ten-a-penny. Or the ones who wanted to be artists who didn't even try; who were too afraid to fail. And what do so many of these people end up doing? They become teachers, that's what; and which is exactly what you and me, Hainault, could end up doing. It's a ghastly thought, I know, but we could be looking at a future of more books, more theories, more classrooms full of the barely teachable; with a lot of piddling common room politics and academic jealousy along with that as well—all that hey-diddle-diddle! And with the two of us consigned to spend our working lives like monks in an academic cuckoo land—a couple of solitary wankers lecturing in medieval English Lit., or some such thing, God help us both!'

If any such help was available, I'd expected him to add.

I'm sure that Chris, like me, realized that our religious differences were not unimportant ones; that our two families wouldn't have considered them of no account either. But for both of us our friendship, and how much we valued it, wouldn't allow that issue, as crucial as it might be, to create any divisions between us. And by not making any mention of it, we wouldn't be taking any chances of that happening, we must have implicitly agreed.

The only time I remember the subject coming up between us—after football training one afternoon—when we'd been talking about the huge, sectarian-based rivalry between Glasgow's Celtic (Catholic) and Rangers (Protestant) football clubs. Chris said: 'Personally, I just don't get it—this never-ending Catholic versus Protestant thing, and how bloody awful it still can get. It's all so yesterday. It's ancient history—back to the bloody dark ages, and where it bloody well all should stay, I say. But then I can't get the hang of religion anyway, can I? I mean, if it's not about everybody trying to live together in the only world we've got, what's it all about, then, I ask you? That's what I'd like to know.' And then with hardly a breath in between, 'But what I'd like to know right now—really like to know—is who's going to be upfront with me against Basildon on Saturday, with all the injuries we've got? If there's gonna be anybody, that is. That 4-5-1 formation Scotty used last week was a washout—a flipping waste of time and energy. And mostly mine.'

From my standpoint, what I'd shared with Jeremy and Chris at BPH was all to the good. Each one, in his open and individualistic way, had helped me see a number of things from a different angle than I might otherwise have. Knowing Jeremy and Chris when and as I had, I'd got an early advantage in life. Some needed insights into the way others thought and felt about what made for good, worthwhile human relationships. A subject of real importance, I'd eventually learned—to which one's full attention needs to be paid at all times. ('People who need people,' and all that.)

I've not seen nor heard much of either Chris or Jeremy since leaving Blenheim Park High. Chris gave university a miss to play professional football, most notably for Charlton Athletic. But his injury-plagued career wasn't a long one. He married a red-headed Irish-Australian girl, and eventually emigrated to Sydney, NSW, where he coaches professional football. Jeremy went to Cambridge, where he read political science, having chosen to view politics as theatre of the most serious and influential kind, most probably. As a member of the diplomatic service, he has worked abroad for several years, most recently in Prague.

13

Ursula Haldane was a child of the theatre—on her mother's side of the family, at any rate. In fact, she was only an hour away from being born in one; in Lincoln during the Rep's final performance of the 1937-38 season. Her mother Celia had had to abruptly leave the backstage party that night to make it to the hospital only minutes before Ursula chose to make her very first entrance; and in very good voice too, apparently. A very pretty and an accomplished performer, an audience favourite, Celia Brome had been with the Rep since 1935. Carrying her baby well, and with the help of her stage costume, a nun's habit, Celia had been onstage that night, looking as pure as snow, quite untouched by any man. (By September that same year she was back onstage appearing as a fast, nubile 'It' girl in a knock-about comedy.)

Billy Haldane, Ursula's handsome, debonair father, was a 'Brylcreem Boy,' a Royal Air Force officer. He and Celia had met in London where she was appearing in her first West End show. A love match, they'd married less than a year later; and Celia had gone happily enough to live in married quarters at RAF Scampton, north of Lincoln, quite prepared to play the role of a Flight Lieutenant's wife to the best of her ability. Being at her darling Billy's side was all that mattered, all that would ever matter to her, she'd told her theatre friends, and she'd meant it.

But the Lincoln Rep soon came calling. One night, sitting in the stalls, Celia had been recognized by someone with the Rep. After some deliberation and encouraged by her husband—he was sure his wife was missing theatre even though she'd never said so—Celia linked up with the Rep as an associate rather than on a weekly, full-season basis. Billy was very happy for her. He told her, 'I love watching you onstage, darling.

And I love it all the more knowing I'm the one going home with you afterwards.'

One of Ursula's earliest memories is sneaking into the wings to watch her mother onstage and getting a delighted hug from her when she came off, with the stage manager looking on disapprovingly.

In 1943, Billy Haldane, by then a Squadron Leader, ran head on into the almost inevitable. After one bombing mission too many, he became a casualty of war, suffering serious head injuries he was months getting over. And after which Celia left the Rep and never went onstage again; caring for Billy round the clock became her first and foremost mission in life. Which he'd felt quite bad about, but loved her all the more for it. After recovering and moving to desk jobs in Suffolk and Bedfordshire, Billy retired in 1948. He and Celia settled down in a village near Luton.

When Ursula at sixteen announced she wanted to be an actress, her mother wasn't all that keen on the idea; she could see her, rather, as a Portia-like lawyer. Celia had had to admit, though, that she was hardly in a position as a former actress to try persuading her otherwise. Her father, however, was all for it. If she was sure she wanted that and got into a quality theatre school in London, he told Ursula, he'd support her every way he could. He said too he felt badly about messing up her mother's stage career, and that maybe she could help him make up for that in a roundabout way—or at least feel a little better about it by being the best actress she could be. 'And if you're as good as your mother, stick with it—follow your star, follow it all the way.' He'd be cheering her on every step of the way, he said.

After training at the Central, a season in rep in Brighton and another in Ipswich, Ursula went to the Bristol Old Vic; and in her second year there got her first of several leading roles. In 1960, the stately Theatre Royal on King Street was a more than useful and an exciting place to be doing anything. Peter O'Toole's *Hamlet* had played there in 1958—'a landmark of post-war British theatre,' with a prince of Denmark who was 'a real figure, easily understood by a new generation of urgent, serious, intense young theatregoers.'(Nicholas Wapshott. *Peter O'Toole.*)

Ursula Haldane's star was on the rise quicker than she'd ever hoped it could be.

The BOV was also the place that Ursula got started in any sort of serious way with a man. His name was Teddy Bentley.

Teddy was handsome in a rough-hewn, Richard Harris sort of way: tall, square-shouldered, solidly built, with a slightly re-arranged nose. Big Teddy had once been a very useful rugby forward—one you wouldn't want to be tackled by too often if you planned on leaving the field under your own steam. For Ursula, Teddy made all the other younger men around her seem like mere boys, with an inner strength too she'd seen before in her father. She warmed to his lack of pretense, his look-you-in-the-eye honesty, his never pushy, non-presumptious attentions to her. And soon she was aching to be held in his manly arms. She told him she thought he was treating her like some sort of rare flower, and not long after that they became lovers—passionate but also always considerate lovers. They were straight with one another about having a career to establish, however. 'I've got something to prove to the old man,' he said. 'When I decided to get into theatre he was sure some sins of his forefathers had been visited on his head.' In a way Ursula felt she had something to prove to her father as well.

Five years older than Ursula, in his third year with the BOV when she got there, Teddy was getting typecast more often than not because of his size and physicality; but admitted he'd have cast himself no differently if he'd been the director. He told Ursula, 'If I don't stop doing what I seem to be good for as an actor, and get myself into directing somewhere, I'm going to bore myself right out of the business.' Directing was what the no-nonsense northerner from Leeds had had in mind for himself ultimately, in any case. He wanted to have happen onstage what he thought, what he knew could and should be happening up there. Lacking trust in his own artistic vision and in his ability to get it clearly in view on the stage wasn't a problem for Big Teddy.

Ursula and Teddy had about six months of passion—for each other and their work—at Bristol. The next season Teddy returned to his native Yorkshire to take an assistant director's job at Hull. There wasn't any question of his not going, or of Ursula not staying in Bristol in order to stay together. That wasn't a priority for either of them, as good as they'd been together. The idea of hitching their careers to one another's wasn't a viable one for either of them.

Ursula knew that the BOV's AD Richard Plunkett had had a hand in getting Teddy his position in Hull. But when she heard that BOV board member Bernard Glyn-Davies may have helped with that as well, she'd wondered why. Glyn-Davies, a Bristol barrister, had a friend from his law school days practising in Hull at the time who also had connections with the Hull Rep, Ursula was reliably informed.

In actual fact, the two lawyers hadn't had anything to do with Teddy's move up north. But it wasn't long after his departure, however, that the unmarried Glyn-Davies was showing much more than a casual interest in Ursula, and not only as an actress.

The Welsh-born Glyn-Davies—a Weston-Super-Mare resident as well as having a flat in Bristol—had plenty of things going for him, including Kenneth More-ish looks and also the actor's pleasant voice and affable manner. He was always impeccably groomed and courteous to a fault as well. There was, too, his balconied house in Weston-S-M overlooking the Bristol Channel, and a forty-eight-foot, mahogany-cabined sailing boat he'd mentioned just in passing.

That summer, staying in Bristol to look for a flat, Ursula was invited to go sailing with G-D., just the two of them, and had enjoyed the day immensely. And not long after that, G-D. snapped up his opportunity to woo her—a gently-paced, by-the-book courtship, with all the proprieties being observed. Although they'd sometimes dine and spend the evening in his Bristol flat, there was never any pressure from him to have her stay the night. There was a decorum about Bernard's attentions that Ursula thought wouldn't have been out of place in a Jane Austen novel.

Ursula didn't need any telling that Bernard loved her. So after a few months, when he told her just how much, she wasn't surprised. And not overly surprised either when he followed that up by asking her to marry him. She'd told him she'd think about it, and fully intended to do just that. She knew, of course, she'd become very fond of Bernard—but also knew that she didn't feel for him what she'd felt for Teddy. But as her mother told her: passionate love can be fleeting, and the lasting, deeper sort usually develops more slowly. 'Never count on a fast, jump-into-bed starter staying the course,' Mrs. Haldane had told her, speaking from experience, probably.

Ursula accepted Bernard's proposal of marriage a few weeks later. He'd been considerate and thoughtful—calculating, even—and infinitely patient in the waiting. He'd anticipated they'd have to agree on a couple of issues before she'd say yes, and he was right. He said that having children or not was entirely up to her; and with or without children, she'd be free to pursue her career as long as she wanted to, as long as the work was available.

Bernard reasoned that in all probability their work would eventually take them to London; that they'd have a home base to work from and enjoy a reasonable amount of normal domesticity.

No reason for Ursula to stop following her particular star by marrying Bernard, then.

It wasn't supposed to have happened: Ursula getting pregnant after ten months of marriage. A man of fixed habits, Bernard had uncharacteristically got carried away one becalmed afternoon in Bridgwater Bay, jumping the gun by a few hours his usual Saturday night congress with his wife. ('It's quite possible I'm here courtesy of a German dry white Mumsie's rather fond of,' Jace said.)

But from the day their daughter came on the scene, Bernard and Ursula had eyes of love and wonder for the marvellous little being they'd made together. Bernard couldn't believe he'd been so ambiguous—indifferent, even—about having children, he told Ursula. She reportedly said later the main reason why men love their daughters so much is that they don't have to do much to be loved by them; and because they can leave most of their raising to their mothers, pleading ignorance of the things that matter most to women. Jace isn't sure if she ever did do anything wrong in her father's sight—which on the whole, she felt, was a positive thing for her, sustaining her emotionally. When she was younger she'd always felt the need to have all the love and understanding she could get from her father, with her mother being away so much.

Ursula went back to work as soon as she could after Jacinth's arrival, putting in another season at the BOV—with Bernard's backing, of course. They'd found a live-in nanny, Bea Tibbles, a pleasant single woman in her fifties, whom they both liked and trusted, and who treated Jacinth like a granddaughter she'd always wanted.

But trouble was accruing. Althea Glyn-Davies, Bernard's imperious mother, who lived with her also widowed sister Dierdre (whom she treated like a housekeeper) in the nearby family home, thought her less-than-dutiful daughter-in-law's place was at home caring for husband and daughter. Mrs. G-D. badgered Bernard about this from time to time. She hadn't been overjoyed, to begin with, when her son had chosen an actress for a wife.

The next season, Ursula leapt at the chance to join the prestigious Birmingham Rep, which meant she was back in Weston-S-M only one day a week—only increasing her mother-in-law's antipathy towards her. But Bernard wasn't going back on his word to Ursula, and she remained at Birmingham for two seasons. And the next year—still following her brightening star—Ursula joined the RSC for its long season in Stratford-on-Avon and London. And during which Bernard's mother convinced him to take a stand, insisting that his absentee wife make a choice, once and for all—between her family and her career.

After a long but never acrimonious meeting in London, Bernard and Ursula agreed to separate. She told him she'd already signed to do two good roles the next season with the RSC—and also that his mother was right about her dismal failure as a wife and mother. She said they couldn't avoid facing the hard and difficult truth any longer: that he and Jacinth deserved so much better than she was willing and able to give them. That she was sure that in the long run—and perhaps more immediately than that—they'd both be better off without her poor impersonation of a wife and mother. She told Bernard, 'I don't expect your forgiveness, of course, letting you down as badly as I have. But I hope neither of you will end up hating me.' She said that leaving Jacinth to go on having certain hopes and expectations about their future together would be more hurtful for her than putting an end to an untenable situation. 'I'm certain she'll realize that when she's older.'

Jacinth told me her father said she wasn't to feel unloved by her mother, to ever think badly of her. 'And maybe I never did think that, probably because I'd got used to her not being around, to not needing her. But young as I was, I also thought that if she did love me she'd had a strange way of showing it. I think I felt worse for my father than for myself. Besides, I now had my daddy all to myself. A daddy I knew would always be there for me, who loved me from head to toe—and who was never happier than when he was making me happy.'

Ursula encountered the third man she'd ever loved—an unlucky third one—in her second season with the RSC. Suddenly, there he was: P.D. Beaumont, in all his beautiful but also manly glory. A newly-arrived company colleague with a shiny, rising star of his own to follow as well, P.D. was a hard-to-resist, golden-maned cavalier of a man. (Someone in his family tree had in fact fought on the king's side in the Civil War.) P.D. had loved several women and they him. But he was openly proud of his absolute lack of resolve when it came to getting married, and had remained single. Just two weeks into rehearsals, and the love affair between the two was on, blazing away for all to see. P.D. had run away pell-mell with Ursula's affections. He told her their destinies were forever enjoined; that there wasn't a reason in the world why they couldn't be the next Olivier and Leigh. (There'd been nothing forever or in their stars about that particular personal and professional union, however.) It sounded good to Ursula, anyway. She filed for divorce and the golden couple got married as soon as the papers came through.

But if Ursula had the makings of a Vivien Leigh, a roaring boy like P.D. was more in the mould of a Burton or an O'Toole. An English version and a cross between the Welsh and Irish stars of stage and screen, P.D. might have become, like each of them, a household name. But there was a problem—a big problem P.D. couldn't overcome. His initials—for Porteous Dermot, names he detested—could have stood too for 'Problem Drinker.' (And also, from Ursula's standpoint, for 'Personal Disaster,' Jace said.) But P.D. vehemently denied having any such a problem until the reality of it had put paid to his career.

Two years into the marriage, keeping his alcoholism under the carpet became impossible for P.D. He started missing rehearsals, unable to account for his absences, and his lines were all over the place. He had a car accident, breaking an arm, and was arrested for driving under the influence. The RSC had had no alternative. The company informed the media of P.D.'s unavailability due to health problems it wasn't at liberty to discuss. But throughout the profession the word was out on P.D., of course. He was unable to find work anywhere.

He tried various treatments that didn't work out for him. He was clinically depressed as well as being an alcoholic. It wasn't long before he began bitterly resenting Ursula's continuing success. He abused her mentally and emotionally, and sometimes physically. He was also tomcatting around with other women, often not knowing whose bed he was in when he woke up. Ursula left P.D. twice, but went back to him both times after he'd pleaded for another chance—inexplicably so, as her friends and colleagues saw it. She finally put her second, five-year-long, devastated marriage behind her for good. She couldn't take any more.

All passion spent indeed.

Meanwhile, Bernard Glyn-Davies hadn't remarried. He'd not been looking to, apparently. Jace thinks he may even have entertained the idea of remarrying Ursula after her divorce from P.D. She said, 'For a lawyer, and the very logical and deliberate man he was, Daddy was a bit of a dreamer, I got to realize.'

At the age of fifteen, Jacinth moved to London to live with her mother in her Brook Green flat in Hammersmith. Ursula Haldane had got custody of her daughter following a series of events over a period of years that Jace had meted out to me piecemeal in no particular order, also over a number of years.

Of course, at the very centre of what had happened to so drastically change Jace's young life was her father's demise in 1978. A shatteringly painful experience Jace never has found easy to talk about, so deeply affecting her as it had at the time, and on into her adulthood. Also, before and after this traumatic occurence, there'd been the unexpected departures of others close to Jace as well in her childhood and youth in Weston-S-M. Her grandmother, Mrs. G-D, had died after a brief period of quickly deteriorating health, and a few months later, Bea Tibbles, racked with arthritis and phlebitis, had had to go into a seniors' care home. And her Great Aunt Dierdre, whom Jace had got on well with, sold the house she'd inherited from her sister and bought another in Torquay to be closer to her married daughter.

After Bernard G-D's shockingly sudden passing after a brain aneurysm—he'd gone to work in Bristol as usual that morning and Jace never saw him again—she lived for a period with her uncle and aunt, Mark and Carrie Blaydon, in Guildford, Surrey. The Blaydons had a daughter about Jace's age. And it was while living in Guildford that Jace, accompanied by her aunt, began seeing something of her mother, who was living in London. (Bernard had taken Jace a couple of times to Stratford to see RSC shows of Ursula's.) Carrie Blaydon may have been acceding to her brother's wishes in this regard, and doing so in collaboration with Bernard's good friend and legal partner, Ian Callister.

Jace told me: 'Callister was instrumental in getting the legalities settled—in line, very probably, with my father's instructions. And Mumsie getting custody may have depended too on her finding something better and steadier than her iffy, always insecure, gypsy-like career on the stage. Mind you, Mumsie's never admitted anything like that, not to me; and if it was true, I very much doubt she ever will.'

In any event, when mother and daughter were reunited legally, Ursula was working for the Morris Digby theatrical talent agency, just off the

Strand not far from Charing Cross, on whose books she'd been since early in her stage career. In a matter of two years or so, Ursula was to become Digby's business partner (but never his lover, as some thought) and in time took over the agency from him. Also, Bernard had left more than adequate monies for Jace's upkeep and education, as well as a substantial trust fund for her when she turned twenty-one.

Even though missing her father so very much, Jace hadn't been unhappy living with the Blaydons. 'But I was extremely curious to see how much I was like my mother—maybe more interested in that, funnily enough, than in whether I'd like her, and like living with her,' she told me. 'Luckily, however, living with Mumsie turned out well, I think—for both of us. Of course, Mumsie spoiled me—making up for the past, probably.' And Jace had liked the idea of living in central London; she was a city girl at heart.

Inevitably, Jace got to see a lot of good theatre, only a tube train ride away. And it was only a matter of time before she realized, being like her mother, that the stage was for her—utterly convinced that this was a world she wanted so much to be a part of; the only world for her. Like her own mother with her, Ursula didn't encourage her daughter to get into acting, but didn't discourage her either. But with their downstairs' neighbour and landlord, Horatio Lambert, it was another story. Raich regaled the impressionable Jace with his theatre stories, read and discussed plays with her, especially Shakespeare, and told her, 'Jacie Girl, if the stage isn't your natural milieu, I'll eat my hats, even the good ones.' And after RADA and her early successes, he couldn't resist the occasional 'Told you so, sweetie.'

14

On the face of it, the Christian education of every CPM kid up to the age of sixteen was my father's responsibility. Dad had been the church's Sunday school superintendent since 1962, almost as long as I'd lived. He treated Paul and I at CPM much as a headmaster would with sons enrolled as pupils in his school: not interfering with their instruction and disciplining for the sake of proper procedure and school morale. For teenagers at the church experiencing any ambivalence in matters of Christian faith and practice, however, it was Mrs. Marjorie Cromwell they had to look out for. Mrs. Cromwell was CPM's CYC/AC—Chief Youth Counsellor/Activities Co-ordinator—as well as being the always well-prepared teacher of the seniors' Sunday school class (for fourteen-to-sixteen year olds).

An enthusiastic and personable woman, Mrs. Cromwell did her job at CPM with all due diligence, as no doubt she did her everyday one as a social worker. For my liking, however, she was a shade too zealous and overly watchful so far as her charges/clients at the church were concerned. In fact, someone with my 'form' at CPM couldn't afford not to look out for her. I'd labelled her 'Olive'—in jokey deference to her grand old Puritan surname and England's post-Civil War Lord Protector, Oliver C. Olive, aka Big Mother, was watching you.

Olive would certainly have considered me different from my brother in a few important ways. Paul was as good a student of Christianity as he was a secular one, for one thing; for another, he was seriously considering going into the ministry. And as for what Olive might have on me, rumour had it that she kept detailed files on every CPM teenager, taking stock of each one's spiritual progress on a quarterly basis. If true, the most recent entry in my file might have read something like this:

> Showing signs of doubting God's way for him, trusting less in the Holy Spirit's guidance. School companions may not be helping him in this regard. Possibly a continuing, long-lasting reaction to the death of his dear mother. Timothy is hard to read at the best of times, and he likes to keep it that way. No BACKSLIDER ALERT on him as yet, but continued watchfulness and prayer for him is a must. Must trust too that his father and brother can help Timothy through this rough patch. I'll probably need to talk to them both at some expedient point.

In any event, any suspicions Olive might have had about the state of my spiritual health were probably warranted. I was indeed having spells of wanting to serve both God and Mammon, sometimes one, sometimes the other. After going to the theatre in London to see Jean Anouih's *Becket, or The Honour Of God*, I'd returned home that night determined to be on the side of the archbishop's angels—and just a day or so later I was back on the king's side, not wanting meddlesome priests or anyone of that sort telling me how I should conduct my affairs. Know your enemy as well as the good guys; that was Olive's Christianized mantra. She seemed to have well-tuned antennae, an early warning system, alerting her to any friskier lambs looking to escape the church family fold. There wouldn't be any lost lambs on Olive's patch, God willing (and why wouldn't he be?).

One April afternoon, after Sunday school—I would soon be sixteen and free of Olive's class for good—the Rev Trev was suddenly at my side. He wasn't usually around the church on Sunday afternoons. He wanted to see me in his study, if I didn't mind.

'I better tell Dad. He'll wonder where I've got to.'

'That's all right, Tim, I already have.'

I couldn't remember ever having been in the Rev's study. It felt rather like being summoned to headmaster Podge Hodge's room at BPH. All told, though, I reckoned I had more to worry about being invited into the Rev's inner sanctum. My progress as a BPH student was on record, whereas what was being expected of me at CPM was harder to gauge.

With his usual quick and easy smile, the Rev Trev said he was glad to hear how well I was doing at school academically, and with the football and cricket as well. 'As a Christian lad it's a good thing to be seen as both intelligent and athletic, a very good thing,' he said, but didn't elaborate any further.

The view from the study window behind the Rev's desk was almost completely obscured by a close-by tree's profusion of pink blossoms. The Rev swivelled his chair and motioned towards the window. 'You know, Tim, that tree out there—just a short while ago it was a rather sad, grey, skeletal sort of thing. And now look at it! The blossoms and the foliage—all that new life on display, the wonderful gift of spring! And you know, Tim, that's exactly what I see when I look at you—you and every other young person here at the church. All the new life, the gifts and the promise of summer you all have, which I see every time I look at you. And it gladdens my heart to think of the future of this church being in your hands.'

He was leading up to something, of course.

He went on, 'I think Mrs. Cromwell is right, you know.' Not about me in any specific way, I hoped. 'She thinks we should have some Christian career counselling at Cliff Place—so that young people can think not only about what they're going to do after school, but also what they can do for the Kingdom on an ongoing basis, in their own individual way. Anyway, Tim, they tell me that you're also very good at the drama you're doing at school.'

So that was where he was going.

The Rev stayed on track. 'I've always thought, Tim, that a good story—a short story or a novel, a play or a film—helps get some truths across to people in a very effective, non-intrusive way; like what Jesus did, telling all the parables he did.' That being so, he said, he was thinking of having a 'dramatic presentation' at the church, and asked if I'd be willing to help out with it; to use my talent for that kind of thing for 'the greatest cause of all.' He assured me, however, that he wasn't putting any sort of onus on me to say yes. 'I'm not saying we won't be going ahead with something if you say no. But with you on board, Tim, I think we'd be putting our best foot forward, for the Kingdom's sake, with a venture like that, I really do.'

What a clever Rev Trev you really are, I thought.

Of course, I'd wondered if the Rev had been put up to this by Olive. Along with a few others, she didn't think the church's adult ministry programmes adequately served the interests of sixteen-year-olds. She thought that kids in their mid-teens—caught in that 'dangerous gap' between youth and adulthood—were largely being left to fend for themselves at a very critical stage in their personal development, especially spiritually; that they needed something more than weekly worship services and youth group meetings and outings to keep them under the church's protective roof. 'They're the church's future, its greatest asset,' she reminded CPM's senior laypersons. 'We need to tap into their talents to keep them interested and committed.'

In any case, for reasons probably best described as decidedly mixed ones, I acceded to the Rev Trev's request, and got more than I'd bargained for—and possibly the Rev Trev had too, for that matter. I did three productions in my two remaining years at CPM. I appeared in the first one, an adaptation of John Bunyan's *The Pilgrim's Progress*; directed and appeared in *The Last Error*, a Biblical drama; and written and directed the third, *Altar to an Unknown God*, a contemporary drama with a title borrowed from scripture.

I doubt, though, that my short theatrical career of sorts at CPM did much to help me overcome any spiritual challenges I'd faced during that critical period in my teenage years—or that I'd done a great deal for anyone else's spiritual good, for the great cause of the Kingdom, either.

Theatrically, with a large, mostly commandeered and less than eager cast and crew, *The Pilgrim's Progress* wasn't up to much. Directed by Moira Midgley, the Rev's wife, I'd played the central role of Christian, the pilgrim who sheds his burden of sin and presses on, buffeted by temptation and opposed by evil forces on every side, to finally reach the Celestial City. (I'd not been typecast, then.) Mrs. M. had allowed me to do pretty much as I'd wanted as Christian—not a good thing for any actor on any stage, of course. Still, the production, all three performances, was well-attended and enthusiastically received. But what's done for the Kingdom, for a captive audience, isn't likely to come under much in the way of critical scrutiny, of course.

There was one memorable moment in the play, however—but having little to do with performance quality, unfortunately. It was a scene in which I was kneeling before a cross, repenting of my sins and being ministered to by a trio of holy maidens, the Shining Ones. Playing the SOs were Philippa 'Pippa' Harwood, a recent past interest of mine; Jacquie Midgley, the Rev's daughter and my brother's very steady girlfriend; and a dazzling CPM newcomer, Annabel Vickers. I'd been seeing Anna on the quiet—but not quietly enough for Pippa and Jacquie not to have noticed, apparently.

As the scene came to its reverent close, the quiet, gentle Pippa had to step forward and say, 'Thy sins be forgiven thee,' which she did quite convincingly. But Jacquie, putting the sign of the cross on my forehead, looked at me in anything but a forgiving way. Then the blonde-tressed Anna, looking positively angelic, had to replace my tattered, sin-stained cloak with a bright, shiny new one, which she did, whispering in my ear (off script, of course): 'There you are, you naughty boy, you.'

I wasn't inclined to do another play at the church, citing my A level school studies. But Mrs. M. suggested something be done on a smaller scale with only interested people, and proposed doing the quite well-written *The Last Error*, which I eventually agreed to do. Mrs. M. then suggested I direct as well as play the role of Pontius Pilate's military commander in Jerusalem—a double duty I'd taken on without thinking it through. But Mrs. M. and everyone on and offstage rallied around me, doing their jobs enthusiastically and conscientiously, and Anna in particular. I'd cast her as Pilate's much younger wife (his second or third, maybe?). We had a scene together in which our distrust of Pilate and feelings for one another were expressed in a subtle but also unmistakeable fashion. Anna looked great—both demure and sexy at the same time. She had talent, took direction well, and contributed a lot in making the play work as well as it did. (She'd not told me or anyone else that she'd done leading roles, including Shakespeare, in high school in Gillingham before coming to Southend, which I found out later from her parents.)

The original idea for *Altar to an Unknown God* I'd got after coming across something Spanish philosopher Miguel de Unamono Y Jugo had written in *The Tragic Sense of Life* (as quoted by Graham Greene in a memoir): 'Those who believe that they believe in God, but without passion in their hearts, without anguish of mind, without uncertainty, without doubt, with an element of despair even in their consolation, believe only in the God Idea, not in God himself.' The play has a Prodigal Son parable-like theme—except in this case it's a father and two daughters.

The plot revolves around Elaine Blake, a well-brought up Methodist girl raised in a fictional seaside town in Essex. Always more adventurous than her older sister, Elaine leaves home to go to university in Norfolk, where she gets involved with a handsome, engaging and articulate agnostic, Malcolm Crowther. (My take on Jeremy Burgess, perhaps.) Bringing Malcolm home to meet the parents, Elaine realizes she'd made a monumental mistake—an error that eventually forces her to have to choose between her strict father's obdurate, black-and-white beliefs, which her mother and sister have never questioned, and her own exploratory, still-in-the-making ideas and convictions.

I needed, I knew, a trio of justifiably confident actors for Elaine, the boyfriend and her father. I chose Anna for Elaine right away. She said I'd surprised her, but also encouraged and motivated her by the confidence I'd shown in her. It hadn't been a difficult choice, I told her; that I had good reason to believe she'd be the Elaine I was looking for. I'd assured her too that I'd get her some strong onstage support, which I did. I managed to persuade Jeremy to play Malcolm. (Playing himself too?) I'd also appropriated an actor from the locally-based Pilgrim Players, an interdenominational chancel drama group, who'd had some professional experience, to play Mr. Blake. As I'd thought they would do, the three worked very well together—and at certain moments, too effectively for the comfort of some in the audience, perhaps.

I'd not set out to write a controversial play—nor had I; not as I saw it, anyway. Without question, however, with its open-ended closing scene, *Altar* . . . hadn't delivered the satisfactory denouement, the Prodigal Son story's outcome, that many in the audience had anticipated. Conceivably, too, it had raised issues of faith some viewers were reluctant to have examined in any sort of public forum at the church. As for the response mattering most to me, the Rev Trev said the play had been performed very well; that something like that, prompting people to examine what they truly believe, couldn't but be helpful. And Dad had said pretty much the same thing.

Interestingly, though, about a fortnight later, Olive supplied her Sunday school class with a written exegesis, with relevant Bible texts, offering some 'analytical commentary' on certain issues my play had raised, a copy of which she'd forwarded to me—and no doubt to the Rev Trev as well. In her accompanying note, she wrote: 'With an open, searching mind like yours, Tim, I'm sure you welcome each and every response to your play, both pro and con.' Judging by Olive's 'review' of *Altar* . . . she'd found my argument neatly phrased and nicely dressed up dramatically, but sadly lacking any real substance. As she'd said in her note as well, 'Your devil's advocate approach isn't the problem for me. It's that in my view your play reflects all too often an inadequate appraisal and appreciation of the deeper, not always easily accessible eternal truths of God and His ways in the case of both Elaine and Martin, the latter in particular.'

In any case, with *Altar* . . . I'd blown my cover with Olive, it would seem—as had Anna too, I expect. For Olive, with Anna and me, the less than beneficial effects of our recent collaborations, offstage as well as on, were showing up all too clearly. And although probably undecided about which of us was most to blame for unhelpfully influencing the other, Olive would have concluded we were both in some trouble, spiritually speaking ; that all the signs were there of our having veered off the faith's straight and narrow we'd had so clearly mapped out for us since we were children.

15

Jace signed on for two terrific and vividly contrasting roles for the '87 Chichester Festival in Sussex's bucolic South Downs country. She reprised the part of Kate Hardcastle in Goldsmith's *She Stoops to Conquer* she'd played for the Bristol Old Vic, and with the same director, Tristan Major, who'd wanted none other; and then taken on the title role in Shaw's *Saint Joan*. Jace had made the transition from the one character to the other with a startling, consummate ease, weighing in with two splendid performances. (*The Observer* on the first: 'Goldsmith might have had Jacinth Glyn-Davies prophetically in mind for the beautiful, witty, designing Kate, who in concert with her eligible but often bemused and always captivated lover, combine to make the dramatist's case against sentimental comedy so effective, and his piece the funny, engaging play it will remain when played like this.' And *The Guardian* on the other: 'Glyn-Davies gives us an awe-inspiring and yet also human and womanly maid of Orleans—one that any man worthy of the name would follow and fight any battle for, and perhaps as well secretly long to fight over and win for himself.')

Saint Joan was directed by Teddy Bentley, Ursula Haldane's old flame at the BOV in the early 1960s. Teddy and Jace had never met before. She said, 'Teddy's a director I'd work for anytime in anything. And it's not hard for me to see either what my mother once saw in the man—and, if I'm not mistaken, what she still sees in him, and what he probably still sees in her. I wouldn't be surprised at all if there's something starting up again between the two of them. In other words, stay tuned.' In fact, Teddy and Ursula had already started seeing another again after so many years in the spring. Jace remarked: 'You know, Tim, for all I know, maybe they never did forget one another—and which might help explain why they've both been divorced a couple of times.'

I didn't tell Jace what Big Teddy told me over a Shaftesbury Avenue pub lunch. He said: 'Of course, the fact is, Ursula should still be performing. She was a great talent. They'd be calling her Dame Ursula if she hadn't just upped and walked away like she did. But we all know why, of course. Some untoward circumstances she could have avoided if she'd kept her wits about her, that is, instead of letting her heart rule her head at least once too often. On the other hand, though, if she'd watched her step more carefully, there wouldn't be a younger version of herself around to admire, would there? And as an actress, the daughter is maybe an improved version of the mother. Anyway, Tim, someone for both you and me to admire and be grateful for, if for different reasons, wouldn't you say?'

Jace's closest girlfriend since their RADA days, Emma Kirk, came to Chichester to see *Saint Joan* in late July. After the congratulations, the catching up chit-chat, Emma had a surprise for Jace. She said that while on holiday in Greece in June she'd met a lovely man—a thirty-four-year-old, never-been-married history professor she was certain she loved and whom she didn't think she could live without. And she was just as certain that the man felt the same way about her; he'd not said anything, but it was in his eyes, she said. 'I could hardly believe what I was hearing,' Jace told me. 'It was like something straight out of "Good-bye Mr. Chips".'

She'd told Emma she was very happy for her, wishing her luck with her academic. But admitted to me, though, she was worried about her friend, and what exactly was going on with her. 'She didn't seem to be the Emma I've always known. The chap was all she could talk about—as if everything in her life was already revolving around him, seeing him as someone she could gladly sacrifice everything for, her career included. And this, mind you, from a heart-and-soul feminist like our Em, would you believe? She's talking like someone I'm going to have to get to know all over again. I've this feeling too she's not telling me everything, that she's holding out on me about something.'

A few days and a phone call later, Jace got out of Emma that Gareth Burnett lectured at Sheffield in New Testament history; that he was the son of a C. of E. clergyman who'd also kept the faith of his father's. Jace said, 'I was flabbergasted. I mean to say, is this going to be a case of having to have her Gareth and his God too? What is the girl thinking of, I ask you?'

Listening to Jace you'd have thought that Burnett had 'form,' as the police say. I said, 'And what did you say? Did you ask her what she thought she was doing?'

'No, I didn't. But it was on the tip of my tongue. To tell the truth, I didn't know what to say. And her parents didn't know what to say to her, either, apparently.' And said she could see why, describing the Kirks, who were both teachers, as 'card-carrying unbelievers.' But added, 'But I think Emma knew what I was thinking. Because she said the chap had assured her he loved her as she is, for who she is; that he wouldn't dream of forcing anything he believed on her.' And that respecting her 'sacrosanct individuality' would always remain a 'must' for him. 'Well, for Emma's sake, I hope her lovely man is a man of his word. It would be pretty scary for her if he isn't, don't you think?'

Gareth and Emma announced their engagement at Christmas that year, and their plans to marry the next summer after Emma had completed the rep season in Ipswich. 'And getting married in church with her father-in-law officiating,' Jace reported. Only confirming, she said, her troubling fears for Emma—'a friend who seems intent on running away and hiding on me.'

Jace asked, 'How did it go, then?'

'Very well, actually. It was a good evening all round.'

'You enjoyed it, did you?'

'Yes, I did.'

'Well, there you are, then.'

My father had decided to pack it in as Cliff Place Methodist's Sunday school superintendent to make way for a capable younger man, The church had held a special Sunday afternoon service in September to honour him for his twenty-five years of faithful, unstinting service. If I'd not got a note from the Reverend Midgley inviting me to attend, saying it would mean a lot to my father if I could make it, I wouldn't have known a thing about it.

In his remarks, Dad gave a very good account of himself, seldom referring to his notes. He spoke of his conversion as a youngster in Hook Norton, and of his large debt to the Timsons. He said he'd learned from Anthony and Agnes that one witnesses as a Christian through 'the total fabric of the life experience, when we are least aware of publicly demonstrating something, but are simply caught up in the toils, heartaches, glories, depths and peaks and mundane chores of life.' And that having a Christian experience like that is what turns 'emptiness into fullness, washed-out grey failure into shining brightness, aching loneliness into relatedness.' (He was quoting from Malcolm Boyd's *Christ and the Celebrity Gods.)* What my father had had to say that afternoon—I've got a video tape of the whole ceremony—encapsulated, I thought, the way he'd always lived his life, both publicly and privately.

I'd not been in Cliff Drive Methodist for nearly five years, not since Christmas 1982, during my second year at Nottingham, and I wasn't quite sure how welcome I'd be made to feel in surroundings some might be feeling I'd been only too glad to have put behind me. But a number of people came over to me to say hello—among them the Midgleys, of course, and also the Cromwells. (Did I see in Olive's eyes some sadness and regret over a lamb in the fold who'd got clean away?) And I got to talk to the Harwoods, and to Mrs. Vickers as well. Speaking of whom, neither Pippa nor Annabel were there that afternoon—both of whom had married someone they'd met at university and had moved away from the Southend area. Their absence had left me feeling a mixture of both relief and disappointment—something like that, anyway.

It had been a busy, quickly passing summer that year for me as well. I was working on a TV adaptation of H.G.Wells's *The History of Mr. Polly*, a three-parter, with rewrites to do, deadlines to meet, conferences to attend. I'd got my first commission for the telly the previous year to adapt George Gissing's late nineteenth century novel, *New Grub Street*—about a clever and unscrupulous writer whose success is aptly described in the last-but-one *Oxford Companion to English Literature* (edited by Margaret Drabble) as 'the triumph of self-advertisement over artistic conscience.' This had been aired in March, well-watched and positively reviewed.

I'd got to Chichester for the openings of *She Stoops to Conquer* and *Saint Joan*, naturally, but hadn't returned as often as planned, particularly earlier in the summer. Although this hadn't gone unnoticed by Jace, she'd complained hardly at all, and then only mildly. As she knew I was aware, Jace used her Sundays and breaks between performances to get in some serious down time, lying low, doing what she called her 'Greta Garbo "I-vant-to-be-alone" thing.' She'd said once, however, 'But I do make the odd exception, you know—and with you, Tim, it's an exception I'll always make, as I'm sure you've realized by now. But I'm not at all sure if in realizing that you're going to pull up your socks and get yourself down here more often than you've been doing.' I might have said in my defence that I'd not wanted her to feel pressured to take our relationship up another level; but I'd refrained from that, letting my coolness under the fire of passion prevail. I've always been quite good, not unlike my father, at keeping my deeper feelings under chink-free wraps.

But that approach, not an easy one to adopt where Jace was concerned, wouldn't prevail much longer. On a Saturday night in late June, after a *Saint Joan* performance, as I was dropping her off at her flat, Jace said, almost matter-of-factly, 'Tim, why don't you come in—and if you want to, stay the night? If you don't mind not getting your money's worth at the hotel, that is, of course.' And just like that—spending the night in so glorious and delectable a fashion as we did, with a repeat performance the following night—the level of passion between Jace and I got turned up at least two notches, maybe three. We'd taken our next step in becoming one another's significant other.

After that, I got myself down to Chichester every remaining weekend that summer, having got . . . *Mr. Polly* finished and out of my hair; and for this having to put up with some moderately gentle jokes at my expense. Jace said, 'Well, it seems a woman's got to do what a woman's got to do, to have the pleasure of your exclusive and intimate company, Tim Hainault.'

We did manage a six-day holiday, our first together, roaming around Cornwall, squeezed in between her *Saint Joan* closing and the start of rehearsals for a pre-West End run of *The Importance of Being Earnest* at Greenwich. And during which I thought we'd broken some new ground while covering certain aspects of love we'd previously talked about in more general terms (and mostly too through the eyes of others—writers, mainly, from Shakespeare through Fielding, Sheridan, Byron, Keats, Dickens and Eliot to Storey, Larkin, Kingsley and Martin Amis and Stoppard.) The sort of discourse—as we'd both admitted this time—that had allowed us, up until then, to take a safe, non-commital sort of position on the whole subject.

16

Anna—Annabel Vickers. We knew each other for only two years. Then off we went to university—she to Sussex, me to Nottingham. That was in 1980. I saw her again during the Christmas holidays the following year at Cliff Place Methodist; and we'd also had lunch together in Southend. I've not seen Anna since then.

Of all the girls of my youth I knew Anna best. So much better than Pippa Harwood, who I'd grown up with. (That 'all the girls' isn't to imply there were rafts of them.) And it was Anna I'd let get to know me better than any other girl. I'd let my ever-present guard down when I was with her. Also, Anna had a knack of knowing where I was going with something sometimes before I did.

From the Sunday she'd first turned up at CPM in the summer of 1978, Anna was turning boys' heads and making girls envious. I was in the church foyer that day talking to Stewart Simpkins, my only real pal at CPM, when she walked in the door. (Like me, Stew was almost certainly on Olive C's 'to watch' list; she'd have regarded us as birds of a feather.) Stew said, 'Hey, Tim, turn yourself around and see what I see—a vision, a dream walking! I'm not kidding you.' I could see what he was going on about. Who wouldn't have done? Anna was a smashing, ash blonde, green-eyed stunner. In the sanctuary, Stew and me sat at the end of the row behind hers, hoping to get an occasional side view of her. (Sneaking looks at girls in church was something of a ritual with us.) Stew said, 'Remember, pal, I saw her first.'

I was content to let Stew and one or two others make their moves on Anna. I wasn't just standing idly by, however. I'd made some selective eye contact with her to let her know I was interested. And also letting her know that I could bide my time with her; that this was one laddie who wouldn't be a pushover. A well-reasoned way, I thought, of getting noticed by a classy girl who could afford to be choosy. (This had worked with Marnie Boulting at BPH, anyway.)

In fact it was Anna who made the first move—in what I was to learn was her usual and straightforward manner. Getting me alone in a church corridor—I think she'd been waiting for me—she said, 'Looking for me, were you, Tim? So, then, when are you and me going to get to talk? Anytime soon, d'you think? Just name your time and place, and we'll get things moving between us, all right?'

After we'd got together a couple of times, she said, 'You don't want to be seen with me around the church, do you?' So I told her about Olive Cromwell's unwritten rules for dating: that a CPM boy and girl should only be seeing each other exclusively, and have serious, long-term intentions on their minds; not just trying it on with one another, in other words. To which Anna remarked, 'Well, if Mrs. Cromwell's into unwritten rules like that, let her come and explain them to me herself, so I've got them right. And anyway, aren't there enough written rules as it is, without piling on a bunch of unwritten ones?' Clearly, Anna wasn't going to let Olive or anyone else at the church have her jumping through their hoops like a performing animal at a circus.

But we did decide, though, to stay under Olive's radar; to pay scant attention to one another at the church while continuing to see each other regularly at carefully planned times and places. I think we both enjoyed playing our deceptive, undercover lovers' game at CPM. Anna said, 'You know, Tim, I'm not sure we should be as good at this as we are.' In the meantime, neither of us made any pretence of not seeing anyone else—just as long as it wasn't someone who went to CPM.

Getting to know Anna was never boring or predictable. Of course, in that regard, she had the advantage of me, having some local sources of information to go on. Anna went to Southend High for Girls, as did Pippa Harwood. I was confident, though, that Anna wouldn't be tapping into Pippa or any other CPM girl to get the goods on me. But a school friend of hers, Jane Matheson, who'd transferred from Blenheim Park to Southend, knew me, Jeremy Burgess and Marnie Boulting, having been in the same classes as the three of us. Jane also knew Chris Penlow and had been friends with one or two girls who knew me through him. But Anna never mentioned anything that Jane may have told her about me. In any case, she was more than capable of sizing me up, as she could anyone else we both knew.

There was plenty of 'he said, she said' with Anna and me—no lack of any free and easy communication going on between us. Unlike any other girl I'd spent time alone with, especially a church girl—Pippa in particular. I felt I could discuss anything with Anna; and I got to expect nothing but the straight goods from her.

Sex was a topic we got onto quite often. Talking about it seemed better for us than not talking about it when it came to keeping our physical feelings for one another under control. Anna was characteristically forthcoming on the subject: 'I think sex is marvellous—one of God's great gifts, and so on. I'm orthodox C.F. & P. on that.' (Christian Faith and Practice, she was making reference to.) 'But I don't agree with kids who say, hey, if it feels good, let's do it. I don't think you can get away with that, emotionally or psychologically, having sex just for the fun of it. Maybe boys can—but girls, I don't think so. And that's apart from any Christian guilt feelings coming into it. The point is: I don't see getting myself used like that, as most teenage girls are. Afterwards, feeling good isn't what you're going to be feeling.' Having me down as well as she did, Anna wouldn't have expected much of an argument from me on that, and I was happy to oblige her.

Still, with Anna and me, it wasn't all talk and no action, of course. But what action there was we'd somehow managed to keep within the common sense limits we'd agreed on—but not without a high degree of difficulty, admittedly. And in managing this, it was always more a matter of Anna's will power than mine.

We were in the last week of rehearsals on CPM's *Pilgrim's Progress*. Anna said, 'You take your acting very seriously, don't you?'

'Well, I don't want to look stupid up there, do I? Not if I can help it.'

'I'm surprised you're as patient as you are, actually. It can't be easy for you with the likes of us up there with you—not taking it seriously, and not having the talent for it, either.'

'They're not all like that. You're certainly not. I look at you up there and I see actress written all over you.'

'Well, if you do, I don't know how, the little I have to do onstage. But you, on the other hand, seem to know what you're doing. If you didn't, with the part you have, it would be pretty farcical, the whole thing. I'm very impressed, actually, Tim. The conviction in your voice—saying the things you have to say—and the way you look at me as a Vanity Fair tart, and then so differently as a Shining One at the cross, it really is something, you know. Well, I think it is, anyway.'

'Well, thank you, Anna.'

She curtsied after a fashion. 'But I do have to ask one thing, though. What you're doing onstage—it is acting, isn't it? The character of Christian and Tim Hainault, the guy himself—they're not like two peas in a pod, are they?'

'Do you think they might be, then?'

'Well, to tell the truth, Tim, I can't tell. But that's probably just me. I sometimes have trouble deciding what is and what isn't, even though I pretend I don't. And maybe that's because I don't want to know—that knowing might spoil the fun for me.'

I said, a month or so later, 'No, Anna, like I said, Jeremy has a steady girlfriend, and has had for quite awhile now.'

She said, 'Helen Bartlett, you mean?'

'Right, the very same.'

'Helen's in my year at Southend.'

'Yes, I know.'

'I don't know her at all. But I see her after school a good deal—at Victoria Circus, waiting for a bus. She meets a boy there; a good-looking, fair-haired boy. They're very good friends, obviously. Their hands are all over each other.'

'Really?'

Anna looked at me—one of her searching looks. 'What makes me think I'm not telling you anything, Tim? And that maybe it's something you're not telling Jeremy? I thought Helen and him were joined at the hip.'

'Well, they're still a twosome, anyway.'

'Tim, am I missing something here?'

I compressed my lips, tilted my head. 'All right, Anna, I'll tell you. Keep it to yourself, if you would, please. Jeremy and Helen are—well, the fact is, they're putting up a front, pretending they're involved; something they're not, not anymore. They think it will help cover up the fact that Jeremy's homosexual—at least until he leaves home for university, anyway.'

'And Helen's willing to go along on that?'

'I think it was her idea. Either hers or Mrs. Burgess's, one or the other.'

'So his mother knows?'

'Oh, yes. It's not for her sake; it's for her mother's. Jeremy's grandfather was the vicar at St. Andrew's in Westcliff for thirty years, and his wife is still a parishioner. Mrs. Burgess thinks it would kill her to know about Jeremy, her favourite grandson; and she doesn't want the people she rubs shoulders with every Sunday to know, either. Anyway, Jeremy's mum asked me to stick with him as a friend and not to tell anybody about him and Helen; that that might help discredit the rumours she said were floating around, I guess it was.'

'And you're okay with that?'

'With Jeremy's homosexuality, you mean?'

'Yes, I suppose I do'

'Yes, I am okay with that. It just doesn't matter to me. Jeremy and me, we like each other's company, and we always have. We have a lot in common. We've a liking for many of the same things—things most kids don't want to know about. We understand the way our minds work. And we're tolerant about our differences. All of which makes us good friends, allies, good companions, whatever; and if anybody has a problem with that, that's too bad. And I hope I don't protest too much for you.'

'No, no, Tim. You don't protest too much for me at all.'

'But you're surprised, right?'

'Well, I am a bit. But maybe not the way you think I am—the way I know I am.'

'What way's that, then?'

'Well, Tim, in the last few minutes, I think I've got to know you better—and what I've got to know makes me like you better than I already do. Actually, Tim, I'd say you've just gone up in my estimation, I guess it is.'

'I have?'

'Oh yes, Tim, you definitely have.'

She smiled, put an arm around me and kissed me on the cheek. We looked into each other's eyes, then shared a kiss—this time mouth-to-mouth.

Anna said, 'You don't have to tell me, of course, if you don't want to. But I was just wondering how things are these days between you and Marnie Boulting?'

I said, 'Maybe I should ask how things are between you and Richie Dennison.'

'Okay, sure. I'll go first. I'm not seeing Richie anymore. That's all over and done with. And that's all that needs saying about that, I think.'

'Okay. And maybe all that needs saying about Marnie and me is that that's all over and done with, too. Besides, her father's been moved by his firm to Manchester, and the rest of the family will be joining him there in the summer.'

'I was just wondering, that's all.'

But she'd also asked me another time about Pippa Harwood and how did that stand? And I'd told her the thing between Pippa and me was more an idea of our respective parents than it was ours. (Shading the truth a bit there, I think.) The Hainaults and the Harwoods were old friends and the two families had done quite a few things together, I told her. 'Besides, I can't say I'm very keen about families at the church getting connected through marriage like they do, anyway. There's something insular, too cosy and close-knit—stifling, even—about it, don't you think?' She'd readily agreed.

In fact, Anna and I had already agreed, some months before, that before chasing each other with any real intent, we'd wait until we'd got out into the wider world at large, where we'd each have some honest-to-goodness choices to make about something as important as that. That way, if we did end up together, we'd realize and appreciate what clever and lucky people we will have turned out to be, she said.

By the time Anna and I did *Altar to an Unknown God* at CPM in March '80, neither of us cared very much how many people at the church knew about our feelings for one another. There wasn't much we could have done about what people might have been thinking in that regard, in any case. The two of us had provided the romantic interest (all words, no actions) in the Biblical drama, *The Last Error*, CPM's previous dramatic offering in the autumn of '79; and with that we'd also provided enough proof for some of how close we were off the stage as well, apparently.

While rehearsing *Altar* . . . Anna said, 'I'm curious, Tim. Being the big-head I am, I'm wondering if you wrote the part of Elaine specially for me. The thing is, you see, I was wondering why all those lines were so easy for me to learn, why I knew straightaway I could do the part convincingly. And then I realized that a lot of Elaine's thoughts and feelings are very much like mine. It was like we'd sat down and talked for hours and you'd taped our conversation. You had me down like nobody ever has, seeing things in me other people, especially boys, don't see; and don't care if they see or not, either. And you know what, Tim? I thought I'd be crazy not to be crazy about a guy who understood me like that. But then, I thought, having a guy know me like that might not be so good after all. He'd always be one step ahead of me. So I'm thinking: is this a guy whose arms I should be running into—or a guy I should be running away from as fast as I can?'

'So what did you decide?'

'I'm still thinking about it,' she said, and laughed.

The pressure was off. We'd just finished our A levels; we'd both studied hard. And we'd worked hard too on *Altar* . . . and worked well, we believed. As we may have seen it, we deserved a break—and why not a reward of some sort as well?

I said, 'Anna, if you're not doing anything Saturday evening, would you like to come over to my place?'

'Your father will be there, will he?'

'No, as a matter of fact, he won't be. He's away for the weekend—at a church conference in St. Alban's.'

'Oh. Are you having a party, then?'

'No, I'm not. It would be just you and me.'

She gave me a long look, then said, 'Of course, Tim, why not?' She said her parents were going into London that night, and wouldn't be home until late.

When Saturday night finally arrived, we watched some telly and talked. And after some prolonged and intensive necking, we went upstairs.

'You've got some protection with you, Tim, I hope?' she said. Which I had. She didn't seem at all surprised.

In bed, we wrapped ourselves around one another. I tried to be patient, but it wasn't easy. Afterwards, though, she said it'd been lovely for her. (It has been bloody marvellous for me!) I didn't think she was just saying that. She also said how wonderful it'd been, breaking our duck together—cricket jargon for scoring your first run in an innings.

We never did have the opportunity for a second innings, however. Anna was away for most of the summer.

Jeremy told me once that sexy church girls like Anna can't help attracting upstanding, clean-living young men like me, who often end up marrying them. 'They really do want to be good girls, you see—just like the girl Daddy married. But wanting to be good, and being good—well, it's not the same thing at all, is it? So do watch your step at that church of yours, won't you, Hainault?'

Anna and I both applied for English studies at Nottingham; but she'd had to be content with Sussex instead. And which meant that the idea we'd had about chasing each other in earnest after leaving home remained just that: a nice idea. But if we both had gone to Nottingham, however, things might very well have turned out quite differently for Anna and me, I've often thought. In fact, I'm sure they would have done.

17

Raich Lambert went to see Jace as Gwendolen Fairfax in *The Importance of Being Earnest* quite a few times—at the Greenwich and Haymarket openings, and at least twice more after that. Wilde described the play as a trivial comedy for serious people—for people who needed to be made fun of for their own good, who live to impress, influence and control the rest of mankind as if with a God-given right to do so, he meant, I suppose. But as Raich said, 'It's damned good fun, anyway, whichever way you slice it. It's one of the short list of plays outside of Shakespeare I just can't see enough of, that sends me out of the theatre like I've had a champers too many.' He told me he'd seen more than a dozen different Gwendolens in his time, and worked opposite three of them as Jack Worthing—but for his money, Jace had made 'even the best of them fade into the shadowy recesses of what passes for my mind these days.' He said he'd immediately sensed as much soon after her first entrance with her line, in response to Worthing having told her she was quite perfect: 'Oh, I hope I'm not that. It would leave no room for developments, and I intend to develop in many directions.' And Raich added, 'And as with Gwendolen, so with Jacie Girl—a gel who'll be developing in all sorts of ways and directions, I'll be bound, offstage as well as on. And believe me, m' lad, I know of whom and of what I speak, considering the host of women whose paths I've crossed over the years, for my sins.'

Jace considered Gwendolen an 'absolute delight' to play and a totally refreshing change after Shaw's Saint Joan. But she saw her too for the 'basically mindless and insensitive upper class gorgon-in-the-making she is—already too much like her mother, with something bordering on the sinister behind all that prettiness, style and witty repartee'; a certain kind of young woman Wilde had probably run into far too often in London drawing rooms and salons. Jace had had to remind herself, she said, of something Olivier had said when playing a character you dislike: that what in fact you have to do is find every way you can of liking the person you're playing. 'Which made me readier to play the part than I would have been, I think.'

Raich paid his money for a seat in the stalls to admire Jace's Gwendolen once more in March that year. The next morning he lost his footing on the frost-slick steps outside the Brook Green flat, falling and breaking a hip.

In hospital, Raich was cheerfully optimistic, telling his visitors he was like his classic Rover he'd kept for several years in a lock-up—'just needing a part or two to be up and running like a charm.' But he'd told Ursula—the one person he knew he couldn't put anything over on—that he wasn't feeling 'up to snuff at all.' And he'd talked about having had 'a jolly good innings, knocking plenty of boundaries and a six or two'—but wasn't feeling 'at all comfortable at the crease anymore, not seeing the ball as I like to see it, big as a balloon.' Ursula said he hadn't sounded at all like himself; not as she'd always known him to be.

About a week later, Raich was gone; everything had shut down on him very quickly. He'd told Ursula—one of the last things he said to her—that a quick, neat and tidy exit was his style, anyway: just as he'd have written it himself if he'd had any choice in the matter. She said, 'Dear Raich really did love Jacinth and myself like family, you know. And maybe better than family considering how families can be sometimes, his included. I'm going to miss Raich more than I can imagine right now, I know I am.'

Jace wasn't taking Raich's final exit too well, either. She told me, 'It's really strange, something I've never experienced before—but I'm finding I'm having to drag myself down to the theatre these days. Raich just loved me as Gwendolen, he told me. And I should be doing every performance in his honour, loving the work as he did, as we all do. But somehow I don't seem able to look at it like that. It's more like I'm irritating some internal injury I've suffered now that he's gone. And I'm sad everytime I have to play Gwendolen again. I think I'm going to be relieved and glad to be done with her—to take a break, and, if I'm lucky, get started with somebody else as soon as possible.'

Raich was buried in the family plot in Highgate Cemetery—next to the parents who'd distanced themselves in life from him, his father in particular. There were no other relatives still alive to mark his passing. An ex-wife was thought to have survived him, but nobody knew her whereabouts. Ursula and Raich's longtime friend and agent Tom Skilton had looked after the funeral arrangements. There was a pretty good turnout of mourners—nearly all former theatre and television colleagues and associates. Laying aside the Common Book of Prayer's prescriptive words and the customary funereal clichés, the officiating minister went off book with his 'Good night, sweet prince: and flights of angels sing thee to thy rest'—parting words I think Raich would have appreciated as much if not more than any others.

A Sunday morning in July, going on for midday. Jace and I were having our usual brunch—orange juice, mushroom omelettes, toast and marmalade, and coffee, prepared by me, also as usual. But this time, not as usual, at my place in Putney.

I'd awakened beside Jace that morning in her bed in the upper Brook Green flat for the first time. And for which there was a simple explanation: her mother didn't live there anymore. Ursula had moved into the lower flat, after a makeover to replace Raich's wood-panelled, men's club-like decor. 'Well, isn't this a treat?' Ursula had said to Jace. 'From now on we'll have a choice to make with our two T.s, won't we?' She'd meant the 'your-place-or-mine?' choice; her 'two T.s' were Teddy Bentley and myself, of course.

It had been Raich Lambert's after-death largesse that had supplied his two dear girls with the wherewithal to make a choice like that, obviously. In his will he'd given Ursula and Jace joint-ownership of the free-and-clear Brook Green property; and also some investment holdings, his furniture and books. (He'd left the Rover to Tom Skilton.) Both mother and daughter were recipients as well of something of a different sort of value Raich had left his solicitor to hand over: packages including a letter, some mementoes of occasions spent together and an enlarged photograph of himself with each of them. One with Ursula (as Portia), taken backstage at Stratford, where they'd first met, at the height of her troubles with P.D., and another with Jace in her Gwendolen costume at the Haymarket opening. Each photo Ursula and Jace had had custom-framed, then placed prominently on display in their living rooms.

Some fifteen months later, Jace showed to me what Raich had also included in her package: pseudo-adoption papers making her his supposedly legal daughter, at the bottom of which he'd written 'Paternally and eternally yours' over his signature, and had dated the document 'Today and forever.' Jace also told me that in his letter to her mother Raich had made her a penned, decorously-worded proposal of marriage—allowing him, he'd written, to go to his grave believing that in accepting him she'd be acknowledging that they'd been man and wife in mind and heart, if not on paper, and that they would always be one in that way. Jace said, 'Raich was a lovely man and a loyal friend. And also an incurable romantic, of course; and in that respect, I think, may have reminded Mumsie a little too much of her two previous husbands.' Both her father and P.D. had been romantics in their own different ways, she thought. 'But you won't say anything to Mumsie about this, will you? She'd think I was using you to get out of her what I've always wanted to know: what she'd have said to Raich if he'd asked her to marry him to her face, instead of from the "other side." If Mumsie had had to look into those soulful eyes of his and given him a straight yes or no, I'm talking about.'

I took this to imply that Jace's views in one important respect hadn't changed much since we'd decided to live together. For after *The Importance of Being Earnest* closed, she seemed to have put any such romanticized views of marriage in their proper place—'in a sensibly realistic context'—and had quoted Gwendolen's final line in the play to support her 'plainly rational' contentions. With her marriage to Jack Worthing settled, and in response to his line that it was 'a terrible thing for a man to find out suddenly that all his life he has been speaking nothing but the truth'—and could she forgive him for this?—Gwendolen replies, 'I can. For I feel sure that you are sure to change.'

If Emma Kirk was running away and hiding on Jace she wasn't doing a very good job of it. Or Jace wasn't letting her dear friend get away from her that easily—with the first of those things much more likely the case than the second. In any case, the two were keeping in touch by telephone as consistently as before, it seemed, with Jace frequently bringing Emma's name up in conversation. Also, they'd kept up their once-a-month Monday luncheon dates in a favourite restaurant of theirs on St. Martin's Lane. Not only that, Jace had agreed to be at the church on time to serve as one of Emma's bridesmaids at her July '88 wedding in Aylesbury, Bucks. She said, 'Em said she couldn't think of me not being there to share the happiest day of her life with her.'

And as the wedding date drew nearer she admitted she was rather looking forward to being part of the ceremony. 'Well, it's a part I've never played before, and in a lovely setting like that too. Like something out of Thomas Hardy.' (The next month she'd be going before the cameras for the first time to do a BBC-TV adaptation of Hardy's *A Pair of Blue Eyes*.) Jace had also enjoyed traipsing around London helping Emma choose her wedding dress and the bridesmaids' mode for the day. (Emma's mother hadn't shown much interest in this or any other of the nuptials' preparatory doings.)

Gareth Burnett and Emma were married in Aylesbury's ancient St. Mary Church, situated not incompatibly in a square sided by seventeenth and eighteenth century buildings. The groom's father, the rector, conducted a traditional C. of E. Solemnization of Matrimony service, which had included the standard selection of hymns for the occasion, and the familiar processional and recessional organ music. And throughout all of which Jace couldn't help being fascinated by what she'd got herself into, she'd told me later in the day.

She said, 'The novelty of it all—maybe that was part of it for me. I haven't been in a church since my schooldays in Guildford, when I'd taken no notice whatsoever of what was going on. It was all that lovely language too, I expect—so perfectly worded and phrased, and often poetic, Shakespearean, even. But as I'd expected, of course, the substance of what was being said so beautifully—the wedding vows particularly—was a bit too much for me, I'm afraid.'

She'd marvelled at the sincerity and conviction in the eyes and the voices of both bride and groom considering the promises they were making, she said. 'But it wasn't only the vows. It was everything that was being said and sung—and all of it taking place in the sight of God, which I had no sense of whatsoever. My part in the proceedings was just a performance—with me smiling or looking appropriately solemn as required. Just doing what an actor has to do to make people believe you in the part, but knowing too that I was wrong for the part. I even got to wondering if I might somehow be jinxing things for the bride and groom—you know, like a sceptic at a seance, or something.'

I had to smile. 'No, Jace, no need for you to worry on that score, I'd say. That's not how it works.' To which she said, 'Well, how would I know how it works? Something I'm not familiar with like that?'

'Well, certainly, not how it works the way Emma and Gareth would see it, anyway. What they did today, making the vows they did, was a very private thing—just between themselves and their God, with nobody else involved. And if, just if, their marriage doesn't work out, I can't see either of them holding anyone but themselves responsible for that—if that'll help put your mind at rest at all.'

'Well, yes, I think it will do, coming from someone well versed in such things, Tim. Thank you, darling.' This said in all seriousness.

Back at the hotel, she got into bed and snuggled up to me. She'd told me earlier that she was tired out—but obviously wasn't ready to go to sleep right away. 'And you know something, Tim? If Emma is to be believed, you and I are meant for each other, too.'

'Really? Emma thinks that, does she?'

'Well, that's what she told me last night. She claims to have known as much the first time she saw us together, that night at the flat, having dinner with Mumsie and Raich; the way you and I were together.' At the time, she said, Emma was off men altogether after a bad experience with someone when she was at RADA, and wasn't sure if she'd ever want a man in her life again. 'Maybe you remember me telling you that about her. Anyway, when she saw us together that night that all changed, apparently. She started believing again, amazing herself too, that there was a man, a good man, out there somewhere just waiting for her to come along. But this time to be patient, not to force anything—to just let it happen. And sure enough it did—on a tour bus in Athens. Her professor came down the aisle and asked her if the seat beside her was taken; and, as they say, the rest is history. And she said if you and I can't see, after all this time, that that's how it is for us too—the way it is for her and Gareth—we must be blind, or not very bright, one or the other. In that take-it-or-leave-it way of hers, of course.'

'So what did you say to that?'

'Well, what could I say? Except that she'd given me something to think about. For both of us to think about, wouldn't you say, darling?'

After Jace got back from some location work in Cornwall as Hardy's Elfride Swancourt—and before taking on another much less saintly Shavian woman from the previous one, making her National Theatre debut as Vivie Warren in *Mrs. Warren's Profession*—she and I had arrived at a meeting of the minds on one thing of more than ordinary importance so far as our relationship was concerned. We decided to try living together; and with Jace having convinced me to do the logical thing and move in with her at Brook Green.

Clearly, not the leap of faith and commitment Emma and Gareth had made together that fine July day in St. Mary Church—but for us, a step of some significance, all the same. But perhaps, rather, a misstep, as my father might have viewed it. But as Gran told me, 'I know your dad knows how much you love the girl—and that someone like her doesn't come along very often, just like your mum did for him. So like I told him, you had to do something—but you couldn't do anything more than the girl is going to let you, obviously.' To which he'd not said a thing—just nodded his head.

18

PAUL JOHN HAINAULT
April 12, 1960 – August 16, 1980

'And we know that all things work together
for good to them that love God, to them who are called
according to his purpose.'
–Romans 8:28

He will never grow old or go unremembered.

My father is right, of course. My brother Paul will never grow old, forever fixed in our minds as we last knew him; the experiences we'd shared with him like scenes in a film that never change. Paul will always be remembered—if not always as clearly and accurately as he once was, as the years slip by. Some things stay with you with a remarkable clarity, however. But again, memories of him can also convey and mean different things as each time one revisits them or, more likely, when one is revisited by them. Remembrances come as they will—randomly, at any time, mostly without any attempt made to bring them to mind.

Another thing, too: as some experience or other I'd shared with Paul comes back to me, what is recalled rarely amounts to very much, to any sort of cohesive whole—only bits and pieces of events and conversations, and sometimes no more than moments; a quick snapshot, a pointed look or a fleeting glance. And if indeed these unbidden and disjointed recollections of my brother serve any discernible purpose, they more often than not remind me of the differences between us, rather than the things we'd had in common.

As kids, when we were younger, with only two years between us, we played together quite a lot, of course—but I don't recall dogging his footsteps with any regularity. We had our own games to play, by ourselves or with others; a pattern that developed early on and became more pronounced and noticeable as we continued on into our youth. My time-consuming interest in sports and his inveterate lack of anything of the kind, for instance. (Although he did sometimes play tennis, after a fashion, in Chalkwell Park with his girlfriend Jacquie Midgley, the Rev's daughter, and also enjoyed hiking with Dad, if that counted for anything.)

We played miniature golf together once or twice, I recall, while on holiday in Cromer—the only time I remember playing anything of a sporting kind with him. After one such occasion—I'd beaten him by at least ten strokes—he said, 'You really do like winning, don't you? Even an excuse for a game like this? But so what? What does that prove?'

'It proves I'm better than you at this.'

'Well, yes, you are. If you just go by the scorecard. But maybe, playing like I did, I'm better off than you, anyway.'

'How's that, then?'

'You won, I lost, true—but I think I'm happier than you. Because I played the game in the right spirit, just to enjoy it, win or lose. Isn't that what a game's supposed to be? Something to enjoy? A way to relax?'

Always thinking a little deeper about things than most people our age—that was typical of Paul. My brother was always old for his age.

What he chose to read must have had a lot to do with that, I suppose. It was always serious stuff like philosophy, psychology (particularly Jung's), secular and Church history, Bible commentaries and biography—hardly ever any fiction, unlike me. And with him, of course, there was the theology too, starting when he was early in his teens—almost exclusively the Wesleyan variety; very little Calvinistic stuff. Paul had quickly dived and delved in the deeper end of Dad's front room library pool.

But, like Paul, I'd enjoyed Bible stories too, packed as they are with human interest. The competition going on, with God and man constantly having a go at one another over something or other, the battle royal of good and evil, appealed to me. But by the end of Acts my interest had dropped off sharply; and only five books into the New Testament, too.

But not for my brother. True to form, he was very keen too on what his namesake, the apostle, had had to say in his fourteen letters to various churches and associates; on mainly theological matters I wasn't in the least interested in getting my head around. Important matters to do with what a Christian is expected to think and believe—the vital 'underpinnings and the bedrock of the faith of faiths,' as Olive C. told her senior Sunday school class—and during which Paul was by far the most eager and ready participant; while I, on the other hand, remained virtually silent (to either hide my ignorance of or indifference to whatever was under discussion).

On his eighteenthth birthday, Paul announced to Dad and I that he'd decided to go into the ministry—after several months of 'wrestling with myself over several lesser ambitions.' Jacquie M., who was with us in the restaurant that evening, and already in the know on this, looked as contented and settled about his decision as he did. The Rev asked Paul to tell the congregation about his decision the following Sunday, which he did in an articulate but also unpretentious manner. He'd quoted and commented on the words of St. Paul's to the Romans. (The text that Dad was to choose for the bronze plaque he'd had mounted in the CPM sanctuary in Paul's memory.) And after which not a few in the congregation that day had expressed to Paul how gratified his news had made them; nobody from CPM had entered the ministry for more than two decades. Quite a few had congratulated him on his remarks and his ability as a speaker as well.

Also, that summer, with the Midgleys away on holiday, Paul preached his first sermon, again referring to a Pauline letter, this time to a fellow evangelist, Timothy—to instruct and encourage his younger protégé, who might have been temperamentally timid, my brother said. His text, relative to St. Paul's own ministry: 'Nevertheless I am not ashamed: for I know whom I have believed, and am persuaded that he is able to keep that which I have committed unto him.' And once more he'd got himself a lot of complimentary attention after the service.

Later that same day, he said, 'Sorry about that, Tim—all the fuss people seem to be making over me, saying the things they are about me.'

'Hey, Paul, there's no need to apologise. It doesn't upset me at all, if that's what you're thinking.'

'Well, if you say so. I thought it might be getting to you. You know, putting some pressure on you.'

'What sort of pressure?'

'Well, mostly, to fall in line with what I'm doing—or at least to think about it. That maybe that's what Dad wants for you too. And a few others want for you as well.'

'What, me? No, I don't think so, Paul. Dad's very pleased about what you're doing, and proud of you, sure—but I think he's got much more modest ambitions in mind for me; like being found every Sunday in a pew somewhere, preferably a Methodist one. He'd be very content with that, I think. And anyway, Dad's not the sort of chap who wants more than his fair share of good things, is he?'

But I'd known where Paul was coming from, however. Gran Gadsden claimed that Paul John was named after the apostle and John Wesley, arguably the two greatest preachers the Church has ever seen—and myself after St. Paul's missionary colleague, and secondly (as Charles) after the Methodists' founder's younger brother, the prolific hymn writer. (I'd always thought I'd got my second name from my maternal grandfather.) In any case, to my knowledge, Dad has never acknowledged such a thing.

Also, another time, Paul said to me, 'I know people think that when Saint Paul talks about being "called" he's always talking about going into the ministry—but they're wrong. The truth is, we're all called, whatever we do for a living, to represent Christ in some way or other. We're all servants of God.'

The truth of it was, however: my brother was far more suited and better equipped than I to be one of God's trusted agents in any sort of setting. I only had to look at what Paul had up and nicely framed on his bedroom wall—some colourful, decorative calligraphy he'd done himself, and done very well, reminding me of the painstaking work on display at Prittlewell Priory done by monks some centuries back. Words from the sixteenth century Sarum (Salisbury) Primer, author unknown, that are still used as a benediction or a benedictory hymn:

'God be in my head,
And in my understanding;
God be in mine eyes,
And in my looking;
God be in my mouth,
And in my speaking;
God be in my heart,

And in my thinking;
God be at my end,
And at my departing.'

For Paul, these were words to live by. But as I'd said to him once, words easier to live by for monks, ensconced and isolated in a strict religious community, rather than out in the temptation-torn world at large.

'You're probably right, Tim,' he said. 'A prayer like that doesn't give you much leeway to be mindful of anything other than spiritual things. The way I see it, though—if it's sex and marriage we happen to be talking about here…' (How had he known that?) 'If that was fine with Martin Luther, a monk who finally saw the light, then it's fine with me. Within marriage, I mean, of course.' And with Jacquie too, I presumed. (My CPM pal Stew Simpkins said that despite her proper, Rev's daughter decorum, he was convinced that Jacquie M., or Midgette, as he sometimes called her, had a sexy, 'still waters run deep' streak.)

'Yeah, maybe it was okay with Luther, having a good time in bed—but it wasn't okay with Saint Paul, was it?' I said. I must have been in the mood for an argument that day. 'Paul said it was better not to marry; to only tie the knot if you're burning up with sexual desire. That doesn't sound to me as if the apostle was that well-versed on what a nice and healthy marriage is all about.'

'Yes, well, it's quite possible Paul was speaking from experience, in a specific, very personal way. About having a wife who'd given him a lot of grief—as some think he'd had in mind when mentioning his "thorn in the flesh."'

'So, if Paul did have a wife, she may have been too sexy for him, is that what you're suggesting?' Yes, I was in the mood all right. 'Whereas, with Luther, his wife wasn't sexy enough for him, maybe. That along with his wine and beer, he also enjoyed a good time between the sheets, which he wasn't getting.'

Paul smiled. 'Nice try, Tim—but I'm not going to bite. Your questions are probably not serious ones, anyway. But if they are, maybe you should try them on a tried and true man of the cloth who knows all about having a wife. Like the Rev says, his door is always open.'

Now who wasn't being serious? Have a chat with the Rev about sex? Paul knew I'd rather have a tooth drilled without freezing. Although it might have been marginally better than talking about sex with Olive C.,

I thought. She wouldn't have batted an eyelid; not been deterred by any embarrassment a third degree along those lines might have been causing me.

There'd been the *Playboy* incident as well. Someone had slipped a copy in among the magazines and other literature in the church vestibule, with Stew S. the chief suspect. And Paul may have been among the number of those who felt I was part of a conspiracy of silence in the matter, as well as suspecting I was a member of the *Playboy*-reading 'underground movement'at the church.

He'd said to me, 'The thing with that, it isn't just the air-brushed female flesh on view, and the fantasizing that that sets off.' The 'self-pleasuring' (*Playboy* jargon) that goes with that, he might as well have said. 'It's what it does to objectify women, to get you thinking of women as just things to be used for your own gratification. And it's not just the photos either. It's what's on every page, from cover to cover. The food for the mind that's on offer—what you're digesting—and the moral and spiritual harm it's doing to you. And also for the poor, unsuspecting woman you happen to be chasing at the time.'

He wasn't preaching at me, trying to force his views on me. Paul was like Dad in that respect. He took the view that it's your life to do what you will with it. In one of Olive's class discussions, I recall him commenting on the freedom we're given to choose Christ and his way or not. He said, 'God never was interested in making us perfect in a perfect world, like puppets whose strings he could pull. In other words, we're allowed to be human somebodies—not just automated somethings—to try making the world a better place for everyone we have any dealings with.'

Paul would have made one of Christ's more competent and trustworthy spokespersons, I had to think.

Paul never did train for the ministry. He'd gone ahead with his plans to go to Exeter to read psychology before going to theological college. He said this would help him 'see the world as it is, and people as they are—to show them, hopefully, how things could be better for themselves and for others.' But Paul wasn't to get his degree, either.

On that tragic day, another Saturday—August 16, 1980—Paul had been with a party of Christian students at Exeter on an itinerant evangelical mission on the English Riviera in the South West. ('Working for the Kingdom and having a good deal of fun doing it,' as he'd described the venture.) And once again I'd been off that day in pursuit of some sporting pleasure—this time playing cricket for Westcliff C.C.'s second XI at Loughton in my first season with the club.

I'd arrived home around eight that evening to get the terrible news. The police had called at the house that afternoon, in response to a message from Lyme Regis in Dorset (in *The French Lieutenant's Woman* country). There'd been a traffic accident that morning on the outskirts of town—a very bad one. The Volkswagen passenger van Paul and his group were travelling in had collided on a curve with a heavy transport lorry that had lost its brakes. Paul had died at the scene, and a companion at the hospital; while three others had been injured, two seriously.

This isn't happening, I thought, and may have said out aloud as well.

My stricken father seemed to have aged ten years in a matter of hours. And for me, under the sorrow and the pain, there was already a layer of fast-hardening anger as well. I couldn't but help see Paul's death as the epitome of abject pointlessness—a cruel instance of a good and promising young life getting snuffed out—and for what possible reason? The anger I was feeling wouldn't be denied. I doubted I'd be capable of giving Dad the sort of comfort and support he'd be looking for from me—as much as I'd wanted to provide something like that for him. Certain reactions of mine to what had happened were already too strong and assertive to allow for that. And although Dad and I were probably closer that awful day than we'd ever been—as survivors in a family now cut in half so arbitrarily—it was also the day, I'm sure of it, when the distancing, a distinct apartness, began to wedge its way and develop between the two of us.

INTERVAL*

1 9 8 9 After Jace's successful debut the previous autumn with the NT in *Mrs. Warren's Profession*—'getting it in right proportions with a Vivie Warren whose physical charms and proper etiquette belied her steel trap mind and cool, hard centre,' as one critic had it—she went into rehearsal in February the next year for *Half Truths, Full Spin*, a new play at the Savoy, playing a London PR consultant who'd subtly sunk a 'big fish' corporate client for betraying and ruining a young woman, her dearest friend. And in this part too Jace had again gained herself a swathe of good reviews. Then *A Pair of Blue Eyes* aired in April and was highly praised, making Jace an overnight household name in the U.K. And in

---

* There is no exact point you can point to, of course; but going into your thirties, the tempus fugit factor kicks into a higher gear. Time becomes more of the essence; the days, months, years start to click by faster like quick, passage-of-time, calendar page dissolves in an old film. And there's more urgency to fulfil your potential, your ambitions, to establish yourself professionally. To reach high levels of achievement—or for an artist in whatever field, create a body of work recognizably out of the ordinary. In any case, that's how it was for Jace and me. Going into 1989, Jace was about to establish herself in British theatre's top ranks. I had written two well-regarded, successful plays, and been recognized as an adept, imaginative adaptor of novels for television. For me, though—and for others too—the one question was never far from mind: what had I done lately for the stage? *Entrances and Exits* was written in 1984-85, produced in '85-86. With me, the play's the thing, as always; it's always about my next play. Jace and I had settled in well together. We both liked the thought of having each other to come home to, to eat, sleep and relax with. The fact is, though, it was probably always the work that mattered most for each of us; where the main focus was. Of course, life goes on, and things of significance of a personal sort were happening for both of us. But other than becoming more used to and comfortable with one another, our own personal relationship was, in effect, in the doldrums—quite static, in limbo—in a state of arrested development that seemed to have gone unnoticed or ignored. To all intents and purposes, nothing was going forward for us as partners in life and love—hardly any more for us than for two characters in a play (so far as the audience is concerned) during the interval between the acts.

August she was back with the NT pulling off another personal success as Irina in Chekhov's *The Three Sisters.*

I had two TV scripts aired during the year—*Of Human Bondage*, which was well-received, and an adaptation of my own *Writing and Loving, Loving and Writing*. That went well too, and again brought the D.H. Lawrence cognoscenti out into the open; and again I'd managed to stay out of the arguments. A colleague of Jace's at the National, who'd watched the teleplay, said that one advantage of getting involved with a writer rather than another actor—probably the only one—is that his or her movements are easier to keep track of.

Also in August, Ursula and Teddy Bentley gave Jace and I short notice that on the following Friday they were getting married at the Kensington register office, having a restaurant reception close by, then taking off for somewhere in Derbyshire for the Bank Holiday weekend. They were planning a full-scale honeymoon over Christmas on a Mediterranean cruise. 'Maybe this was always meant to be, if there's ever anything meant to be about something like that—and let's keep our fingers crossed it'll be third time lucky for both of them,' Jace commented. Teddy moved in downstairs with Ursula, a temporary arrangement until they'd found something else. Teddy told Ursula he could be a kept man only so long; and that the four of us under the same roof would be too cosy and close for comfort, anyway.

1 9 9 0 And so on into the century's and the millennium's last decade Time marches on, with never, for the still living, any falling out.

More accolades for Jace in the summer on her debut with the RSC at Stratford-on-Avon. She'd been an enchanting Helena in *A Midsummer Night's Dream* that wisely hadn't tried to out-innovate Peter Brook's legendary white box, trapeze-rigged version in 1970. And she'd followed that with *Romeo and Juliet,* in which, the critical concensus was, she'd made a Juliet 'to die for'.

In my top-of-the-house, hideaway lair in Brook Green, I was working on another TV adaptation: Thackeray's *Pendennis*, his second major novel after *Vanity Fair*. About the disheartening misadventures of a would-be-lawyer-turned-journalist—another writer—and the four women of various types, characters and class levels he'd been attracted to. I'd also finally completed 'the next one'—a stage play, of course—titled *Romeo Scores*! A comedy-drama slated for workshopping with Jamie Kingston at the Manchester Library Theatre; for production in March 1991. About a handsome, football phenomenon, a born striker, and his adoring girlfriend, whose dad was Manchester City F.C.'s chairman—with conflicting bigwig family and club loyalties involving City's famous rivals, Man. United, coming into play. A contemporary take, obviously, on Shakespeare's classic tale—well, with a nod in its direction, anyway—and with a far from happy ending, but certainly not as tragic a one as the Bard's.

In July, Aylesworth's, the London legal publishing firm for which my father had worked more than forty years, was absorbed by a conglomerate, moving from Bell Yard to Chancery Lane—and Dad, making a move of his own, opting for retirement. If he'd suffered any loss of identity and self-worth as a retiree I'd not noticed any. He said he was looking forward to ticking off some things he'd always wanted to do.

1 9 9 1 I spent five weeks early in the year in Manchester working with Kingston and the Library Theatre on *Romeo Scores*! Worked squeezed in between rehearsals for other shows; lots of late nights doing rewrites. With an inventive set, and using rear projection screens, the play was a rip-roaring success, quickly selling out. Quite a lot of non-traditional playgoers in the crowd, some of whom were wearing United or City colours, and rooting, sometimes audibly, for one club and family or the other. It got some good reviews and also some less good ones. For some, whatever they'd been expecting with my next one, this definitely wasn't it. The contrary opinion: I'd gone off on a tangent, skipped down a side road leading away from where I should be going as potentially a dramatist of distinction. This sort of naysaying surfaced again when, the following year, a BBC Manchester telly version I'd adapted went down a treat with viewers all over the U.K. In addition, a *Romeo Scores*! touring company was put together for the 1991–92 season and played to full, appreciative houses in Liverpool and Sheffield (two other two-football-club cities) and also in Leeds, Hull and Newscastle. Plans to mount a London production fell through, however, for never fully explained reasons.

Jace was again at Stratford—as Cassandra in *Troilus and Cressida* and Julia in *Two Gentleman of Verona*. More well-deserved critical plaudits for her, none of which she'd let turn her head. 'I'm just on a lucky streak,' she said.

A raven-haired Canadian beauty by the name of Leona Fielder was also at Stratford that year. Fresh out of RADA, she'd got a play-as-cast contract with the RSC and an instant Equity card, working at the lower, supernumeraried end of the company's cast lists in several plays. I'd noticed her, though. If I'd tried to say I hadn't, Jace would never have believed me. She said that Kell Marleau had noticed Ms Fielder in a college theatre programme in Vancouver, where he'd directed a show for the Playhouse; and he'd advised her to get some top quality training in London. 'If she goes anywhere, I'm sure Kell will be claiming most of the credit,' Jace commented.

At Gran Gadsden's eighty-fifth birthday party in Hook Norton in April, Dad had turned up with a companion, Yvonne Blaydon—a very presentable-looking widow from Rochester he'd met on a trip to Israel. Gran said it was good to see him 'back in the land of the living at long last'; and that now perhaps he'd dismantle 'that bedroom shrine to your mum he's got in Westcliff.' But Dad's relationship with Mrs. Blaydon was over by Christmas. So far as Gran could tell, she said, he'd scared the woman off; that she'd realized he'd always be comparing her with Mum.

Also, at Gran's big bash—held in Hookey's community hall—I'd got talking to Les Plunkett, captain of the Hook Norton Cricket Club. I'd talked too much, agreeing to turn out for the team that summer. I've played regularly for the club every season since. (The occasional Sunday Jace had come to Hookey to watch a match, driving down from Stratford, not too far distant, she'd caused quite a stir, making me the envy of not a few teammates.)

1992 Kell Marleau kept in touch regularly with Jace by phone, and got over from wherever he was in Canada twice, sometimes three times a year, not wanting to miss anything she was up to, and also to see his parents in Ireland and France. He'd always spend more time with Jace than with the two of us, and even more so the past two years, visiting with her in Stratford. This didn't concern me at all. The friendship he and Jace enjoyed, as strong as it was, wasn't intrinsically the sort that had kept either of them from finding or maintaining a special relationship with someone else—as it had always been between them. Kell had phoned Jace to tell her how upset he was about not being able to get over that summer to Stratford to see either Jace's finely-drawn Cordelia in *King Lear,* or her scintillating, irrepressible Kate in *The Taming of the Shrew*. He was going to be far too busy preparing for his first season as AD with The Citadel in Edmonton, Alberta, he'd informed her.

Playing opposite Jace in *Shrew* as Petruchio was Matthew Norden, Teddy Bentley's Albert Finney-like protegé and fellow Yorkshireman (and also a client of Ursula's). Onstage he and Jace made a brilliant match for one another. Matt and Sloane Ranger Ali Partington, an RSC publicist, were living together in Warwick that summer. The four of us, becoming friends, had some good times together. More often than not, Ali and I would find ourselves providing an audience for Matt and Jace and their actors' talk and repartee.

Leona Fielder was back for a second season with the RSC, getting a small part or two. I bumped into her and another actress in town; they were leaving a pub as I was going in. I'd probably imagined it, but both women, who knew who I was, seemed to look at me as if wondering where Jace was, and maybe some other things about the two of us as well. Also, in Leona's dark, glorious eyes, there was a flash of interest in me of more than just a casual sort, although I'd probably imagined that too.

Other than with *Romeo Scores!* on tour in the north—I'd gone up for the Newcastle closing and the Leeds opening—there wasn't much doing for me that year. Just homework for me alone in Brook Green, occupying myself with research, note-making and a first draft for a play—about English WWI nurse Edith Cavell, who was executed in Belgium by the Germans, supposedly for spying. I'd integrated with the text some WWI poetry. I was chronically drawn, it seemed, to the past—to another time in England; interested in people with little in common with my own generation, in their speech, manners or values. My liking for history in general as well as my adaptations of nineteenth century novels had had something to do with this, conceivably. I wasn't making much progress, though, and had started again. I was still slogging my way through the first act by the end of the year. But I'd had a very good second summer of cricket in Hookey, however; which pleased me a good deal. Also, I'd seen a lot of Gran, who organized the home match refreshments for the club. There wasn't much she wasn't still into in Hook Norton; but wasn't as sprightly as I'd always known her to be, I thought.

In August, taking Gran's advice at last, Dad sold the St. John's Road house in Westcliff and purchased a top flat overlooking the Thames Estuary in a four-storey, 1980s' building near Chalkwell station. And in October he left for a month-long trip to Italy (Rome), Greece (Athens) and Turkey, to see Ephesus, this time tracing some of the steps of St. Paul.

He was going alone this time, not with a tour group, he wanted Gran to know.

1 9 9 3 Neither Jace nor Matt Norden were at Stratford for the RSC summer season. In September, however, they were opposite one another again, this time at the National in London—as Benedick and Beatrice in *Much Ado About Nothing*. And once more the pair had made well-matched sparring partners, verbally scoring off each other so often, particularly in the early rounds of their romance. This onstage encore for the two had been a fortuitous, unanticipated one. The NT, in approaching each of them, had made no mention of the other; neither one had thought the other available, in any case. (Ali Partington was no longer with the RSC either, living in London with Matt—patiently keeping track of his social activities, especially with other women, someone had tartly remarked.)

Both Matt and Jace had left the RSC reluctantly—she was by then an associate company member—neither one being able to stay with the company because of large and small screen commitments. Matt was making a new film version of John Osborne's *Luther*, some of which was being shot on the Continent. Jace had an exhausting daily schedule, mostly in London, making a series for ITV called *Cass Cartwright, QC.* As Cass, in an all-women chambers in Lincoln's Inn, while representing mostly female clients—sometimes feminists, sometimes more traditional women put upon by men—she enjoyed giving the legal establishmentarians, always men, some twitchy moments; and a lesson or two whenever possible, particularly in the court room. The first eight-show series was a runaway hit, and ran for two further years. Jace couldn't go anywhere now without being recognized; and got herself more or less permanently on the tabloids' 'set-up-and-knock-down' celebrity list.

Leona Fielder wasn't at Stratford that summer either. She'd done some rep at Derby during the winter—after which, we were informed by Kell, he'd persuaded her to return to Canada to work with him at The Citadel in Edmonton in 1993-94. He'd dangled under her nose no less a role than the Egyptian queen-enchantress in Shaw's *Caesar and Cleopatra*. Kell said Leona took all of five minutes to decide to take him up on his offer.

Another thin year for me—just a one-show TV script for an ITV police series; but my first original one, however. I'd abandoned the Cavell play. I'd started on another about playwright and poet Christopher Marlowe, dealing with his rivalry with Shakespeare, some suspected criminal as well as espionage activities, and his rather mysterious death at twenty-nine in a Deptford tavern fight in 1593. A good deal of research had been involved. But that wasn't going particularly well, either.

Gran was advised by her doctor, because of a heart condition, to cut back on her community and church activities, to watch her diet, the social drinking and smoking. She said he might just as well have told her to pack up living.

1 9 9 4 Not a good year for me. Things happen—and they did. By mid-year, having turned thirty-two, that unassailability, that blithe sense of untouchableness, had deserted me. Gran Gadsden had a debilitating stroke early in April, totally incapacitating her. She told Dad she didn't much care for the quality of life she could look forward to, preferring to have God call her number and have done with it. In the middle of May she got her wish, seemingly glad to get on with whatever awaited her next. Dad and I were deeply saddened. For both of us, Hookey wasn't going to be the same place with Gran not there. I may have come to rely on her pithy, straightforward advice more than I'd realized. I'd had no doubts at all that she'd loved and cared about me much as Mum had.

'Abide with me' was sung at Gran's funeral at St. Peter's—and that same question asked again: 'Where, grave, thy victory?' Words I'd last heard sung two years before at Wembley Stadium, with a military band accompaniment, prior to an F.A. Cup final. I'd not joined in the singing on that occasion either. Gran was laid to rest in the family plot in the churchyard.

At the funeral service, Dad had for the first time set eyes on Sally Grainger, a vivacious, easy-on-the-eye, fifty-six-year-old; a Banbury resident and erstwhile Hookey GP's daughter Gran had known and liked since she was a child. Dad and Sally started seeing each other a few weeks later. Gran, I'm sure, would have approved; and been grateful in time to Sally for making Dad the happy man he is today.

Jace didn't attend Gran's funeral. She was in France on location near Clermont Ferrand making a film, *The Last Time I Saw Vichy*—about a popular, photogenic historian (Jace) searching for the truth about her English mother's involvement with French collaborators and the Resistance in WWII.

Ten days later, in Banbury, at Gran's solicitor's, I was in for the surprise of my life. Making sure I'd never get the chance to thank her—she'd not said a word to me about it—Gran had left me Queen's House, lock, stock and barrel. She had discussed it with Dad, however; he couldn't have been more pleased for me. 'Tim's a Hookeyite at heart, I know he is,' Gran had told him; and that she hoped I'd never sell the place, that it would always stay in the family. (Obviously, Gran would have had to be presuming I'd eventually have a family of my own.)

Jace was back in London for the weekend in mid-June. I was in Hook Norton; she'd not told me she'd be in town. I phoned her as soon as I got to Hookey; she'd left a message. She said we needed to talk—something I couldn't remember her having said before. 'But not over the phone,' she said. She was making me nervous. I said I'd return to Hammersmith just as soon as the day's cricket match was over.

Jace and I decided to stay closed-mouth on what had taken place between us that evening. (So far as I know, not even Ursula or Kell ever got an explanation.) There'd not been a great deal said, in any case. Jace and I didn't spend much more than an hour talking; a conversation punctuated by several and sometimes lengthy silences. Jace left the flat soon after ten o'clock; she'd booked herself into a hotel. She was returning to France first thing in the morning.

For Jace, then, it had happened. It could have happened to me, although I'd never thought it would. His name was Marc Lalerne, a Parisian actor she'd met on the film set in France. As self-protective as she'd always been when it came to liaisons with people she was working with, she said she'd tried, but managed only so long to ward off the advances of the divorced Lalerne. And: 'But we'd both known the day we met, of course.' When the film was finished, she was planning to spend a month or so with Lalerne in Paris and on the Normandy coast. 'I think this is it, this is meant to be,' she'd said. (Shades of her mother and P.D.?) 'I'm so sorry, Tim, I really am,' she said, and seemed to mean it.

Sadly, but perhaps not so strangely—as shocking and devastating as this had been for me—there was almost a sense of inevitability about it as well, I'd realized afterwards. Conceivably, we'd both seen this coming for some while. We'd virtually stopped talking about anything other than mundane day-to-day things; and, of course, the work we were doing, anything work-related—not much else. Ostensibly, we'd tacitly colluded in tabling any discussion about where things might stand between us on a personal level for another but never dawning day. Neither of us, probably, had wanted to know—or, in actual fact, admit what we did know. What, actually, is there to discuss when, over time, the love two people have for each other has slowly eroded—that was clearly now falling short of the love they'd expected to give and receive in roughly equal measure for the foreseeable future?

Jace wanted me to stay on in the Brook Green flat—'what with your work space set-up on the top floor, for one thing,' she said. When she'd got back from France, returning for work reasons, she said she'd likely be taking up a RSC colleague's offer of a flat in Earls Court. She'd been doing some thinking about a future without me for awhile, it seemed.

And a future without Jace I'd needed to think about too. Making an adjustment like that wasn't going to be easy. I knew. But keeping busy would help, I knew too. Fortunately, there was another TV adaptation job to hand: Evelyn Waugh's first novel *Decline and Fall.* Also, with the Marlowe play idea shelved for the time being, I'd moved on to the next century, to the Restoration period, with a view to doing something about the introduction of women on the English stage.

For the next while, then—it couldn't be helped—that's how it would have to be for me: the writing a 'go' and the loving on hold. I was certain of one thing, though: I wouldn't be content without love in my life for any extended length of time. Notwithstanding love's various problems, recognizable as such or not, and the heart-wrenching let-downs that almost inevitably go with all that.

TWO

1

The arrival of another year: 1995. As usual, a time for forsaking the old and taking on the new—at least so far as my work was concerned, anyway. In my personal life, though, when it came to the company of women, looking for someone new had hardly crossed my mind.

I was in fact still missing Jacinth. Often I'd find myself wondering what she'd have thought and said about something or other. I could have given her a bell, of course—we'd remained good friends—but not at the risk of seeming to want to turn back the clock with her.

So each and every day it was off to work with a single-minded passion. By the end of January, after weeks of research, I'd got something promising down on paper—for a big, ambitious play about Restoration playwright and poet, William Congreve.

Ideas for plays come and go easily. But once in awhile, as in this instance, one comes along you sense from the start has some staying power; that continues to excite and fully absorb you from start to finish. A project receiving every day your inner critic's approval; one you feel is within you to write and carry off well. But a job of work too requiring a daily act of faith; a belief that your fanciful conjurings will one day catch the fancy too of a producer, and a large if largely faceless audience.

Plays and fiction with a historical background sometimes have their beginnings with the hope of finding an answer, or something like one, to some leading questions the real-life protagonist of the piece had left unanswered—as with my play about Congreve I'd eventually titled *Congravino*. The question in Congreve's case: why did he, in 1700, at the age of thirty and at the top of his game, choose not to write another play in the remaining half of his life? And this after the London production that year of what is generally regarded as his finest play and ahead of its time, *The Way of the World*. (Which wasn't as well-received as each of his previous plays had been, however.) In any case, a decision for which English dramatic literary history is the poorer for having been made.

With the evidence to hand, however, not in any way an easy question to answer. Congreve was a complex and enigmatic, secretive man; a writer who chose to hide as much as he could behind his words on paper. And possibly with a dual personality of sorts—with a need to give expression to his exceptional gifts as a dramatist and poet as well as fulfil his aspirations to be generally regarded as a bona fide gentleman in society at large. So, along with his literary work, he'd sought and made the right connections to secure a useful sinecure as a civil servant. And never a rakish man about town—a type he knew well and wrote about—he felt that a good, well-informed mind and a clear conscience best suited his self-image. Congreve, nevertheless, loved women—but always with discretion; and always women with intelligence and talent as well as beauty who could inspire as well as excite him. He wrote hundreds of letters, as the literate often did in his day—but not one written to or received from either of the two great inamoratas of his life has ever surfaced, as almost certainly he'd not intended one would. As a writer in need of an audience, of course; but in working to be the man he saw himself as, the fewer the watchers and listeners the better for him.

It hadn't taken long to realize that to tell its story my play would require a good measure of imaginative speculation based on what facts were to hand—par for the course when reconstructing historical events in a dramatic or fictional form, of course. That the play would not so much uncover the every why and wherefore of Congreve's life as explore as thoroughly as possible the mind-and-heart territory he moved in. In fact, in its telling, a story more about the journey travelled than the destination arrived at.

As I tell it, the story begins on a wintry day early in 1729, in the vestry at Westminster Abbey following Congreve's funeral and burial service. Two elegant middle-aged women in full mourning commiserate with one another over the passing of the man they both had loved and would never stop loving. Under their veils their fine looks haven't deserted them. One is Henrietta—the young Duchess of Marlborough, as she was always known. (Her mother Sarah had the same title). The duchess had made the funeral arrangements, making sure Congreve's last resting place would be close to hers in the abbey. The woman with her is Anne Bracegirdle, one of England's most celebrated post-Restoration actresses, but by then retired from the stage. Through Congreve—their Conny—the two had known each other for some twenty years and become friends, having learned to appreciate what the other's love had meant to him. Anne says: 'Conny's work, his fine and true words, will surely last and live on, for you and me especially.' And Henrietta: 'He was a fine work in himself, too, a true and loving man. That is what will always remain with me.'

Then in moments switching back in time to an Inner Temple lawyer's chambers in 1691, to discover the twenty-one-year-old Yorkshire-born Conny, newly arrived from Ireland, where he'd been educated (most recently at Trinity College, Dublin). Congreve didn't take long to convince his head of chambers that a legal career wasn't for him. He'd already published a moderately successful novella of love and intrigue, *Incognita*, that same year, which he'd written using a pseudonym to hopefully stay on the right side of his father, a military officer, who wasn't literary minded.

Starting to make a name for himself with his classical poetry translations, Conny finds the beckoning world of writers, actors, singers and musicians opening up for him. Socially, too, people are drawn to him with little effort on his part, especially women. Asked the secrets of his success with the ladies he tells an envious friend, 'I have none—except I look ever for qualities of mind in a lady as well as for her physical attributes. And seeing this in my eyes and in my manner towards her, most ladies are accordingly well-pleased, I find.' And certainly pleasing for an extremely attractive and accomplished singer and lute player, Arabella Hunt—and the attraction is mutual. He writes an ode *Upon a Lady's Singing* (1692) for Arabella, calls her his 'dear angel' and writes to her that she makes 'every Place alike Heavenly wherever you are.' It pleased both as well to keep the time spent together behind closed doors strictly to themselves—the kind of romantic attachment of choice for him; to be conducted with all due discretion.

When Conny and Anne Bracegirdle's paths cross, however, Congreve's attentions to Arabella fall off a cliff. Known in the 1690s as London's 'Darling of the Theatre' and 'The Universal Passion,' Anne becomes at once his private passion—which in fact comes as a great surprise to him, knowing his own cool and collected self as well as he does. Conny meets Anne for the first time early in 1693 during rehearsals for his first play, *The Old Batchelor*, at the Theatre Royal, Drury Lane. And undoubtedly it is Anne's excellent and captivating Araminta that immeasurably helps secure the play's spectacular success.

Much to Conny's liking, Anne has always conducted her private affairs judiciously—in her case dispelling the 'loose woman' image of actresses especially prevalent in the late seventeenth century. Anne lives with her widowed mother, whose husband had left her well-provided for, in a townhouse just off the Strand, not far from her socially well-placed sister, Frances Porter, and her lawyer-husband Edward. The Porters take to Conny, Frances in particular, and invite him to take an upper suite of rooms in their Surrey Street house, which he does; and where he is to remain for the rest of his days. Anne also has a floor to herself in her mother's house, with both hers and Conny's living arrangements making their assignations the easier to accomodate. Also, Frances and Conny enjoy their witty and sometimes flirtatious dinner table conversation; and he keeps in touch with her too when he is travelling. In one letter to her, he refers to an earlier one she claimed not to have received, which he describes as having been 'very passionate.' But adds: 'For my part I keep the Commandments, I love my neighbour as my selfe, and to avoid Coveting my neighbour's wife I desire to be coveted by her; which you know is quite another thing.' As well she did. In fact, Frances is in two minds, to encourage or not her younger sister's romantic involvement with the personable and perhaps too persuasive playwright. But, in any case, neither Conny nor Anne see marriage ahead for the two of them. For him, as a gentleman in the making, marrying an actress hardly merits serious consideration. And for Anne, given her highly successful career—her Shakespeare is much lauded and in demand too—and her existing and foreseeable circumstances as her mother's sole legatee, a husband is more or less a redundancy.

Conny's second play, *The Double Dealer*, also in 1693, isn't as successful as his first despite the admiration and unqualified support of his friend and mentor, playwright and poet laureate John Dryden, the grand old man of English letters. A production, though, in which Anne scores a personal triumph as the virtuous Cynthia, a role Conny has written especially for her. And whose lover in the play seems to press Conny's own suit to the actress—the first but not the last instance when his feelings for Anne overlap into his art; and which at times proves confusing for both of them. Anne also plays the romantic lead in each of his three remaining plays—Angelica in *Love for Love* (1695); Almeira in his only tragedy, *The Mourning Bride* (1697); and Millamant in *The Way of the World* (1700).

Professionally, at any rate, the two could do no wrong; together they dominated London's theatrical landscape in the 1690s.

With the arrival of the new decade and century, however, what the pair expected to continue on indefinitely between them, onstage and off, comes to a gradual halt. *The Way of the World* turns out to be their last collaboration. (And again a show in which Anne's reputation doesn't suffer despite the play's lukewarm reception.) She'd excelled as the fascinating and mercurial Millamant, arguably Congreve's most memorable, finely-drawn female character—and perhaps, like Anne herself, the stage's earliest version of one of Ibsen's or Shaw's free-thinking 'new' women, some two hundred years later.

Actually, *The Way of·the World* is a harbinger of the significantly changing things to come for Conny and Anne, professionally and personally. For one thing, he'd not expected the play to succeed, knowing it was too subtle in form and substance for the new century's punters. As he writes in the play's dedication: 'Little of it was prepar'd for that general Taste which seems now to be predominant in the Pallats of our Audience.' He tells Anne, though, that he has at least one further substantial play in him, with 'as good a part as I've written for you in it, I am certain.' But the play's a phantom in his mind; it never materializes.

Conny has in fact seen the writing on the wall for the sort of truthful and insightful play about how people are and possibly can be that he wants to write, that he has in him to write—with this realization coming in the wake of the controversial clergyman Jeremy Collier's *A Short View of the Immorality and Profaneness of the English Stage* (1698). Congreve defends himself and his work in print against Collier's vituperative diatribe—but not very effectively, having used rational arguments in what was essentially an irrational debate. But despite his diminishing prospects as a dramatist considering the number of theatre managers with wet fingers raised in the wind, Conny remains convinced that Collier is wrong about his work. He still believes his plays, as best exemplified by his latest one, contribute rather than the opposite to the overall moral good of society; that they affirm the constant need for fairness, mutual respect and true civility in both one's public and private dealings, helping to offset the harmful effects of human appetite and ambition he sees every day on every side.

And yet, while always trying to apply principles like these in his own affairs, Conny isn't so sure he has the strength of character enabling him to maintain the moral integrity required to conduct himself in such a way at all times. In 1699, while working on *The Way of the World*, he admits to Dryden his 'unsettled state of heart and soul' is sorely troubling him; that his 'spiritual malady' is threatening to 'incurably overwhelm me.' But the moral support Dryden offers him, however, is stopped for good the next year by his death, which Conny feels deeply. He'd always highly valued his mentor's true friendship and ready counsel (his Tory sympathies and Catholicism notwithstanding). And later that same year, Conny confides in Frances Porter—expecting more help and understanding from her than he'd have got from Anne—that he is consulting privately 'with both High Churchmen and zealot enthusiasts of the reformed churches' in the hope his 'personal religion will be fixed and put in good working order.'

One cleric of the first sort Conny visits with is Archbishop Gilbert Burnet of Salisbury, well-regarded in English society, high and low. Like his longtime friend, fellow Whig and advisor to King William, John Locke, whose philosophy Conny greatly admires as well, Burnet had long espoused the idea that Christianity is eminently sane, rational and reasonable in all areas of human activity. Then, closer to home, Conny crosses the river to talk with George Cockayne, a Noncomformist pastor in Southwark who'd been a friend and ministerial colleague of John Bunyan's. (*The Pilgrim's Progress*, published in two parts, the first in 1678, the second two years later—and soaked up by Conny in his youth—had made the former tinker Bunyan a well-known literary figure as well as a preacher, with its vivid picture of uncompromising Christian faith in contrast with the destructive worldliness of Vanity Fair.) Cockayne tells Conny that 'a tree is known by its fruit, good or bad, as a man is by his work,' and, sad to say, in his view, his enquirer's plays do not reflect well on their author or the current state of his soul.

Over the next few years Conny keeps his head down, professionally and personally; and especially after Anne's affections become centred on a cousin of his, Robert Leke, Earl of Scarsdale. She'd had no compunctions either about working with 'reformist' theatre managers whose productions Conny considers 'sickly-sweet in sentiment and inherently false about man's nature and, therefore, about his Creator's as well.' His creative attentions turn to verse translations, and commissioned librettos for a masque and an opera on classical themes. (The latter, *Semele*, his last stage work of any kind—regarded as 'a final warning on the dangers of succumbing to the forces of appetite and ambition'—Conny never did see performed.)

Cutting his ties with the stage altogether in 1705, selling his interest in a new theatre in the Haymarket, an unprofitable joint-venture with playwright and architect John Vanbrugh, Congreve concentrates on his duties as the newly-appointed Commissioner for Wines. His social life revolves mainly around his male friends, writers and Whig politicians he rubs shoulders with at the Kit-Cat Club, not far from his lodgings. His womanless state, he feels, is perhaps just as well. He has been spoiled. Women such as Arabella Hunt, who is ill and dies prematurely that same year, and Anne Bracegirdle, especially the latter, do not very often come a man's way.

Then: enter Henrietta Godolphin—making an entrance as only she could have made. The incomparable young Duchess of Marlborough herself—beautiful, brainy, well-read, witty, high-spirited and strong-willed; but also conspicuously married (before a large congregation of courtiers and sundry blue bloods). Her marriage at eighteen in 1698 to Francis, son of the politically powerful Earl of Godolphin—a 'tepid man' and 'bereft of opinions of his own,' Conny is told—was commonly considered to be an arranged one. Conny is first introduced to the Godolphins after a Haymarket Theatre opera in 1705, and thereafter has to resign himself to adoring Henrietta from afar.

Gradually, though, over another six years, this changes—for Conny, unbelievably so. Henrietta invites him into her artsy coterie; and in one of several letters the two exchange about his literary accomplishments, she insists there must surely be more such fine things to come from him. Finally, conceding this in due course, he completes in 1712 a set of poems he dedicates to Henrietta, and which she asks to have him read to her privately at her Windsor Park lodge. And after which, to his astonishment and delight, she unmistakably invites his romantic advances. (With the glaring disparity between his and her station in life, he'd not dared initiate anything of that sort in their dealings.) But suddenly he is sharing passionate kisses with the duchess—as high-born as any woman he's ever known. Henrietta is the eldest daughter of John Churchill, the renowned first Duke of Marlborough and exalted military hero, and his wife Sarah, one of Queen Anne's closest associates.

There is nothing spur-of-the-moment and transient about the duchess and Conny's romantic attachment, however. The earth has moved for both of them; the emotional terrain under them is unrecognizably rearranged. And soon neither one doubts for a moment that their love is anything other than a true, selfless and lasting one—'an ever-fixed mark, that looks on tempests, and is never shaken.'

Affairs in such high circles were not uncommon, of course. But theirs is different; the man is the one of lower status, for one thing, and older for another. And as lasting as this affair is—staying intact for more than twenty years until death intervenes—it was extraordinarily rare. In fact, after a passage of time, both the Godolphins and the Marlboroughs are forced to acknowledge the body-mind-and-heart relationship the two have together forged—with the exception, that is, of the older Duchess of Marl, Sarah. She and Henrietta are often at loggerheads, and especially over the 'bad company, the worst kind' the mother says the daughter is keeping. She rails on at Henrietta in particular about her affair with Congreve, calling her his 'moll.' Sarah continually tries, unsuccessfully, to have the Duke put a stop to it. But with his only son having died in his youth, Henrietta, his favourite first child, is his successor; and as he tells her, 'I am confidence itself in knowing you will always keep to your rightful place as the Marlborough you are—and keep your lover, the poet, always in his.'

In 1723, at the age of forty-two, Henrietta has a daughter, Mary, with the eleven-year-older Conny—a 'love child' she chooses to have despite her doctors' stern warnings about surviving the birth. She tells Conny, 'How better show you my great gratitude for the meaning in life your love has given me? Than to make this life-to-be within me my dearest gift of love to you?' A few months later, holding their baby for the first time, Conny, overcome with relief, joy and wonder, when he is at last able to speak, says, 'Present me the man who dares say God will not suffer this sweet child to come unto him!' Then Henrietta informs him that her husband Francis—the man she'd never loved (nor possibly he her, having always obeyed his father to the letter in all things)—is willing to accept Mary as his own. And in doing so, he assures the girl's full acceptance in the eyes of royalty and his peers.

And so the play, two scenes later, comes to its close in Westminster Abbey.

With Henrietta and Conny at the centre of the action, and the dearth of letters or other material touching on their relationship, the play's second act relies heavily on an imaginative reconstruction of events. In reality, very few at the time had said much about the couple's 'close friendship' and even fewer left any written record concerning it; and certainly no one had published anything on the subject. And Henrietta had in fact joined Conny in death in the Abbey before any version of their story got into print.

In 1733, *The Court Parrot* published a literary hotchpotch of a piece, 'The Secret History of Henrada Maria Theresa,' in which what purported to be fact was dressed up as fiction, roman-á-clef style. The story's title subject is described as the eldest daughter of an aristocrat and military hero in an unnamed European state—and as 'a Lady of Wit and Spirit she took a secret Pleasure in reading Poetry.' Henrada is especially partial to and transported by the romantic verse of a highly-regarded poet of the day by the name of Congravino; and although married to the good Count Adolphus, she is carried away, mind and body, by the handsome, charming versifier. And carrying on 'their Intrigue with such Subtlety' for so long the lovers have a child together—a daughter Henrada 'would always look upon with an Eye of Tenderness and Affection.' The unknown author's lengthy, titillating piece concludes with Henrada repenting of her wayward goings on with Congravino—ostensibly, a morality tale after all, then; one that any reader, particularly one with a sanctimonious streak, might feel the better for having absorbed in its every naughty detail.

As for my leading question when starting out on the play—about Congreve's full retreat from writing drama in the latter half of his life—the linkage made between this and his long, unbroken relationship with Henrietta is clear enough to see. A connection, this—and the developing form it takes—that is entirely of my own making. But in the seldom easy-to-explain way a story will take its own course in the telling of it—with character development playing so much a part in this—so with *Congravino*. At certain points in the play, in various ways, even the author himself is taken by surprise. And, in retrospect—as recently as three years or more after its completion—the play occasionally speaks to some state of mind or heart of mine in unexpected ways as well.

2

In June 1995, I went to see Jace in one of the year's biggest successes so far: a new play at the Garrick called *Inventing Herself.* Directed by Teddy Bentley, Jace had turned in a tour de force as Margot Fallon, a Labour cabinet minister and former orphanage girl and, as a tabloid reveals, at one time a West End call girl—playing the character from the age of eighteen in the early 60s and on into the mid-'80s. After going back after the show to congratulate her, we'd gone for a drink.

It was almost entirely shop talk. She said Julian Caverley had come to see the show, and that my name had come up in conversation. He'd told her that he and I had talked a few times recently about this and that; that I was in good spirits and keeping busy. 'I said that probably means you're talking about something you've been working on, and getting somewhere with—and we left it at that,' she told me. 'If I'm right, I knew I wasn't going to get a squeak out of him about it—a new play, I suppose it is.' Other than my agent Gerry Atherton, Julian was the only one I'd talked to about *Congravino*. Julian had given me a good deal of time reading the first draft, discussing it with me; and had been very positive about it, encouraging me no end.

'Oh, by the way, Kell's in town,' Jace said. 'He'll probably be calling you to say hello. He's not going back until the end of the month, he says.'

'Unusual for him to be here this time of the year, isn't it?'

'Yes, it is. But there's a reason for that. He's no longer in Alberta, in Edmonton, with a season to open in September. As a matter of fact, he was planning to return here for good when the Stratford Festival called him in for talks, and a week later gave him an offer he couldn't refuse: as assistant AD next season, and a three-year contract as AD the following year.' The job had opened up after the previous incumbent had suddenly resigned. A caretaker AD had been appointed in the interim.

Well, well. Mister/Monsieur Marleau had landed himself, it would seem, in a field of four-leafed clovers. After nine years in Canada—teaching and directing at the National Theatre School in Montreal, and freelance directing stints there and in Toronto, Winnipeg, Vancouver, for the Shaw Festival and at Stratford, as well as an an AD job in Halifax prior to the Edmonton one—Kell had got himself to the top of the country's theatrical pile. The Stratford Festival, near London in Western Ontario, is a world class company; Canada's theatrical pride and joy.

'He's like a kid about to be given the run of a sweet shop,' Jace continued. 'He knows he's going to have his critics, of course—but they'll be in for a big surprise if they're thinking he's not up to the job, he says.'

'Yes, I can hear him saying so.'

'Yes, well, that's Kell for you. The self-confidence comes out of his pores. He says he's already got people from coast-to-coast calling him. Also, Leona Fielder is going to join him in Stratford next year, apparently. She was a stunning Cleopatra and an unforgettable Desdemona for him in Edmonton, he says. A protégé of his, as he sees her, I expect; and maybe a faithful disciple of his too, probably.'

I didn't comment; making as if Leona Fielder's relationship with Kell, onstage or off, wasn't of any interest to me. Jace said, 'I do hope the girl isn't giving Kell any more credit and gratitude for her development than he deserves, as an actor or as a person.' My sentiments exactly, I thought.

Kell was already planning his first season in charge, Jace said. 'He's asking me for suggestions for plays—and I don't need to tell you why either, do I?'

'He wants you over there to do something with him, something you've always wanted to do, probably.'

She nodded. 'Directing me has always been one of his great ambitions; it would be absolutely bloody marvellous, a glorious experience, blah, blah, blah. I managed not to laugh in his face, however, but only just.'

'Good for you. He'd have been cut to the quick.'

'But I did tell him, though, that just because we've been such close friends for so long doesn't mean we can work well together—that we both could end up thinking that that's one experience we'll never need to repeat, thank God! To which he said, "And Tristan and Isolde didn't love each other, either." He's going to keep on at me about this, I know he will—like a dog with a bone.'

Not unexpectedly, the subject of Marc Lalerne didn't come up. I'd heard she was still seeing him, but also a fellow cast member in *Inventing Herself* she'd first met at Chichester, Trevor Langford. And she'd probably heard too that I was seeing someone as well, also an actor—Belinda Tranter—who'd played Julie Capp in both the original Manchester production and TV version of *Romeo Scores*! Belinda was now in London working on a TV police series as a CID detective sergeant, bringing her savvy, no-nonsense Lancashire persona with her.

When Kell phoned later that week, he made a point of telling me that Jace and Langford were just friends; that she didn't like going unescorted in public and he was obligingly filling the bill for her, which was probably true. He didn't mention Lalerne. Kell's campaign to keep Jace and me close until we'd come to our senses and realized the error of our ways in breaking up—what he'd called 'a monumentally daft act of wilfully self-inflicted harm'—was still in full swing, it seemed. I think he saw himself as a go-between of sorts; a self-appointed one, of course.

Kell had had some business in mind in calling me as well. I knew he'd always admired *Writing and Loving, Loving and Writing* and had directed it twice in Canada. He said he was thinking about it for one of the two smaller Stratford Festival venues in 1997. 'If I decide to do it, I'll let you know through your agent, of course. And if it's a go, maybe you could pop over to see it, and also take part in one of the Festival's "Playwrights in Perspective" seminars.'

He wasn't to know, of course. Should the SF do the Lawrence play, his chances of getting me there to see it, and also take part in the seminar (even that)—with the prospect of my seeing Leona Fielder as well—would have improved by quite a margin.

My father had a changed look about him the day he married Sally Grainger, I was sure of it—the look of a man I'd not really expected to ever see again. On a sunny summer's day in July that year, in the Oxfordshire countryside in all its glory, he and Sally had expressively and eagerly exchanged their traditional vows before God in the chapel at Bloxham School, near Banbury, where she'd once been the resident Matron-nurse. It was as clear to me as daylight—the moment the couple had turned from the altar to face the congregation as man and wife—that Dad's years of ingrained sadness were at last behind him. (Gran Gadsden said to me once, 'It's like your dad's always wearing a hair vest under his shirt, doing penance for something or other only he thinks he did or didn't do.')

Dad had been a revelation as well at the reception in the marquee in the school grounds. He'd danced with his wife, navigating her fluidly around the plywood floor with the assurance of a paid on-duty partner at a 1940s-'50s tea dance. He must have been taking lessons. I remember Mum ruefully recalling his always reluctant clumping around at dances in Hookey when they were courting.

In his remarks at the reception, Dad's best man, Norman Harwood, probably said it best: 'I don't think Art saw Sally coming, but when she did come his way he immediately saw her as the someone he'd been waiting for, whether he'd ever known it or not, for a long, lonely time. The first time the wife and I saw Art and Sally together, we knew that either the good Lord, or one of his angels, had had a hand in getting them together. And today, I'm thinking, we've now got plenty of company feeling pretty much the same way, wouldn't you agree?' He'd had to pause for awhile for the outburst of assenting applause.

Two other CPM friends of Dad's, Hugh and Trish Manning, told me he may have lost the regard of one or two at the church because of Sally. 'But I'm sure he's told you about that,' said Trish. Actually, he hadn't. And so I learned that the widowed Sally was a divorcee after an earlier failed marriage; that she'd had Rosalind, her only child, with her first husband, Clifford Halcomb, and not with her second, Dennis Grainger, a Bloxham School housemaster, as I'd thought. And that a few at CPM, having taken certain New Testament verses into account, believed that marrying a divorced person wasn't on for a thoroughgoing Christian. Trish said, 'We told your dad to take no notice of talk like that, that he didn't need friends like that anyway, and he agreed he didn't.'

Sally, like Mum, was a Hook Norton girl. Her father was at one time the local GP, and also choirmaster at St. Peter's, before moving to Oxford when Sally was twelve. After her father's death, she'd carried on as he had supporting St. Peter's and other local causes. A nurse at the Radcliffe in Oxford, Sally had fallen hard for Halcomb, a surgeon; and ignoring some well-meant advice, she'd married him. She'd then made a second mistake in thinking a child, a daughter, would settle down her wandering-eyed husband, which it hadn't for very long. Getting a divorce—her store of forgiveness had run out—Sally resumed nursing in Oxford, then in

Banbury, where she met and married the gentlemanly Grainger; his first marriage. And after his move to Bloxham School, she'd joined the staff there as well, becoming a mother-figure for a host of boy boarders before the school went co-educational. Following Dennis's untimely death in his mid-fifties, Sally joined forces with Rosalind as a partner in her daughter's bakery and lunch-and-tea shop in Banbury, across from the Cross on South Bar. Still single, Rosalind was a home economist and nutritionist; and working well together, mother and daughter had opened a second outlet, also a going concern, on the High in Oxford, with plans afoot for a third in Stratford-on-Avon.

Between romantic attachments, Rosalind had gone unaccompanied to the wedding; as I had. Slim and eye-catchingly attractive like her mother, but fair-haired and very possibly favouring her father in looks and colouring—and bright and personable along with that—my new stepsister was as easy as pie to like. And not at all by chance, we'd found ourselves in each other's company more often than not that day. She told me she'd not even started thinking of Dad as a stepfather (nor me as a stepbrother, I had to think). 'But don't get me wrong, will you? I really believe Mum has found herself a lovely husband. It's just a thing, I think, that daughters have for fathers who disappear on them. You know, you go on loving them for no good reason, anyway. I know for a fact that I didn't love Dennis the way he deserved to be loved. The dear man loved me like a father should love his daughter. And I've got this feeling, a very sure feeling, that your dad is going to love me just as well. So I've a very good chance, I believe, of being able to make amends with your father, and to love him better than I did Dennis.'

I didn't find it hard to believe, either, that that was indeed what Rosalind would do.

At first glance, seeing the couple at a distance, I had thought Kenneth Branagh and Emma Thompson were among the wedding guests—the way they'd looked in the *Fortunes of War* TV series—only to find it was in fact Pippa Watts, née Harwood, and her architect-husband David. Pippa was beautifully turned out, very easy on the eye, poised and gracious—as I might have realized the girl I'd foresaken as a kid in Southend would turn out to look and act like. I'd not seen her since the early '80s. She and her husband looked good together, and perfectly content with one another. Fortunately for me, Rosalind and Pippa carried much of the conversational load between the four of us as we talked. Not much in the way of any one-on-one exchanges with Pippa, but she did say, 'I was sorry to hear about you and Jacinth, by the way. Your dad was very sorry about it too, I understand.' (Dad should have known that anything said to Norman would almost certainly get passed onto his wife, and so on.) Pippa may have been wondering as well why there wasn't any sign that day of my having found a replacement for Jacinth.

When I told Rosalind about Pippa and myself as kids, she said, 'Well, I did just wonder about the way I saw her looking at you, when you were talking to her husband.'

'Oh? What way was that, then?'

'Well, she could have been comparing the two of you, I thought.' She smiled. 'And going by what you've just told me, maybe she was trying to decide if she'd let you get away too easily—or if letting you go was the smartest thing she's ever done.'

On a Saturday night five months later, Belinda and I were having a drink in the Edgar Wallace after seeing a show at the Aldwych, which we'd agreed to disagree over. 'Well, enough of that, anyway,' she said. 'D'you realize, Tim, we've been dating for what—six months, is it now? And d'you know something? I'm starting to wonder what it is exactly we think we have going for us. What we think it is we're up to with one another, going along like we are.'

I knew what was coming; I'd heard it before. We'd been talking the week before if whether or not it was time to warm up things between us a degree or two. We'd agreed when we'd started out not to get into anything too suddenly. But for her, however, this hadn't precluded having some fun together in bed, as I'd mistakenly thought it had. After a few dates, though, I couldn't help but know better.

I'd more or less avoided the issue by spending more time than ever that summer in Hookey, concentrating on *Congravino* and playing cricket. Even so, every time we met or talked, Belinda would invariably prod me—more jocularly some times than at others—about what she'd characterized as my 'no sex, please, I'm skittish' posture. And once again, on this occasion, there'd been little to add to what I'd already told her; that my reluctance to have sex with her didn't mean I didn't fancy her that way. She never had looked convinced. 'I'm not sure I can explain to myself, even, what the problem is,' I'd added. 'Knowing full well how much I'd enjoy being with you that way.' Considering this, looking even more dubious, she'd said,

'Well, okay, I get your point. But in saying that, maybe you're also saying we're just not making a good connection, you and me, and I don't mean just physically; in quite a few other ways too. I mean, we're not talking grand passion here, I know. But with you, Tim, where you seem to be coming from, I get the feeling we're not talking about passion at all. And if that's how it is, why are we even bothering?'

When we didn't end up that night going back to her place or mine, I think we both knew it was just about curtains for us. And a few days later, over a non-recriminatory lunch, so it proved to be. But buried as deeply as I was in *Congravino,* however, I may have been effectively insulated from any ensuing regret—not something, though, I'd had any reason, all told, to feel very good about.

3

Hook Norton was beginning to have a sirenesque-like effect upon me. Tucked away in some gently-rolling countryside a few miles off the busy A34, about halfway between the tourist Meccas of Oxford and Stratford-on-Avon—as well as lying just outside the eastern boundary of the beseiged theme park the Cotswolds have become—Hookey was as good a haven as any to escape to from The Big Smoke's hectic clamour. No question about it, I was spending considerably longer periods of time than ever in Hookey, not only in the summer that year (1995), but also during the following autumn, winter and spring months as well. One reason for this: the renovations I was having done at Queen's House—a new kitchen and bathrooms in particular. Also, I was starting to develop a proprietary sense about the place that the rented flat in Hammersmith couldn't possibly have prompted in me.

But there were other reasons as well: my steadily growing involvement in local community affairs. I'd become firm friends with the cricket-playing vicar of St. Peter's, Ashley Bonnar. In his early forties, Ash had somehow persuaded me, over a draught in The Pear Tree after a match, to serve on a fund-raising committee to help keep his historic workplace in good nick. (Like many other places in the English countryside the tourists never go near, particularly churches, the late Saxon St. Peter's has some features of interest: some now being restored murals of Biblical scenes, white-washed over to save them from Henry VIII's Reformation storm-troopers, and a Norman font with signs of the Zodiac carvings, to name just two.) The convivial and always engaging Ash never brought up the name of the One-on-High he served when talking with me. He must have assumed I was one of the legion of 'hatch, match and dispatch' C. of E. constituents who might, if pressed, admit to a belief in God, but who'd rather you hadn't asked, thank you very much. I'd also taken on the captaincy of Hook Warden C.C.—again for reasons I wasn't as clear as I should have been about. One thing I soon realized, though: the job involved more committee work at both the club and the county level than I'd bargained for.

There were family considerations, too. Dad and Sally were now in nearby Banbury, not much more than a ten-minute drive away. They'd both sold their flats and purchased a handsome, refurbished mock-Tudor house sitting back from the Bloxham Road. (In Essex, in Chalkwell, Dad had missed his garden in Westcliff; but only half the size of the one he now had to look after.) There were more signs of Dad having changed since marrying Sally. On a Sunday in August, the newly-marrieds attended matins at St. Peter's, had a pub lunch, and in the afternoon turned up to watch a Hook Norton C.C match—all of which Dad had seemed to be more than comfortable with, surprising me somewhat. Obviously, he couldn't have been happier being beside his beloved Sally, whenever or wherever. Although the name Sally Hainault had taken a bit of getting used to, my fetching, svelte and never dull stepmother—who knew her theatre, as it happened, having started going to the Oxford Playhouse in her teens—was as easy to get to know, and as likeable as her daughter. (Sometimes the way Roz and I talked when we were alone may have had something more than the brother-and-sisterly about it, getting on as well as we did.) Sally was also in Hookey during the winter as well. She was on the same committee as I was at St. Peter's; and also helped out in several ways with the Christmas Eve pageant and carol service, and other special events.

Lastly, but not the least of it, there was the work I was getting done in Hookey. Much more of *Congravino* got written in my Queen's House study than in the one in Brook Green. I think, as the play started to take shape, I may have got myself stuck with the sort of notion a writer can sometimes get—for no logical reason whatsoever—that in a certain place or space the writing will go easier and better there; a highly debatable notion, to say the least of it. It's possible, too, the quiet, mostly trafficless walks I was able to take in and around Hookey had helped with the mental stocking up and stocktaking the creative writing process demands of you, sometimes to the exclusion of any other considerations. (Charles Dickens had relied on a three-hour walk routine while faced with his current novel's ever-pressing instalment deadlines.) Also, my phone rang less often in Hookey than in London.

The fact is, though, writers can write anywhere—especially the writing going on in your head, which never ceases once you've got your teeth into something you believe will work. It's a case of wherever—if not whenever—for those who do what I do.

The sixth and final draft of *Congravino* was at last completed in mid-May, 1996. And with the last page finished, I'd felt an urgent need—a release of sorts—to get out of the house. I strode down to The Bell, just a three-minute walk from the house, for a celebratory drink or two, raising a glass of best bitter to myself and my play.

About halfway through my first pint I was joined by a couple of cricket teammates, both of whom had their own ideas about the make-up of Hookey's first eleven that they were intent on making known to me. I think I'd surprised one of them, who I knew had seen himself as the team's next captain, by how much I knew about the club's record in the '90s and the current players' varying abilities—all of this courtesy of Ash and his encyclopaedic mind. But time passed well enough that night, however—as it usually does if you keep to what you have in common with the people you're passing the time with.

The next morning, after sleeping in longer than I'd intended—not having anything on my mind to write to wake me up—I mailed a play script to Julian in Bristol, where he was the Old Vic's AD; then drove down to London to deliver another one to Gerry Atherton. Gerry said, 'Good God! At long last! I thought you were never going to let go of the thing.'

A few days later Julian phoned. Commending me for my rewrites, he said, among other things: 'Tim, it's the best new play I've read in a long time, and I must have read dozens of them. It's right up there, as a period piece, I think, with "Amadeus" and "The Madness of King George." It's a big, beautiful play, it really is, Tim.' And: 'Anybody doubting you had a major play in you somewhere is going to be doing, as somebody said, "a Tour de France bit of back-pedalling."' (Julian's 'somebody' was Martin Amis—in answering a newspaper piece Andrew Motion, the poet laureate, had written about the controversy his own biographical assault on Philip Larkin, as a poet and as a man, had stirred up.)

Julian's reaction was a great and sweet relief for me. His artistic judgment and integrity, his directorial skill—and his personal qualities as well—I have admired and appreciated since our days in Nottingham, where his belief in me and my abilities had meant everything to me. The part Julian had played in the success of *Writing and Loving* . . . and *Entrances and Exits* remain incalculable.

Bringing up Julian's name the next day, Gerry said, 'Look, Tim, I know how much he likes the play, how much you'd like to have him direct it, that it would be a cert for Bristol's 1997-'98 season. But like I said, we've got to start, give it a go first with the National or the RSC, no place else. That's where this belongs—and I'm betting one or the other of the two will think so too.'

'Gerry, don't worry about Julian. He'd be the first to agree with you. Like us, he only wants the best for the play. And besides, he's already told the BOV he won't be back for the '97-'98 season. He's going to be assisting at Chichester in '98. And just between you and me, he'll be taking over there the next season from Des Thurlow, who is moving on to the National.'

'Well, that's fine, then. We'll give the NT first crack, okay? An exclusive look-see—but with a deadline, one we'll keep to. They'll know, of course, who is next in the queue, wanting to see a script. After all, word about a play like this one is almost bound to get around, isn't it?' And he grinned.

Gerry knew the NT's routine with a new play, of course: the script department's evaluation before getting to the literary manager's desk, and the preference given to the writer-in-residence when it came to new material. And once over those hurdles, getting a final going over by directors and selected colleagues before determining the play's fate; the usual process. Also, I wasn't expecting any special treatment. I was a two-play wonder, with my previous London stage credit, the success though it was, going back ten years to 1986. Gerry, however, aware of the lead time companies needed to plan their seasons—and why he'd wanted the play finished three months before it was—gave the National no more than a six-week period to decide on *Congravino*. 'They won't squawk, getting pressed on this,' he said. 'They'll know we know what we've got; they'll know after one quick read through. And, as I say, they'll know who's up next, who the competition is.' Every season since 1963, it had been the same story for Britain's two theatre flagships: getting the quality material and the best hands on-board with which to rule the British theatre's high seas.

More than four weeks later, in the first week of July, nothing heard from the National other than confirming the script's arrival. Gerry said, 'I wasn't expecting them to get back any sooner than they have to, anyway. It's that big fortress mentality they have over there. No matter who comes calling, never lower the drawbridge except slowly and condescendingly, that sort of thing.'

'Understood, Gerry.' How else could a playwright, wanting his stuff showcased for the first time at the National, expect to be treated?

Sunday, July 14 found me at Blenheim Palace in Woodstock, Oxfordshire—but not there for a guided tour. I was there to play on the stately pile's vast back lawn for the Oxford County Cricket Association's selects against the Duke of Marlborough's XI, a very useful squad, in a charity match for the National Trust.

Rising to the occasion—given the quality of my surroundings and the opposition—I'd had a good outing, knocking a quick forty-three before getting caught on the boundary, and also taking a pair of wickets. Unfortunately, though, not in a winning cause; despite a wagging tail we'd lost by twenty or so runs. Still, having Dad, Sally and Roz there to applaud me on helped make the day the fine one it most certainly was for me.

I'd been to Blenheim before; twice, in fact—the first time with the family as a kid, which I don't remember much about. Then once again, less than a year back, while still working on *Congravino*. The palace had been gifted to the first Duke of Marlborough as a right royal reward for his victory over the Bavarians and the French at Blenheim, Germany in 1704. A direct descendant of the Duke's, Winston Churchill, my father's hero, was born there in 1874.

There's a scene in *Congravino*—a historically correct one—in which the duchess Sarah, at a family gathering at Blenheim, remonstrates with her daughter Henrietta for ignoring her like 'a servant there to snuff the candles.' And in the high-ceilinged, ornately decorated and tapestried rooms I'd walked through on my second visit, I could almost hear the fractious exchanges between mother and daughter over their several differences. And none more fractious than over Henrietta's hard and fast attachment to William Congreve—something Sarah had never been able to stomach.

In a corridor off the Great Hall, I'd gazed intently at images of the two women, sitting next to each other in Closterman's huge formal family portrait painted in 1693. Only just in her teens at the time, Henrietta was prominently positioned, her head above her mother's and almost level with the Duke's. In her proud, serious face, the individuality and spirit as well as her grace and femininity were already on view—allowing a look in advance at the woman who would count loving and being loved by Conny as valuable a thing as the advantages her nobility and wealth had given her. Someone has written: love is a great leveller. And someone else: love changes everything.

After the participants' after-match shindig at Blenheim, I'd driven on to London, where Gerry had phoned me the next morning. He said there'd been nothing in the post from the NT that day—their *Congravino* deadline date. Then, at three in the afternoon, he phoned again.

'They've just got back to us, by special delivery,' he said. Followed by a nicely-timed, two-beat pause. Then: 'I am, I'm happy to say, Tim, the bearer of good news.'

Good news!? It was bloody brilliant news! *Congravino* was a 'go' at the National; provisionally scheduled for an autumn '97 opening at the Olivier. (It would open in December, in actual fact.) To be directed by British theatre's latest wunderkind, Daniel Morgenheim, who'd made a fast, dazzling name for himself with his riveting *Titus Andronicus* and enchanting *As You Like It* for the RSC. (A recent 'steal' of the NT's.) Congreve and his two leading ladies—as I'd read their minds and gauged their hearts, anyway—would again live and love in London Town, this time onstage almost directly across the river from where he'd lived half his life. I couldn't wait for what, conceivably, could be a night of vindication for me as a dramatist. But wait I was going to have to, of course.

In the meantime, scratching an itch—what else to do but work?—I'd started on a TV original I'd called *The Chief*, a working title. Yet another historical piece—this time London in the 1880s. About newspaper editor and journalist, W.T. Stead—one of a new breed: the investigative reporter. (A colleague was the young George Bernard Shaw, who didn't care for Stead's sensationalism or his 'Crosstianity.') Aided by The Salvation Army, Stead exposed the city's well-established 'white slave traffic,' a prostitution racket involving the use of young girls the establishment preferred not to know anything about. I was interested not only in Stead's reforming zeal and journalistic skills, but also the strong attraction he had for women—high society ladies, bluestockings, madams, harlots and Sally Ann lassies alike.

No such similar gift of attraction where the ladies were concerned in my case, however. Then again, I probably wasn't trying conscientiously enough for their attention. I should have known better. As Willy the Great has Biron say in *Love's Labour's Lost*, which I'd seen that summer at The Barbican:

> 'For where is any author in the world
> Teaches such beauty as a woman's eye?
> Learning is but an adjunct to ourself
> And where we are our learning likewise is:
> Then when ourselves we see in ladies' eyes,
> Do we not likewise see our learning there?'

4

A grey but not cold day in London: the first Sunday in 1997. No change in my Sunday mid-day routine: a short jaunt across the road, through Brook Green's elongated island-in-the-road park and tennis courts, to The Queen's Head.

'Afternoon, Tim.'

'Afternoon, Bri.'

The bartender at my local poured me my usual pint, not needing to ask. 'No Rob today?' he inquired.

'No, not today. Miranda's parents are in town for the weekend.'

'Oh, oh. Sounds like things are getting serious.'

'Yes, they could be.'

'Ah, well. Comes to most of us sometime or other, the old comeuppance, doesn't it just?'

Rob Barclay and his live-in girlfriend were my neighbours, Ursula's downstairs tenants. Rob was an architect and a Chelsea F.C. and Middlesex C.C. supporter, all of which gave us plenty to argue good-naturedly over; and Miranda an English teacher and regular theatre-goer. The three of us got on very well together. Miranda couldn't understand, she said, my lack of a girlfriend—'a straight, good-looking guy like you.' Rob said he was holding Miranda off from trying to set me up with a nice-looking, artsy girlfriend of hers. 'You better keep holding her off, then—if you value our friendship at all,' I'd told him.

'I'll have some lunch today—onion soup and the shepherd's pie,' I told Bri. 'I'll be in the back. And if anybody asks, don't tell them I'm here, please. I've got some reading I want to catch up on.'

I settled myself in a booth at the rear of the pub, overlooking the back terrace and garden (unused in winter). The Queen's Head had a country pub ambience about it, which I liked. Walk in the door and you wouldn't know you were in central London. The Head was deceptively larger than a first-time patron might think; quite a bit longer than it was wide.

Nose stuck in my book, I'd not seen her come through to where I was, not much more than five minutes later. But she'd seen me all right.

'Hello, Timothy.'

I looked up—and almost immediately snapped the book closed. And at which moment any thoughts of late Victorian politics were gone for good. Standing before me, smiling a shade hesitantly, was a sleek and stylish, quite stunning-looking young woman. At first, for a few seconds, I'd not recognized her.

'Leona Fielder,' she said.

'Yes, yes, of course! Well, hello, hello, Leona! What a lovely surprise!' Both the adjective and the noun were right on the mark. I slid out of the booth, not as smoothly as I'd have liked to. We shared a showbiz buss. For me, though, not the usual obligatory ritual; I could have called her 'darling' and meant it.

'May I join you?' As if she'd needed to ask.

Still trying to avoid sounding lame, I said, 'Well, what can I say? Who'd have thought? You being here, out of the blue like this! I'm tempted to use a Bogart line in "Casablanca." You know: "Of all the gin joints in the world . . ."—that one.'

'Well, yes, it is quite a coincidence, finding you here like this—seeing the place in passing and deciding to pop in for some lunch, as I did. But being here, in the neighbourhood, in your neck of the woods—that certainly didn't happen by chance, I have to admit. I came to Hammersmith looking for you, to knock on your door. I must have just missed you.'

She'd been to a party the night before with some actor friends, she said, and my name had come up in connection with the National's announcement about *Congravino*. 'I was so happy to hear it, Timothy, knowing something about your work as I do. So I thought, before returning to Toronto, I'd try getting in touch with you—you know, to renew acquaintances, congratulate you, wish you luck, and so on.' As it happened, Belinda Tranter had also been at the party, and she and Leona had got talking. 'So I just upped and asked her if she had your number, just like that,' Leona said.

'And my home address as well?'

'Well, if I couldn't get hold of you, I thought I'd drop you a note. Anyhow, Belinda was happy to oblige me. She had her address book in her purse.' And, smiling: 'She also said she hoped I'd have better luck with you than she'd had—just her little joke, she said.'

'Yes, that sounds like Belinda.'

Leona had spent Christmas and the New Year in the U.K., visiting relatives and friends; and the last few days, staying in a West End hotel, the easier to do some shopping and see some theatre. 'London still has the same allure for me, and I think it always will. My father, who's English—well, more English than Austrian—thinks he's to blame for me becoming the Anglophile I guess I am.' She said her father, a trial lawyer, had always been very much a part of the ex-Brit scene in Vancouver.

She continued: 'So, anyhow, I woke this morning and got this sudden impulse—which I don't get all that often, let alone get to act on one. That instead of phoning, I thought I'd try tracking you down, to see you. Don't ask me why, though, okay? I just wanted to see you as well as talk to you. Talking on the phone isn't the same, is it?' Then, after a pause, having fixed her lovely, compelling eyes on me, and without a flicker of reticence in them: 'And, I suppose—I have to confess—I also wanted you to see me; to get a good look at me as well.'

The pleasure was all mine. This was an extremely beautiful woman sitting across from me. As with a lot of attractive young women, I find, some extra living helps turn the once less well-defined prettiness into an exquisite, more finely-contoured beauty. Leona's striking facial features, her expressive eyes in particular, were accentuated and enhanced by her nape-length, salon-shaped, coal-black hair. And with her subtle, artful make-up and elegant attire—high-collared camel coat, pearl-white blouse, her knee-length black skirt and high-heels, revealing long, shapely legs—there wasn't any trace of the actress-gypsy type I'd remembered from five years back in Stratford-on-Avon. In any event, undoubtedly a woman well worth the seeing—a veritable feast for any man's eyes. And for any man as well, a woman most definitely to be seen with. I'd revelled in the looks I'd got from Bri and quite a few other chaps in The Head that afternoon, plainly envying me the unquestionably 'fair to look upon' company I was keeping.

And, for any man too, in all likelihood, a woman to look out for; to be on one's guard with whenever in her close company. Coming to mind, again going back to Leona's days with the RSC in Stratford, I recalled what Jace's co-star Matt Norden had had to say about her: 'Ah, yes. That very foxy Canadian charmer! A Pacific Coast Lorelei, a siren if ever I saw one.' I'd wondered at the time if he'd ever tried it on with Leona, and had been rebuffed. If she had turned Matt down, it would have been a startlingly new experience for him, I'd had to think.

She asked me about *Congravino*. I'd said a number of things, but hadn't gone into any details. But I must have said enough to whet her appetite. She said, 'Seems like fascinating stuff, my kind of play, with two women characters I very much like the sound of. When I'm done with Stratford, I'll be back here in a shot to catch it, all eyes and ears.'

As she'd hinted at earlier, Leona was more than conversant with my two London stage successes (and also some of my television work), commenting on them knowledgeably, especially *Entrances and Exits*. 'Natasha Fenner's one contemporary part I've always wanted to do, but I've never even got the chance to audition for,' she said. She'd also been very much taken by the Julie Capp role in *Romeo Scores*! 'You do seem to have a way with your women, don't you?' She'd seen the TV show on PBS in the U.S. It had been surprisingly successful over there, where round-ball football hasn't the prominent place in popular culture it has in the U.K., obviously. She'd enjoyed talking to Belinda at the party about originating the role—'a working experience she said she'll always look back on as a very special one.'

Leona said she'd had a very useful and satisfying first season with the Stratford Festival in '96. Kell Marleau had been very pleased with her work, particularly with her Olivia in *Twelfth Night*. ('If music be the food of love, play on.') 'I'm looking forward to what's coming up for me this season. Having another shot at Cleopatra, how could I not be?' But this time Shakespeare's, not Shaw's—having to take the measure of Mark Antony, a different relational dynamic altogether from the one with Caesar, of course. 'A huge challenge for me, anyhow, that I do know. But Kellison's on my case, assuring me one way or another that I can trust him to see me through; that I'm going to make a Cleo we're both going to be proud of. Kellison prods me a lot, but encourages me a good deal too.'

'Oh, by the way, Timothy, do you know Sean Blake?' she asked a minute or two later.

'No, not really. I've just met him socially, that's all. I did see his "Backstreet Ballads" in October. I was very impressed.' Blake's season at the Donmar in Covent Garden had got him a good deal of favourable attention around town, I said.

'Yes, so I hear. I worked with Sean in Derby. He wasn't happy when Kell whisked me off to Canada, but he seems to have forgiven me. I had dinner with him this week. He's trying to persuade me to come back here.'

'Is he, now? And are you listening?'

'Oh, yes, I'm listening all right. I told him I'd talk to him about it in the summer. He said he'd like to get over to see my Cleopatra, which I hope he does. I've developed quite a bit since he last worked with me. I'm going to send him a tape of my Olivia. The CBC filmed a "Twelfth Night" performance for television. But no mention of this to Kell, though, please, if you don't mind, Timothy.'

After I'd settled her mind on that, she said, 'I don't think my father will be jumping for joy if I do come back here, though. He was so happy when I returned to Canada. We've always been close, of course. There's only the two of us, and it's been that way since I was little.'

Nathan Fielder had emigrated to Canada in the '50s, living in Toronto before moving to Vancouver, where he'd met and married her American, Seattle-born mother, a professional orchestral violinist. Her parents had divorced when she was six—'a long, twisty story'—involving some differences harking back to her father's family history. His parents were Austrian Jews from Vienna who'd moved to Paris in 1938, and a year later, after his mother's death, to London. Nathan had had 'a raft of differences, particularly religious ones,' with his father, and also with his twin brother; and after moving to Canada he'd changed his name from Fiedler to Fielder. 'Another long story,' she said. 'Anyhow, he's never remarried. He claims he's never been able to find a woman who could make both of us happy.'

It had started to rain quite heavily when we left The Queen's Head. I'd persuaded her to let me drive her back to her hotel.

As we turned into the Strand, I said, 'Could you do me a favour, Leona, and send me a "Twelfth Night" tape as well? I'd like to see it. And if you do decide to return here to work, I could pass it on, if you like, to one or two others I know would be interested in seeing it too.'

'Yes, of course, Timothy, I'll be very happy to. And thank you for asking. It was very thoughtful of you.'

I pulled up outside the hotel. It was still raining.

'Don't get out, Timothy. Thank you again for lunch, for a lovely afternoon. I'm very pleased with myself, acting on that impulse of mine this morning. I was very lucky it paid off, and turned out as well as it did, too.'

She leaned across and kissed me. On the lips, just briefly, but not a peck, either—and smiled. I didn't want to think of her smiling like that at some other chap, but I had no reason to think that she shouldn't, of course—just hoping she wouldn't, that's all.

She got out of the car. She smiled again and waved, turned and went quickly into the hotel. My last view of her, through a rain-streaked, misted-up car window, could have been a better one.

On the drive back to Brook Green, her perfume was still in the car. And suddenly I knew that that would be just the start of it. I'd be replaying over and over in my mind, minute by minute, the time I'd spent that afternoon with Leona Fielder, I could count on it, I knew.

5

It may not have been entirely coincidental either when, late in May, Jace and I ran into each other in the cafeteria-in-the-crypt at St. Martin-in-the-Fields in Trafalgar Square. We'd sometimes lunched there in our bookshop crawls in the vicinity, and also sat in occasionally on a lunchtime organ recital in the 1720s' church upstairs. (Handel had also played the church's state-of-the-art organ. His patroness, the Duchess Sarah of Marl, and her daughter Henrietta had found yet another reason to argue: over the compositions of Handel and Bononcini, with the young duchess preferring the latter's.)

Jace had been busy in front of the cameras in England and Italy, continuing on with her *Cass Cartwright, QC.* telly series, as well as playing English WWI nurse Catherine Barkley in a BBC-PBS American production of *A Farewell to Arms*. With the older, more experienced Catherine, who cares for and loves the wounded American soldier, Frederick Henry—an autobiographical rendering of young Ernest Hemingway's romance with Agnes von Hurowsky in Milan in 1918—Jace had weighed in with another fine piece of work. (After she'd called things off with the novelist-to-be, Agnes, according to Hemingway, had completely 'gypped' him.) Jace said the film's U.S. director, Brad Neufeld, thought that losing Agnes had coloured Hemingway's relationships with women from then on; and that this had continued showing up in his man-woman relationships on the written page. In telling me this, I wondered if Jace was reminding me that Julian had said something like that about my playwright Terry Hankin's dealings with Natasha Fenner in *Entrances and Exits*—and what Jace had at the time thought a veiled reference to what had happened between me and Sam Tolliver in Nottingham.

About to leave for a ten-day junket in the U.S. to promote *A Farewell to Arms*, Jace said she'd be seeing Kell over there; that he wanted her, if possible, to see his *Antony and Cleopatra*. 'He's very proud of it. It's packing them in, got rave reviews. Leona Fielder's nothing short of brilliant as Cleo, he tells me. Of course, I know what he's up to: he wants to show off the company to me. Like I said, he's going to keep on and on at me to do something with him over there.'

It seemed I was going to have to ask—even if by doing so I'd be admitting that I didn't know. I said, 'So what's happening with you and the National, then?' The talk about the NT's Daniel Morgenheim casting her in *Congravino,* I was alluding to, obviously.

She said she'd be seeing Morgenheim again as soon as she got back from the States. She'd read for him, opposite two possible Congreves, as both Anne and Henrietta."He says he's only got me and two others in mind for the actress and the duchess. He wasn't going to tell me who the other two were, naturally. He tells me he's leaning towards me as Anne rather than Henrietta, which is fine with me. They're both smashing parts—but if the choice was mine I'd be picking Anne, anyway. She's the more mysterious one, I think. I get the feeling too that Morgenheim thinks you wrote the play with me in mind for Anne; and which even if that were true I know you'd never admit to it. Has he ever asked you about that? Or asked you anything about casting?'

'No, Jace, not a word from him about that. My meetings with Morgenheim and any others in the brain trust over there have always been solely about script matters. And resulting only in some light rewriting, I'm pleased and relieved to report.'

She nodded. And after that not much more said about *Congravino*. What had been said, however, had left me with few if any doubts, either then or at any other point over the next month, that it would be Jace in either one of the women's roles.

But I was in for a jolt.

A fortnight after Jace got back from America, word got out that Morgenheim had settled on his three principals. It was going to be Alun Craddock as Conny, Olivia Lennox as Henrietta, and as Anne none other than Sam Tolliver. I was bowled over. I wasn't the only one.

What had gone down between Morgenheim and Jace depended on who you were talking to. Jace herself wasn't talking to anyone; in the media or to her friends. The story the NT stuck to was that while in the U.S.

Jace was approached by New York stage and film director Drew Schaeffer about doing Blanche Dubois in *A Streetcar Named Desire*—to open on Broadway in January '98—and that she'd chosen to do the Tennessee Williams classic prior to any decisions being made on the women's roles in *Congravino*.

Jace never did give anyone reason to think that this wasn't a true version of events. This didn't stop talk, though, that she'd opted for Blanche only after Sam and Lennox had been cast. She did finally tell a *Guardian* interviewer: 'The thing is, I've always hankered to play Blanche. And when the chance to do so presented itself—to play her in New York too—I couldn't say you're on quickly enough. After all, I might never get the chance again. There's quite a risk in doing this, I know. I'm going to be compared with some very fine American Blanches, not to mention Vivien Leigh. But you have to believe you can bring something of your own to this or any other role, as others must believe as well—and then just get on with it.'

Also, there was talk in New York of Jace repeating the role in a new film version, again with Schaeffer directing. I could see emulating Vivien Leigh's outstanding stage-and-film double as Blanche appealing to Jace in no small way.

Jace told Ursula she hoped her decision hadn't been upsetting for me. In relaying this to me, Ursula said, 'I know one thing: Jace is sure you're going to be absolutely delighted with what Tolliver and Lennox are going to do with your two splendid women. And I couldn't agree with her more on that.' And which Jace eventually got around to telling me herself.

Sam Tolliver also phoned, saying how thrilled she was to be originating another of my characters. 'It was wonderful being your first Jessie Chambers, of course, Tim. But now, being your first Anne—and for the National, too—I just know this is going to be twice as wonderful for me, I'm certain of it. It's going to be something very special for me; and as I'm hoping so much it will be for you too, Tim, darling.'

For her part, Sam wasn't saying anything to either affirm or deny a story that the NT had in fact chosen her over Jace for Anne, making her their first choice for the role; and that although I'd not had casting approval, I'd supported the choice. (And in line with that, what did that say about any current feelings of mine of a personal sort I might have for either Jace or Sam, former lovers and leading ladies of mine?) This latter sort of talk I wouldn't have got into to save my life, of course.

In any event, I was glad to get out of London that summer and hang around for longer periods in Hook Norton—and where I'd not done much of anything other than play cricket, playing my part to help keep the team on its way up the league ladder.

Getting to know Leona Fielder wasn't going to be easy—with the distance between us necessitating a gradual, low-key process. We'd exchanged notes and some press cuttings, made the occasional phone call, and that was about the extent of it.

I did get to know something about her as an actor, however. I'd watched the *Twelfth Night* tape she'd sent me several times. Leona's Olivia was a polished and artful piece of work. She'd achieved and maintained a delicately poised balance in creating the role—between her character's privileged, pampered and flattery-ridden upbringing and the 'princess' complex this had given her, and the very human woman one could relate to, who'd wanted to love and be loved without having a clue how to go about it. Of course, the actor herself—her looks, the way she moved, her affecting mannerisms, the pleasing alto speaking voice and mid-Atlantic accent—had added to the whole, keeping me in the palm of her hand from start to finish. I'd passed the tape on to Julian; he'd been impressed too.

She sent me some photos and two reviews of *Antony and Cleopatra*, and about which she'd written: 'I surprised myself by what I've been able to do with the part, and quite a few others too, I'm sure. I enthralled my father, anyhow. And my Antony, Corey Bax, is so talented and marvellous to work with, which was the other half of the battle for me.' And a square-jawed, handsome chap her Antony was, too. 'Kellison was very clever, actually. He asked if we'd read the play, and when we both admitted we hadn't he told us to keep it that way until rehearsals; and also not to read anything about playing the characters. He talked about what Olivier said about doing the play. That the verse was so beautifully written that even someone with half an ear could catch it and get it; and the same thing too with handling the play's emotional depths. Olivier had assured Vivien Leigh that it would all fall into place for them, go clickity-click for them.' As indeed it seemed to have done for Leona and Bax as well. The *New York Times* reviewer said 'the very passionate, all-consuming connection between the pair was palpable, in the air they breathed—and in the audience's too—and never abated despite knowing it would eventually be the death of them.'

Also, there were two bits of news from Leona of more than passing interest to me—one in late summer, the other in early autumn. They were to have two very different effects upon me.

Firstly, she wrote that Sean Blake had flown over to visit with her, seeing her Mariane in Moliére's *Tartuffe* as well as her Cleopatra, and had persuaded her to make the move to London when the SF season was over. 'So that's it, I've burned my bridges. Kellison is very disappointed, giving me that basset hound look of his, but says he understands, that he couldn't blame me; that it was a move I would have had to have made, and sooner rather than later.'

Then, in October, there was a phone call from her. She said she was going to have to put everything on hold for the time being. Her father was in hospital, seriously hurt in a traffic accident—internal injuries, fractured arm and leg, cracked ribs and a concussion. 'I'm going to Vancouver as soon as I'm finished here. I'm not sure how long I'll be there—until the New Year, anyhow. I'm still hoping, though, to get to London in time to see "Congravino," as well as get together with Sean Blake, of course.'

And in a note with her Christmas card, she congratulated me on *Congravino*, having seen some English newspaper reviews. Also, her father was out of hospital, but had a lengthy convalescence ahead of him. She wrote: 'He needs me right now, more than he's admitting. He says he can get somebody in, but I know he'd much rather have me around the place. I'm really sorry about this, missing your play, having to delay getting over there. And not getting to see you as soon as I wanted to. Sean is very disappointed, I know that.'

I wrote back, saying I was sorry too; but also that good things are always worth waiting for. And informed her she could catch *Congravino* at the Chichester Festival in the summer, and in which the NT production's three principals would be reprising their roles, but this time directed by Julian Caverley. (A special arrangement of mine and Gerry Atherton's with the National and the CF's artistic director and the NT's AD-in-waiting, Desmond Thurlow.)

'The play's the thing'—if, of course, the thing is a play. And the National's powers that be, in their collective wisdom, had assessed *Congravino* as such, obviously.

But then, of course, a play is only a play in performance. And just as obviously, although conceived and perceived individually, a play is an experience one shares with others. The playmakers and the audience must come together to make the play happen. It goes without saying that a play that gets onstage does in fact happen; which isn't to say, though, that it is a 'happening.' In Tom Stoppard's view, what one experiences in a theatre is ideally an 'event,' a 'happening'—something taking place you sense won't easily be forgotten; that your presence there will strike you as being more than circumstantial, having some personal significance for you. And I am still given to thinking, considering the critical and general response to the play, that the first and every subsequent performance of the NT's *Congravino,* in all respects, was an event, a happening, as Stoppard would have recognized it as such.

To say that a good job was done by the company would be a huge understatement. What unfolded onstage at the Olivier was brilliant—a complete, all-round success assured by the NT's always first class production values; the superb cast (with the triumvirate of Craddock, Tolliver and Lennox faultlessly leading the way); and the never less than sure-handed and often inspired direction of Daniel Morgenheim. The production fully deserved the plaudits the company garnered, the box office receipts it chalked up. The NT's *Congravino* was indeed a play, in the best and fullest sense of the word.

And, personally, a very heady and thrilling experience: four grey months of winter on London's South Bank 'made glorious summer' for me. Also, an early Christmas present that went on giving through to the end of the run in late March '98—one I expect I will always cherish. I must have watched the show, playing in repertory, more than a dozen times. I couldn't stay away. The show had provided me with a measure of artistic vindication as well.

How quickly, however, the normality of the writer's solitary existence reasserts itself, as indeed it must. Once the book is launched, the play up and running, however well-received, it's back to the work place, to the waiting blank page. Engaging oneself again in the same self-communing routine in search of some new literary territory one can explore and exploit. A writer always has something further to prove: that you still have something left worth saying, and can still say it as well as you'd ever said anything.

I'm frequently reminded of a comment by John Fowles (*The Magus, The French Lieutenant's Woman, Daniel Martin*, etcetera). Fowles had also spent some of his youth in the Southend, Essex area, incidentally. After being ballyhooed and fêted in Boston and New York on the publication in the U.S. of his first novel, *The Collector*—even wined and dined by Gloria Vanderbuilt in her Central Park apartment—Fowles, in a September, 1963 diary entry, noted: 'I too have felt like Cinderella all this week. A play could be written on Cinderella at the ball; and not have a child's line in it. But all glitter and anxiety.'

The kind of play I may well write myself one of these days.

6

Kell eyed me like a copper might a prime suspect in the interview room. 'So what's this I've been hearing about you and Sammy Tolliver?' he asked.

'So what have you been hearing, then?'

'As if you didn't know.'

'Well, it depends, doesn't it? Maybe you could be more specific?'

'Okay, if I must. I'm told Tolly's on the loose again—free and well clear of husband number two. And that hearts are stirring again between the two of you.'

'Ah—that one.'

'Yes—that one.'

'Yes, well, I'd check my sources if I were you, Kell. There's a lot of misinformation circulating out there.'

Kell wasn't being fair to Sam, either. She'd lost her first husband in a mountain climbing accident after nine years of marriage—a good marriage, by all reports. And had done all she could to keep her second one from falling apart; as I'd learned after getting reacquainted with Sam during *Congravino* rehearsals. Also, before that, Julian had been a reliable source of information on such things; he'd kept in touch with Sam, going as far back as Nottingham.

'You mean, not even a little, harmless fling?' Kell pressed. 'Just for old times' sake?'

'No, Kell, not even for that—and maybe especially not for that.' He looked less than convinced. 'Yes, It's true, Kell, I do love Sam's Anne Bracegirdle, I'll give you that. But that's really as far it goes.'

A pause, then a sudden, smallish smile crossed his face. 'Well, ol' chum, I am relieved to hear you say so. After all, we all know the history between you and Tolly Dolly, don't we? And we wouldn't want a repeat of that, would we? Getting yourself burned by an old flame all over again—not what you or any man needs.'

'Well, thanks for your concern, Kell, anyway.'

'You're welcome. You know, Tim, I'm convinced there are women—and Tolly's such a one, I'd bet on it, who can keep an otherwise very clever chap coming back for more of the bad old same, and without even trying. Something genetic, that they can't help doing, possibly.'

'Yes, well, every man to his own femme fatale, right?'

Kell couldn't possibly have known, of course: that at a Christmas party at the Craddocks', I'd looked over at Sam and wondered just how different, how much better a second time around with her might turn out to be.

Kell was pleased, though, I could tell. Since the breakup with Jace, he'd evidently derived a good deal of satisfaction from the absence in my life of a woman I might be getting close to. Previously, he'd asked about both Belinda and Sophie Jenkins—the latter a BBC-TV drama producer he'd called my 'executive bird in The Bush.' (The BBC's Television Centre is in Shepherds Bush, just up the road from my place in Brook Green.) One or two, although nobody close to us, had got the idea that Sophie and I were enjoying as good a personal relationship as our professional one, a story neither of us had been bothered about enough to deny.

Kell and I were having dinner at Mediterranean Maxie's, a favourite French noshery of his in Covent Garden. Towards the end of January '98, this would have been. He'd also been in London in December, during which he'd seen *Congravino* three times; and which he'd phoned to tell me was 'the best evening I've had in a theatre for donkey's years, not counting anything of my own, of course.' Why he was back in London so soon, and inviting me out for dinner I had no idea. I couldn't remember ever eating or doing anything with him without Jace being present.

He'd been in New York for three days before flying on to London, and was full of news about Jace and her 'absolutely fabulous, just fabulous' Blanche Dubois on The Great White Way. *A Streetcar . . .* was selling out and being held over until the end of April, and could be transferring to another theatre after that. Also in April, the film version would be going ahead in New York and New Orleans. A large spread in the glossy, iconic *Vanity Fair* magazine featuring Jace was also in the offing. 'Jacie's the biggest and the classiest Babe Broadway's had for several seasons,' he enthused. 'Oh, and Jacie said to tell you she couldn't be more thrilled about the success your play is having.' She'd left for New York before *Congravino* opened. 'And also to give you her love, she said.' Or was it really just her warm, possibly affectionate regards?

Then it was about the Stratford Festival's past season; how well it had gone, especially *Antony and Cleopatra*. I listened and responded as if he was telling me something I didn't know. And also to tell me about his upcoming season, as well as his longer-term plans for the company.

He said he was going to miss having Leona on board. 'We've been working together for four seasons in a row now, at the Citadel in Edmonton and at Stratford. The girl's just coming into full bloom as a classical actor; she's just about there. But that's how it goes, isn't it? The wheel turns, and life goes on. And I do have a couple of women who are ready for bigger things, though, so not to despair.'

Leona and I had agreed to keep the contact we'd had in London and since to ourselves. I didn't want Kell badgering her at all about any relationship we were having. 'No problem, that's fine with me,' she'd said—a shade too enthusiastically for my liking perhaps.

Kell continued on singing Leona's praises. 'The girl's a very good actor. Professionally, I know her inside out—she's very open that way. She'll talk to you, and work with you every way she can to find out and do what you're looking for from her. Her concentration is phenomenal. She's always very focussed, and wants your focus on what she's doing as well. But once out of the rehearsal room or the theatre she's practically a stranger; doesn't seem to want to know you. She doesn't hang out much with her colleagues like most actors do, especially in a town the size of Stratford. She seems more than content being a loner. The girl's a riddle wrapped up in a mystery, you might say. One of the guys in the company calls her our very own "dark lady of the sonnets".' He said a story that she's seeing co-star Corey Bax (also Jewish) was a lot of rubbish. 'Being able to keep a secret like that in Stratford is beyond the realms of possibility.' Kell did say, however, that Leona had befriended and become attached to Barton Heddle and his wife Lois, spending a lot of time at their converted farmhouse a few miles out of town.

A veteran, highly respected actor, Heddle was the only member from the original 1953 company still with the SF. Kell said, 'Leona looks up to Bart, wants to learn what she can from him. But the main attraction for her could be Lois, a retired psychology professor. Lois taught at the U. of Western Ontario in London for more than twenty years. And very keen and sharp on things literary as well. She's written on psychological factors affecting characters in novels and plays; she's probably been some help to Leona with that sort of thing. Still, it's a bit odd, all the same, the connection she's made with the Heddles. For one thing, they're practising Christians; regular Anglican churchgoers. And if Leona's got religion in common with the Heddles, then I'm a Dutchman.'

Also, Kell told me what I already knew about Leona's father's accident and her return to Vancouver. 'I know she's always been very close to her father—a real Daddy's girl, if you ask me—but why she's staying out there so long, and not getting herself over to London, I find more than a bit puzzling. Then again, with Leona, who can tell what's going on with her from one moment to the next?'

Feigning no more than a polite interest in all of this about Leona wasn't easy, especially when tempted at times to question what I was hearing. If the short time—the all of three hours or more—I'd spent with her counted for anything, I couldn't square Kell's guarded 'loner' with the warm, vivacious and gregarious woman who'd sought me out the year before in my Hammersmith local.

But Kell, as I might have known, hadn't got me to Maxie's just to talk about Jace or Leona, or how life in general was treating him.

With the huge serving dish of bouillabaisse Kell had recommended on the table, we were also into the main course—conversationally, that is—he must have had in mind for me from the outset. He said, 'This is just a flying visit for me this time, actually. I have to be back in Stratford next Monday. So would you mind giving Gerry a bell first thing in the morning and see if the three of us can get together before the week is out? I've got some serious business to talk over with you two. To cut to the chase, I want to have your lovely, one hell of a play for my '99 season. And believe me, Tim, ol' chum, I'm going to be all business with this, I kid you not.' He'd not be expecting any favours, playing the friendship card, anything like that, he said. 'I'll be coming in, straight and true, and hard too, with a solid, competitive offer I know will get me into the game. And once in, it's going to be bloody hard to get me out it, you just watch!'

Someone at a nearby table laughed—but not an eavesdropper, of course. I couldn't help smiling, however.

'Yes, all right, Tim, be my guest: amuse yourself at my expense. And maybe ask me what I'm smoking these days if you want. But don't underestimate me, ol' chum, that's all. Being an underdog doesn't faze me one bit. I'll be in there, getting my licks in, playing for keeps.'

'God forbid, Kell. I know you too well to think otherwise.'

He had to know what he was up against, however. I told him that the New York producer Freddy Flaxman wanted exclusive North American rights for runs in Chicago, Boston and The Big Apple in the spring or autumn of '99.

'Yeah, so I heard when I was there,' he said. 'Flaxman's already putting out feelers to Drew Schaeffer to direct; hoping he can bring Jacie with him, probably. But Freddy's only talking ten weeks, max—and I'm talking six months, running the whole season.'

'Also, the Guthrie in Minneapolis is interested.'

'Well, come one, come all. But like I said, whoever comes in for it is going to be in for a right royal scrap.'

'And if you did get the play, you'd be directing, I assume?'

'How'd you guess?' He grinned. 'And to save you asking, either of the women—Bracegirdle or the duchess—would be Jacie's for the asking.'

I smiled. 'You read my mind. You do realize, though, you'll be on your own with that, don't you? I very much doubt there's a thing I could say to sway Jace on that.'

'Yeah, well, as m' mam used to tell me when I was a kid: you make your own luck, so stop mooning around just wishing for things. And how right the old darlin' was. It's not up there somewhere in your stars, is it? It's in your own self—right, ol' chum?'

People can quote Shakespeare—William the Great—at me anytime they want, and know for sure their point has been well and truly made, of course.

A fortnight later I got a note from Leona. Hoping that all was well with me, she wrote: 'My father is still having his problems. He's not recovering as well as expected and won't be getting back to work, which he loves and lives to do, for some while yet. Also he's been diagnosed as clinically depressed, but refuses to take any anti-depressants saying nobody is turning him into a zombie. Anyhow, I've decided to stay here for a few more months, probably until June or July. I'm missing theatre, of course, but not as much as I thought I would, and that surprised me. I should be so lucky, I know, but I've been working since the day I left RADA. Maybe I needed the break, a sabbatical, which I know an actor's not supposed to wish for. But sometimes you do something you know isn't in your own interests, but you feel is the right thing to do, and I guess that's what I'm doing—or think I'm doing, anyhow.'

Leona signed off: 'Affectionately.'

In mid-March—the dealing over with—Gerry said, 'Tim, why don't you call Marleau and give him the news? He'd prefer to get it from you, don't you think?'

'Yes, you're probably right.'

After getting through to Kell—and informing him he'd got *Congravino* for '99—there were at least ten-seconds of silence on the line, except for an intake and expulsion of breath. Almost certainly a drag on a ciggy—one of Kell's imported Gitanes, probably—followed by a release of smoke.

'Did you hear what I said, Kell?'

'Oh, yes, dear ol' chum, I heard you all right. My ears are working fine.'

He sounded choked up; or needed to stop smoking without delay, more likely the latter. He coughed and cleared his throat, getting out, 'Thank you, thank you, Tim, you lovely man, you. I just can't thank you enough, can I?'

'No need, Kell. It really was all business with Gerry and me, you know. The way you wanted it.'

'Yes, yes. But thank you, and bless you real good, anyway.'

Some more throat clearing, which seemed to improve things for him. And then it was back to business. 'The agreement—as per my latest offer, I take it?'

'Right, Kell.'

'And all signed and sealed? And in the mail?'

'Crossing The Pond as we speak.'

'Good, good.'

Another drag and release. 'Look, Tim, ol' chap, you won't mind if I let you go now, will you? I need to let all this sink in. Do a bit of pondering, maybe some honest-to-goodness exulting, and have a drink or two. I'll drop you a line, okay? Express my feelings and gratitude properly, in black and white, all right, chummy?'

'Just as you wish, Kell.'

He was probably already reaching for his telephone number listings—wanting me off the line to get some calls made as soon as he could. His first call—I'd bet on it—to Jace in New York.

7

By May, things had taken a definite turn for the better for her father, Leona phoned to tell me. He was not only much improved physically, but had got himself out of the 'psychological black hole' he'd fallen into as well. 'The mind thing turned out to be as bad if not worse than the physical injuries,' she said. She'd insisted he see a therapist who'd been recommended to her; she'd had to push him hard to keep his first three or four appointments. 'And a month and fifteen sessions later, his black depression was gone, like a dark storm cloud blown away by the wind. And it wasn't just a case of getting back the father I've always known, either; he was a changed man. I'm talking a day-and-night difference here. He looks like the same man, but he isn't. I'm going to have to get to know him all over again—that's how much he's changed.' She said she'd spare me the details for later. Nathan Fielder was planning to return to work in September.

And there was this latest thing he'd sprung on her as well. He'd announced he was off to San Francisco for a week, and while there would be seeing his ex-wife, Leona's mother. It was all arranged. Like him, Merle Fielder had never remarried. 'I don't think they've seen one another or even talked for twenty years or more. When I asked him what was going on, he said, well, that's what the two of them were going to find out, wasn't it? He smiled like a man of mystery and told me to stay tuned—and that was it. Anyhow, the thing is, I'm returning to Toronto next week. I'll be staying for a few days, then go on to London. I should be there before the month is out.' This was around the middle of July.

The next time she called, about a week later, she'd had some more news. And this time something I knew immediately I was going to need time to get my head around, not to mention get some feelings sorted out as well.

I should have seen it coming, but I hadn't.

She told me: 'I'd promised Kellison I'd see him in Toronto before I left. A couple of weeks before he'd sent me a copy of your play, saying he couldn't get me out of his mind for Henrietta. I said I'd read it, anyhow. He knew, of course—that I'd love the part, the play, everything about it.' She said she was now a little in awe of me; that *Congravino* had put me, as a dramatist, 'very high up there, sky high' in her estimation. 'Anyhow, we had lunch in Toronto. But not just the two of us, it turned out. Kellison had someone with him—none other than Simon Jago, who's going to play Congreve for him; who just happened to be in town that day from New York. And a couple of hours later, there I was reading Henrietta with him at Kellison's place—and which went very well, more than well, for all three of us.' And with Kellison standing by, nodding and smiling like a godfather, she said, Jago told her she just had to do the play; that she was made for the part. 'The two of them had been lying in wait for me.'

Kell had mentioned Jago in the letter of thanks he'd written me for getting the play, saying he was hot on his trail. An English-born Canadian who'd been with the SF in the late '80s, early '90s, Jago had since had three excellent seasons at the Guthrie in Minneapolis, and more recently turned in a highly-praised Iago in *Othello* at New York's Lincoln Centre. In his letter, Kell hadn't mentioned he was going after Leona as well, however.

Leona said that Kell told her he was getting more confident by the day that he could persuade Jace to do Anne Bracegirdle for him. 'That's a big part of his pitch to me, of course; working with Jacinth and Simon Jago. He wants the three of us—that's his Plan A. And we all know Kellison, don't we? What he wants he goes for like a hound after the fox. Anyhow, as you can imagine, he's left me with a giant-sized dilemma on my hands.'

She said she wanted to do Henrietta 'like crazy'—but also wanted so much to get over to London. 'I can't decide for the life of me which one I want more.' She sighed. 'Of course, I know you can't make up my mind for me, Tim, you or anybody else. But if you've got an opinion, whatever it is, one way or the other, I'd like to hear it—either now or sometime soon.'

I took a breath. I was in a quandary of my own. What was it she'd rather have me say? Anyway, I went ahead regardless. 'All right, Leona, for what it's worth, I'd like to see you over here as soon as you can make it. I think it would be good for your career. But also because I'll see more of you onstage, I'm sure, and with some luck, see more of you off it as well—for purely selfish reasons, in other words. On the other hand, the thought of you as Henrietta is a very fascinating thought—and it's getting more so the more I think about it.' I said I'd a feeling that if she did do Henrietta, that Olivia Lennox's performance, as fine as it was, might possibly lose some its lustre for me by comparison. 'If any of that is of any use to you, Leona.'

There was a pause on the line. Then—so quietly I could hardly hear her—she said: 'Thank you, Tim. Thank you for that.' And two or three beats after that: 'I think you've just made making my mind up that much easier, Tim—f or what that's worth.' Getting off the phone, I couldn't help feeling I'd just consigned myself to a further year-and-a-half of spasmodic and unsatisfying long distance contact with Leona.

In any event, whether or not anything I'd said had affected Leona's decision in any way, that was exactly what I would be facing—starting right then and there.

Jace surprised me by not returning to London later that summer after her stage and film commitments with *A Streetcar Named Desire*. I'd thought she couldn't stay away any longer than she'd already done. Instead, however, she'd opted to do *The Philadelphia Story* on Broadway in October playing Tracy Lord (who else?), with Simon Jago as her ex-husband Dexter Haven; and directed again by Drew Schaeffer, with Freddy Flaxman producing.

Running into Ursula at an opening at the Haymarket, we'd got talking. She told me that Jace was fine, that she'd managed to get a welcome break in the Saratoga area in upstate New York, away from the city's summer heat and humidity. 'She stayed at Drew Schaeffer's lakeside place, apparently. Which could have been her way, of course, of telling me that what I'm hearing about the two of them is true—that he's playing away from home with her. And if so, I'd have thought she'd have been smarter than that—and him, too. The man has a wife with money, which probably explains how he lives so well. They have a daughter too. As you can tell, I've been doing some snooping.' And also: 'I was talking to Jace just the other day, actually. She tells me she's going to do your play in Canada next year, doing the Bracegirdle role. I might have known that Kell Marleau would eventually have his ambitious way with her.' She looked at me, narrowing her eyes. 'I think I've just taken you by surprise, haven't I? Sorry about that, Tim.'

'Yes, Ursula, you're right, you did surprise me, actually.'

'Well, it's not been announced yet, I understand. And I'm sure Marleau the Marvellous will be letting you know all about it soon enough; and crowing between the lines like he does.'

'He did leave a message for me today, actually.'

'Well, there you go, then. You will act surprised, though, won't you? You'll spoil his fun if you don't.'

Ursula also told me that Kell had got Arthur Miller's *All My Sons* in his next year's line-up, which Drew Schaeffer would be directing. 'I don't know if Marleau knows it or not, but that means Jacinth's going to have some close and possibly distracting company in Stratford, for part of the season, anyway.'

When I got back to Kell he told me he'd clinched a deal with Flaxman to run the SF's *Congravino* and *All My Sons* in repertory in New York in a five-week, November-December time slot. Obviously, he'd been thinking a few steps ahead, securing the rights to *Congravino* until the end of the year as he had. Both Jace and Schaeffer had very likely known about the New York deal before signing on with the SF. Kell had played his cards well.

Before ringing off, he said, 'Oh, yes, one other thing, ol' chum. Whatever you may have heard about Jacie and Schaeffer, about her being at his summer place in Saratoga, and so on—well, his wife and daughter were with him up there, too. Just thought you'd like to know, anyway.'

I'd spent Christmas at Dad and Sally's in Banbury, celebrating as well with Roz and Karl, a Swiss chef she'd met in Berne, and who'd be moving to Oxford to work in the New Year. I'd gone to a couple of parties in London over the holidays and enjoyed myself—but not nearly as much as everyone else seemed to be doing. Wherever I went, whatever it was, I'd find myself wishing Leona was by my side.

On the work front, my television original, *The Chief,* was going into production in the spring. Also, I was having another go at the Edith Cavell play—but this time, on Sophie Jenkins's advice, as something for the box; and shifting some of the focus away from the nurse-martyr to a wounded soldier-poet. It seemed to be helping.

Meanwhile, Leona was in Toronto where she'd done David Hare's *Amy's View* for longtime SF actor/director, and a friend of the Heddles, Laura Welby. After which, back in Vancouver over the holidays, she'd stayed on into mid-January to witness her parents exchange wedding vows for the second time around. She said, 'I was in a daze most of the time. Of course, I was very happy for them, but I was also wondering what on earth did they think they were doing?' She couldn't remember ever having been in a synagogue before. 'I'd felt like a fish out of water. It was all pretty strange for me.'

A wintry night, at home alone in Brook Green, just lazing around—and for awhile thinking of one Canadian West Coast girl while listening to another: jazz singer-pianist Diana Krall's *If I Had You.* (The CD, *All for You,* was a salute to the 1950s' Nat King Cole Trio.) Krall's 'warm and strangely knowing' voice, 'like wild honey with a spoonful of Scotch'—as the anonymous CD insert writer had so well described it—had floated from the Manhattan recording studio's monitors 'like the smoke from a film noir cigarette':

> 'I could show the world how to smile,
> I could be glad all the while,
> I could turn the gray skies to blue,
> If I had you . . .'

8

26B Caledonia Street,
Stratford, Ontario N6A 5W4
April 18 '99

Dear Tim:

I'm having a lazy, pajamas-and-housecoat sort of Sunday. It's cloudy and very cool outside, a good day to stay in. In Vancouver they'll be in shorts jogging in Stanley Park, for sure. Hope everything is going well for you, healthwise and in every other way.

Rehearsals are going well. We start previews next week. Kellison feels I'm on track with Henrietta. I'm getting a lot from Jacinth and Simon. Sometimes I can't believe I'm actually working with Jacinth. My time with her with the RSC doesn't count, of course. We never exchanged a word onstage. I've admired her since before then, first seeing her as Natasha Fenner in 'Entrances and Exits' in London when I was seventeen. I was on a student exchange with a school in Sevenoaks. That night I knew for sure I wanted to go on stage. I told her this when I was with the RSC and she said she hoped I wasn't thinking she had a lot to answer for, and if so to blame it on Natasha Fenner, not her. She also said being the first Natasha is something she's proud of and will never forget, and how grateful she is to you and Julian Caverley for giving her the role. I think I told you I've never played Natasha as much as I wanted to. I've identified with her as an actor and as a person for quite awhile. Like her I've found it difficult at times to cope with the changes and the unknowns that go with the job, and the changing ideas you get about yourself. Like Natasha says, who you think you are can be influenced by the various and chameleon-like things you're expected to do as an actor. When I mentioned this to Jacinth she said she knew what Natasha, and me as well, were saying. She said sometimes she'd wonder when she was playing Natasha if she was, more or less, just playing herself, knowing her character like she did. Also she said she'd learned one important thing more than any other from Natasha, that it's best to check whatever is going on in your private life at the rehearsal room door, because if you don't you can fall down on the job considering the head and heart thing you have to do to create a character.

I'm going to tell you something about myself, I've decided, and I don't mean as an actor. I've got quite a few confusing things going on in my head right now. I was talking to my father the other day. And the thing is, I still can't get over how different he is from the person I knew as a kid. Back then and for a lot of the time since then, my father could never say or do anything wrong. I think I've always seen him as the kind of man every other man should be. I'd sometimes go to see him in action in court and I thought him the smartest and the wisest person in the room, including the judge. And I wanted to be a lawyer too, a defense counsel like him. That is until I did a play at high school, and that changed all that. And did it ever! I played the blind girl in 'Wait Until Dark.' And I was hooked. Anyhow, I'm not sure now what I'm supposed to think and do to keep my father happy and proud of me, and that goes for my mother too. And he's telling me another hard-to-believe thing. That he and Mom are going to London in June for a family reunion. He and his twin brother Jacob haven't had anything to do with one another for over 40 years, more my dad's doing than my uncle's, to tell the truth. There were just the two boys. There was a big blow up between them over a girl, who his brother later married. Dad fell out with him about that and a lot of other things, and the same thing with his father, only worse, particularly when it came to religion. Grandfather Fiedler was a very devout man, while Dad didn't have any time at all for religious belief of any kind, not in the slightest. I got to know and like Uncle Jacob and his family when I moved to London to go to RADA, but I never told my father. I reckoned he'd think I was being disloyal to him. I was only four or five when Dad started telling me there wasn't a God in heaven or anywhere else. That it was all a fantastic myth and a very bad and terrible joke. He told me the Jews had badly and sadly fooled themselves and the rest of the world about that—or how else to explain their awful history, and the Holocaust, most of all? We'd had relatives who'd died in the gas chambers at Auschwitz, apparently. I trusted my father completely and believed everything he said was true. And now my parents and my aunt and uncle are also going to Paris and

Vienna on a sort of family history tour, and will be including Auschwitz in their itinerary. Amazing! That really is the only word I can think of for all of this, although 'stupefying' might come close as well.

I really hadn't intended to go on about all this family stuff when I started this. I'm not sure if it's of any interest to you. But that didn't stop me, did it? So I may as well tell you the rest and be done with it. Anyhow, what happened, after seeing the therapist I'd forced my father to go to, out of desperation, really, he started going to the local synagogue, and also having private sessions with the rabbi, who is a well-known author on Jewish history and religious law, I found out. I was flabbergasted. Dad said I could ask all right, but he wasn't sure he could even start to explain what was going on with him. He told me he'd looked in the shaving mirror one morning and saw someone who wasn't really there at all, without a visible sign of any life in his eyes. And during his therapy he'd realized what his problem was. If he was ever going to find himself, find a true self to be true to, he was going to have to open up the shutters he'd had over his eyes for so long and acknowledge and embrace his Jewish birthright and heritage, and take hold of what he called his 'personal reality.' He also said he'd understand totally if I couldn't fathom or accept this, considering the way he'd raised me, and that he'd never hold that against me. Also I found out from my mother that the divorce was mainly over their religious differences. In fact, she told me that she'd wanted to return to her Jewish roots and faith. Her ambitions as a musician weren't really a factor in their marriage breakdown, apparently. Anyhow, here we are now, my parents and me, in a sort of once removed, live-and-let-live situation. The family unit's together again after all this time, but only technically, you might say. Which is ironic and pretty sad, wouldn't you say? And it's left me wondering which is which when it's reality you're talking about. Has my father finally got it right after all those years of getting it wrong, or is it the other way round? I'm not really sure why I'm telling you all this, not sure at all. All I can think is that your play may have something to do with it. Something to do with the way Congreve looks at life, trying to sort out what's important, what matters, and what isn't. I guess, though, telling you what I have, I've added you to the short list of people I confide in. There isn't a lot of them. I can count them on one hand.

Anyhow, I think I'm getting writers' cramp. And to think the only thing I was going to tell you was that my parents are coming for the 'Congravino' opening and staying for a few days. I'll be introducing them to you, of course. I've not said anything to them about our friendship, by the way. My mother would only start asking questions. I think she's wondering why I haven't a 'significant other' in my life by now. I'm hoping we can get together by ourselves while you're here, but if we can't, let's be sure to if you can get back over here again before the season is out. I'd love you to see my Rosaline in 'Love's Labour's Lost.' Nicholas Lirani, who's very clever and imaginative, is directing. I'm feeling good and very positive about the whole thing. Playing my lover Biron is Corey Bax and it's great to be working with him again. He was my Antony two years back and it was a terrific experience for me, and I think it was for him too. We really clicked just like Kellison said we would, and I feel it's going to be that way this time too for both of us. Corey says he's going to have to start calling me his 'other woman.' Last summer he married a bright and pretty woman who reads the news on a Toronto TV station.

So see you in a few weeks' time. I'll have to be as patient as I can be until then. But the way time is flying in rehearsals should help with that. I think it's going to be a bit nerve-wracking for me on opening night, knowing you're out there in the audience somewhere. On the other hand, it's going to be good knowing you'll be silently urging me on to be the best I can be as your Henrietta, which I very much want to be, of course. Am I right in thinking you've always been a little in love with your duchess? You will tell me someday, Tim, won't you?

Affectionately yours,
Leona.

9

Rather than being met, I'd rented a car, a Pontiac Firebird, at Toronto's Pearson airport and driven to Stratford via Woodstock, which has an old town hall modelled on the one in its namesake in Oxfordshire. I'd arrived around four in the afternoon, a Sunday late in May. Two hours later I was having dinner with Kell at The Church—an exclusive Stratford eatery that had once served food and refreshment for the soul on a pay-what-you-can basis placed on an offertory plate. And where, accorded all due deference as the local mover and shaker he was, Kell was given his usual upper level, high-arched window table. After we'd both ordered the prime rib, he asked, 'Are you really going back on Tuesday?' He was more than a little peeved, I think.

''Fraid so, Kell.'

'I was hoping you'd be sticking around a few days, see some other shows, meet some people in the company.'

'I'd like to, Kell, but I can't. My latest for the BBC got delayed a couple of months. They brought in a new producer with a new budget, involving some script revisions they wanted yesterday, what else? In fact, it came close to my Victorian white slave traffic original getting postponed indefinitely.' (Sophie Jenkins never did fully explain what had brought this about, having left the BBC to join ITV in April.)

Kell had already made clear his reluctance to talk much about *Congravino*, opening the next evening—something I'd understood completely. As he'd told me, 'I've done all I can do, the ball's not in my court any more. The company's as ready and primed as it can be—and now, as they say, the proof is in the pudding. Every show's a new journey for everybody involved, isn't it? How you get to where you want to go is always an adventure, a bit of a mystery tour.' He'd said that a few times before, I could tell; and mixed in with his practised coyness, some cool confidence was showing through too.

But he was more than ready to talk about his darlin' Jacie, of course.

'She's into her usual pre-show, lying low routine, getting her game face on,' he said. 'Which explains why you haven't been able to get hold of her, if you've tried, that is. She's booked into a hotel somewhere, God knows where, probably in London, where she's less likely to be recognized.'

He said the two of them were working a treat together. 'We're on the same wavelength, reading each other's mind like billy-o. And it's been pretty much the same thing with Simon and Leona as well. And I've not had a word out of anyone of 'em about what Morgenheim and Caverley did with Craddock, Tolly and Lennox in London and Chichester.' Presumably, Kell didn't know that Jace had phoned Julian twice about certain aspects of her role. 'Actually, Jacie's been bloody marvellous, a real sweetie. She's been so open and helpful with everybody—about anything affecting the show, I mean, of course. I don't think there's an actor here, particularly among the younger ones, who doesn't look up to Jacie, seeing her as epitomizing what it means to be an actor in every sense of the word; someone with only the interests of the show as a whole in mind at all times.'

And at which point the look of pleased satisfaction on his face drained away. He said, 'By the way, Drew Schaeffer's coming in tomorrow for the opening. I thought you might like to know. You may find yourself stuck with him for awhile after the show.'

'Well, I'm sure I'll survive—and him too, I expect.'

'It won't be a tad awkward for you, then?'

'No, not for me, it won't be. Why, should it be?' Silly question; I didn't want to encourage Kell in the slightest.

He said, 'Well, he might be looking you over, sizing you up. You know, be curious about a long-time former lover of Jacie's, that sort of thing. Speaking of whom, the two of them, I'm afraid I led you astray about Jacie Girl's trip upstate to Saratoga last summer. Something was going on between them, even then.'

'Yes, so I heard.'

'The talk is that his wife knew as well, and chose to look the other way. Something to do, some say, with how much she loves him; and how understanding she is about the occasional emotional dangers and the necessary expediences that sometimes come with the sort of work he does. Some such bunk, anyway.'

'Expediences?'

'Yes, it is a bit of a laugh, isn't it? His having to keep some of the actresses he wants for his shows happy in every possible way—like that's part of his job description, can you believe? Anyway, since last September, it's been a "your place or mine?" scenario they've been playing out in New York—with his wife and daughter conveniently located most of the time in the family townhouse in Boston. Of course, he'll be staying with Jacie while he's here in Stratford, and also when he comes back in June to work on "All My Sons," obviously.'

I said, 'You know, Kell, you're not telling me anything I don't already know. The secret's out; it got to London months ago.'

I might have been talking to a deaf man.

'I don't think it's going to last, in fact I'd bet on it,' he said. 'Schaeffer's never going to stop loving his exquisite, well-heeled and very accommodating wife; everybody who knows him will tell you that.' Apparently, Kell's main informant was Simon Jago; he and his wife lived in New York and socialized with the Schaeffers. 'Melanie Schaeffer lets her husband see their daughter anytime he wants. He absolutely adores the girl. They're always doing things as a family. He was in Massachusetts with them for Christmas. Jacie spent hers with me in Toronto, as you probably know.'

My irritation with this recital was probably showing. I was tired from the long day's travel and not really up to going along with talk I wasn't interested in; and which was making me tired so much the more.

Seeing this on my face, Kell said, 'Anyway, Tim, I'll tell you this about Drew Schaeffer—no, really, this doesn't have anything to do with him and Jacie, except professionally. The man's a bloody fine director. *Streetcar* . . . and *Philadelphia Story* were brilliant. And I have every reason to believe it will be the same thing here with the Miller play. So dare I hope, ol' chum, you'll get back over here to see it?'

Schaeffer had had conversations with Miller about his play, and Kell was hoping to get the American master playwright to Stratford for the opening.

One thing Kell said Miller had told Schaeffer I'd found especially interesting. Soon after writing *All My Sons*, the play that had launched his career, Miller said he'd realized something that had stayed with him ever since. As Kell had it: 'The one true thing true art is, more than anything else, and influencing the artistic process from beginning to end, is a large shot, an overflow even, of love and human sympathy, emanating from the artist's deeper inner self.' It had been something of a head and heart process like that, I believed, I'd found detectable in William Congreve's plays, particularly in his last one; and I'd tried to reflect this in my version of both the man and his work.

A few minutes on and the weariness took an even stronger hold on me when Kell told me what the SF's media relations manager Trish Greenham had lined up for me the next day—and in particular an interview with Marissa Ford, a Toronto journalist with a reputation for knowledgeable and penetrating features on the Canadian performing arts scene. Over and above the *Globe and Mail* theatre critic's review of *Congravino*, Ms Ford would be doing a lengthy reflective and analytical piece on the play itself for the country's leading national. 'Watch yourself with this one, Tim,' Kell advised me. 'She's a very attractive and personable thirty something, very nicely packaged altogether—but never forget, there's a sharp and incisive mind ticking away all the time behind those pretty green eyes of hers, and which she'll use like a scalpel if she's a mind to. Still, ol' chum, I expect you've dealt with your share of such types before, and have your own engaging and canny ways and means of dealing with them, whichever way they come at you, right?'

A vote of confidence isn't always as reassuring as one can only assume it's intended to be, of course.

I phoned Leona as soon as I got back to the hotel. There was no answer. She'd been out for dinner with her parents. When she called, we'd quickly established the chances of getting together by ourselves while I was in town were non-existent, as I'd feared. By the time I'd be done with the media the next day, she'd be home resting up for hers and the Festival's very big and festive first night.

Two days later, back in London, it would be more of the same for the rest of the year for us—occasional notes, letters and phone calls; small, intermittent tokens of our interest in each other I knew that I, for one, would find harder by the day to be content with.

Red-blazered musicians with trumpets and drums, on an exterior balcony of the Festival Theatre, sounded out the traditional first night fanfare for the dressed up throng gathered on the lawns and pathways below them, beckoning their audience to move into the theatre and participate in an age-old ritual of catharsis—intended 'to show mankind himself, and thereby to show to man God's image,' according to Tyrone Guthrie, the SF's co-founder and first AD. The sort of statement the tall, hawk-eyed and charismatic Scotsman—British theatre's 'fiery angel'—wasn't reticent in making; although arguably, in this instance, expounding a premise only the first half of which is still valid for the majority of today's providers and consumers of literature of any sort.

With the onstage proceedings as familiar as they were to me, I was, nevertheless, soon drawn into another time, another world, in Congreve's London. And in minutes I was fully caught up in the goings-on laid on before me, appreciating the various circumstances and vicissitudes of life for the once admired seventeenth/eighteenth dramatist and poet—or at least as I'd chosen to present them, anyway. And as with a play's every new production, as any produced playwright will tell you, there were occasional surprises in store for the author as well. Obviously, the incidents and the dialogue were of my making—but there were moments when some previously unappreciated meaning or inference came to light for me; when a scene's central dynamic was changed by some unforeseen emotional flashpoint, in an unexpected moment of deeper empathy, sympathy and understanding between two characters.

But things such as these rarely catch me completely by surprise, however. I've learned to expect the unexpected from any character when watching anything of mine. For that matter, turning one of my pen-and-paper people into a flesh-and-blood, mind-and-heart, fully realized human entity—as a skilful and sensitive actor is able to do—will always have for me a sense of both the extraordinary and the mysterious about it. (And never more so when the character is a woman, one of those other beings from Venus, or wherever; each and every one of whom will probably always have for me an element of the unknowable about her.)

The question persists for me, then: whether it's possible for the author, the director and the actors to realize with any certainty what in actual fact, collaboratively, they've been party to on any given evening or afternoon in the theatre.

It had been an excellent night in the stalls for me. All the vital onstage signs were very positive ones; everything in fine working order for Kell and his SF company that warm, late May evening. The clever, sure-footed direction; the good use of the distinctive thrust stage (Guthrie's Old Vic colleague Tanya Moiseiwitsch's innovative design, later reproduced at

Chichester); the three leads' beautifully-crafted performances, augmented by a truly supportive cast; the superb technical work and production values—all present and correct to make a complementary whole.

After the show, in the jam-packed dressing room, in the general pandemonium, I'd dutifully but also sincerely expressed my pleasure and satisfaction with the evening's 'stage traffic'—to Kell, Simon, Jace and Leona in particular. Of course, neither they nor anyone else connected with the company would think of asking me to make comparisons between theirs and the two previous U.K. productions. (Nobody has ever yet put me on the spot like that with any play of mine, at any rate.) In the dressing room too I'd got to meet the well-countenanced Nathan and Merle Fielder. It was clear to see where Leona had got her striking physical assets. In congratulating me, Mrs. Fielder said she'd been lifted in both mind and spirit in having seen the play—a kind and thoughtful thing to say, I thought. Hard for me to tell, though, if she'd had anything other than the play in mind, considering the steady, straight-on look she'd settled on me and her subsequent glances my way I'd caught in one or other of the make-up mirrors.

The Festival's Board chairman, Felix Manzer, oversaw the celebratory reception like a circus ringmaster. I was paired in the receiving line and at the head table with his stylish, well-preserved wife. The loquacious Arlene Manzer had been very much taken by the play; she'd tried to draw me into a discussion I'd eased myself out of by acquiescing with her (á la Samuel Beckett) that my play was indeed saying whatever it had had to say to her. Manzer himself was closely attending the evening's number one VIP, the lady Lieutenant Governor of Ontario, a young fiftyish widow and former provincial judge, who could have passed for Sigourney Weaver's twin sister. Kell and his also single assistant AD Nick Lirani; Jacinth and Drew Schaeffer; and Leona and Simon Jago made up the rest of Manzer's complement of first night notables. Jago's clothes designer wife Jane had had to remain in New York for business reasons. Trying to overcome the ambient din in the room, Leona and I had hardly had time to talk before someone was whisking her away to meet somebody or other.

With Kell and his three leads under seige for most of the evening, I'd shared some engaging conversations with Schaeffer and Lirani, particularly with the articulate American. He'd been most complimentary about the play and its trio of principals, but a shade less so about the production as a whole. (He'd had a question or two on certain directorial matters, presumably.) With his fair hair and good looks, his smooth, Great Gatsby-like manner and mien, I could see the man's attraction for Jace, personally as well as professionally—as Kell must have done as well, grudgingly so, probably.

The longest one-on-one conversation I'd got into—and the one I'd enjoyed the most—was with cast member and Leona's good friend, Barton Heddle. ('Saint Bart' to Kell, apparently.) I'd been impressed by Heddle's poet laureate John Dryden, Conny's faithful friend, in *Congravino.* I remarked on the mentor-and-protégé intellectual affinity as well as the father-and-son-like relationship he and Jago had registered so well in their scenes together. Also, I'd managed to get out of him some recollections of the SF's early days, working with the likes of Guthrie, Alec Guinness, Irene Worth and James Mason. Bart Heddle wasn't a name-dropper, though. His physicality—he was a sizeable, lion-maned, imperious-looking man—belied his self-effacing gentleness and modesty. Explaining his wife Lois's absence that evening—she was with a hospitalized sister in Montreal—he told me how much she'd liked the play. They'd seen it in London at the National. 'Lois was really looking forward to meeting you. She asked me to invite you, if you can get back here later in the season, for a home-cooked dinner with us. I think I should warn you, however. One of Lois's joys in life is to get a writer's feet under her table and get as deeply into his or her head as she can.'

I spent a fair amount of time trying to catch Leona's eye. I was tempted, wanting so much to talk to her properly, to ask her to leave and go somewhere with me. But I'd thought better of it, not wanting to put her in an awkward situation of any sort. Consequently, I ended up getting what I may or may not have deserved—no more than two or three minutes alone with her in a side exit corridor, where we'd been interrupted by others leaving the reception. Also, her parents were outside waiting for her.

I couldn't stop myself. I'd kissed her straight away, gently but also eagerly enough for her to have noticed.

'Well, well, Tim,' she said.

I smiled, but not really apologetically. 'I know, Leona. I've been thinking about doing that for a long time, too long, obviously. I'm sorry if I startled you.'

She smiled. 'Apology accepted.'

Neither of us seemed sure about what to say next. For me her closeness had muddled my thoughts.

Leona collected hers before I did. 'What you said, Tim, in the dressing room, I want you to know just how much that meant to me, even if I can't put it into words the way I'd like to.' She didn't have to elaborate. I'd told her I'd loved everything about her Henrietta; that she'd been everything that Congreve—both mine and Simon Jago's—could ever have wanted in a woman. A woman Conny couldn't have resisted loving or ever stopped loving; that for him there could never have been any other woman. Leona's eyes had sparkled like sunshine and rain on water.

There were more voices as people came into the corridor, a party of five or six. We snatched another kiss before saying goodnight—just being casually demonstrative the way showbiz people are with one another, as anyone passing by us would presumably have been thinking.

10

CONGREVE: LIFE AS GOOD ART

MARISSA FORD reflects on Timothy Hainault's CONGRAVINO at Stratford

Historical fiction, drama or film has its charms and curiosities. A genre, however, that arguably works best when its relevance to the way we live now, and how we might wish to improve on that, is made apparent without the sniff of a lecture about it. And in that respect Timothy Hainault's drama about Restoration playwright and poet William Congreve, *Congravino*—presently onstage at the Stratford Festival and running until November 6—would seem to have succeeded. The British playwright's absorbing piece isn't as far removed in sense and sensibility from the contemporary scene as one might be inclined at first to think. Not just concerned with the making of good art—a timeless topic, in any case—the play has to do as well with making life itself a creative endeavour, and with fulfilling one's human potential in an often inhumane world; with what living well inescapably involves on a day-to-day basis. Rather more specifically, however—as Hainault has his celebrated and yet also very private dramatist eventually see it—living the good life in its best sense is more achievable when one discovers the inner means to love constantly and well some special other, and having the good fortune as well to be loved in like manner in return. But central to the play and impossible not to notice is the conspicuous difference between the pre-modern then and the postmodern now. Although Oliver Cromwell's Puritans had been sent packing (and the theatres open again to reflect that with a racy, worldly vengeance), religion was still very much in the social, cultural and political mix in Britain at the turn of the seventeenth and eighteenth centuries.

When 21-year-old William Congreve moved to London in 1691 to study and practise law, the first stirrings of the British Enlightenment were being felt in the corridors of power, in academia and also in the Church. Christianity—correctly understood—continued to be regarded as the wellspring of sound thinking, right values, acceptable conduct and the only basis of good government (in line with John Locke's generally-held ideas that reason and Scriptural revelation were reliable allies, as spelled out in his *The Reasonableness of Christianity* in 1695). In fact, Locke's calm, collected and rational religious ideas—considered fit for the best educated of persons—were already in vogue at Canterbury and throughout the Church of England in the early 1690s. Also, for all the Restoration period's materialistic and jaded attitudes and practices—as evidenced by what was then on the London stage—the literary lions of the land were as much in lockstep with Locke's views as not, along with society in general.

And it was the literary crowd young Congreve sought out soon after arriving in London—in places such as Will's Coffee House on Bow Street, where the grand old man of English letters, John Dryden, held sway. A religious man, a poet and playwright, Dryden admired Congreve's classical verse translations and befriended the bright, talented, young Yorkshireman. (Although brought up in Ireland and educated at Dublin's Trinity College, Congreve wasn't the Erin boy some have thought he was.)

He'd brought with him to London a short novel, *Incognita*, for which he quickly found a publisher. As *Congravino* tells it, he used a pen name mainly to keep his literary aspirations from his stern father, a country estate manager and old soldier. And yet like his father—as an older Congreve told a singularly unimpressed Voltaire—what he aspired to most in life was to be acknowledged as a gentleman. By that time, he'd stopped writing for the stage.

Hainault says delving into history to find your story often begins with a question: why this or that happened, usually to someone you'd not have expected it to have happened. 'You hope to come up with a possible explanation or two, but it's probably more about looking for answers than it is finding them,' he says. In this instance, the question: why had Congreve stopped writing plays so abruptly in 1700 at the height of his powers and fame as London's leading dramatist?

In Hainault's search for answers, in Act One, Congreve considers drama his true métier, even his calling in life, after the huge success of his first play *The Old Bachelor* in 1693, followed by *The Double Dealer* and *Love for Love* over the next two years, and his one tragedy *The Mourning Bride* in '97. In 1700, however, with the mixed success of *The Way of the World*—arguably his finest but also last play—Congreve sees the writing on the wall for the kind of drama he's writing and wants to write. From the start, his work had mirrored the world around him as he'd clearly observed it, the way people were; but also in his view, how society could be if the majority were open and honest with one another. The artificiality and vapid sentimentality of plays by the likes of Colley Cibber were about to take over the London stage in the name of decency and moral propriety—the kind of fare Congreve sees as not only short on artistic merit but inherently untruthful as well, and as such of not much moral worth either. And if that was what the London public wanted, as the theatre owners and producers saw it, then Congreve was no longer their man.

In *Congravino* Congreve also had his reasons for walking away from the theatre of a more directly personal sort. It had to do with how he saw himself and wished to live and conduct himself—how 'he wanted to write his own life, if you will,' Hainault says. He made reference to a quote from a Congreve biography by David Thomas (1992) in the play's program notes, pointing out that the playwright's 'whole life seemed an urbane and studied attempt to transform life's inevitable vicissitudes and disappointments, through a series of deliberately planned rational strategies, into a harmonious and pleasing pattern.' And in *Congravino* we see Congreve attempting to achieve an equanimous state of mind and heart like this in everything he puts his mind to, says or does.

What Congreve saw as best for his own well-being had been increasingly reflected in his plays as well as in his poetry. With his work for the stage there is a steady progression from earlier Restoration comedy and drama, in several respects, to be traced and tracked. Cleverness and success is no longer to be equated with what is good, with personal fulfillment and peace of mind; or appearances and wit with reality and wisdom. (Samuel Johnson was to write some years later: 'Wit can stand its ground against truth only so long.') In Congreve's last two plays, for instance, Norman Holland writes in his *The First Modern Comedies*, 'The hero retreats from the social world of deception and illusion to a personal haven of psychological truth and emotional sincerity. He discovers the heart behind the mask.'

The heart Congreve's later dramatic heroes discover is one he himself is in the process of finding as we see him in *Congravino*. 'I don't think it's much of a stretch to believe that his religious beliefs played no small part in Congreve's search for self-worth, for the soundness of mind and heart he was looking for,' Hainault says. Making his case in a relaxed, take-it-or-leave-it manner (he'd done this before, of course), he continued, 'The rational means Congreve tapped into to access the harmonious sense of well-being he was seeking are linked to what he sees as his reasonable duty to God and, with that, to his fellow man as well. A supposition the letters we have of his lend a fair weight of support to, by the way, or as I read them, anyway. I'm theorizing, of course, but as I see it, as Congreve moved on in his thirties—and now seriously questioning his ambitions in life—the more he seemed to appreciate the importance of being "a good shepherd of one's own soul," an idea that until then had been just so many words to him.' Words, in fact, Hainault puts into the mouth of Major Congreve as he sends his son off to London, along with a gift of a pearl-handled razor. And his father's admonition to take all due care of his soul in a city as full of temptation as London invariably came to mind whenever the success-hunting young writer looked in his shaving mirror.

Giving his soul's needs the attention he's certain they require, Hainault's Congreve seeks out the helpful company of both lay and clerical religionists. His chief confidante in conversations like these was Dryden, the aging poet laureate and father figure who'd become more committed to Christian thought and practice as he'd grown older. Dryden had given up writing for the theatre just as Conny, as he called him, was establishing his own lofty reputation as a playwright, and being lauded too as his mentor's worthy successor. Also, there'd been a meeting too with no less a clergyman (and writer) than Jonathan Swift, whom Congreve had known at Trinity in Dublin.

And some advice too from another man of the cloth, if a different bolt of cloth—a Southwark Non-Conformist pastor, George Cockayne, a former close associate and biographer of John Bunyan. In his youth, Conny had avidly read Bunyan's best seller *The Pilgrim's Progress*, published in the1680s, as *Congravino* has it; and was prone to associate London with the book's year-round Vanity Fair, where everything was for sale and all of it worthless for either mind or soul. And so Conny says: 'I have good reason not to purchase property in London, since that might have me in the eyes of many so much more a part of the place than I am, and standing mostly for what the place mostly stands for.'

One denizen of Bunyan's Vanity Fair, however—and who like his fellow lost reprobates was to be avoided at any cost—was Lord Carnal Delight; and whose residence there young Conny wasn't likely to have overlooked. Let loose in London, Congreve had continued to delight in the frequent and close company of beautiful women; and all the more so if the woman who'd caught his eye had her share of brains or talent, preferably both.

Both before and during his long-lasting liaison with the dazzling Anne Bracegirdle, London's most admired and celebrated actress, there'd been other women. And in particular there'd been an accomplished singer and lutist, and also a poet and playwright—very good looking, the two of them, of course—and to both of whom Conny had professed to love ardently, in letters and in verse as well. But neither one he'd loved as he had Anne, the London theatre's 'Universal Passion,' who'd played his leading female roles. But a love, all the same, neither one of them ever declared openly to anyone.

For one thing, and not the usual thing either, as the common perception then of actresses as wantons would suggest, Anne had an unreproachable personal reputation she wanted to maintain just as much as Congreve did his as a prominent civil servant. Marriage was never in the picture, of course. Gentlemen, or would-be gentlemen, did not give their names to actresses. And, in any case, in *Congravino,* Anne wasn't looking to marry Conny. With so strong a sense of her own personality and individuality—much like Millamant's in *The Way of the World* whom she'd played—marriage would not have allowed Anne the freedom of thought, belief or movement she was convinced her very nature and being depended on. Finally, after the two had disconnected romantically, Congreve implied in verse that Anne and love had played him falsely; a highly questionable claim, involved as he was by then with Henrietta, the young Duchess of Marlborough.

When Congreve first met the duchess in 1705 after an opera at the new Haymarket Theatre, the bright, attractive 24-year-old Henrietta had been married for seven years; the wife of Francis Godolphin, son of the first Earl of Godolphin. Congreve loved her at first sight, and in due course she became the love of his life for as long as he was to live, and he hers.

Based on the available evidence—and certainly as we see them in *Congravino*—the love Congreve and Henrietta had for one another was the real thing, unconditional and unstinting. Their unfaltering romance was a 'marriage of true minds,' admitting no impediments, never altering when alteration found—an 'ever-fixed mark' for each of them. Their relationship had lasted a decade when they'd had 'a love child' together—a daughter, Mary, of whom Henrietta says in the play, after his death, 'I look on her every day and see her dear father, and I am reminded once again of his constancy in love, which blessed me at every turn.' Henrietta had insisted he be buried in Westminster Abbey, dictating every aspect of how he was to be publically remembered. Her inscription on his memorial plaque referred to 'the happiness and honour' she'd enjoyed in his company. And prompting her mother Sarah, the older Duchess of Marlborough, to remark, 'I know not what happiness she might have had in his company, but I am sure it was no honour.' (Mother and daughter were not close, argued over most things, and at loggerheads most of all over Congreve; Sarah habitually called Henrietta his 'moll.')

As with Anne, the more so with Henrietta for Conny, however: their love would never be on public display or ever openly acknowledged by society. Given the difference in class and social standing between them—Henrietta was in fact the Marlboroughs' ducal successor—there'd been no possibility whatsoever of their ever marrying. A divorce for her would have been unthinkable, completely beyond the pale.

In *Congravino*, the paramount importance of Congreve having at different times both Anne and Henrietta in his life couldn't have been made any clearer than Hainault has made it. In his twenties—in the more public phase of Conny's life as an acclaimed playwright—Anne was for him not only his secret love but also his muse as well. After meeting Anne during rehearsals for his first play, he'd written a part for her as his romantic heroine in each of the four that were to follow. In the latter, much less public part of his life, however, with Henrietta at the centre of everything for him, he was never to look twice at another woman. Congreve had found in the duchess and the love they'd shared the equilibrium, that haven of psychological truth and emotional security which for him made for harmonious and pleasurable living. In other words, Henrietta had enabled him to 'write' the rest of his life much as he'd wanted to. Just so long as he had Henrietta as his constant friend and lover, what else would he ever want or need in life? What else could possibly matter to him? To all intents and purposes, Conny's life with Henrietta was in itself a work of art. For she too had served as his muse, but on a deeper mind-and-heart level in an infinitely more significant and affecting way than had Anne.

Hainault's Conny has few if any troubling doubts about the morality of his illicit attachment to Henrietta (or of the effect it might be having on the status of his eternal soul). In fact, they both see their unlikely and yet enduring relationship as a redeeming and restorative factor in their lives; as all part of some life-changing and fulfilling divine plan they could never have conceived themselves. There's a telling and touching scene, early on in their relationship, after Henrietta's near-death case of smallpox threatens to marr her beauty. She meets Conny for the first time after her recovery, and lifting her veil she fears the worst. But with no visible shock or hesitation, Conny tells her he sees only the woman he loves and adores, heart and soul; that nothing would ever change her God-given beauty in his eyes. And months later, in another scene, after her blemishes have faded faster than expected, she tells him: 'Because you never saw my offending marks, I stopped seeing them too. And no longer serving their disheartening purpose, they were thus sent expressly on their way.' (Her mother acknowledges her daughter's renewed prettiness in person, but sees no difference, though, in her less than pretty manner towards her.) And Henrietta goes on to tell Conny that his love has a miraculous power to make all things right again in her life; that 'your love must have healing qualities of every sort for me.'

In the main, though, Hainault doesn't dwell on any connections between the couple's love for one another and their love for God. He touches on anything of that sort, in most cases, almost incidentally; as if, like his two lovers, he takes them for granted. For instance, there is a convivial, high-spirited scene towards the end of the play in which Conny is drinking and playing cards with some cronies of his. And all at once, seriously and sadly, Alexander Pope complains to Conny that in attending so much to the young Duchess of Marl, he'd forsaken his good friends and, worse still, neglected his literary gift as well. And Conny replies, 'I must ask you, then, dear Alex, to understand me best in this one thing: that the lady you speak of, she *is* my gift. The lady is no less than everything to me, indeed the very making of me—a present to me within the giving of only God himself. And loving her, as she indeed loves me, is now the art in life I aspire to create more than any other.'

All told, *Congravino* is an engrossing and entertaining piece of theatre, fully deserving of its success in the U.K., as it will almost certainly enjoy here too. All told, though, the play's romanticism and particular kind of high-mindedness, and its relevance in contrast to the way life is lived now is hardly your average postmodernist's cup of tea. Still, as Ionesco said in 1985, his work wasn't intended to condemn and ridicule society, but rather 'to show what man may become when he is cut off from all transcendence.' And as no more contemporary a playwright and insightful a chronicler of our times, David Hare, says: 'If a writer doesn't have a sense of the other, by which I mean spirit or soul, I don't want to know.'

The Globe and Mail
Saturday June 5 1999

11

A quickly passing summer for me that year; in the always beckoning Oxfordshire countryside. Each time, driving to and from Hookey, the more it seemed like going and leaving home. Hook Norton's success and my own good form on the cricket field, as well as having helped make the club's new pavilion a reality, had played a contributory part in that, I reckoned. (But which isn't to say the pull that London has for me seemed to have lessened much.) My social life, such as it was—just about all of it in Hookey—consisted almost entirely of after-match or late evening pub get-togethers, committee meetings and the occasional good, square meal at Dad and Sally's in Banbury. In reckoning I survived on food out of a tin or a packet, or on so-so pub nosh, my stepmother was only half right—but closer to the mark in thinking that Dad and I had spent too little time in each other's company for too long a time; and in considering our attempts at any meaningful communication as 'more like something in the 1930s than the '90s.'

The work I'd thought I could gently ease my way through during the summer while staying clear of the city's 'madding crowd' was just a nice thought, it turned out. With the rewrites for *The Chief* finally out of the way, I wasn't able to relax for long, however. My agent Gerry Atherton had excelled himself, coming up with one, then two script commissions for major screen projects—one scheduled to go before the cameras in spring 2000, the other in the summer. The first, a television three-parter about Charles Dickens in America, a BBC/PBS (U.S.) joint production; and the second, an even more exciting challenge (and a first for me): an Anglo-American feature film production of *Congravino*. Hard to believe, but Conny and his two lovely women were destined for the big screen. The deadline for the television script was January 1, 2000; with an only slightly less demanding one, January 15, for the film. Suddenly, just like that, in the space of ten days, I'd got my work well and truly cut out for me.

With *Congravino*, working with one's own material, the choices of what to include or leave out would make the job so much the harder, I'd realized, of course. Writing for the cinema is always about paring down and getting on with the story. About adapting his own play, *The Madness of King George III*, for the screen, Alan Bennett writes (in *Writing Home*): 'Film is drama at its most impatient, "What happens next?" the perpetual nag. One can never hang about.' Whereas with the telly, with the viewers closer to the characters, you can dawdle a bit, Bennett maintains.

Telling the Dickens story as I'd chosen to entailed probing as insightfully as possible into some personally affecting experiences of the novelist's between his two stateside visits, some twenty-five years apart, and dealing with his problematic relationships with parents, wife and children, as well as his affections for his sister-in-law Mary Hogarth and actress Ellen Ternan. In other words, I was probing into the private man behind the public figure, as one is duty bound to do. And I'd found myself keying on a discerning point Peter Ackroyd had made in his definitive Dickens biography about the author while he was in America for the second time: that 'despite his conviviality and his need for friendship and love, he was in many respects an utterly private and enclosed man. He needed time alone; time for writing, of course, but also time for the kind of self-communing through which, as he said, he was able to "understand my own feelings the better." The isolated child was also the isolated man and he needed that isolation, however temporary it was; he hugged it to him as if in its enclosure he might remain true to himself.' I knew the feeling.

And as for that—my own need for friendship and love, and, as a writer, the enclosed and isolated sort of man I might well be developing into—the absence of a woman in my life, a significant other, wasn't going unnoticed by those I was closest to; although never remarked on in my presence except by Kell, along with an inference or two from Sally. But then nobody knew what was in fact going on with me in that particular department: the waiting-for-Leona game I was playing. (Although, in reality, I'm sure Leona would have been as surprised as anyone to realize the extent and depth of my feelings for her.) It was, of course, all that mileage over land and ocean that lay between us; that would always be the main problem. Separation, however much of it, isn't the end of love between lovers, true—but it's rarely the start of something that leads to love, either.

I'd told Leona about the work I'd let myself in for over the next few months. She said she was happy for me, particularly about the *Congravino* film, and wished me all the best with it. I said, 'I've never had two things on the go like this—hard-and-fast jobs, I mean, not the speculative stuff. It's a bit of a slog; it's about all I can think of right now. Even taking some time out to eat and sleep makes me feel I'm skiving off, letting my concentration slip, or something. Not that I'm complaining, though, of course. I'm up to my neck, sure, but in my element, obviously.'

'Yes, Tim, I can imagine.' And could understand too, she said, how single-minded I'd have to be about what I was doing. And could appreciate too, she assured me, that loosening up the time to get back to Canada before the SF's season was over might present a problem for me. 'Which isn't to say, Tim, I'm letting you off the hook about coming—because I'd be very disappointed if you didn't.'

'I know, Leona. And I'd be very disappointed not making it too.' And wanting to please her—but mindful too of my deadlines, and playing it as safe as I could—I'd committed myself to some actual dates: the last ones available to me, actually. I told her I'd be over for the Festival's closing weekend at the end of October to see her *Love's Labour's Lost* and again in *Congravino*.

After expressing her delight, she said, 'Tell you what, Tim. When you come, maybe you could stay on an extra day or two. We could spend a bit of time together here and in Toronto. Think about it, anyhow, all right?'

An incentive to get back to my work if ever there was one.

Sally had anticipated as much: Dad's rambling days were numbered. She'd finally got it into his head that going off alone for jaunts into the countryside, even with a mobile, wasn't on for him anymore; but not before his GP had told him the same thing. His doctor had been treating him for some heartbeat irregularities. And not long after that, after a spell he'd had behind the wheel on a side road—he'd swerved off into nothing more solid than a hedgerow, fortunately—Dad had had to concede too that his driving days were over for the time being as well.

Following a battery of tests, his medical advisors determined that bypass surgery was required—news Dad had accepted with equanimity, and on which he'd taken an optimistic slant. He told Sally the operation would make a new man of him, wipe the worry from her eyes, and let her concentrate again on helping Roz with the business, which he knew she loved doing. 'Loving you, that's what I love doing,' she'd replied. He'd probably said it was the same thing for him as well. He and Sally's autumn love for each other—after, metaphorically, a summer-long absence of it in their lives—was as clear to see as sunlight streaming through a window, four years on in their marriage though they were.

Dad was to go under the knife in a private clinic in Oxford run by an old surgeon friend of Sally's. 'Waiting for God is one thing—waiting for the NHS is another,' she'd told me. She'd phoned in October to confirm that Dad's surgery was scheduled for later in the month, for Friday the 29th, and assuming, I had to think, that I'd do everything I could to be at the hospital for Dad. But I couldn't be in two places at the same time, of course. I was due that same day to fly to Toronto for the SF's closing weekend. I'd not got around to mentioning this to either Dad or Sally.

Of course, there wasn't much of a decision to be made. I cancelled my airline ticket and phoned Leona. She said, 'There's no need to apologize, Tim, there really isn't. Where else would you want to be?' She asked me to be sure to let her know how the surgery had gone. I told her there was no reason to think that it wouldn't go well, that no complications were expected. 'Well, let's hope and pray there won't be, Tim,' she'd said. ('Pray?' I'd thought.) 'I'll be thinking positive thoughts for him, anyhow.' Had she read my mind?

'Thank you, Leona. I'm going to be sorry, I know I am, to miss your Rosalinde—systematically blowing Biron's mind and heart, as she does. Still, I will be seeing your Henrietta again in New York, lucky me—and have her work her magic on me once more, only more so, probably. And best of all, of course, get to spend some time with the actress herself.'

'Up close and personal, you mean?'

'I most certainly do.'

'Yes, well, so do I, Tim. But for me, I think, a case now of believing it when I see it.'

'I'll be there, Leona, I promise.'

'You're crossing your heart and hoping to die, are you, Tim?'

'Even as we speak, Leona.'

Six days after his hardly run-of-the-mill surgery, which he'd come through with flying colours, Dad was home again—in good spirits and raring to get back to normality ASAP; but still on a half-a-day bed rest schedule, which Sally was keeping him to religiously.

Sally was in the kitchen, serving up some afternoon coffee and freshly baked scones. Dad was upstairs taking a nap.

'Are you sure you won't stay for dinner, Tim?' she asked.

'Thanks, I'd love to, but I really can't. I've a meeting first thing in the morning I'm not quite ready for.'

She nodded. 'Yes, well, you've spent a good amount of time here as it is, I realize, and which I'm very grateful to you for. It's meant a lot to your father, I know it has. I know, I'm making you feel awkward, Tim—no need for me to be grateful, and so on—but I am grateful, like it or not, so there you are.'

Into our second cup, she said, 'Before you go, Tim, I'd like to show you something.'

In the study, she asked, 'Have you seen these, Tim?' She'd pulled out three bound scrapbooks, one older looking than the other two. She didn't seem surprised when I said I hadn't. The older book went back to the seventies, containing Blenheim High theatre programmes and photographs. In another, Dad had conscientiously collected my professional press cuttings (both stage and television) including programmes, promotional material, reviews, magazine articles and captioned photographs, starting with my first play at the Nottingham Playhouse. There was provincial as well as London press stuff covering my stage plays. Sally told me, 'Your agent kept your dad informed when and wherever one of your shows was on.' Gerry hadn't said a word to me; on my father's instructions, probably.

The more recent scrapbook, devoted entirely to *Congravino,* was only three quarters full, a work in progress. To get hold of the latest entries—the Toronto and Montreal reviews and articles including Marissa Ford's lengthy piece and the SF programme—he'd enlisted the aid of my by then widowed (but still circulating) Aunt Pam, now living in Toronto. 'Pamela told your father you must have got some of your talent for telling a good story from your grandfather,' Sally said. 'She says she still enjoys having Art on about their father's genes showing up in his, which I found amusing.'

She continued, 'You know, Tim, your father doesn't seem able to get enough of your "Congravino." You'd almost think he was obsessed with it.

I'm sure he hasn't told you, but we ended up seeing it five times, twice at Chichester as well as in London.'

'No, he didn't tell me.'

'He's got the play script too, which he studies like he's doing a thesis on it. There are lines underlined and notes in the margins on nearly every page. He can quote lines at the drop of a hat. And judging by the library books he's borrowing, I think he's checking your research, too.'

'Does he discuss the play with you, then?'

'Oh, yes. He says he likes hearing my opinions, that I'm more theatre savvy than he is.'

'He's not said very much to me about it.'

'No, well, he wouldn't have. He knows you're not keen on talking about your work. He's read what you've told interviewers about that. But he did say that one of these days maybe the two of you could sit down and have a real good discussion about what you've written.'

'About "Congravino" in particular, did he say?'

'No, he didn't. But I assuming he'd have that in mind, certainly. I have a theory. Your father's got this idea, I think, that the better he gets to understand your plays, especially your latest one, the better he's going to understand you, Tim. Who you are, what you think and believe, what's important to you—as an adult, I'm talking about. I'm not sure he feels that he's ever really got to know you, Tim, not since you left home—not the way a father usually wants to know his only son, anyway. But like I say, it's just a theory of mine, that's all.'

And, when I thought about it, perhaps not such an outlandish theory of Sally's at that. And, for her, there had to be something sadly amiss between Dad and I to have had a theory like that come to mind in the first place.

12

I phoned Kell; he'd needed to know. I reached him in Toronto. He'd accepted my explanation with no more grace than he'd reckoned it deserved, I suppose it was. He'd been expecting me in New York the second week in November to help promote the *Congravino* opening at the St. James's. But with the Dickens script not close to being finished—and at the beck and call as I was of director Colin Izzard and the producers for more script conferences than I'd bargained for—I'd had to beg off. Still, I remained as determined as ever to see my play on Broadway. Telling Kell this, he said, 'I should bloody well think so too, chummy. You probably won't ever get another chance.' (Closing night was December 11, a Saturday.)

He also said, 'Well, when you finally do show up, let's hope you'll be here in time to help me with Jacie Girl.'

'Help you how, exactly?'

'Help her as only her two dearest and loving friends can, of course. A double dose of the sort of advice she knows she can count on, as always, coming from both of us.'

I didn't much care for the sound of that.

Drew Schaeffer had reared his clever and handsome head again, apparently.

Whatever it was that Jace and Schaeffer had had together personally had come to a rather abrupt end in late summer, Kell said. 'And I couldn't have been happier about it, I don't have to tell you, I'm sure.' He didn't. Simon Jago told him later that it was questionable whether or not Jace had ever expected Schaeffer to leave his wife for her. But he hadn't done so, clearly, and the two had stopped seeing one another. (Maybe his wife had put an elegant foot down at long last.) How sad either one had been to part they'd kept strictly to themselves.

'The thing is, Tim, who knows if it really is over between them?' Kell went on. I was afraid he was going to. 'I know Jacie was planning to return to London before the year's out, she told me she was—and back in London she most certainly should be, as quick as she can, as you agree with me, I know you do.' Well, I did know, at any rate, that Jace was in demand in the U.K.—that both the National and the RSC, and also Teddy Bentley at the Old Vic, were lining up to get her on their stages in 2000. 'But now Schaeffer's right back in the frame, would you believe? He's whispering sweet somethings of one kind or another in Jacie's shell-like. He's pressing the dear girl to stay in New York and join Millennium Three—a new theatre company the three amigos, Freddy Flaxman, Jago and Schaeffer, have put together.' Based in New York, with a film and video production arm as well, the company was planning to present an American and international (including Shakespeare) classical bill of fare. Also, Los Angeles, Chicago and Boston were to be included in a tour itinerary. 'Anyway, Schaeffer and Jago, between them, have got Jacie's full attention. They're dangling some choice roles under her nose, you can bet on it.'

He couldn't have missed the sigh with which I'd preceded my response. 'Well, you know, Kell, I really can't remember Jace letting anyone influence her about what to do next, except her agent, possibly. Unless, of course, you're suggesting that this time she'll be letting something other than professional considerations affect her decision.'

Which was, of course, exactly what Kell was suggesting. 'Yes, well, that's it, isn't it? The fact is, I can't see Schaeffer caring very much at all about what he has to do to get Jacie Girl to join his happy band, just as long as she does. I've got this feeling—and it's not a pleasant one—that the tricky blighter, with that smile and smooth way of his, that he won't think twice about playing fast and loose with Jacie's emotions, if that's what it takes. And without turning a manicured hair, I can see him justifying any personal pain he's caused her just by reminding her of the artistic and financial good he'd done her.' And with a fair imitation of Schaeffer's sonorous, well-articulated voice: 'Sorry about that, darling—but I could have sworn it was all business with you as well.'

It had to be said: 'Well, Kell, as I see it, whatever Jace and Schaeffer decide to get up to together, professionally or personally, it certainly isn't any business of mine—or yours either, for that matter. And I'd be very surprised indeed if Jace didn't see it that way as well.'

Not in any way the kind of response Kell had been looking from me, of course. But he was going to have lump it, wasn't he?

But it wasn't just Kell, obviously; I was going to have to phone Leona as well. She too had been expecting me to be there for the *Congravino* opening on The Big White Way, of course. Her usual bright, charming and communicative self, she'd phoned just the day before to tell me where she was staying in Manhattan; that she'd told the hotel's protective front desk staff to put my call through to her room. And also about a restaurant she liked and thought I would too.

This time, though, Leona didn't even try to hide her disappointment over my opening night no-show. This she'd indicated as much by her silences on the other end of the line—I'd heard background sounds of police or ambulance sirens during the pauses—as by anything she'd said. She did remind me, though, of what she'd said before; about seeing me when she saw me, and having to have to leave it at that. And also, 'Maybe, Timothy, the next time you call, it'll be from a Manhattan number. That way, we'll both know where we are, and what's up, won't we?'

We didn't talk for long. She had to go; she'd got things to do, she said.

13

I thought I'd surprise Leona in New York—not the best idea I've ever had.

Keeping my travel plans to myself, I flew into Kennedy the last Saturday in November. I booked into the Chelsea on W.23rd—a three-night reservation I'd made on a whim. (The hotel's historic literary associations—on its facade are name plaques for former guests such as Mark Twain, Tennessee Williams and Dylan Thomas, the last of whom had died before checking out—had appealed to me.) I'd not wanted Kell getting into the act, marshalling me around, and possibly setting something up with Jace, for either the two or the three of us.

The two Stratford Festival shows at the St. James's on W.44th were playing in repertory, with Saturday and Sunday performances for both *Congravino* and *All My Sons.* (The Monday was dark.) Aware that by 10 p.m. NY time I'd be battling jet lag and probably not winning, I decided to give my play's Saturday evening performance a miss, and take in the Sunday matinee instead. And anticipating going back after the show and surprising Leona, I reckoned we'd have something to eat before catching the Miller play in the evening, and then go on somewhere afterwards. First thing on the Monday, I wanted to do some work in the NY Public Library—I'd greatly benefitted from its Berg Collection of Charles Dickens correspondence—and after that, from midday on, I'd planned on spending the rest of the day with Leona.

Things started off well enough. I'd thoroughly enjoyed the play. And when I'd made my appearance in Leona's dressing room, she'd fallen on me as one might have a long lost brother. We'd hardly disengaged, however, when there was a knock on the door; and invited to enter was none other than another visitor from London, Sean Blake.

The still boyish, good-looking artistic director at the Donmar in Covent Garden (he was well into his thirties) wasn't any more pleased to see me, I think, than I was to see him. He'd seemed relieved and pleased, though, when Leona told him she'd had no idea that I was in town as well. As he saw it, I suppose, his rights of first access to Leona that weekend were no longer in question. He'd flown in on Friday evening, some twenty-four hours ahead of me (and would be flying out, as I would be as well, on Tuesday morning). Also, unlike me, he'd been expected. I knew, there and then, where I stood in the line for Leona's company for the next day or so.

Blake's interest in working with Leona must have gone up a few notches, bringing him to New York in the middle of the season as it had. He'd sat in on the Saturday evening performance of *Congravino* as well, expressly to see Leona, obviously. And she, in turn, was giving him as much of her attention as possible. She was going to have dinner with him that evening—at the Algonquin's Rose Room, she informed me. He was pulling out all the stops for her.

And there was more disappointment to come. Leona and Blake had made arrangements for lunch and visits to the Empire State building and the Guggenheim on the Monday. Not only that, she told me apologetically, she would be attending a dinner party at the Flaxman's Central Park apartment that evening, along with Jace and Kell, Drew and Melanie Schaeffer, Simon Jago and his wife; and another coup for Millennium, Broadway's latest favourite flavour, the tall, dark and handsome Warren Kester. He and Leona would be making up the dinner pairings, presumably.

Leona said she wasn't exactly sure why she'd been invited. 'I'm not that keen to go, actually. But as Simon says, turning down an invitation from Freddie Flaxman, cocking a snoop at him like that, wouldn't be the smartest thing for any actor in New York to do. Kellison tells me that Jacinth isn't jumping at Millennium's offer, being very cagey about it. He's advising her against it, saying she should get back to London where she belongs. His theory is that Schaeffer has me in mind if Jacinth turns him down. Mind you, though, nothing like that's been said to me'

I felt my throat constricting as I asked, 'And if Millennium does come in for you?'

'Well, I'd listen, I know that—you know: good work, good company to be in, and pretty good money, I suppose. And New York, New York—all that jazz too, of course. But then there's you, Tim—what you're telling me—and Kellison too. In his view, for an actor with any real classical ambitions, it's London, or nowhere. A risk I must dare to take, he says; it's now or maybe never for me, and so on. He says he's seriously thinking about going back himself when his contract's up. There's also Sean as well, of course. He's very serious about getting me to the Donmar. He must be, I guess, coming over to see my Henrietta, and making the sounds he's been making.'

Reasonably confident his Donmar contract would be renewed in March, Blake was tentatively planning his 2000-'01 season. He was considering a Mamet play and also *The Misanthrope,* each with a role Leona would be 'spot on for,' he'd told her. Leona as Moliere's Celimene, whom the infatuated Alceste calls 'a baited barb of beauty,' would be something to see, I couldn't deny.

In any event, the schedule I'd had in mind in New York for Leona and I wasn't even in shreds; it had disintegrated altogether. (A 'shambolic balls-up,' Kell would have called it—'a laugher or a cryer, take your pick.') I stayed longer in the NYPL than I'd planned on the Monday, and in the evening went to a New York Rangers hockey game at Madison Square Garden. (Not a lot of goals for my money, but quite a few fights, though.) It wasn't cricket, certainly.

Still, Leona and I did manage a late afternoon phone call, around forty minutes long. I might just as well been calling from a central London number. In short, just more of the same for us: a means of communication leaving a lot to be desired.

We talked about the SF's *Congravino* the previous day. I'd told her in the dressing room I'd found the performance as fresh and focussed as I'd remembered it in Stratford, if not even more so—buoyed up as well by having a Broadway audience to play to, perhaps. I'd reiterated too that her Henrietta had very likely moved up a degree or two in its overall impact and effectiveness, if anything—as effective and affecting as before. There wasn't a lot more I could have added that I'd not already said. I did say, though, 'You were using the same spell that had worked on me at Stratford, obviously.'

But actors rarely swallow whole what people tell them about their performances, in dressing rooms or anywhere else. And again, if I was hearing correctly what Leona was saying between the lines on the line—I'd also suspected as much in Stratford on opening night (when I could see her eyes)—she may still have been nursing some misgivings about her performance in comparison to Olivia Lennox's young duchess in the

London and Chichester productions. She'd read, I knew, the London reviews, and also what I'd said on record about the excitement I'd felt seeing Lennox and Sam Tolliver (and Craddock as well) 'get into the heads and under the skin' of their characters as comprehensively as they had. There is, perhaps, a frisson only playwrights experience seeing a character of theirs brought off the written page and on to the stage for the first time, and in so fine a fashion. (Whether or not, though, I'd made a complex and hard to explain connection, emotionally and psychologically, with the actresses who'd first played my characters—if not in Lennox's case, but certainly in Sam's, with her Anne Bracegirdle and her much earlier Jessie Chambers, and also with Jace's Natasha Fenner and Belinda Tranter's Julie Capp—that was decidedly quite another matter I will probably never get to the bottom of.)

With a carefulness I'd got better at with practice, I said, 'Anyway, Leona, the more I think of your Henrietta, there really isn't a thing, nothing at all, I'd have liked to have seen you do differently with her.' Music to her ears, she'd said that had been.

There wasn't much that Leona didn't know about what was presently onstage in, or scheduled for London in 2000; and in some provincial centres as well. 'That's because I'm always picking up British papers, and every week the Sunday Times, devouring its culture mag section,' she said. 'Which reminds me, Tim, how come I had to read in the paper about a new London production of your D.H. Lawrence play? In February, isn't it? With London's bright new lights, Vince Dunleavey and Alicia Fewster, no less, as Lawrence and Jessie Chambers.'

'Didn't I tell you?'

'Not a word.'

'Sorry about that. I thought I had. Sometimes, when I'm writing, I can lose track of what's going on just the other side of my door.'

'Yes, of course, Tim. That old and tired excuse writers seem to be so fond of.' Said with a little scoffing laugh. 'Who is directing, by the way?'

'Julian Caverley, I'm very happy to say.'

'Yes, I'm sure you are, Tim. And good for him too, getting what he richly deserves at last.' She knew, obviously, he'd directed the original production; and that if life was fair he'd have also been at the helm in London as well. Speaking of which, she said, her good friends in Stratford, Barton and Lois Heddle, who faithfully made an annual early-in-the-year theatrical pilgrimage to London, had already got their tickets for the

Writing and Loving . . . remount. 'Bart's heard about you being here, by the way. I was talking to him in the hotel coffee shop this morning. He asked me if I thought you'd mind if they looked you up in London. Lois is itching to meet you. He was wondering if you might like to have lunch, or dinner, with them.' I said I'd like that, and asked her to pass on my home phone number to Bart, which seemed to have pleased her.

Heddle had assumed, I suppose, that Leona and I would be seeing each other while I was in New York. I conjectured too if he and his wife, especially Lois, knew in any detail about the attachment Leona and I had formed. Presumably, though, Bart hadn't taken it for granted that Leona would be in London in February. If he had—as I'd reckoned it, anyway—why hadn't he suggested the four of us get together while he and Lois were in town?

About that—Leona's coming to London—she'd added little to what she'd said the day before about her discussions with Sean Blake. She did tell me her former agent in the U.K. was no longer in the business; and also that Jace had suggested she contact Ursula. She asked, 'D'you think she'd even consider representing me, the distinguished list of clients she has?' I said I didn't see why not. I reminded her that both Ursula and Teddy Bentley had been highly impressed by her work in *Congravino.* (But perhaps more dressing room plaudits she'd not accepted at face value?)

She said she'd be spending Christmas—'well, Hanukkah, anyhow'—and celebrating the incoming new millennium with her parents in Vancouver. 'We may also pop down to San Francisco for a few days. My mother's connections with quite a few people down there run pretty deep. She wants me to meet them.' And also said: that if she did get an offer from Millennium Three, she'd not be discussing it with her parents. 'I don't have to guess what they'd say, specially my mother. She's got a sister in New York, for one thing.'

She admitted she'd still not come to terms with what had happened to change her father so much; and why and how this had played the part it had in bringing her parents together again. 'I still can't fathom it. It's like Dad and Merle—I still have trouble calling her Mom—are using another language I'll have to learn to understand what's going on with them, what they're really all about. Mind you, I could be trying to understand a lot harder than I've been doing so far, I guess. The funny thing is, though, Tim—and this is quite ironic, it really is—I'm the one who's responsible, in a way, for the new man and reclaimed husband my father has turned into. D'you recall me telling you I'd lost patience with him, how I'd strong-armed him to go see a psychiatrist to deal with his depression? A last-gasp therapist, you might say—by the name of Lee Slazenger. He'd been recommended to me, actually, by Lois Heddle. I'd been bending her ear by long distance about my father.'

Slazenger had studied with Lois at Western, and, like her, he hadn't got himself entrenched professionally in either the Freudian or the Jungian camp, Leona said. But neither one, however, could live with Freud's inability to perceive religious experience except as a pathological problem. 'Also, Lois has always been drawn to Jung's exploration of the creative faculty as reflected in art of every kind—and about which, she says, Freud admitted to having no explanation.' And she said that along with Slazenger, a practising Jew, Lois considers Freud's reductionist and deterministic theories as extremely sad and fatalistic, leaving people at the mercy of their impulses; and, as a result, stuck with a very problematic sense of personal identity—with one's future possibilities left up in the air. (Something along those lines, anyway.) 'To tell the truth, Tim, just so long as Slazenger could keep my father going to him, I was going to count my lucky stars, and keep my fingers crossed on both hands. My father had already dumped two other therapists after only one session.'

(As she spoke, I'd been reminded of an exhaustive, in-depth study I'd read about, that had concluded the only thing any 'trick cyclist' knows for certain is that the people they treat, when given half a chance, like to talk.)

'Anyhow, Tim, I think I've told you the rest—my dad's three months of therapy with Slazenger, his synagogue going and the sessions with the learned rabbi, all that. Of course, my father knew how taken aback I was, to put it mildly, by the effect this had had on him; and particularly by the brand new sense of his own self he said he'd gained. But he was reluctant to talk about it in any detail. He said there was a lot of explaining to himself he still had to do, let alone to anybody else; and that even then he wasn't going to expect anyone to make much sense of it.'

Leona had talked to Lois Heddle about her father's remarkable transformation, and had inquired as well about Slazenger. Lois said her former student was known to espouse logotherapy—a psychoanalytical method originated by psychiatrist, Viktor Frankl. But not a course of treatment Slazenger used exclusively, however. Lois had been quick to add too that Slazenger hadn't consulted her in connection with Nathan

Fielder's treatment; and that she'd prefer not to comment further on the matter, if Leona didn't mind.

Viktor Frankl's name rang a bell. After getting off the phone, I'd mentally fast-forwarded through some of the psychology I'd read (de rigueur for a writer of my sort), both Freudian and Jungian. And before long I was back in time to one of Olive Cromwell's classes at Cliff Place Methodist in the seventies. My brother Paul was weighing in as usual, making a point during a discussion, backing up a point of his with something he'd read written by Frankl from his *Man's Search for Meaning*—one of several books Paul had recommended to me; and, as it happened, one of the few I'd actually got around to reading. An Austrian Jew, the lesser known third member of what was sometimes called 'The Viennese School of Therapy,' Viktor Frankl was the school's odd man out, having taken a clearly different therapeutic approach than had either Freud and Adler, developing and applyinging his logotherapy methodology. As Frankl's seminal book title makes clear, his theories and work focus on 'the will to meaning' in man's constant search for fulfillment and satisfaction in life—in sharp contrast, he maintained, to Freud's 'the will to pleasure' and Adler's 'the will to power.'

Leona said she'd not as yet read Frankl's book, but intended to sooner or later. 'I'm sure I can find a copy in New York, if it's still in print. Lois says it's not heavy-going stuff, a lot of it biographical, and written in down-to-earth terms. When I see my father next, it could be a conversation starter for us, if nothing else. Like they say, there's nothing like a book—or a film or a play, for that matter—to get people talking, and maybe opening up about things that actually matter to them, whether they'd intended to or not.'

Sally would almost certainly have agreed with her on that. But then Leona went on to say, 'Mind you, I can't say I've ever been much good at sharing anything with anyone, on a personal level, I mean. I'm not a "heart on my sleeve" sort of person. I tell myself, I'm playing it smart, of course. That it's a self-protective thing—like, knowledge is power, and the more people know about you, the more power they have over you, that kind of thing. But then again, I guess, that's where love and trust come into it, in a relationship, one that counts for something, I'm saying. The sort of wonderful relationship that Bart and Lois have—the way they are so consistently with one another.' Then interrupting herself: 'Good God, it's quarter to five! I've got to go! I can't go to the Flaxmans looking like something the cat dragged in.' As if she ever could have done.

We said our goodbyes. Talking about love and trust with Leona, about experiencing a relationship together that counted for something, was something for another day—one I could only hope wouldn't be too far distant.

14

Back in London, it was immediately back to the blank page for me—to my own world as a writer, getting the Dickens and the *Congravino* scripts completed. The January deadlines for both were quickly bearing down on me. Except to go out for groceries and an occasional pint and sandwich at The Queen's Head, I was holed up in the Brook Green flat for most of December, lying low, out of sight, like an informant under wraps in a MI5 safe house.

Except for one overnight stay—on Christmas Eve—I didn't get back to Hook Norton until late January. I'd gone to the service of carols and lessons at St. Peter's that night with Dad and Sally. Sally had missed only one such service since leaving Hookey as a teenager. My good friend and fellow cricket player, the Reverend Ash Bonnar, kept any surprise he'd felt in seeing me in his church to himself. Presumably, he'd counted me in with a fair number of local residents who are never to be seen in St. Peter's at any time in the year other than for this one traditional service, without which Christmas wouldn't have been the same for most Hookeyites, I expect. I'd spent Christmas Day in Banbury, where it had been just the three of us. Roz and Karl, her husband-to-be that coming summer, had gone to his parents in Switzerland for Christmas.

Sally said she'd read that the Bristol Old Vic was putting on *Congravino* in March. 'Your father wants to see it, surprise, surprise. Are you thinking of going at all?' I said I'd likely be making the trip sometime during the run, and Sally had wondered if perhaps we could go together. 'Yes, why not?' I said. 'Maybe we could stay overnight somewhere. I would be happy to drive you down.' She smiled. 'That would be lovely, Tim—and not nearly so tiring for your father, too.' And the chances of lessening the distance between Dad and I with some discussion about the play had just improved quite a bit, she was probably thinking, too.

Letting myself loose in London for a few hours after completing the Dickens script—I'd needed a haircut, for one thing—I'd also picked up a copy of Viktor Frankl's *Man's Search for Meaning* in one of my usual bookshop haunts on the Charing Cross Road; and which I'd started reading on the tube back to Hammersmith. It isn't a long book; I'd finished it the next night. (First published in German in 1946, and in English in the U.S. in '59, my copy was the revised '84 edition.) It occurred to me that Leona might have been hoping I'd brush up on my Frankl to facilitate some further discussion between us on the man and his logotherapy.

Along with his two more famous Viennese contemporaries, Frankl was carrying the religious and cultural baggage that came with the trio's common backgrounds and heritage. But as their careers developed, Frankl's psychiatric regimen and practises could hardly have been more different from those of Freud's and Adler's. Frankl never strayed far from the synagogue. His logotherapy is inherently based on a belief in God—or, if you prefer, in a 'Super-Meaning.' The system's all-important central premise is the role the transcendental plays in shaping one's life; a process of both mind and heart providing the inner wherewithal to live as a creative, fully-realized human being. In sum, a means of being one's own true self, at home with oneself, and able to express that self in a manner you and others can live with and benefit from, both emotionally and psychologically.

Frankl wrote that logotherapy may conform to some of the training and licensing requirements of other schools of psychotherapy—that a logotherapist 'may howl with the wolves, if need be'—but, at the same time, be in fact 'a sheep in wolf's clothing.' He claimed that in the history of psychotherapy there isn't a less dogmatic therapeutic system than his. 'My interest does not lie in raising parrots that just rehash "their master's voice," but rather in passing the torch to independent and inventive, innovative and creative spirits,' he wrote.

Without doubt, personal experience had left an indelible mark on Frankl, significantly influencing his psychiatric theories. During World War II, he'd been a 'guest' of the Nazis in four concentration camps including Auschwitz, for three years in all. In its initial form, the manuscript of his book he'd sewn into the lining of his overcoat, only to have it discovered and destroyed by a camp guard. Single-minded and undeterred, Frankl used whatever scraps of paper he could find and keep hidden to start again. By the time he was released, he'd virtually completed his book's first draft.

In the unimaginably inhumane and deadly light of his camp experiences, which make up a significant portion of his book, Frankl is unable to accept the view, contrary to Freud's, that when people are reduced to the worst of extremities, they revert to brute, animalistic instinct. In the camps he learned first hand that distinct, revealing differences emerge among people in such circumstances. Individuals made choices reflecting a state of mind and spirit that was exclusively their own, and in clear contradiction to Freud's dismal contentions, Frankl points out. In fact, he says, suffering and hardship (the unavoidable sort, that is) is potentially one of three ways of finding meaning in life, depending on the attitude with which one faces such things; one can adaptively change even extremely negative experiences into positive and hopeful ones and, consequently, become a stronger and better person for it.

Each of Frankl's two other ways to meaning, however, would seem to be for most the preferable routes to go. The first involves achieving or accomplishing something in life that presumably is beneficial in some way or other to others as well as for oneself. The second entails discovering what is recognizably satisfying to you as being good, honest and true, and sometimes beautiful as well—and that may or may not include encountering one special other whose love and uniqueness you experience, and to which you respond to in like manner. (Personally, I'm looking to have it both ways, combining the two.)

There is, however, a catch, if you like, in all of this. In Frankl's logotherapeutic scheme of things, there is that problematic transcendence factor he insists on; the indispensable key, as he sees it, to the good life as he would have you envision it. Two forms of transcendence, in fact, as Frankl has it. There is, to begin with, what he calls 'self-transcendence,' which he describes as directing one's thinking and actions away from selfishly ambitious concerns and toward the needs of those whose lives intersect with yours. And then as well, of course, there is the experience of transcendence in its generally understood sense, bringing with it vision and strength from a higher source outside of yourself through religious/spiritual revelation and consciousness. (As would seem to be necessary when the self-transcendence isn't working for you as well as it should be.)

Something Frankl had written too on the subject of happiness also reminded me of what my brother Paul used to talk about: the commonly-held perception of Christians as the world's quintessentially 'unhappy campers,' and how the 'worldlings' had got it all wrong. In his book, Frankl maintained that the pursuit of happiness is in fact a misleading myth. 'Happiness cannot be pursued, it must ensue,' he wrote—that, rather, a human being is 'in search of a reason to be happy.' And that happiness comes only when one is actualizing one's human potential by finding purpose and meaning in one's everyday existence on an ongoing basis. And which logotherapy can help with when a quality existence like that isn't happening for you.

Viktor Frankl, as a psychiatrist and logotherapist (and well-rounded human being), had remained, it seemed, 'a sheep in wolf's clothing' until his death in 1997.

Two days left to go in 1999.

Sam Tolliver phoned to confirm my attendance at Julian's New Millennium's Eve party on the river at Chelsea. (Sam and Julian had been living together for several months, and there was talk, no more than that, of the two putting things between them on a 'go for it' legal footing in the spring.)

'You're bringing someone, I presume?' Sam said.

'Why? Should I be?'

'You're not, then?'

'It doesn't look like it.' Leona would be on the other side of Canada, wouldn't she? 'No, I found, when it came down to it—with all the lovely possibilities at my disposal, as you can imagine—I couldn't settle on a clear-cut first choice.'

'Oh, dear! I am sorry, luv,' she said—but far from abjectly sorry, obviously, catching as she had the vein of humour in my voice. 'You know, Tim, you really are getting to be a bit of a lone wolf these days, aren't you?'

I said I thought that might be best for me, that role, in this instance, at any rate. 'Seeing in the new century with someone—you know, the customary big hugs and kisses, and so on—it doesn't seem appropriate, somehow. Maybe meaning something I wouldn't want it to; promising something I have no intentions of following through on, that sort of thing.'

'That's rather old-fashioned of you, isn't it, Tim?'

'You're probably right, Sam. But perhaps that's my problem: being born too late for the times I got plonked down in.'

'Really? You know, Tim, that sounds suspiciously like something someone who's living in the past too much might say. Who needs to start looking ahead for a change.'

I laughed. 'Point taken, Sam.'

'Well, I do hope so, anyway. Oh, by the way, Tim. You wouldn't happened to have got a call from Alicia Fewster, have you? In the last week or so?'

'No, I haven't. Should I be expecting one?'

'Well, maybe she's planning to waylay you at the party on Saturday instead. Just giving you some advance warning, that's all, Tim. Don't fret, it's just your mind she's after, not your body—although, for all I know, maybe it's both. Anyway, Alicia's been peppering Julian with questions at rehearsals about your Jessie Chambers, and phoned me as well. She asked Julian if I'd mind. She's done her homework all right. All that big fuss after the original production, and so on. About the effect Jessie would have had on Lawrence and on his writing if he'd married her, all that. She knows you and Julian worked on the script together, and about our discussions, the three of us, about all that. And also about changing the order of the "Writing" and the "Loving" in the title. The girl knows about things I've forgotten.'

'Oh dear, oh dear. Not that again.'

'Yes, I know. Some things just won't go away and die a nice, quiet death, will they? Leavis may have been dead for twenty something years, but his "thought police" are still out there, hunting down dissenters. The thing is, anyway, Alicia's noticed the occasional subtle change you've made from the original. I think she feels you and Julian may have changed your mind on a few things about Lawrence and Jessie and their relationship, and how this might play in to what she's doing with the character—something like that, I suppose it is.'

'You think so?'

'Seems to me it is, anyway. But in any case, I wasn't going to offer an opinion, was I? I've no idea about how it was for Lawrence and Jessie, how her love and his writing affected their relationship, and I'm not sure Julian knows either; and come to that, maybe no more than you do, Tim. It's very complicated, isn't it? Mixing up one's art with one's love life, unavoidably, like that; doing your best to determine and sort out where your real passion lies.'

Later, it occurred to me I could have told Sam I'd made some headway in trying to sort out that very thing since my *Writing and Loving* . . . days in Nottingham. But not something, though, she'd have reckoned as anything approaching progress, very probably—not without my having brought Leona's name into the conversation at some point, I had to think.

MORE RECENTLY

I have never been so sure of anything: I loved Leona Fielder, heart and soul. And I would always love her, I knew; knew it in my bones.

I'd called for her at her cousin's place in Cricklewood. The way she'd looked that evening, the way she'd looked at me, coming downstairs into the hallway where I was waiting for her—and there it was, taking hold of me and locking me into the emotional reality of what I was feeling for Leona, mostly inexpressible though it was. I'd forgotten, somehow, just how stunningly beautiful she is—'her gorgeousness herself,' as Kell had once referred to her. (A singular beauty like that in anyone isn't easy to describe; coming closest perhaps is Shakespeare's 'Such stuff as dreams are made on,' and, more interestingly if less famously, Oscar Wilde's 'A form of genius.') I'd not said much more than hello to her, but I'd not needed to; she could see in my eyes what was in my heart, I was certain. I wanted her in my life for the duration. This one true thing I suddenly knew—in that one, all-revealing moment—at 6:05 p.m., Wednesday, February 3, 2000. Just like that.

We went for dinner to Macklin's in Dean Street in Soho. I'd been introduced to Macklin's and the Macklins—Tony, the chef, and his wife Margot, who managed the place—by Julian. I'd taken a quick liking to them both, and wasn't sorry for it. Tony had been a commiserating schoolmate of Julian's at Harrow, which they'd both detested. I'd taken a liking too to the food Tony was doing wonders with; and also to the quiet, intimate surroundings in which to enjoy it. We'd got the back corner table I'd wanted. With its overhead, long-corded lighting fixture providing an almost third degree-like arc of of illumination, concentrated rather theatrically on just the two of us, the chances of our saying anything without the eyes either confirming or denying the words on our lips as we spoke were practically non-existent.

Leona had landed in London five days earlier than she'd planned to. I'd been out of town for a new play festival and playwriting seminar at Durham University, leaving her to arrive unmet at Heathrow. She'd flown in the same day she'd received a very early morning call from Ursula, her new agent, urging her to get to London ASAP to audition for a major BBC and PBS-TV production of Henry James's *Daisy Miller*. After reading several times over the next two days—'I was so loosey-goosey, figuring I didn't have a ghost of a chance,' she said—she'd landed Daisy, the typically Jamesian innocently audacious American miss abroad in late nineteenth century Europe. Also, she told me, there could be as well some 'just as amazing' stage work for her later in the year and in 2001. In addition to Sean Blake's concerted campaign to have her join him at the Donmar, Teddy Bentley was showing a keen interest in her for Maggie in The Old Vic's *Cat on a Hot Tin Roof* in the autumn; also, Julian had told her he was keeping her prominently in mind for his 2001 Chichester Festival company.

'I'm starting to wonder if there could be something in that stars-in-alignment stuff after all,' she'd enthused. 'One thing's for sure, anyhow: things can change in a shot for you, can't they? Just last week I was stewing over turning down Millennium Three in New York, and wondering if I'd been out of my mind.' But the offer, however, wasn't to replace Jace, who'd decided to return to London (to Kell's abundant satisfaction). Freddie Flaxman had already signed Carly Farringer for the roles Schaeffer had wanted Jace for, apparently. 'Obviously, it was supporting stuff he'd lined up for me.' All this I'd learned on getting back to London, after trying several times to get through in response to her phone messages.

Over our cocktails, Daisy Miller was clearly first and foremost in Leona's mind, not unexpectedly. Director Terence Courtland had told her that Henry James, with his Daisy Miller, for one, had significantly influenced how women had since been portrayed in fiction. 'I wasn't quite sure what that might mean in trying to play her, though. As well versed as you are in nineteenth and early twentieth century literature, Tim, maybe you've an idea or two on that.'

I offered a few thoughts. 'Well, James's views on relationships between the sexes were regarded as advanced for his day and age,' I said. 'Critics still consider his psychological insights, with a Freudian slant, as relevant today. I had a lecturer at Nottingham who rated James's psychology as superior to his brother William's.' William's *Varieties of Religious Experience* (1902) is still studied and well regarded. 'There's an old joke in academic circles: that William was a humourist who wrote about psychology, and Henry a psychologist who wrote novels. Anyway, the thing is, Leona, Daisy was flirting with quite a few modern ideas, so you may find getting into her century-old head easier than you thought it was going to be.' I'd mentioned too something that T.S.Eliot had said about Henry—that there seems to be a search going on in his novels for definite signs of spiritual life, and sometimes in the oddest, least expected places.

She said, 'That's interesting. And something I should be looking for in Daisy somewhere, maybe. I'm sure Bart and Lois could help me with that while they're in London later in the month. If anyone can detect signs of that sort in literature it has to be the Heddles, either one of them. They're both up on either of the James boys, and know their Eliot too.' (About a fortnight later, having dinner with the Heddles, talking about the James brothers, Lois commented, 'William wrote that the great use of a life is to spend it on that which outlasts itself; and that's what both he and Henry, I think, never stopped trying to do, each in his own individual way.')

Leona told me about the Heddles' long association with St. James's Anglican in Stratford, Ontario, prominently sited diagonally across from the Festival Theatre on the banks of Lake Victoria—and where, at either of the venues, mankind's spiritual needs and yearnings always get a good hearing, they'd maintained. Leona said that Bart had first got serious about his 'often questioned but remarkably durable faith' as an English Lit student of Northrop Frye's at the University of Toronto. What Frye had had to say about literature and the Bible (and comprehensively set out in his *The Great Code*)—that the one cannot be properly understood without a good working knowledge of the other—had made a lot of sense to Bart, and started him looking into the question of God, which up to then he'd 'cavalierly ignored,' he said.

'You talk a lot about the Heddles,' I said. 'You seem to be pretty close to them.'

'Yes, you're right, Tim, I am. It's hard not to get that way, actually. I was drawn to them almost immediately. They're so different from so many others you run into. It's a lot of things about them. The ease they have in their own skins, their collectedness, I guess you could call it—as individuals, but also as a beautifully matched pair, connecting the way they do, which you can't help sensing is the status quo with them. And the way they connect with you, you can't miss that either. They include you, you can tell; you just know and feel that they care. I don't think I could stay away from the Heddles if I wanted to, however hard I tried.'

I was intrigued. I said, 'And what about their religion—what d'you make of that?'

'Well, it sure works for them, no question of that. Until I met Bart and Lois, I'd not really given religion a serious thought. I couldn't see what any of it had to do with me—or, come to that, with anybody or anything. Their psychology, though, Lois's in particular, I thought might be of some use to me sometime or other—but that was as far as it went. But as for anything else, making them the way they are—and so consistently too—that's been a bit of a mystery, a conundrum for me. It's a whole mix of things with them, of course—their philosophy and theology as well as the psychology. Something they've individualized, their own special blend; their whole approach to life. It's a sort of balancing act they pull off before your very eyes, leaving you wondering how they do it; and wishing you could experience something like that with someone yourself. And it's not like they talk and go on about it. You're left, for the most part, to make of it what you can about the way they are.'

'Your parents know about your friendship with the Heddles, of course?'

'Oh, yes. I've told them a few things. They know the Heddles are not Jewish, of course—but not about their Christianity, let alone how deep it goes with them. I wouldn't think so, anyhow. I don't think they'd have gone around asking questions about the Heddles when they were in Stratford. No, I think they think that Bart and Lois, like most professional people these days, are non-believers, sceptics, secularists, what have you.'

'And you can't see yourself telling your parents anything different?'

'No, not anytime soon, I don't. Right now, our relationship is complicated enough as it is when it comes to religion. It's a sort of a no-man's-land between us we don't care to wander into; it might be too upsetting for all concerned.'

I wasn't about to poke around any further into Leona's relationship with her father, and, it would seem, with her mother as well. But I was curious, as she must have guessed. She said, 'I did get around to reading Viktor Frankl's book, by the way.' If she'd suspected that I had too, I couldn't tell. 'His experiences in the camps I found very harrowing. Of course, his fortitude, his spirit in the face of such dreadful things was absolutely amazing; in fact, I was quite dumbfounded by it. I could see the connection, of course, between what he'd gone through and the psychological theories behind his logotherapy. But I'm not sure I'm ready yet—in fact, I know I'm not—for his Super-Meaning, or his God, either one. I did talk to Lois about it, just listening more than anything else—but not to my father, when I was in Vancouver. Lois thought it might be best if I didn't. She said he might think it intrusive of me, going into his psychiatric treatment with Doctor Slazenger. And besides, as I've inferred, I don't think my father's ready for that any more than I am. I think he's far too conscious of the man, the father he was to me when I was growing up; what he taught me, how he influenced me back then. And now, imposing himself, his new self on me, is the last thing he wants to do, I guess. Like with me and the Heddles, it's for me to find my father, as he is now, in my own time and way.'

She sighed, and said, 'Well, anyhow, that's more than enough of that, I'm sure.'

She told me she'd had dinner in Toronto with Kell, who'd been sad and wet-eyed at the thought of running a company without her being part of it, saying it was going to take a lot of getting used to for him. 'But we had a few laughs too, looking back on some of our adventures together.' In the theatre, she'd meant, I assumed. (But with Kell, who could tell?) He'd also filled her in on Julian's lavish new millennium revels—second-hand stuff he'd gleaned from his several London informants; he'd been in Paris with his father and stepmother. He'd told her about Julian and his hostess Sam's engagement announcement that night, and their midsummer wedding plans; and also about me and Belinda Tranter hooking up for the evening, neither of us having turned up with someone. (I'd felt it necessary to say, albeit rather sheepishly, that Belinda had had no more intentions of getting anything going with me again than I'd had with her.)

Kell's main interest, though, had been in Jace's comings and goings since arriving back in London, she said. There'd been good reason why, while in the U.K. in December, he'd not managed to get hold of her, he'd told Leona. She'd gone to ground in Yorkshire with her friend and former RSC co-star, Matthew Norden. The two had eventually surfaced at Julian's splashy party, and their big news was soon out and doing the rounds among the guests. Firstly, they were on for, and noticeably up too for Daniel Morgenheim's *Antony and Cleopatra* at the National in May. Jace had agreed to do Cleo only after Matt had been confirmed as her Tony. And secondly, as nobody onboard that evening needed telling, they were very much an item on a personal level as well. And, the word was, that after a fortnight of love in the sun on a Greek Island, they'd be moving in together in his place in Notting Hill. Leona said Kell told her he couldn't believe I'd reportedly said I couldn't have been happier for the two of them. 'But he didn't explain why, though, and I thought it better not to ask,' she'd added.

But then Leona may not have needed to. To begin with, she'd already known about Jace and Matt. Jace had told her in New York that she and Matt had spent a small fortune on transatlantic phone bills; that as far back as their RSC days, Matt had never stopped believing that one day they'd end up together—and that maybe Matt had had that right all along. Leona said a friendship had developed between Jace and herself as the long Stratford Festival season had worn on. 'Around the time Jacinth and Drew Schaeffer called it quits, this was. We'd kept it to ourselves, though. As you know, Jacinth isn't one to get too close to anyone in particular in the dressing room. It's not her style, and not mine either. In fact, in that respect, we're both like your Natasha Fenner, wouldn't you say? Anyhow, we both got a bit emotional saying our goodbyes in New York.' Leona's friendship, when she'd needed some, was a godsend, Jace told her; and that she was looking forward to having her to see and talk to in London. (Had Jace put Leona straight, then, as to where things stood and had remained for nearly six years between the two of us, no matter what she may have heard from Kell?)

'Well, hello, stranger.'

I looked up from my filet mignon to see Margot Macklin smiling down on me. She must have been in the office when we'd come in. An attractive, gaminesque forty-year-old who looked at least five years younger than she was, Margot could make her navy blue suit 'uniform' seem both business-like and alluring at one and the same time. I introduced Leona, telling Margot about our *Congravino* connections. 'I knew you had to be an actress,' Margot said. They'd talked briefly about Toronto; the Macklins had friends there with whom they'd exchanged visits. The two women seemed to like one another—if it's possible to tell something like that.

Before taking her leave, Margot said to me, 'Somebody told me you were giving up your London flat and moving permanently to Oxfordshire. It's not true, is it?'

'No, Margot, it isn't. I'm not even thinking of it.'

'Well, thank God for that. We don't see enough of you as it is. And besides, what could possibly make you think you're a country boy, anyway?' And after a quick dart of a look Leona's way: 'As Tony says, the sort of sophisticated, accomplished and desirable woman you're partial to may like an occasional weekend in the country, but never very much more than that.'

Leona smiled; and said after Margot had gone, 'Well, Tim, am I right in thinking I've just been given a quick once over?'

I smiled. 'Yes, I think you probably have.'

'Just looking out for a man she feels needs looking out for, is that it?'

'Yes, something like that. I wouldn't say that Margot was displeased at all with the company she found me in tonight, though.'

'Wouldn't you?' An exquisite raised eyebrow with this. 'Even though your lady friend doesn't know me from Eve?'

'She doesn't need to. Margot's got this idea about me, you see. As she sees it, when it comes to women, I've been keeping myself high up on a shelf like a fine figurine I'm afraid of getting chipped or cracked. Maybe a ceramic Round Table knight King Arthur could trust with his life, and his wife, she says.' Leona smiled, as only she could. 'Yes, well, Margot can turn an amusing phrase when she puts her mind to it—but not always with much in the way of truth in any of it.'

'Oh, yes?' She sipped some wine. 'She's right, though, about you not being a country boy, I suppose?'

'Well, half right, anyway. My grandmother, who left me the house in Hook Norton, always thought I was a Hookeyite at heart. She believed I'd eventually find that life in the big city wasn't all it was cracked up to be; that keeping your head on straight and your heart in the right place isn't easy to do in a city like London, or maybe in any city, for that matter.'

'You must have meant a lot to your grandmother, by the sound of it?'

I nodded. 'And Gran meant a lot to me too. She always had time for me, especially after Mum died. Her "very own lovely lad," she'd call me. And more recently, after I started going regularly to Hook Norton to play cricket, we'd talk a lot together. She told me about her parents, about her life; about her husband and her "darling Daph,' my mother, who I'd only known when I was a kid, of course. And about my dad too, when he and Mum fell in love as teenagers. And other family things she thought I should know. Knowing where you're from always helps, she told me. Gran was always very easy to listen to; and funny and perceptive with it, too. Quite a few things she told me have stayed with me. For instance: don't just let things happen to you; think them through, try and find out what they're telling you. And always expect the unexpected—and if it's not good, try to make something positive out of it. Which she said you usually can do with a bit of pluck and downright luck—along with some faith in the good Lord, not to mention a prayer now and again.Things like that.'

'She was a religious woman, then, was she?'

'Well, not as some might think being religious means. She liked having her fun, enjoyed dancing and playing whist, and her smokes and large brandies. Actually, she'd gone to church, the Church of England, all her life, and could quote the Bible or something from the Prayer Book more or less accurately, when it suited her to. But she liked to say too, "I don't believe in organized religion, and I never have—I'm C. of E., for God's sake!"'

Leona laughed—a sight and sound to wonder at, to be mesmerized by, if you weren't careful. I concentrated on the food in front of me; I didn't want to be caught gazing at her like some gobsmacked halfwit, and seemingly unable to deal with anything on a rational level in her company.

She said, 'You know, Tim—what your grandmother said, about not letting things just happen to you without trying to make some sense of it. Isn't that what you had Natasha Fenner say to the playwright? Or something of the sort, anyhow?'

I grinned and nodded. 'Yes, Leona, something very much like that, actually. At the time, though, when I was writing that scene, I had no idea I was echoing something Gran Gadsden had said to me. But writers soak up so much, like a sponge, and don't always realize where they got some of what they're putting down, or why it's stayed with them, somewhere in their heads.'

'Yes, well, that's probably true for most of us, don't you think? Something you think or say you're convinced is your own take on whatever it is, without knowing any different. Things you believe represent your own individual take on things without knowing any different. But what I wonder about too is how that sort of thing can add up over time—to the point of making you unsure about anything you know, and about yourself too. It's as if you're not connecting the dots; that there could be some sort of pattern emerging, in a lot of it—that you're just not getting, missing out on.'

'I know exactly what you're saying, Leona.' My mind could still function reasonably well in her close, intoxicating proximity, then. 'A design for living, so to speak—that's been developing behind your back, as it were. And maybe one you're not sure you'll ever be able to alter, going forward, into something different.'

'Yes, that as well. I mean, you can't go on living aimlessly, going from pillar to post, living haphazardly like that, not giving a thought to where you're going with your life. It'll be over before you know it. You've got to be going in a direction of some sort. And like your grandmother said, Tim, that's also going to involve looking back, assessing where you've been, how you've got to where you're at. You know, Plato's point about the unexamined life, and so on—taking that seriously.' She recalled Lois Heddle having said something like that—that though life has to be lived forward, it can only be understood backwards. 'She was quoting somebody—Kierkegaard, I think it was. I've actually read some of his stuff, believe it or not. I've been hanging around too much in the Heddles' library, I guess that's what it is.'

I poured her some more wine. She'd been going gently with the Beaujolais. We both had—the better to keep our wits about us that evening, no doubt.

Our boyishly handsome waiter (a between-jobs actor or dancer, possibly) arrived with the dessert. He'd again deferred to Leona in particular, like a performer to royalty in a command performance, after-show reception line. After which Leona had conversationally changed gears. She said her cousin, who ran a real estate firm in West London, was hunting down somewhere for her to live, and until then she'd be staying in Wimbledon with her uncle and aunt. And also that she'd be returning to Toronto in a few days' time; her earlier-than-expected departure for the U.K. hadn't let her get everything cleared up there. She said she wouldn't be long, about five or six days at the most.

I asked, not as casually as I may have sounded, 'You'll be back the week after next, then, will you? By midweek, for sure?'

'Oh, yes, I'm sure I will.' Her marvellous, expressive eyes focussed on mine. 'Did you have something in mind, then?'

'Yes, I do, Leona, as a matter of fact.' I said that *Writing and Loving*... was opening that week, on the Thursday, and I was wondering if she'd like to go with me. (Hoping like mad she would was infinitely closer to the truth of it.)

The merest of pauses before she'd broke into one of her matchless smiles. 'Yes, of course I'll go with you, Tim! I'd love to, I'd be thrilled to!' I think I'd blinked; her smile must have dazzled me. She said, 'You weren't thinking I'd say no, were you, Tim?'

'Well, I wasn't taking it for granted you'd say yes, either. I'm absolutely delighted you did, though, of course. Thank you for that.'

'Don't be silly, Tim. I'm delighted you asked. I should be thanking you. In fact, I'm going to. Thank you so much, Tim. It's going to be wonderful, a real pleasure, I know it is.'

We smiled, almost shyly—both of us temporarily short perhaps on what to say next. We went back simultaneously to attacking Tony's delicious raspberry cheesecake. (Authentically Times Square, New York style and quality; the best in London, he boasted.)

I broke the silence. 'Well, anyway, Leona, maybe I should let you know what you're in for—at the opening, I mean. My claque's going to be there in numbers—all the usual suspects; a full gang turnout, some of them going back to my Nottingham days. And my father and Sally will be there too, of course.' She looked at me somewhat quizzically. 'The thing is, Leona, you're going to be—well, something of a surprise for quite a few of them, I think.'

'Am I?'

'Most definitely.'

'Who on earth is she, pray tell? Where did she suddenly spring from? That sort of thing?'

'Well, that, certainly. They've all got used to me flying solo, staying under the radar, where women are concerned, you see. Jacinth spoiled me for other women, made me far too picky for my own good, some think, Margot among them, probably. Some others even think I'm off women altogether. Gerry Atherton, my agent and good friend, seems to think I've not only lost the urge, but the knack as well. He says he doubts I could pull a bird—one that's worth pulling, anyway—to save my sad, lonely life.' She smiled. 'Believe me, Leona, I'm going to enjoy seeing Gerry's face when I walk into The Savoy with you. But please don't think I want you with me just to show you off, like a trophy, will you? I'm going to be proud to have you beside me, Leona, that's true enough—but that's not it at all, what it's about; that's not how it is with me. I never have dated just for the sake of it; wanting to have a woman on my arm for appearances' sake. I've not even gone to one of my own first nights, a special night like that, with someone.'

'Haven't you, Tim? Why ever not?'

'Well, I suppose I told myself that far too much would have been read into it if I had. I simply couldn't be bothered having to deal with that sort of thing.'

There was mischief now in those dark, expressive eyes of hers. She said. 'Of course, three of your big opening nights, they didn't really count, did they? In each case, the woman you were very eager, I'm sure, to have beside you, dangling on your arm, wasn't available, was she?'

I had to smile, acknowledging her palpable hit. 'Nice one,' I said. The trio of women she was alluding to, of course, had been otherwise occupied onstage, playing my female lead—Sam Tolliver (in *Writing and Loving . . .*); Jace (in *Entrances and Exits*); and Belinda Tranter (in *Romeo Scores!*).

'You didn't think I'd have missed that, did you, Tim?'

She enjoyed my wry expression. 'And how did you know I didn't take anyone with me to the "Congravino" openings in London or in Chichester?'

'Oh, that didn't take much finding out. Remember me telling you about Kenna Watson?' She and Leona had been in the same year at RADA. Kenna Weston had played Arabella Hunt in both U.K. productions of *Congravino*. 'Kenna and I have been exchanging cards and occasional phone calls since leaving RADA. It was Kenna who told me. You strike her as a good man going to waste for no reason she could think of, she said.' And after a sip of coffee: 'But tell me something, Tim—if you want to, of course. Having to explain me to your parents, and to that gang of yours, all that to-do—how come you can be bothered this time with all that, with all the fallout from that you seem to be expecting?' I replied without any hesitation, 'I'll tell you why, Leona. It's you, Leona. It's as simple as that. You're the reason. It's you I want to be seen with at The Savoy, Leona—you, and only you. There just isn't anybody else. It never occurred to Margot and the others, you see—that there was someone, a very special someone, I dearly wanted to be seen with; someone I couldn't possibly accept a substitute for. Then again, why would that have occurred to anybody? I'd kept you to myself, hadn't I?—as you'd kept me to yourself, as we'd agreed to. Although, for me, it wasn't always easy doing that, mind you. You kept coming to mind so much. There was always something to remind me of you. I nearly spilled the beans more than once.'

'It was the same thing with me, Tim. There were times, after you came to Stratford, when I wanted so much to talk about you to someone or other—well, certainly the Heddles, anyhow. Particularly when we got to talking about "Congravino"—always then.'

'Yes, well, with me, Leona, that kind of thing—thinking about you, wanting to talk so much about you—goes as far back, I think, to that rainy afternoon in January '97, when you came looking for me in Hammersmith.'

She nodded, and smiled. She'd probably known as much at the time.

After a sip of coffee, she said, 'On the plane coming over, I was thinking of some other times I'd been in London. To begin with, as a child, with my father, which I couldn't remember very much about. And certainly nothing about my relatives over here; we'd not gone anywhere near them. The summer school exchange in my teens, though, that was something else again. I remembered a lot about that; and, most of all, seeing Jacinth in "Entrances and Exits" in London. And then, back in Vancouver, in theatre school, meeting Kellison for the first time. He was looking for a girl for "The Crucible" at the Playhouse, and he picked me, telling me how promising I was. So there I was, a few months later, flying to London to audition for RADA. And after RADA, straight to the RSC in Stratford, and actually getting on the same stage with people like Jacinth. And then, of course, seeing you, Tim—and hardly ever without Jacinth tagging along.'

'I think it was me, rather, doing the tagging along.'

'Well, whatever. Still, I'd not gone unnoticed, had I?' I grinned. 'Do you remember, Tim—when we first laid eyes on one another? In the Dirty Duck?' (As RSC people, for who knows how long, have dubbed the Black Swan pub in Stratford-on-Avon.)

'I most certainly do.'

'Yes, I thought you might have done. Anyhow, I thought I'd be sure to run into you again, when you were by yourself—just accidentally, of course—but no such luck. And the next year, I didn't even try. I was being ridiculous, I finally realized. And when I left the RSC, I thought that was that; that I'd forget you. But I never did manage that, for some reason;

not even after I'd got back to Canada. It was this absurd idea I had: that we must have been meant to meet; that it hadn't happened by chance. I read your plays, and anything I could find written about you. I had your photo blown up; taken off the backcover of a script. I tacked it up in my apartment in Edmonton—but always took it down if anybody came over, to save myself some embarrassment; and the same thing in Stratford. Actually, I still have it, packed away somewhere.'

'I'm assuming you didn't tell Kell anything about me, then?'

'Oh, God, no! Not a word. But then I heard about you and Jacinth breaking up—so there I was, at it again, trying to put you and me in the same frame, in the same picture. That's what I must have been up to, it must have been, when I tracked you down in Hammersmith.'

'As I remember it, Leona, you said you were just acting on a sudden impulse—something you couldn't quite explain.'

'Well, I couldn't, could I? Not then. It was too soon, I knew, far too soon, to be opening up to you like that—for myself, let alone for you. I couldn't imagine what you'd have thought, how you'd have reacted. We didn't know each other in the slightest. I'd have come across to you as some wild, delusional woman, or something, just talking a lot of nonsense.I could have scared you off for life. I couldn't let that happen. I was going to have to be patient, bide my time, I realized. Although having to wait as long as I have, that I wasn't expecting. But like you said once, Tim: good things are worth waiting for.'

I had to be careful. I couldn't stop smiling. I didn't want to have coffee dribbling down my chin.

Leona had taken charge of the conversation; but that was fine with me. 'So, anyhow, Tim, here's how it is with me. I'm here, in London, to find work, to advance my career—that's very true. And I'm absolutely thrilled to have gotten Daisy Miller, of course. But that's almost beside the point, really. The main reason I'm here is because of you, Tim. I think, and I believe, that there's a future for you and me to share—that now I can actually say that, and be sure that I'm making sense, complete sense. That there is a pattern—a design for living—that you and I, Tim, can work on, and work out together. I really do believe that's true, Tim. That the time has come—finally—for the two of us to start connecting the dots; to see what we can come up with together.'

I reached across the table and covered her hand with mine. She was reading my eyes like a book, and now I was reading hers too. But Leona, like me, also wanted to hear the words spoken, I knew. I said, 'I love you, Leona.' She said, 'And I love you too, Tim.' I said, 'With all my heart and mind, I love you.' She said, 'And I love you, Tim—with all my heart and mind, too.'

If the table between us and the chairs under us had all at once started floating upwards, carrying the two of us out through an open roof and into the night sky over the city, I don't think either of us would have noticed.

That night I slept the sleep of a blissfully contented man. The next morning, I was actually singing in the shower. All was well with me again. I phoned Leona to say good morning and tell her that I loved her. It was good, incredibly good, to have the loving back in my life once again—along with all the hope that comes with that.

It took me half the day, well into the afternoon, to get back to the writing.

POSTSCRIPT:

SUMMER 2002

The book was my idea; the title, *Loving and Writing, Writing and Loving*, was Leona's.

Leona read the manuscript as I worked on it, chapter by chapter, after which we discussed it. Quite a number of changes, particularly in the later chapters, reflect her insightful comments. Being included in the creative process like that, she said, had helped her understand me that much better; and at times herself as well. And this had also helped, she felt, to bring about the commitment we'd made to one another on that hazy, mid-August day in 2002 in the Chelsea register office, becoming man and wife.

But, of course, not the only factor leading up to a decision of such consequence as that.

After filming *Daisy Miller*, Leona rented a flat in Camden Town. When her lease came up for renewal a year later, she agreed to move in with me in Brook Green. She'd stated, however, that she wouldn't necessarily be seeing our cohabitation as a trial marriage, much less as merely a prelude to one; and I'd concurred with her in that regard (although with some disappointment I'd managed to keep to myself). In any case, deciding to marry wasn't a taken-for-granted eventuality for either of us.

We had got into the habit, though, of talking about how best to stay as close as we could be, and not just physically. Further developing an all-round sense of togetherness was important for both of us.

One conclusion we'd arrived at in our discussions along these lines: that being able to consistently believe what we felt for one another, and, in turn, feel what we believed—that that would be the key to achieving what we were looking for as partners; as partners in every sense of the word. (Something to be striven for, if not easily attained, as Philip Larkin maintained in *Further Requirements;* that is, if one is to write both truthfully and well. But also 'a common human condition' hinging on one's ability as well to live life in a productive and satisfying fashion, Larkin had undoubtedly implied.) In effect, then, loving one special and significant other—one of Viktor Frankl's ways to meaningfulness in life—is a fully operational function of the mind as well as the heart.

At first, the Fielders, and Dad and Sally as well, had almost certainly looked askance at whatever it was they'd thought Leona and I were up to in forming the relationship we had. Neither couple had likely had much hope (if any at all) of it lasting for any length of time. But we'd stayed in touch, however. We'd had meals together with the Fielders and also with Dad and Sally in London in 2000 and '01, when in each instance any uneasiness between us hadn't shown itself at any point. Leona said, 'I think my parents are slowly warming to the idea of there actually being a you and me, Tim, wouldn't you say? And I've never felt anything other than entirely comfortable with both your dad and Sally.' And I'd said that it was possible our parents were seeing and sensing a coming together between us with more depth to it, and also a permanence about it, than they'd been expecting. (In any event, at the wedding, both parental couples had looked considerably more than merely resigned to the day's proceedings, smiling often and easily enough, I'd thought. And the next day, the Fielders had joined the Heddles on a day trip to Windsor—the Stratford Festival had had Bart understudied that weekend—and later in the week had visited with Dad and Sally in Banbury.)

Starting as far back as early in 2000, Leona and I had always felt free to talk to the Heddles about personal matters affecting our relationship—as they had with us about theirs. In '02, early in the summer, we'd travelled to Canada, staying for a week with the Heddles in Stratford; and taking in four shows, including Kell's thoroughly bracing *The Tempest.* (Kell had renewed his contract with the Stratford Festival, and also taken out Canadian citizenship, having now established himself as one of his new country's cultural icons.) What Leona saw in Bart and Lois wasn't difficult to see.

It was a good place to be—in the Heddles' warm, inclusive company, communing together as the four of us had. Whether it was Bart or Lois doing the talking, it was all the same to me: I couldn't get enough of what either had to say.

Bart told us about his air raid warden father's brave death in a rescue attempt during the London Blitz; and about his mother's faith in God and never failing fortitude throughout and after the war. Mrs. Heddle had spent her last twenty years plus as a paraplegic on volunteer committees for various charities. On another occasion, Lois remarked that she would have given up her teaching career in a flash to have had a child. She'd suffered three miscarriages, the last of which she'd been fortunate to survive, affecting her health permanently. On her doctor's advice, she and Bart had decided against adoption. Also, Bart had made mention of a blank verse play of Christopher Fry's, *A Sleep of Prisoners*, he'd appeared in during the '70s in Toronto, when the Cold War still weighed heavily on people's minds. As Meadows, one of four British WWII soldiers interned in an abandoned church—each dreaming of various, still relevant moral and spiritual conflicts involving certain biblical characters, starting with Cain and Abel—Bart had had the play's final soliloquy, voicing Fry's central premise. He'd had the words down to a T: that ' . . . our time is now when wrong comes up to face us everywhere, never to leave us till we take the longest stride of soul men ever took . . . The enterprise is exploration into God . . .' And he and Lois agreed they'd each endeavoured to live by Fry's words on a daily basis; and that this had had much to do with the love and the togetherness they'd experienced as a couple over the years. For each of them, they'd told us, living with and looking into the not always easily understood 'through-a-glass-darkly things of God' had made life's various vicissitudes that much less difficult to deal with, whether affecting them head on or in a more general way. (And a thought probably prompting Bart's prediction that New York's tragic 9/11 experience would trigger an 'indiscriminate and largely ignorant onslaught' on faith and religion—that in the West, particularly, would impact detrimentally, as well as ironically, on both Christians and Jews.)

For Leona and me, the tricky issue of religion would always have to be factored in so far as our relationship, our togetherness was concerned—as the two of us had known well enough from the beginning. We'd not shied away from talking about this either, having become increasingly inclined to look more diligently into Bart and Lois's 'things of God' (and my father's and Nathan Fielder's as well), and also Viktor Frankl's 'will to meaning' and blueprint for a well-lived life—for Leona for the first time, and for me, more seriously than in my childhood and youth when, like many other such kids, I'd taken the reality of God as a given. ('When you think about it, we'd both be setting out from pretty much the same starting point,' I'd told her.)

Back in London, Leona and I aired an underlying concern neither of us had managed to shake—about going off on separate and divergent tangents in search of spiritual enlightenment, self-knowledge and fulfillment in our lives. (By necessity a particularly individualistic quest, in any case.) Each of us was apprehensive about running into some potentially divisive theological snags—'relational landmines,' Leona called them. A decision needed making—and make it we did—to leave the other free to follow his or her own exploratory path to God. (Or to try to find meaning, identity and direction in our day-to-day existence, both individually and together, by whatever other available means.) A choice, once made, we knew instinctively had been the right one. Otherwise, claiming to love one another unconditionally could ultimately amount to just mouthing the words. What each of us meant by love in forming and working to strengthen our relationship couldn't be defined, in either mind or heart, and be put into everyday practice by any other means, we agreed. For us, as partners in life, it was the breakthrough we'd been looking for. And had culminated in the fully fledged commitment we'd made to each other that August 2002 day in Chelsea—resolved as we were to find in each other that 'ever-fixed mark' of true love of William Shakespeare's. And as the "Star of Poets" (in Ben Jonson's estimation) concluded his 'marriage of true minds' sonnet (116), as only he could have:

> 'Love's not Time's fool, though rosy lips and cheeks
> Within his bending sickle's compass come;
> Love alters not with his brief hours and weeks,
> But bears it out even to the edge of doom.
>   If this be error, and upon me proved,
>   I never writ, nor no man ever loved.'

CPSIA information can be obtained at www.ICGtesting.com
Printed in the USA
LVOW072245121011

250244LV00003B/1/P